D0560787

The Shadow Players

THE
SHADOW PLAYERS

Linda Sole

ST. MARTIN'S PRESS

NEW YORK

Library of Congress Cataloging-in-Publication Data

Sole, Linda.
    Shadow players / Linda Sole.
      p. cm.
    ISBN 0-312-08292-4
    I. Title.
  PR6069.038S48   1992
  823'.914—dc20   92-21915
                                         CIP

First published in Great Britain by Random Century Group.

First U.S. Edition: October 1992
10 9 8 7 6 5 4 3 2 1

The Shadow Players

Chapter One

I screamed for help as I ran across the desolate waste of the saltmarshes, my long dark hair whipping into my eyes and sticking to my mouth. Stumbling through the muddy pools in a desperate attempt to escape, I'd fallen and scratched myself on half-buried broken glass, but in my fear I was scarcely aware of the pain. The man could run so much faster than I, and he was gaining on me. I gasped for breath, feeling my chest begin to hurt as I redoubled my efforts to reach the one person who could save me.

I'd been warned not to stray too far, but I loved the solitude and the wildness of the Blakeney marshes. Although some people found their eerie stillness frightening, I'd never been afraid of the marshes . . . Until now. Glancing back, I caught a sobbing breath. My pursuer was catching me up, his long stride outpacing mine with ease.

He was so close now that I could hear the rasp of his breath, and his feet thudding over the muddy sand and coarse grass. I gave a despairing cry, and then, as if the effort had been too much, I faltered and pitched forward, sprawling face downward. I felt the wetness and the grit on my skin and in my mouth, then he was on me. I fought him, scratching, kicking and biting until my face, arms and legs were torn and bleeding. His superior strength prevailed and finally he held me imprisoned beneath him, my resistance crushed. His hands were round my throat, squeezing, restricting my breathing. Defeated, I lay looking up into his face, mutely pleading, begging for my life. He was going to kill me. I knew he was going to kill me. I was eleven years old and I was going to die. This man had made up his mind. There was such a strange, wild look in his eyes, then he seemed to falter, his hold slackening as if he were unsure.

'You shouldn't have laughed,' he said in a choked voice. 'The old bitch laughed at me, too . . .'

My lips were almost too stiff with fear to form the words as I whispered, 'Please, don't hurt me. I didn't mean to laugh at you.'

I stared into his resentful eyes, sure that he would not listen to my plea and that I would die, and then the blackness took hold of my mind, blotting everything out.

★

I came out of the blackness slowly. At first I was aware of a feeling of suffocation, as though layers of cottonwool were pressing down on my face. I tried to push them away, but my hands wouldn't obey me. It was like being in a nightmare and knowing that I wasn't dreaming, that it was all too real. Then I became aware of the pain. My throat was sore and I ached all over. It hurt. It hurt so much that I felt tears begin to slide down my face. Their saltiness stung my flesh.

'Michael . . .' I whispered. 'Michael, please . . .'

Where was he? I wanted him, needed him so much. He was my daddy and he had always protected me. I cried his name aloud and then I opened my eyes.

It was so strange. I'd thought I must be at home in my bed at Hazeling, but I was in a small bare room that I'd never seen before. As my eyes began to focus, I was aware that two people were standing at the foot of my bed. Who were they? I didn't know them. Where was I? What had happened to me?

The woman moved towards me, her smile gentle and reassuring. I saw that she was wearing some kind of a uniform. My panic receded.

'Are you a nurse?' I croaked.

'Yes. It's all right, Aline,' she soothed. 'You're being looked after. No one will hurt you now.'

'Excuse me, nurse. I'd like to talk to Aline.' The man moved forward, ignoring the nurse's frown. He smiled at me, but the smile didn't reach his eyes. 'I'm a policeman, Aline. Inspector Robinson. You don't mind talking to me, do you?'

I stared at him in silence for a moment. He was a large man with greying hair, and his face was so stern that I was frightened. People only looked at you like that if you'd done something naughty.

'Are you really a police inspector?'

'Yes, Aline. I'm here so that you can tell me what happened to you.'

My anxiety mounted. 'Have I done something wrong? Are you going to put me in prison?'

He shook his head and smiled. 'Not unless you tell me you've robbed a bank.'

My eyes went to the nurse. 'I'm in hospital, aren't I? Am I ill?'

'There was an accident. You were ill but you're going to be all right.'

'Please leave this to me.' The policeman glared at the nurse. 'I want you to tell me what happened, in your own words, Aline. You mustn't be afraid to tell me the truth.'

I was confused. What were they talking about? His manner seemed somehow threatening and it upset me. I was becoming more and more aware of how sore I felt. Putting up a hand to touch my cheek, I winced.

'Your stepfather was there, wasn't he?'

I felt a prickling sensation at the back of my neck. There was something about Michael . . . something that worried me.

'Michael . . .' I whispered. 'I – I don't know.'

'He was there on the marshes when it happened, wasn't he?' Inspector Robinson leaned towards me, his face intent. I thought that he looked as if he was ready to pounce on me.

'I don't know,' I said. 'I can't remember. I don't know what I've done . . .' My voice rose and I plucked at the sheets, looking to the nurse for help. 'I want Michael,' I cried. 'I want my daddy.' Tears sprang to my eyes. 'Please tell my daddy to come.'

'You haven't done anything, Aline.' The nurse's expression was accusing as she looked at Inspector Robinson. 'She's upset. I think you should leave, sir.'

He frowned, clearly very annoyed with her. I thought he was going to insist on staying, but as I began to sob, the nurse gathered me into her arms, glancing back at him.

'You will have to go,' she said. 'If you force me, I shall call the doctor.'

'I'm sorry, Aline,' he said. 'I didn't mean to upset you. A policewoman will come and see you later. Perhaps you will tell her what happened, because we do need to know.'

As he went out, I clung to the nurse. 'Don't let him come back again, will you?' I begged. 'He frightens me. I don't know what I've done . . .'

'It's not what you did.' She frowned, hesitating. 'Don't you remember what happened just before you came into hospital?'

'I don't remember coming here at all.' I trembled in her arms. 'What's wrong with me? Why can't I remember?'

'It doesn't matter,' she said, stroking my hair. 'Don't worry about it now. Sometimes people forget things when they've been ill. You may remember tomorrow or the next day.' She smiled at me. 'Shall I get you a glass of water now – or would you prefer orange juice?'

'Only if it's fresh. My mother doesn't let me have squash.'

'I think we can manage that.' She looked thoughtful. 'Shall I ask Sister to telephone your mother and ask her to come in?'

'Yes . . . but I'd like to see Michael, too.'

'Is he your stepfather?'

'He's my daddy,' I replied. 'Not my real daddy, because he died in a plane crash when I was little, but Michael's like a proper father.'

She went away without saying anything, but there was a peculiar look on her face, as if she thought I'd said something strange. I lay back on the pillows, closing my eyes and trying not to cry. It was difficult because I hurt so much, and I was frightened. The nurse said I hadn't done anything wrong, but I must have done. That policeman had been so stern and cross. I knew that people only acted that way when you'd been really bad. So what had I done?

I sat up as Michael and my mother came into the room. The nurse had kept her promise to ring them. My mother was dressed in one of her favourite Chanel suits, with a white silk blouse, real gold chains and neat Cuban-heeled shoes. She looked as if she'd had her hair done that morning, and somehow that reassured me: everything was as normal, despite the anxious look in her eyes. Beside her, Michael was less immaculate, in his baggy cords and darned sweater. There were tiny flakes of paint clinging to the hairs of his sweater, so I knew he must have come straight from his studio.

'How are you feeling now?' my mother asked. 'We were here all night but you were un – you were asleep.'

'I feel a bit sore,' I said, my eyes going past her to Michael. He looked at me in funny way, somehow guilty, and his gaze dropped from mine. 'What happened to me? There was a policeman here earlier. He frightened me.'

'You had an accident, that's all.' My mother frowned at Michael as he murmured a protest. 'Don't you remember anything, Aline?'

'No . . .' I glanced at Michael again. 'Were we on the marshes?'

Before he could answer, the door opened and the nurse came in, the one who had been there when the policeman upset me. She smiled at me, then turned to my mother.

'The doctor is waiting to see you, Mrs Courteney – and a police inspector.'

'The police . . .' My mother glanced at Michael, her alarm obvious. She fiddled with her handbag, then seemed to make a decision. 'Yes, I suppose that's inevitable, though my husband has already told them all he knows.'

'We'll come straight away,' Michael said, running nervous fingers through his hair. 'We have to face it, Sheila – ' He broke off and gave me a reassuring smile. 'We'll be back soon, Aline.'

As he moved towards the door, the nurse made an awkward, embarrassed sound in her throat.

'I'm sorry, Mr Courteney. They asked to see Mrs Courteney alone.'

4

Her cheeks were flushed. 'Perhaps you would like to wait outside for a while?'

'Wait out—' Michael was angry. I saw his hands clench into fists. 'Aline Marlowe is my stepdaughter.' He glanced towards me, something hovering in his eyes, then nodded. 'Very well.'

After the door closed behind them, the nurse fussed about the bed, tucking in the sheets and tidying the cabinet by my side. I sensed that she was wasting time, and I was somehow disturbed. Why had she made Michael wait outside? I wanted to talk to him.

'I'm thirsty,' I said. 'Can I have another glass of orange, please?'

For a moment she hesitated, then nodded. 'I expect it's all right,' she said and went out.

As soon as her footsteps had died away, I hopped out of bed and opened the door, intending to call Michael in. But he was sitting in the corridor with his head in his hands, and something about him made me hesitate. Then he looked up and saw me, and his expression was so exhausted and defeated that it frightened me.

'You'd better get back in bed,' he said sharply, as if he was angry with me, blaming me for something . . . 'Your mother and I will be in in a few minutes.'

Hearing voices as a door opened further down the hall, I fled back to my bed. Why was Michael angry with me? Why would no one tell me what I was supposed to have done?

'You haven't eaten many of your grapes, darling,' my mother said as she bent to kiss my cheek. 'I've brought you a packet of chocolate drops today – and Michael sent you these.' She laid a sheaf of comic books on the bed. 'Though why you like them I shall never know.'

'Ooh, thanks,' I cried, as I saw some of my favourites. 'Michael always knows what I like. Is he here? Is he coming in to see me?'

Mother turned aside, fussing with the fruit bowl on the bedside cabinet. 'He was here all the time when you weren't well but now he has to work. You know how absorbed he gets when he's painting. You're coming home in a couple of days. You'll see him then.'

Disappointment made my mouth droop. Michael had only been in that once to see me since I woke up, and even then he had seemed angry and uncomfortable. I had wanted him to put his arms around me and hug me, but a small voice in my head had warned me not to. No matter how I tried, I still couldn't remember what had happened just before I came into hospital, but I did remember how cross he'd been the last time I'd cuddled up to him – that was on the morning of my birthday, when I'd crept into his bed to thank him for his present. It was so strange that I could remember every moment of my birthday, but nothing after that. *Something* had happened to me. Something nasty. I was covered in bruises and my arms and legs were still sore after a week in hospital. I must have hurt myself, but no one would tell me how. They all kept asking me strange questions . . . and a lady doctor had examined me in a way that I didn't much like. She was kind and gentle, but it still hurt and it was embarrassing.

I looked at my mother, sensing that she was hiding something.

'Have I been ill?' I asked. 'Why am I in here – and why does that policewoman keep coming to see me?'

Mother stiffened and her face went tight. 'Don't talk about it, darling,' she said, taking my hand in her own. 'It's all over now. We shall just forget it ever happened.'

'But what did happen?'

'Nothing. I told you, we're not going to talk about it. You were hurt, but you're better now.'

I knew that look of my mother's. It meant that something nasty had happened. I wasn't sure exactly what it was that men and women did behind closed bedroom doors, but I did know that my mother didn't consider it nice to talk about that sort of thing. The girls at school whispered about it, and they'd giggled when one of the older girls got a fat tummy. They'd said she was in the pudding club. I'd wondered what that meant, until I saw the girl in the street with a baby in a pram. I'd asked my mother if that was being 'in the pudding club', and she'd slapped me on the leg for being rude. The look on her face was exactly the same now as it had been then.

'Did I do something terrible?'

'I'm sure I don't know what you did, Aline.' Her voice was sharp. 'I don't want to talk about it any more. Open your sweets. I had to go into town to get them.'

I stared at her, then picked up one of the comics, my eyes pricking with tears. I *must* have done something wicked, or the police wouldn't keep asking me questions, and my mother was cross with me. But what worried me most was Michael's absence.

'Will Michael come this evening?'

'Stop talking about your stepfather,' she cried. 'It's time you grew up, Aline. You're forever hanging about his neck and taking up his time. You're a big girl now. Start behaving like one.'

My bottom lip trembled. I knew Mother loved me, but she could be so sharp sometimes. Michael had always stood between us, softening the harsh words, making a fuss of me, loving me. I missed him so much, and I wanted him to visit me. It made me sick inside to think of him being cross with me, but I daren't say any more.

'Well, I must go now,' Mother said, bending to kiss me again. 'I only popped in for a few minutes on my way to a meeting. I'll come in again this evening, darling.' She smiled her regret. 'I'm sorry I was cross, but it's better if we just forget all this. Better for everyone – especially Michael.'

I stared at the door as Mother went out. What did she mean? Had Michael done something wrong, too? That policeman – the first one with the stern eyes – had kept asking about Michael, insisting that Michael had been on the marshes. Well, of course he had. We always went there together. I spent the time exploring, looking for wild flowers when they were in bloom or shells half-buried in the mud, while Michael painted wonderful pictures of the marshes and the wild birds. Sometimes he painted pictures of me, too, but I was too impatient to keep still for long.

I'd been looking for his lost palette knife that day . . . My stomach tightened with nerves. That was the first time I'd remembered anything at all about the day after my birthday, but I remembered now.

'Don't go too far,' Michael had called as I wandered away, my eyes on the ground.

What had happened next? I screwed up my face and thought about it hard. All I could remember was waking up to find that policeman by the bed. And yet there was something about Michael. I had a vague picture in my head. I thought that he had held me in his arms and wept, but I couldn't be sure. It might just have been a dream. I'd had disturbing dreams since my illness, but I could never remember them when I woke up.

Someone opened the door and poked her head round. It was the policewoman called Lucy. She had soft, pretty hair and nice eyes. I liked her, and I smiled as she came in bearing a gift of sticky buns. She had brought them every day since she'd discovered that I liked them.

'Feel like having a chat?' she asked.

Nodding, I accepted a bun. I knew that the chat would turn into more questions, but I didn't mind. All I had to do was to keep on repeating that I couldn't remember. I wasn't going to tell the police anything, not even Lucy. If Michael had done something wrong, they might send him away to prison. I didn't want that to happen. Not even if he . . . but there my thoughts came to an abrupt end. My mother was right. It was best not to think about it.

★

7

Back at Hazeling, I was more than ever aware that my life had changed. My mother's behaviour towards me was somehow different, though I couldn't have told anyone what had altered. I only knew that it hurt. Sometimes I caught her looking at me as if I'd done something wicked or . . . or dirty, and it made me feel guilty.

I had always thought that it would be exciting to be grown up, but now I wondered. Before the incident on the marshes, I'd enjoyed complete freedom to run and play in the gardens and the woods next to the house. I'd spent hours perched in the branches of my favourite tree. Now it made Mother cross.

'Come down,' she called when she saw me. 'For goodness sake, child, have you no sense of decency? You're too old to be clambering about like that, showing your knickers to all and sundry.'

My cheeks flushed. I was stung by that disapproving note in her voice. There was no one to see me but Michael, quietly working at his easel, and he had never cared what I did. He had even built me a tree house in the woods. I saw him glance at Mother and frown, but he didn't say anything. Why should it matter that Michael might see my knickers? It wasn't so long ago that he'd bathed me and tucked me up for the night, with lots of hugs and kisses. Now he scarcely came near me. He had stopped smiling at me in the special way that had made us so close.

Growing up wasn't much fun after all.

It was later that afternoon that I heard the quarrel between my mother and Michael. I had come in from the garden, and they were in the small parlour at the back of the house. The door was open and I stood in the hall listening to the sound of their raised voices, and felt sick as I realized that they were arguing about me.

'What was all that about this morning, Sheila?' Michael said. 'Aline has always climbed trees. Don't you think you're being a bit hard on the girl?'

'She isn't a child any more.'

'She isn't a small child, I'll grant you that,' Michael replied, and his voice was harsh. 'But she can't be expected to grow up overnight. She doesn't understand what it's all about . . . How can she, when you refuse to tell her?'

'It would upset her more. You always blame me, Michael. I was just trying to teach her to behave like a young lady, instead of the tomboy you seem to prefer.'

'All I want is for her to be happy.' Michael heaved a sigh. 'And you too, my dear. You know I still care for you.'

'Do you?' Mother's voice was icy. 'I'm not sure that you ever did.'

'And what is that supposed to mean? I told you that everything is over between that girl and me. It was an affair, that's all.'

'You've apologized and I've forgiven you. I would prefer not to talk about it.'

'You can hardly blame me, Sheila. If things were different between us . . .'

'I'm not blaming you. I just don't want to talk about it.'

'That's the problem, we don't talk about the things that matter.' Michael sounded troubled. 'This business about Aline – you surely can't believe that I had anything to do with it?'

I didn't stay to hear my mother's reply. I couldn't bear it when they quarrelled, and it was happening more and more. Everything was changing. My world had seemed to be full of sunshine. Until that day on the marshes . . .

I sat on the swing Michael had hung from the branches of a tree at the end of the garden. It was the nearest I could get to the woods. Mother had locked the gate and I was no longer allowed to play there. She had told me that morning that I was to go to boarding school next term. I wondered why I was being sent away from my home. Was it a punishment, because I'd done something wicked?

My head went up as I heard a scraping noise on the other side of the wall. It sounded as though someone was trying to climb it. I had sometimes played in the woods with friends from the village, and they had come through the gate into the gardens. Perhaps whoever it was wanted to see me, and had found it locked. I hadn't been to school since the incident on the marshes. Mother said I was convalescing, whatever that meant . . . I went to the gate and called out, 'Who is it? Who's there?'

There was silence, but I sensed that someone was there. I could hear harsh breathing, and suddenly I tingled with fear and backed away. My breath came jerkily as my heart began to pound.

'Aline . . .' a voice whispered. 'Aline, is that you?'

I stood uncertain, nervous, poised for flight but held by curiosity. 'Who are you? What do you want?'

'Aline, I thought I told you to play near the house.' My mother's voice broke the spell and I jumped as she came towards me. 'I don't want you to go out of sight.'

Even as she spoke, I heard a slithering noise on the other side of the wall, then a thump as if someone had landed hard. I walked towards my mother, relieved that she had come, even though I was in for a scolding.

'I was only playing on my swing,' I said. 'I didn't go out of the garden.'

'Well, I would rather you stayed nearer the house. I shan't feel safe until they catch whoever . . .' Mother frowned and hesitated, then, 'You're too big for that swing now, anyway. You should be doing your school work. The exam for boarding school is coming up next month. If you don't work hard you won't pass it.'

'Can't I just stay at my old school?'

She looked at me for a moment, then shook her head. 'No, I don't think so, darling. You'll be moving up next year, in any case, and I would rather you went to boarding school. It's a different kind of education. I'm sure you will enjoy it once you get there.'

I wasn't at all sure, but I didn't say anything. I just asked when I could go back to school.

Mother looked at me, her expression thoughtful. 'You can start next week, Aline. If you feel up to it.'

'I feel much better now,' I assured her. 'The bruises are all gone.'

I longed to be back at school with my friends. Back to normality and away from my mother's anxious fussing.

I was quiet as Mrs Mayes drove us back from school that afternoon. Usually my mother came to collect me, but on Thursdays she went to a meeting of the cottage hospital board and Mrs Mayes brought me home. Cathy Mayes was my best friend, or she had been until that morning. Now we sat in sullen silence, not looking at each other.

'Is something wrong, Aline?' Mrs Mayes looked at me and then at her daughter. 'You haven't quarrelled with Aline, have you, Cathy?'

'I only told her the truth,' Cathy said, looking scared. 'She called me a liar and hit me.'

'Is this true?' Mrs Mayes glanced at me. Guilt brought a flush to my cheeks as I nodded. 'What did Cathy say?'

'She – she said I was attacked and indecently assaulted on the marshes.' I felt angry and upset. 'What does that mean, Mrs Mayes?'

'It means that Cathy has been saying things she shouldn't.' She frowned at her daughter. 'You shouldn't listen to gossip and repeat what you don't understand, Cathy.' As Cathy bit her lip and looked down, Mrs Mayes glanced at me. 'You *were* attacked, Aline – but you must have known that.'

'No. . .' I shook my head. 'My mother said I'd had an accident . . .'

'Oh dear. I'm sorry, Aline. Sheila obviously didn't want you to know, but how she expected to keep it a secret when it was in all the papers . . .'

I stared at her, my heart skittering with fright. I hadn't known there was anything about me in the papers. They were never left lying around in our house; my mother was too particular. She liked things just so. We had tea in the drawing room in the afternoons, with shining silver and white starched napkins – something I knew none of my friends ever did; but then, Mother was different.

'Who . . .' My throat had gone dry. 'Who attacked me?'

'I'm not sure I should . . . I expect it was a man, but no one knows for sure.' Mrs Mayes frowned. 'I'll talk to your mother, ask her to explain.'

'No,' I said in sudden alarm. 'Please don't. I would rather ask her myself.'

'Well . . .' Cathy's mother hesitated, and I could see that she was embarrassed. 'It is a little difficult . . . Your mother . . . and of course Michael, there were whispers that he . . . Not that I believed for one moment . . . Perhaps that's best, my dear.' She frowned at her daughter. 'Cathy, say you're sorry for upsetting Aline – and you could apologize for hitting Cathy, Aline.'

'Sorry, Aline.'

'Sorry, Cathy.'

I apologized but I wasn't sorry. I would never forgive Cathy for what she'd said, or the taunting way she'd said it. I was glad that I was going to boarding school.

I jumped out of the car as it stopped at the end of the drive to Hazeling. The gate was unlocked. I realized why Mother had insisted on keeping it locked after I came out of hospital. It was to stop the people from the papers getting into the gardens. She had done it to protect me.

I was thoughtful as I walked through the avenue of trees towards the house. What did 'indecent assault' mean? Cathy had sniggered when she said it; that's why I'd hit her. Indecent meant something unpleasant. The word brought a look of disapproval to my mother's face. Showing your knickers wasn't decent. It was like something the girls giggled about behind the teacher's back at school, and I had a vague idea of what it might mean. When I got in, I intended to look it up in a dictionary.

It was not until I was almost at the house that it occurred to me to wonder if the person I'd heard trying to climb the wall at the end of the garden had been the same one who had attacked me on the marshes. The thought made me nervous, and I ran the last few yards home.

*

11

I woke screaming from a nightmare. As I sat up in bed, Michael came into the room, switching on the light at the door. He stood looking at me uncertainly for a moment, then came and sat on the edge of the bed, putting his arms around me. I clung to him, laying my head against his shoulder. It felt so good to be comforted by the man I had always thought of as my father.

'What's the matter?' he asked, lifting my chin with one finger as I stopped trembling. 'Was it a nightmare?'

'Yes . . .' I gulped and gave him a watery smile. 'I was on the marshes and – '

'Aline,' My mother's sharp voice interrupted. 'What's all this for then?'

'I – I had a bad dream,' I whispered. 'Someone was chasing me.'

Michael stood up and moved away as my mother began to fuss round the bed, tidying the sheets. 'Do you remember what happened?' he asked, his face strained.

'Of course she doesn't,' Mother put in quickly. 'It was just a dream. It's all those comics she reads. I've told you they're bad for her. I don't know why she likes them.'

I wondered why my mother was so on edge. It was as though she didn't want me to remember what had happened that day . . . as though she was afraid of what I might remember.

'Well, I'll go back to bed then,' Michael said. 'Why don't you leave a light on for her, Sheila?'

'She's not a baby.' Mother frowned, then glanced at me. 'Well, perhaps just this once. Settle down, Aline. I'll bring you a cup of milk to help you sleep.'

'Stay with me for a while, please.' My eyes pleaded with my stepfather.

Michael hesitated, glancing at my mother's face, then back at me. 'I'll be near if you need me,' he said. 'It was just a dream, Aline. You're quite safe now, I promise you.'

I lay back against the pillows as they went out. I heard their voices raised in anger and I knew they were arguing again.

'I think she ought to see someone,' Michael said. 'These nightmares could be a symptom . . .'

'Nonsense,' Mother snapped. 'It's best if she doesn't remember anything. She'll be going to boarding school soon and it will all be forgotten.'

'That's all that really matters to you, isn't it?' Michael said, his voice harsh. 'You're more concerned about what people might say than her state of mind. It's more convenient if she just forgets. You half suspect me, don't you? You and that bloody Inspector Robinson both!'

'He didn't make any such accusation, Michael.'

'No, but he thought a lot. I could see it in his eyes.'

My mother's reply was lost as they moved away. I lay very still, staring at a tiny crack in the ceiling and holding my breath as I wondered why everything had gone wrong. Was it my fault that my mother and Michael were so cross with each other?

A tear trickled from the corner of my eye, followed by another and another. I hated it when my parents quarrelled, and it was worse than ever when it was about me. I was suddenly glad that I was going to boarding school, away from this atmosphere of tension and distrust . . . And out of reach of whoever had been on the other side of the garden wall.

Chapter Two

Nine years later, the sun was warm on our heads as Julie and I lay side by side on the dry grass. From somewhere drifted the scent of roses, mingling with the sharper odour of the creosote workmen had been brushing on to a slatted fence. It was peaceful and still; the droning of the bees and the satisfying thwack of tennis balls were the only sounds to be heard.

'Only one more exam to go,' I sighed and stretched, turning on my side to look at the girl beside me. 'What are you going to do when term ends, Julie?'

A pretty, slightly plump girl of twenty with fine, pale hair and green eyes, Julie Gorden chewed on the stalk she'd just plucked from the long grass at the edge of the college playing field and screwed up her eyes against the sun.

'Some kind of counselling . . . But you know that, Aline. We've talked about it often enough.'

We had spent long hours sitting cross-legged on the floor of the tiny flat we shared, talking about Julie's experiences on the various field trips she'd undertaken as a student of social and behavioural problems.

'Yes, of course. I meant – are you going to take a holiday before you start work or go straight into a practice?'

'Oh, I see.' Julie looked at me and wrinkled her brow. 'I thought I'd take a holiday and apply for various posts, to be certain of getting something I want.'

'At least you know what you want to do,' I said. 'I don't think I'm cut out to be a helper, Julie. At least, not on the counselling side.'

'You're probably too reserved,' Julie agreed. 'You could go into administration, but I've always thought you would do something . . . artistic.'

'I can't draw to save my life!'

'There are other ways of being artistic,' Julie said, with a faint smile. 'What are you going to do when term ends?'

'Go home, at least for a while. I know my mother thinks I should stay at home and help her with her charity work until I get married.'

'Will you be happy doing that?'

'That's debatable.' I gave her a wry smile. 'I'm not even sure that I want to get married.'

'Marriage . . .' Julie pulled a face. 'I'm not sure about that either. I intend to explore all the possibilities, until I find a suitable man to be the father of my children.'

I grinned at her. During the years we'd spent at college together, we had become very close.

'And where does love come into all this?'

Julie smiled and raised her brows. 'You should know me well enough by now.'

I lay back and closed my eyes. Julie's men weren't exactly legion, but she fell in love easily and went from one boyfriend to the next without apparent harm. Sometimes I envied Julie, wishing I could be more like her.

Men were more difficult for me. Most of the time I went around in a group, forming casual relationships that demanded nothing. The previous year, however, I'd made the mistake of taking a relationship seriously.

It began as I emerged from the library, my arms full of research books. The books went flying as we bumped into each other, and Jerry Cole picked them up. He introduced himself and apologized, then asked me for a coffee. That was the first of several meetings. Some weeks later, he admitted he'd knocked into me on purpose.

'I'd seen you before,' he said, his dark eyes alight with self-mockery as he confessed. 'I wanted to get to know you.'

Jerry was over thirty and worked as a sales rep for a firm which made computers. Tall, dark and loose-limbed, with an attractive smile, he aroused my interest in a way that none of the younger men I'd met at college had. When he asked me out for a meal, I accepted. After that we saw each other whenever he was in town, which was every other week or so.

At first it was just for casual dates – a meal in the Chinese or a concert – then Jerry asked me to go away with him for a weekend at the coast. I knew what that meant, of course, and it took me a while to make up my mind. All my friends had had affairs, and so in the end I said yes. I didn't know him well, but he was fun and I decided it was about time I discovered what sex was like. Sometimes I thought I might be in love with him.

We drove down in his estate car, stopping for a picnic on the way. Jerry had borrowed a friend's caravan, and seemed intent on pleasing me. We had fun that day, swimming and lazing on the beach. It wasn't until after we'd made love that he told me he was married.

'Catherine and I go our own ways,' he said. 'But I didn't dream you were a virgin.' He sounded angry, as if I'd somehow deceived him.

'It doesn't matter.' I forced a laugh. 'It had to happen some time.'

It had had to happen, but it was a total disaster. I was stiff and awkward, and it had hurt like hell. We tried again a few nights later in the back of his estate car, but it wasn't any better. So it didn't surprise me when Jerry told me he was going on a business trip and wouldn't be around for a while. He was letting me down gently, and I didn't blame him. I wasn't a success sexually; though I responded when he kissed me, as soon as he started to touch me in an intimate way, I froze. Maybe I was frigid or something.

It wasn't easy to talk about it, even to Julie. I had thought I was falling in love with Jerry, and it hurt more than I'd expected. In the end, I just told her that it had been a mistake.

'He was married,' I said, and she smiled her understanding.

For some reason, when I went home for the Easter holidays I found myself telling Michael that I'd had an affair. I didn't tell him it had been a disaster, though – just that Jerry had been married and that it was over. We were in the garden. He was painting and I was on my knees, pulling weeds from the rose beds. A puzzled expression came into his eyes, as if he wondered why I'd told him. He looked at me in silence for a long time – so long that in the end I wasn't able to bear it. My eyes dropped and a flush stained my cheeks. I felt somehow cheapened, as if his silence was a reproach.

'I shouldn't tell your mother, if I were you,' was all he said, but I sensed something much deeper, stronger, that was an unspoken reprimand. Since then I'd stayed clear of messy affairs.

The memory of Michael's hurt eyes stirred in me with a sharpness that made me suddenly uneasy. Sitting up, I hugged my knees as I watched four second-year students playing tennis. When term ended I would be going back to Hazeling. I hadn't lived there for years – except for holidays.

'Julie,' I said, 'would you come home with me when term ends, just for a while? We could have some fun together – and you could apply for jobs just the same.'

Julie rolled over to look at me. She studied me for a moment, sensing my unease because we were so close.

'Sure, why not?' she said, smiling. 'I'll pop home for a couple of days then catch the train to Norwich.'

16

'If you ring me, I'll meet you there,' I said. 'Thanks, Julie. I do appreciate it.'

'I like Hazeling,' Julie replied. 'We can spend the summer together.' She wrinkled her brow. 'Is something the matter?'

'No, of course not,' I lied. I couldn't explain the vague fear that lingered in my subconscious whenever I thought about Michael. 'You know Mother likes you.'

'I like your ma,' Julie said, her eyes twinkling. 'And the fantastic Michael. I could go for him in a big way – if he wasn't married to your mother, of course.'

Julie grinned, and I relaxed. She was only joking. She couldn't know that I suspected my stepfather of being unfaithful to my mother; nor could she guess at those other shadowy fears from the past.

'We'd better go,' I said, standing up and brushing my skirt. We had one final lecture on social studies with our most popular teacher before the onset of exams. 'Mustn't be late for old Stringer's last fling. They say he saves the best until the end . . .'

'What are you saying?' I stared at Michael across the drawing room. The sun was slanting through the leaded windows on to a crystal bowl, and the rainbow of light dazzled my eyes. 'I don't understand. She was fine when I came down for Easter . . . wasn't she?'

'You should know your mother,' he said. 'She never gives in until the last minute. It might have been better if she had.'

'What do you mean by ill?'

'Very ill.' Michael's face was white and strained. 'You have to know, Aline: Sheila is dying. It's cancer.'

'It can't be!'

'It seemed to come on all of a sudden, but knowing Sheila, she'd been putting on a show. I didn't notice anything myself until just before she had the tests. She was losing weight the last few weeks, but I thought it was another of her diets . . .'

The shock sent me dizzy and I swayed. I felt as if I was going to faint. Then Michael was there beside me, his hand on my shoulder. His nearness made me pull myself together, and I moved away. Michael's hand fell to his side and a tiny muscle twitched at the corner of one eye.

'Aline, I'm sorry.'

'How long have you known?'

'A few weeks. The doctors did some tests a couple of months ago, but it's too late for surgery.'

17

I felt a quick twist of anger. 'Why didn't you tell me? I could have come home earlier.'

'Sheila asked me not to. She didn't want to worry you while you were taking your exams.'

'To hell with my exams! If she's dying . . .' I caught my breath on a sob, my eyes accusing as I looked at him. 'You should have told me.'

'It isn't going to happen overnight,' he said, realizing that I was blaming him. 'At the moment the pain comes and goes.'

'Is it going to get worse?'

'Yes.'

I felt the colour drain from my face and I turned away, hugging my arms across my chest. My throat was closing with emotion and I found it difficult to breathe. It wasn't happening. Mother couldn't be dying . . . She couldn't!

'I'd better phone Julie and tell her not to come.' It was a stupid thing to say but I was too stunned to think properly.

'That's a bit drastic,' Michael said. 'Why not let her? The house is big enough. Besides, Sheila will be upset if you cancel. She doesn't want a fuss and she likes Julie.'

'All right.' I stared at him, unable to fight back. It was as if all the strength had drained out of me. 'Can I go up and see her?'

Michael looked at me in silence. I felt untidy in my sloppy tracksuit and a pair of worn-out trainers. His expression was disturbing. I thought he was criticizing me.

'I look a mess,' I muttered, flushing. 'I ought to change first.'

'You look great,' he said, but the words were forced out of him. 'What the hell does it matter? Just try not to cry all over her. You know she hates that.'

'Yes, I know. I won't cry, I promise.' I was hurt by his harshness. He sounded angry with me, and I didn't know why. Or perhaps he was angry with himself. I wasn't sure. 'At least, not in front of Mother.'

'That's my girl.' Michael seemed to recover himself. He gave me an encouraging smile. 'Go up to her now. She should be awake. She sleeps for an hour or so after lunch. She'll come down for dinner . . . Doesn't eat much but she tries. Sheila will never give up.'

'She wouldn't want to let the side down.' We smiled at each other in a moment of understanding. 'I'll go up now.'

I felt sick inside as I went out into the hall. My eyes were lowered as I walked to the bottom of the main stairs. Accustomed to the masses of paintings in every available space on the walls, I looked neither to the left nor to the right. It wasn't that I didn't appreciate the beauty of my ancient home, but having grown up amongst the treasures of Hazeling, I took them for granted. Furniture polished to a silken sheen over hundreds of years was a part of the scenery, to be used and abused with a familiar clutter of discarded gloves, scarves and other paraphernalia.

Walking upstairs, I conquered my emotions. My mother would hate it if I cried. I paused in front of a gilt-framed mirror, wiped my eyes and tucked a wisp of dark, heavy hair behind my ear. Then, forcing a smile, I walked on to Mother's room and knocked. I waited until she invited me to enter.

She sounded exactly the same as always. Sitting up against a pile of pillows, Mother looked as immaculate as ever – not a hair out of place, face powdered, lipstick and just a trace of eyeshadow. It should have been reassuring, but somehow it wasn't.

I swallowed hard. 'How did you know it was me?'

'I was expecting you, darling. Come and kiss me.'

I perched on the edge of the bed, taking her hand and kissing her cheek. It felt very soft, and I was aware of her vulnerability. She had always seemed so strong.

'I've asked Julie to stay for a while – is that all right?'

'Of course. It will be good for you to have a friend. I shan't be able to take you out myself.'

'I don't need – ' I stopped myself. Whenever I was at home Mother insisted on taking me everywhere, as if I were still her little girl. 'How are you today? Michael told me about . . .'

She squeezed my hand. 'We shan't talk about it now, Aline. I'm getting on as well as can be expected in the circumstances. Tell me about you. Was your last term at college fun? Have you got a friend – a boyfriend, I mean?'

'Masses of them,' I said. 'Julie and I went to a party with eight friends, most of them men. We had a fantastic time. Stayed out until six the next morning and then took a punt down the river for breakfast in our evening clothes.'

Mother did her best to look as if she approved. 'That does sound fun, darling.'

Once she would have frowned on my staying out all night. I was surprised at the change in her, but then I understood. She was making an effort to get close to me.

'It was a celebration,' I said.

'Yes, of course.' She patted my hand. 'Is there anyone special yet?'

'No.' I avoided her eyes. 'I'm not in any hurry to get married.'

She did frown then. 'It's such a nuisance my being like this. I'd

19

planned so much for when you left college. I wanted you to find someone nice, the kind of man you can trust.'

'I might not get married.' I stood up and walked to the window, and looked down at the lawns leading to the shrubbery. I mustn't be irritated with her, I thought. 'At least, not for ages.'

'I hope you're not thinking of – of living with someone?' Mother was pulling a face as I turned. 'That's not what I want for you, Aline.'

'It's not what I want either.' I smiled, and the tension went out of me. She was just the same underneath, and I was glad. I didn't want her to change too much – not now. 'Don't worry, Mother, I shan't let you down. When I find the right person, I'll get married.'

'Good.' She held out her hand. 'Come and sit with me for a while, darling. I want to hear all your news . . .'

'But that's terrible,' Julie said when I met her at the station a couple of days later. 'You should have rung me and cancelled.'

'Mother wants you to stay. She's trying to carry on as normal, and she says we're to do the same: go out and enjoy ourselves as if nothing were wrong.'

'She's amazing, your mother.' Julie hugged me. 'But what do *you* want?'

'I think we should do as she asks, for the time being. If I stay in the house all the time, I'll just end up crying. You know how she'd hate that.'

'Yes,' Julie agreed. 'But if you change your mind, if you want me to go – just say.'

'I shan't do that.'

I hesitated, wondering if I ought to tell Julie why it was more important than ever to have her at Hazeling, but even as I considered it, I knew it was impossible. It would be too embarrassing for everyone.

'How has Michael taken it?' Julie asked, and I was startled. It was almost as if she could read my thoughts.

'What do you mean?'

'This kind of thing affects people in different ways. I wondered if he was feeling guilty, blaming himself.'

'Blaming himself?' I stared at her, considering. 'Because they haven't got on all that well for years, I suppose. It could be part of the reason he's behaving a bit oddly now. Yes, you might be right.'

'He's always struck me as an introspective, moody sort of a person – perhaps because he spends so much of his time alone.'

'Do you think he has ever been unfaithful to her?' I asked, looking at Julie. 'I mean, had affairs with other women?'

'Do you want the truth?' Julie took a deep breath as I nodded. 'I think it's possible. After all, he's a very attractive man and – well, they've had separate rooms for several years, haven't they?'

It was what I'd suspected, but knowing that Julie thought the same made it worse. 'That's horrible.' I felt angry with my stepfather. 'I hope he does blame himself. He should!'

'Not for her illness, surely?' Julie sighed as she saw I was upset. 'I wish I hadn't said anything, now.'

'It isn't your fault. I always thought their quarrels were Mother's fault, but if he was betraying her . . .'

'She hasn't divorced him.' Julie's was the voice of reason. 'So she must still care for him.'

'My mother doesn't believe in divorce. You don't know her, Julie. She would put up with anything rather than risk a scandal. She's always been like that.'

'She must have cared for him once.'

'A long time ago. Before . . .' Sighing, I changed the subject. 'I've got my car. Shall we pop into Sheringham for lunch, or do you want to go straight to Hazeling?'

'It's a gorgeous day,' Julie said, tucking her arm through mine. 'Why not make the most of it? It might rain tomorrow.'

'This place is always good,' I said as I drew in in front of the sea-facing pub. 'We sometimes used to eat here when I was a child.'

'You see if there's a table,' Julie said. 'I must just pop to the cloakroom.'

Smiling, I locked the car as she made a dash for the ladies. It was quite a while since I'd been to this particular pub, but the restaurant was very good. I went inside, hesitating on the threshold. They didn't seem very busy, so I thought we stood a good chance of getting a meal. Then, as I looked across the room, I saw a couple sitting at a table in the corner, and my heart stood still.

It was Michael, and he was with a young and beautiful woman. They were engrossed in each other, holding hands in a way that could only be described as intimate, and talking earnestly. I kept on staring. Michael was having lunch with a girl almost young enough to be his daughter while my mother was lying in her bed at Hazeling, dying of a painful illness. I was so disgusted that I wanted to march across to their table and tell him what I thought of him.

How *could* he? How could he do that to her? The woman's fingers intertwined with Michael's, and she laughed up at him. Anyone could see that she was fascinated with him. And he appeared to find her very intriguing. It made me want to hit him. As the throbbing began at my temples, I backed away, blocking Julie's path as she came out of the cloakroom.

'They haven't got a table after all,' I lied. 'Come on, I think I would rather eat fish and chips on the beach.'

Nothing could have made me eat in the same room as Michael and his friend. The food would have stuck in my throat and choked me.

Julie glanced at me as I led the way back outside. I think she suspected something was very wrong, but she didn't say a word. Julie knew that I had a temper when roused, and it must have been obvious to my friend that I was ready to let fly.

Somehow I managed to get through dinner that evening without saying anything, but my eyes conveyed a message. He knew I was angry but he went on making polite conversation, asking Julie what her plans were now that she had left college, and ignoring me. After dinner, he said he had to work in his studio. Julie and I watched a horror film on the video. It was nearly midnight before we said goodnight, but Michael hadn't come in. Slipping on a coat, I took a torch from the cupboard under the stairs and walked the short distance to his studio. He was still working, the lights from his huge arc lamps flaring in the darkness.

For a few moments I watched through the window. He seemed very intent on his work, his strokes swift, decisive, almost driven. I couldn't see the canvas, but his face was very strange, obsessed . . . He looked startled as I went in, and stared at me as if I were some kind of a vision. Then, as I walked towards him, he quickly placed a blank canvas over the one he'd been working on.

I saw guilt in his eyes, and I frowned. It was obvious that he didn't want me to see what he was painting. Perhaps it was a picture of the girl I'd seen in the restaurant. Remembering why I had come, I was angry again.

'I saw you at lunchtime,' I said. 'You were with someone. A young woman. You seemed very intimate with her.'

Michael frowned, then nodded as if my words had made sense. 'So that's what's wrong,' he said. 'That was Zena. She's just a friend, Aline. I met her at a gallery where I was selling one of my paintings. She was working there part-time.'

'She didn't look like a casual friend,' I said, my tone sharp with accusation.

He turned away, his face tight. 'Your mother and I have an

22

understanding,' he said. 'Sheila wasn't alone. The nurse was there all the time.'

'So that makes it all right, does it?'

'You're angry,' he said. 'You don't understand, Aline. Your mother and I . . . We haven't shared a bedroom for years.'

'I don't see what that has to do with it.'

'Don't you?' Michael's voice was soft and a little sad. 'No, perhaps you don't.' His eyes were steady as he looked into mine. 'I'm sorry you had to see me with Zena. It was unfortunate.'

'Unfortunate!' I was so angry that I just flew at him, my hand raised to strike. He held my wrist, his fingers long and slender and very strong. I was surprised how strong he was. For a moment we stared at each other, something flickered in his eyes, and I had the strangest sensation. I thought that he wanted to kiss me, and my eyes widened, then I pulled away from him. 'Damn you, Michael! How could you?'

I had ceased to threaten and he let me go without a fight. 'Please don't make a fuss about this, Aline – and don't upset your mother. She doesn't need to know anything she doesn't already know. Do you understand me?'

'Do you imagine that I would be such a fool as to tell her?'

'Then why did you come?' he asked, his eyes narrowing. 'Is it because you were angry with me? You needn't be. Zena is just a friend.'

'I don't believe you,' I said. His words had made me realize that I was jealous – for myself as well as my mother. Once, he had saved his special smiles for me; now we might almost have been strangers. 'Oh, don't worry, I shan't say anything . . . I just wanted you to know that I think you're despicable!'

A wry smile twisted his mouth then. 'It should make you happy to know that whatever you think of me, I think worse of myself.'

'What do you mean?' I demanded, but he shook his head.

Suddenly, he looked exhausted. 'Go away, Aline,' he said in a weary voice. 'I'm tired and I want to be alone.'

'Go to hell!' I said, then turned on my heel.

As I walked back to the house, I wondered why my cheeks were wet. I couldn't be crying. Michael wasn't worth anyone's tears.

After that, Michael was seldom in the house. I believed he was avoiding me, though the excuse was that he had to work. It was as well that we didn't have to meet too often – when we did the tension between us was almost unbearable.

Julie and I went out for a while most mornings. In the afternoons I sat

23

with my mother for an hour or so, talking or reading to her from her favourite books. She loved the classics, Jane Austen and the Brontë sisters, or poetry. Keats was her favourite. I lost count of the times she asked me to read from 'The Eve of St Agnes'. Mostly we just talked.

'What are you going to do with your life, Aline?' she wanted to know. 'You mustn't become a slave to Hazeling, as I've been. I want you to be happy.'

It had never occurred to me that my mother had felt like that about Hazeling. It was of course a huge monster that guzzled money at an alarming rate, but that was because it was old and beautiful and had been in our family for as long as anyone could remember. It was a listed building and therefore it was our duty to preserve it, but I had believed it was what my mother wanted to do. I had imagined myself helping her with all the work she did for various committees and charities. Now I was aware of a gap in my life and I stared at her in uncertainty.

'I don't know. I hadn't thought about it.'

She smiled and took my hand. 'You've had a good education, Aline, and you've lived with beautiful things all your life. Why don't you put that to good use?'

'What do you mean?'

'I think you should leave Hazeling when I die,' she said, ignoring my sharp, indrawn breath. 'Find yourself a job in London – perhaps at an auction house. You know about antiques, Aline. You could work as an appraiser for a while, just until you feel more sure of yourself, then you might open your own business.'

I felt a flicker of interest. 'Do you think I could? I mean, I know a little but . . .'

'You know a lot more than you think,' she said. 'And you can learn. Think about it, anyway; it was just a suggestion.' She smiled at me. 'Could you bear to read to me for a while now?'

'Of course.' I picked up the worn book of poetry from her bedside table. 'Where shall we start?'

We had celebrated Christmas very quietly, and since then Mother had deteriorated a little more each day. Now, as the cold days of January wore on, I knew I was losing her. One wild night, I sat by her bed. Outside, the wind howling in the trees sounded evil. Watching as my mother's breathing became more and more shallow, I knew that it was nearly finished. I watched without tears, feeling relief at this moment of Mother's release – and gratitude for the closeness, the tenderness of the past few days. I had felt more loved during these last hours of my mother's life that ever before. We hadn't talked much, but the understanding had been there.

'She's gone now.'

I felt the touch of a hand on my shoulder and looked up at the nurse. Then I nodded and got to my feet.

'I'll tell Michael.'

'You can both come back later.'

'Yes, of course.'

A numbness was stealing over me as I left the room and walked along the landing as if I were in one of the dreams that had haunted me for years. It seemed a lifetime since Michael had first told me that Mother was ill, though it was only six months.

Michael looked up as I entered the drawing room. He stared at me, and he must have seen something in my face, because he got up and came to meet me.

'I'm so sorry, Aline.'

As his hand reached towards me, I moved away, rejecting his sympathy. 'At least she's not suffering.' My lips were stiff and I felt numbed. 'The nurse is – is looking after her. We can go up later.'

'Yes. I'd better make the necessary phonecalls.' Michael looked at me, and hesitated. I thought he was going to reach out to me again, but he turned away. 'As you said, she isn't suffering now. We must be thankful for that.'

I couldn't answer. I remained with my back towards him, relaxing only when the door closed behind him. For a moment I felt sick and shivery, and I thought I might faint. Then I moved towards the sideboard and poured myself a generous brandy from one of the decanters. I gulped it down, gasping as the liquid stung my throat and made me choke, then refilled the glass. I sank on to the rug in front of the fire, stared into the flames and sipped my drink. The alcohol was restoring me, bringing me back to life and banishing the awful numbness. Bowing my head, I covered my face with my hands as the first sob broke from me. Then I was caught by a storm of grief, the tears I'd held back for so long pouring down my cheeks.

'Aline, my poor darling . . .'

I heard Michael's voice, but I was too upset to move. Even when he knelt beside me, drawing me to my feet and up into his arms, my grief was so overwhelming that I offered no resistance. I stood like a rag doll as he held me close, his lips moving against my hair, whispering words of comfort.

'Michael. Oh, Michael . . .'

25

For a few moments I was a child again. I clung to him, needing to feel the strength of his arms around me. Then, abruptly, he let go. For one intense moment he stood staring at me, then he turned away, breathing deeply to steady himself.

'I'm going up to Sheila now,' he muttered. 'Give me a few minutes alone, Aline. Please.'

I couldn't answer. I was shaking all over, my head whirling. When I finally turned, Michael had gone and there was no one to see the expression in my eyes, no one to witness the grief I knew must be written all over my face.

'You must come up soon,' Julie said over the phone. 'The job doesn't pay much – I'm on probation, but there's a chance of promotion. My father helped me with a mortgage for the flat. It's small, of course, but I've got a spare bedroom, so you can stay as long as you like.'

'I'm so glad things are going well for you,' I replied. 'I might come next week. There are still a few things to settle with the solicitors. It was such a shock when Mr Jones told me that my father had left most of his fortune in trust for me. I knew he'd made a trust, of course, but I thought Mother must have inherited the bulk of the money when he died. She's just had an income for life. Hazeling is mine – there's some weird clause about my not being able to sell it – and I get the capital on my twenty-fifth birthday. Until then I just receive an income, the same as I've been getting since I was eighteen, I think. I must say, Julie, it makes me feel uncomfortable, even guilty.'

'Did Michael know all this when he married your mother?'

'No . . .' I frowned, feeling uncertain. 'I don't think he knew all of it. Mother asked in her will that he be allowed to go on living at Hazeling, at least until the trust ends, to give himself time to sort himself out, I suppose. She left him her own money, just a few thousand pounds. It won't be enough to keep the house going. I'm going to make over most of my trust income to help out.'

'Are you sure about that?' Julie was being a concerned friend.

'Quite sure. I've already signed the papers. You know, I never spend even half my trust income. Besides, I may take a job somewhere. It would be better than moping about down here. Michael is out most of the time, and I get bored.'

'Going to be a working girl like me.' Julie chuckled. 'Good for you. See you soon, love. We'll talk about it when you come up. Perhaps you can find something in London, then we can be together.'

'Yes, that's what I thought. I'll see you next week, Julie. Bye.'

'Bye for now.'

Putting down the receiver, I sat for a moment staring into space. The house seemed so quiet now. Earlier, Mabel, our cheerful daily, had been whistling as she went about her work, but now there was only the sound of the rain pattering against the window. A melancholy sound at the best of times, it was a reminder of my loneliness. I missed my mother far more than I would have thought possible. We hadn't always got on in the past, but I had loved her.

Shivering, I reached out to push a log on the fire. I poked the embers with a sturdy steel iron, mesmerized as a shower of sparks flew up the chimney. The sudden shrill of the phone made me jump.

I hesitated, thinking it might be yet another of my mother's acquaintances making a sympathy call. They had been ringing for weeks now, people I hardly knew. I picked up the receiver with a sigh.

'Aline Marlowe speaking,' I said. There was silence so I spoke again. 'Hello, is anyone there?'

'Aline . . .' The voice was muffled, but definitely male. 'Are you alone?'

'Who is this?' Something about his voice made me wary. 'What do you want?'

'I've been thinking about you. I think about you a lot.'

'Who are you?'

'Don't you know? Surely you remember, Aline.'

'Remember? What should I remember?'

'I remember you . . .'

I slammed down the receiver, feeling angry. It was bound to be a crank call, in all probability someone who had read about my inheritance. The local paper had written a large piece about Mother's charity work and my father's death while flying a light aircraft – that had always appealed to journalists because he was young, rich and dynamic, and his death had had a touch of romance about it – finishing the article with a few lines about Hazeling. The man must have read it. Now he thought it was a joke to make vaguely threatening phonecalls. It was frightening because I was alone in an empty house. If it happened again I might have to have the number changed, though if I found a job in London, I would only be there at weekends or for holidays . . .

I decided that I would tell Michael I was leaving that evening. What I didn't know was that he had something to tell me.

'You're getting married next week?' I stared at Michael in disbelief. 'But Mother's only been dead three months.' My eyes opened wider as I looked at the woman by his side. 'She's almost young enough to be your daughter.'

'Aline, listen to me.' Michael's lips were bloodless. 'It's for the best, really it is.'

'For you! It was going on before Mother died. You lied to me, Michael. You said Zena was a friend. Don't try to deny it.'

Michael's face was tight as he controlled his anger. 'You don't understand, Aline. Sheila and I . . .'

'What difference does it make?' Zena spoke for the first time. 'You must have known that things weren't right between your mother and Michael. Their marriage was over years ago; they stayed together only because your mother didn't want a divorce.'

'How do you know?' I flared, temper making me glare at her. 'I suppose he's told you everything?' I turned on Michael as the bitterness twisted inside me. 'Have you? Have you told her about. . . ?'

'Aline, please don't,' He said, his mouth stern. 'You must believe that I never meant to hurt you.'

'Never meant to . . .' I stared at him in contempt. 'Do you have any idea of how I feel – do you?'

'Aline, please.' he choked on the words. 'You don't know, you don't know how I – '

'I know that you betrayed Mother – and me.'

He stared at me for a moment, then moved towards me, his fists clenching. Zena rushed forward as if to intervene between us, and her arm brushed against a small table, sending a vase crashing to the floor. It smashed into several pieces, and she gave a cry of dismay.

'I'm sorry. I didn't mean to . . .'

'Mother's favourite vase,' I cried. 'You broke it on purpose.'

'Zena couldn't have known. It was an accident.'

'Go on,' I yelled, 'defend her. Well, I don't care any more. I hate her and I hate you. I'm leaving this minute and I shan't be back. I don't want to see either of you again.'

I ran from the room and hurried upstairs. After locking the bedroom door, I began to pack furiously. Tears stung my eyes, but I was too angry to cry. All I wanted was to get out of the house, away from Michael and the beautiful woman he was going to marry.

I took Julie at her word and went to stay with her in London. She asked no questions even though it must have been obvious that something was wrong. After a while, I told her what had happened. Julie looked at me for a few minutes, her face thoughtful, then she said, 'So what are you going to do now?'

'Find a job,' I told her. 'I've signed most of my income over to Michael for the house, so there's not much else I can do. Anyway, I'm not going back.'

'I don't blame you, of course, you know you can stay here until you sort yourself out.'

'Thanks, Julie. I'll find a job then somewhere to live.'

It took a few weeks of searching before I found what I wanted, but I wasn't prepared to settle for anything less than a challenge. The big auction houses offered me secretarial work, but I turned them down. I also turned down the chance of managing a boutique and a flower shop in Mayfair, both of which belonged to friends of my mother. I was determined that when I landed a job it would be through my own efforts, so when I turned up for the interview with Mr Silcott I left all the recommendations from well-meaning friends at home.

Silcott and Barrie was a small but busy auction house, with its offices and saleroom tucked away in a back street just off Soho. Despite the competition from the giants who dominated the London fine art market, Gerald Silcott was just about managing to hold his own – probably because he specialized in bric-a-brac and Victoriana, as he told me with a rather engaging smile.

'Of course I don't turn down the chance to handle the better stuff when it comes along, Miss Marlowe. It's just that I can make a living out of the things other houses turn down.'

'And exactly what does the job entail?' I asked, with a doubtful frown. 'I'm not looking for secretarial work, though I can type and use a word processor.'

'There's a bit of typing involved,' he said, seeming anxious. 'But you wouldn't be stuck in an office all the time. We open the rooms three days a week for appraisals, and people bring in items they want to sell. You would be giving them advice, identifying the goods and giving estimates of what they could expect to get in auction. Sometimes it involves considerable research and you might have to get other experts in.'

'And I would be working with you,' I said. 'I don't want to mislead you, Mr Silcott. I do know something about antiques, but I'm not sure about prices.'

'A bright girl like you will soon learn,' he said, to encourage me. 'You can study our catalogues for the past twelve months, and that will give you a general idea. Besides, I'll be on hand to help you out, at least until you've got the hang of it. Eventually, I shall want you to take over the estimates altogether, releasing me to do outside calls.'

'It does sound interesting . . .' I hesitated. 'And you said that later on there might be cataloguing for large private collections?'

'That's quite a promising area of growth for the business,' he said. 'I'm doing more and more of it, for insurance companies: verifying genuine antiques and weeding out the fakes. That's why I'm looking for an assistant to help out here.'

There was a note of pleading in his voice, and I laughed. I had taken an instant liking to Mr Silcott and I thought the job would be just what I needed to help me get started and blow the cobwebs away.

'Well, I could give it a try,' I said, and smiled as I saw the relief in his face. 'It does sound as if it's just what I'm looking for. I don't think I could bear to be stuck over a typewriter all day, and I'm not interested in managing a boutique.'

'Then that's settled,' he said, looking pleased. 'When can you start?'

'I'm moving into my flat tomorrow,' I said. 'So shall we say Monday morning?'

'Wonderful.' He stood up and we shook hands. 'I shall look forward to it, Aline.'

'It's going to be rather exciting,' I said. 'I'll see you on Monday then.'

Emerging into the street, I was feeling pleased with myself. I'd found myself a flat I could afford, and now I had a job I knew I was going to enjoy. The only shadow hanging over me was the row with Michael. I knew that I ought to ring and apologize, but somehow I just couldn't. To my mind his behaviour was inexcusable, and I wasn't ready to forgive him just yet.

Chapter Three

'It belonged to my grandmother,' the woman said, pulling out a bulky object wrapped in several layers of tissue. 'I wondered if you could tell me what it's worth.'

I took the parcel from her, experiencing the now familiar tingle as I began to unwrap it. I'd been working in the saleroom for almost two years and I still found it exciting when people brought in their possessions. Often the contents were very ordinary – pieces of china or glass that would raise no more than a few pounds for their owners – and it was sad to see the disappointment in their faces when I had to tell them that their treasures were not of any great value. Now and then, though, something wonderful emerged from the yellowed tissue, and I got a feeling for it – a nose, as the dealers would say. I had that feeling now as I removed the last layers, and then I gasped as I saw what was in my hand.

'This is magnificent,' I said, feeling a kind of reverence as I examined the delicate porcelain vase and looked closely at the decoration, colour and factory marks. 'I'm almost certain that it's Chelsea. The blue is right and the richness of the gilding . . . and see the way those birds are painted. I think this is something special, but I would like to confer with my colleague for a moment, if you don't mind.'

Her eyes brightened and she nodded consent. I took the vase to Mr Silcott and he confirmed my assessment, looking excited.

'See if you can get her to leave it for auction,' he said. 'I'd like to have that in the special sale next month.'

I went back to my place at the counter and smiled at the expectant owner. 'Yes, it is early Chelsea,' I said. 'Is it just the one or do you have a pair?'

'The other one is here.' She produced it with a look of triumph from a box at her feet. 'What could I get for them?'

I examined the second vase. It was in perfect condition.

'We would estimate between three thousand and three thousand five hundred for the pair,' I said.

'Good Lord!' Her face lit up with excitement. 'They've been in the attic for ages. I was only expecting enough to pay a few bills. Can I leave them with you then?'

'Yes, of course. If you'll give me your details, I'll have them entered in our special porcelain sale next month.'

'Would you have a look at this for me?'

She produced a very old leather jewellery case. It was round, with an odd little hump in the lid. Opening it, I saw an exquisite set of pearl necklace, tiara, bracelets and eardrops. The necklace was a collar of four strings, with a heart-shaped pendant and a clasp of rough-cut diamonds. There was a similar clasp on the bracelet. They were on the borderline between late Georgian and early Victorian.

'I would like to examine these more carefully,' I said. 'If the pearls are in good condition, I think we could expect upwards of a thousand pounds for the set. Pearls are not making quite as much as they were, but these are pretty. We might get more if a collector takes a fancy to them.'

'As much as that?' The client looked delighted. 'I'll leave them with you, then. I wasn't sure the pearls were real.'

'I think you'll find we shall have a lot of interest in them,' I said, feeling pleased by her obvious excitement.

It was only when she was leaving that I became aware of someone watching me. A man was standing by a wall hung with pictures for viewing before sale. As I became aware of his interest and looked up, he turned away, but I was able to catch just a glimpse of his profile before he moved on. He was tall, attractive and had a lightly tanned complexion with a suggestion of dark stubble. Then I had to give my attention to a man with a large and very black copper tea kettle on a stand.

'What's it worth then?' he demanded in a belligerent tone. 'They make a lot of money so my mate says.'

Discovering a hole in the bottom of the kettle, I began to explain that the value was reduced by its condition. He was a little put out at first and it took some patience to convince him that my estimate was correct. When he left, Mr Silcott came up to me.

'You handled that well,' he said. 'I think I shall be able to leave the appraisals entirely to you soon.'

I smiled at his compliment, then glanced around. There was no sign of the man who had seemed interested in me. Somehow the incident bothered me. Mr Silcott asked if something was wrong.

I shook my head. 'No. No, there's nothing wrong,' I said, but a vague unease lingered at the back of my mind and I wondered why the man had been staring at me. Yet surely I was being oversensitive, jumping at shadows.

It was because I'd started getting odd phonecalls, just like the one at Hazeling after my mother died – silences, then that peculiar muffled voice asking me if I remembered.

'It's not that he uses filthy words,' I said to Julie some time later. 'I almost wish he would. I could cope with that.'

Julie sipped her coffee and then sat back, staring at me, her brow creased in a puzzled frown. 'What exactly is it about these phonecalls that bothers you so much – and how long have you been having them?'

'The first one was at Hazeling, the night I left to come and stay with you.'

Julie looked startled. 'I thought they'd started recently.' She glanced round the flat as if expecting to see someone lurking in the corner. 'How long have you lived here now? Is it two years?'

'About that.' I thought for a moment. 'The calls started again just over a month ago. I've had four now . . .' My skin prickled. 'It's as though he knows me, Julie. I've begun suspecting strangers now. A man looked at me in the saleroom the other morning and I started imagining that he was watching me. I know it's stupid but . . .'

'It's creepy.' Julie gave an exaggerated shiver. 'You think all the calls were from the same man, then? He rang you at Hazeling, and then after a lapse of two years, he starts again. That sounds peculiar to me. What makes you so sure it is the same man? Most of these calls are just cranks picking a number at random.'

'Yes, that's what I thought at first, but – ' I broke off, feeling awkward. I couldn't tell Julie what was really worrying me. 'It bothers me because he seems to know all about me.' I drew a sharp breath. 'Last time, he mentioned the marshes at Blakeney. He asked me if I remembered.'

'Remembered what?' Julie looked blank.

'I – I was attacked as a child.' For a moment my hand moved restlessly on the arm of my chair. 'I told you.'

'Sorry. Of course – you did tell me. You could never remember what happened, could you?'

'No, nothing concrete – just vague pictures. I had bad dreams but when I woke up . . .' I shook my head. 'I'm not going to think about it. It's silly of me to be upset by the calls.'

'You could have your number changed.'

'Yes, but that's such a nuisance. I would have to go ex-directory too,

33

and that makes it difficult for people who need to contact me. Besides, I'm going away the week after next. I shall be in Spain for a month.'

'Lucky you.' Julie pulled a face. 'I wish I were coming with you.'

'I'm renting a studio apartment,' I said. 'You're welcome to come out while I'm there. I thought I might as well take it for the whole of my holiday. Mr Silcott always closes the saleroom down for August; he says the auctions are dead anyway then, so it's easier to shut down.' I picked up my cup and headed for the kitchen. 'Want some more coffee? I'm having another.'

'Please.' Julie followed me into the small kitchen. 'What's up? It isn't like you to be upset by some crank on the phone.'

Smothering a sigh, I leaned against the sink. 'I wish I knew, Julie. Maybe it's just the weather.'

It was difficult to explain the restlessness that had come over me in the past few weeks. It was as if I were waiting for something to happen. I had an unpleasant feeling that there was a presence shadowing me. I'd even had a few disturbing dreams again, something that hadn't happened for ages.

'Is it the quarrel with Michael?' Julie persisted. 'You haven't been home since you left, have you?'

'No. I sent for some things I wanted for the flat, but I didn't go down. I've spoken to Zena on the phone a couple of times and apologized for being rude, but I don't want to talk to Michael. It's no good, I can't forgive him.'

Julie hesitated, as if she wanted to argue the point, then shrugged her shoulders. 'You know best about that . . .' An imp of mischief lit her eyes. 'What you need is a man. I'll see who I can find for you on Saturday.'

Julie was giving one of her parties. It was something she was terrific at: she had lots of bright ideas for making things fun, and she was a fantastic cook. She was also doing well at her job as a counsellor at a clinic, though she didn't talk about that much. She said one of the first rules of the job was that the counsellor must not impose her own views on clients – or friends. But I knew that her work was important and that she was respected by her colleagues.

'I'll come to the party, of course,' I said, 'but I'm not sure that a man is the answer to my problems.' I shook my head as she raised her brows. 'We've done nothing but talk about me all evening. I want to know about your new man – what's his name?'

'Tony Newman.' A dreamy smile came over her face. 'You know, I think he might just be the one . . .'

'I seem to have heard that one before.'

'This time it's different,' Julie said, and I could see she meant it.

'Really? Then I do want to know all about him. I think this calls for a celebration. Let's open a bottle of wine.'

On that Saturday morning I went shopping. One of my favourite pastimes was browsing around the market stalls and little junk shops tucked away in back streets. I picked up lots of interesting stuff, most of it of no real value. Memorabilia from the fifties and sixties always attracted me, in particular old records. I had a huge collection of 78s: Buddy Holly, Elvis Presley, Jim Reeves, early Sinatra, Ray Charles and countless others. It was the thrill of tracking them down that I enjoyed, the excitement when I found something I'd been looking for for a long time.

The stallholders knew me by now and watched with indulgence as I delved into anything new in stock. Sometimes they had boxes full of records, but often a lot of them were broken or scratched.

That morning, I spent an hour or so going from stall to stall, then I saw it, a pristine copy of an original 'Blue Suede Shoes'. My hand reached towards it at exactly the same moment as someone else's. As our fingers touched, I looked up into the man's eyes. They were bright blue and full of devilment.

'You don't really want that, do you?' he said. 'You're much too young and modern to be interested in this – leave it for old fogies like me.'

'You don't strike me as being in your dotage.'

He was in his early thirties, I thought, tall, fair-haired and attractive. His lazy smile was appealing and he seemed very sure of getting his own way, but I wasn't about to give in without a struggle.

'I've been looking for this one;' I said. 'I've got one copy but it's scratched.'

'I've broken mine, but I'll let you have this if – '

'If?' My brows went up. 'I think I saw it first anyway.'

'How's this, I'll buy it and then we'll discuss it over coffee?'

For a moment I was tempted to tell him to get lost, then I saw the twinkle in his eyes and I laughed. 'OK, but I'm going to take some persuading that you saw it first.'

He bought the record and then took my arm. We walked across the square to a small coffee bar, managing to find an empty table in the corner.

'I'm Nick Winters,' he introduced himself.

'Aline Marlowe,' I said, laughing as we shook hands. 'So, what are we going to do about this record?'

'Aline . . .' He said my name as if he liked the sound of it. 'Tell me, how did you come to be interested in old 78s? Most young women are into David Essex or Michael Jackson these days.'

'I've got some of David Essex's,' I said. 'And all of Phil Collins'; I enjoy all kinds of music: classical, jazz, hard rock . . . But I collect old records, amongst other things. It's something I've done for years.'

'It's just that it's unusual in a girl of your age.'

'I'm twenty-three,' I retorted and then saw the satisfaction in his eyes. 'My mother gave me some that belonged to my father when I was a child. He died before I was born but she kept all his stuff. I suppose it was sentimental at first, then it grew into a hobby.' I glanced up at him. 'So how did you get the bug then?'

'It's my age,' he said. 'I'm thirty-four – practically ancient.'

'Don't give me that,' I retorted. 'Besides, music transcends age. It's a matter of taste.'

'In that case, maybe you'd have dinner with me this evening,' he said. 'Since we both have the same rubbish taste in music, maybe we should discover what else we have in common?'

'I'm afraid I'm going to a party.'

'I'm open to invitations.'

'You really do have the cheek of the devil! I suppose I could ring Julie.' I laughed, liking him despite my natural caution. 'It's fancy dress. You wouldn't have time to find a costume.'

'Want to bet on it?'

His persistence was amusing. I gave in with a smile. 'If you can find a costume, you can pick me up at my flat. I'll give you my card.'

His brows rose at that; then as he read it, he nodded. 'So you're an appraiser for Silcott and Barrie. Yes, you would be. It fits very well.'

'I'm glad you approve.'

'Oh, I approve,' he murmured, his eyes brimming with laughter. 'And just to show you how much, I'll give you the record.'

When I answered the door to Nick Winters' ring that evening, his costume took my breath away. He had come dressed as a devil. Or perhaps undressed would be a better word. He was wearing black gymnastic tights, a tail and horns; his feet, arms and chest were bare, apart from some startling stage make-up.

'I suppose you came on the Underground?'

'Of course. Why not?' Nick's eyes gleamed his appreciation. 'May

36

I say that you're the best-looking witch I've seen this side of Halloween?'

I was dressed in a long black dress and a pointed hat, but my costume was amateur beside Nick's.

'We make a good pair then.'

'Your broomstick awaits, ma'am.'

As we went down to the taxi, I felt like giggling. Nick's mood was infectious and I knew the evening was going to be fun.

Julie's party was well under way when we arrived. We could hear the words of Rick Astley's latest hit as we went in. Wearing costumes seemed to have caught everyone's imagination, and the room was full of weird-looking characters. Red Indians, spacemen, and sexy French maids in short skirts and black stockings predominated. Julie made a splendid Cleopatra, complete with a black wig and the flimsiest of tunics.

'So this is Nick Winters.' Julie gave him the once over and smiled. 'I approve, Aline. It's nice to meet you, Nick. I'm glad you could come.'

Nick took her appraisal with the casual good humour I was beginning to realize was an essential part of his character.

'I'm going to like you, Julie,' he murmured, and produced a bottle of expensive French wine.

'What can I get you two to drink?' Julie asked.

'White wine please.'

Nick nodded. 'Same for me please.'

As Julie left us to fetch the drinks, I glanced at the couples attempting to dance in the crush of the overcrowded sitting room. 'Maybe we could find a space to sit and talk.'

'Why not?'

From that moment on, the evening went into overdrive. I was vaguely aware of other people. They came and went, exchanging a few words in passing, but I was in another world, a world that held only Nick Winters and me. We were so comfortable together it was difficult to believe we'd met that day. Nick did most of the talking and I listened, fascinated.

He was, I soon learned, a reporter for a roving TV team, and his stories about narrow escapes in often dangerous situations – war zones or erupting volcanos – were fascinating. I found myself laughing more than I had for ages. The hours fled, and I was surprised when Nick said, 'Perhaps we'd better be leaving. We're keeping Julie up.'

Looking around, I saw that the room was emptying fast. Julie and Tony had begun to clear the dirty glasses and empty the ashtrays.

'Can I help, Julie?' I asked, glancing at my watch as I walked over to her. 'I had no idea it was this late.'

'I'm leaving most of it to the morning – or rather, later today.' Julie yawned. 'Come over about lunchtime if you like. We'll have a snack and chat over the washing-up.'

'All right, I will.' I turned to Nick as he joined me. 'We'd better be going.'

'I've just asked Tony to ring for a taxi for us,' he said. 'I'll take you home.'

'Thanks.' I kissed Julie's cheek. 'It was a wonderful party – and I shall help clear up tomorrow, so don't do it all before I get here.'

'No chance,' she retorted. 'I don't intend to surface until noon.'

'I don't blame you,' Nick said. 'Thanks for a great party, Julie.'

We went clattering down the stairs, calling to other stragglers who were still standing about outside. I felt Nick's arm about my waist as we got into the taxi; his warm breath on my neck sent tiny shivers fluttering through me. Glancing at his flushed face, I realized that he was a little tipsy.

'You smell good enough to eat,' he murmured, nuzzling my bare shoulder.

I was uncertain as he drew me into his arms and kissed me with a gentleness that surprised me. There was nothing hurried about it, nothing demanding. I wasn't sure what I'd expected, but I suppose I was a little disappointed when he released me and sat back, his eyes half-closed. Perhaps he'd drunk more than I'd thought.

When we reached my flat, though, he asked the driver to wait while he accompanied me to my door. Taking the key from me, he unlocked the door, then placed it in the palm of my hand, closing my fingers firmly over it.

'I'm not the kind of guy a nice girl like you should know,' he said. There was a guarded, almost defensive expression in his eyes. 'I'm not into marriage and happy families, Aline, but I want to make love to you.'

'Nick . . .' I gazed up at him, not knowing how to answer.

'I'm not asking you to go to bed with me tonight,' he said. 'I'm just giving you advance warning so that you know the score.'

Smiling, he turned and walked to the top of the stairs, glancing back to wave before disappearing below.

I went inside, closing the door and standing with my back against it for several minutes. Nick's declaration had sent tiny shock waves through me and I wasn't sure how I felt about having an affair with him.

Since my brief experience with Jerry Cole, I'd kept my friendships with men out of the bedroom, which brought most of them to an abrupt end. Nick was attractive and I believed I was already falling in love with him, but I was nervous about starting a relationship.

I'd never blamed Jerry for what had happened that summer at college. It had been my fault that our lovemaking had been so awful . . . There was a nagging suspicion at the back of my mind that I was frigid. A lot of the trouble between my mother and Michael had been caused because she wasn't interested in sex, and I was afraid that I might be like her.

Julie had been right when she suggested that my moods were not just because of those peculiar phonecalls. Deep down I was lonely. I wanted to share my life with someone special; I just didn't know if I could.

Going into the bedroom, I began to undress. The odds were that I wouldn't see Nick Winters again anyway. He was seldom in London for more than a few days at a time, and I was off to Spain for a month very soon.

The doorbell rang just as I finished washing my hair. I wrapped a towel around my head and went to answer it. I almost gasped as I saw who was standing there. A week had passed since Julie's party and I hadn't heard from him. Now he was on my threshold, carrying a bottle of wine and grinning as he saw I was bare-footed, wearing a comfortable old bathrobe and no make-up.

'You look gorgeous,' he said, anticipating my apology as I looked down at myself. 'Are you getting ready to go out or spending a lazy Sunday at home?'

'I've just washed my hair. I was going to spend the day lying around watching TV and – '

'Sounds great,' he said. 'Well, are you going to invite me in – or do you want me to go away?'

I stood back, feeling slightly breathless. 'Come in, please. You'll have to excuse the mess . . .' I indicated the piles of clothing lying about. 'I'm in the middle of packing.'

He glanced at the open suitcases. 'Off on holiday?'

'Yes,' I said, beginning to rub my hair with the towel. 'I leave on Tuesday. I'm renting an apartment for a month on the Costa del Sol.'

Nick looked interested. 'Are they timeshare? We're doing a report on the growing market for timeshared property.'

'I'm not sure, some of them maybe, not all. It's a new complex – very upmarket, I've been told. There are some brochures on the coffee table. Have a look while I put the wine in the fridge.' I took it from him, hesitating uncertainly. 'I was going to pop a frozen lasagne in the oven for lunch. Would you like one too? I've got various bits and pieces in the fridge if – '

'Lasagne sounds fine,' he said. 'Don't go to any trouble for me, Aline.'

I disappeared into the kitchen, switching on the coffee machine. When I came back with two mugs, he had made himself comfortable on the big old sofa I had brought from Hazeling and was immersed in the brochures and literature I'd been given by the travel firm. He glanced up, smiling as I sat beside him.

'It looks great,' he said. 'How long did you say you were going for?'

'Almost a month. The saleroom is closed for August, so I thought why not?'

'I was hoping we could see something of each other.'

'Maybe you can get out to Spain,' I said, trying not to sound either hopeful or discouraging. 'I can give you the address.'

Nick fished in his jacket pocket and brought out a small black notebook and pen. 'Fire away then. I'm not promising anything, but you never know.'

'A month isn't so long.'

'No.' His grey eyes studied me seriously. 'For some people a week would be too long, but you're different, Aline.'

'Am I?' Blushing, I got to my feet. Compliments always made me uneasy. 'I'd better finish drying my hair. Can you amuse yourself for a while?'

'Sure.' He smiled lazily. 'I'll do it for you, if you like. Do you have a dryer or something?'

'You don't want to do that.'

'Why not?' He laughed as I shook my head. 'OK, I can take a hint. Do you mind if I look around?'

'No. Put a record on if you like.'

I disappeared into the bedroom. Emerging twenty minutes later with my hair hanging loose and shining on my shoulders, and wearing an old tracksuit, I was to find Nick reading a worn copy of Thomas Tryon's *Harvest Home*, and one of my favourite records playing in the background. He looked up and gave me a slow, appreciative smile.

'I see we have the same tastes in books as well,' he said. 'I've been meaning to get this paperback for ages. Do you mind if I borrow it? I promise faithfully to return it.'

My heart did a funny little skip. There was something very appealing about Nick's smile.

'Keep it, if you like. I'm going to put the lasagne in now. Will you open the wine for me?'

'Of course.' He put down the book and followed me into the kitchen, watching as I took the wine from the fridge.

'I'm not much good at . . .'

The words died on my lips as I turned and found him looking at me intently. He took the wine and stood it on the table, then put his arms around my waist, drawing me in close to him. We stared at each other in silence, then he bent his head and kissed me softly on the mouth. I hesitated for a moment, then slid my arms up around his neck, my mouth opening beneath the pressure of his. I was trembling when he let me go, and his eyes narrowed in a frown.

'What's wrong?' he asked. 'Have I been getting the wrong signals? I thought we liked each other.'

'I do like you.' I turned away to put the frozen lasagne into the oven. 'It's just that . . . I don't . . . I mean, I need a little time, Nick.'

'No one is rushing you.' His hands were firm on my shoulders as he brought me round to face him. 'I'm not going to force you into anything, Aline.'

'I know!' I looked at him anxiously. 'I'm sorry, Nick. I'm making a terrible mess of this. I'm afraid I'm not very good at relationships.' I took a deep breath. 'You'll think I'm naive or stupid or – '

'No, I shan't.' He took my hand and led me into the sitting room. 'Do you want to talk about it, or shall we change the subject?'

'Could we talk about something else, please?'

'Of course. I seemed to spend most of Julie's party talking about me. Supposing you fill me in with your life story?'

His smile was reassuring, and I found myself telling him about my mother's painful illness, the quarrel with Michael and Zena – things I hadn't been able to discuss with anyone but Julie – and then at last my short, unsuccessful affair with a married man. When I'd finished I suddenly felt embarrassed. What had made me come out with all that? I was usually too reserved to talk about myself.

'Now you'll think I'm neurotic,' I said, hardly daring to meet his eyes.

Nick stared at me in silence for a moment, then leant towards me and kissed me on the lips. 'Thank you for telling me,' he said. 'You're not neurotic, but you could learn to like yourself a little more.'

'What do you mean?'

'It doesn't matter.'

I didn't press him and he changed the subject.

We ate our dinner, drank wine and listened to records. I wanted to tell him about the attack on the marshes and my mother's attitude towards me after it, but somehow I couldn't. It was too difficult to talk about. I'd never felt this relaxed with a man before, but there was still a part of me that held back.

Nick seemed to sense this. He suddenly pulled me to my feet, saying, 'Come on, let's go for a walk.'

We spent the rest of the afternoon walking in Regent's Park arm in arm, talking, laughing, eating soft ice creams and learning about each other. Any tension between us had gone. When we returned to my flat, I asked him in but he shook his head and smiled.

'I've got a plane to catch first thing, but I'll be in touch.'

Regretfully, I watched him go. I was almost sure now that it would be all right with Nick. I felt more comfortable with him than I ever had with any other man. All I had to do was to relax and put everything else out of my mind. I went into the kitchen to wash the dishes left from lunch and had just finished drying them when the telephone rang.

'Hello,' I said, my heart thumping. Maybe it was Nick ringing to say goodnight.

'Do you remember, Aline?' the voice asked, and my blood ran cold. 'Do you remember that day on the marshes when I let you live?'

'Who are you?' I cried. 'Why do keep tormenting me?'

'I don't want to hurt you,' the strange, muffled voice said. 'I just want to talk to you, to hear your voice. Is that so much to ask?'

'No . . . Yes!' I cried, angry and upset. 'You frighten me. Please don't ring me again. Don't ever ring me again!'

I slammed down the receiver, more shaken than I wanted to admit. I didn't like what this man was doing to me. I was beginning to jump whenever the phone rang. I'd tried to put the calls out of my mind, and I hadn't mentioned them to Nick because I'd thought perhaps Julie was right and it was just some crank ringing at random, but now I knew that there was more to it than that. I walked to the window and gazed out. Someone was out there. Someone who knew all about me, knew about that day on the marshes . . . What did he want?

Chapter Four

The heat met me as I walked off the plane at Malaga airport. Joining the throng of holiday-makers crowding on to the inadequate bus to make the short journey across the tarmac, I put on my dark glasses. Everyone was laughing and talking, excited at the prospect of two weeks in glorious sunshine. The atmosphere was catching and I felt my spirits lifting. At least for a while I could be certain that there would be no frightening phonecalls, no odd sensation of being secretly observed.

The sky was a bright cloudless blue as I drove away from the airport, looking for the signpost to Fuengirola. The complex was set back off the road in the hills between Fuengirola and Marbella. On either side of the coast road were tall apartment buildings, sometimes allowing a glimpse through to the sea, stretches of rocky coastline or small sandy beaches. Clusters of gleaming white villas nestled in the hills, and there were bright splashes of geraniums, hibiscus and bougainvillaea, and stretches of tourist shops filled with leather goods, ceramics and souvenirs. Palm trees waved in the courtyards of hotels, softening the harshness of the concrete towers.

It took me three-quarters of an hour to reach my destination. Seeing the large advertising board with the name of the exclusive complex, I turned off the road and followed the signposts up the hill to the reception office. I stretched my shoulders to ease the slight strain of driving as I came to a halt, then checked my hair and make-up in the driving mirror, and went into the office. A pretty Spanish girl looked up from her typewriter and smiled.

'May I help you?' she asked in perfect English.

'I'm Aline Marlowe. I've booked a studio for the month.'

'Oh yes,' the girl said. 'I'm Juanita. I'll show you to your apartment.'

'Is it far? Shall I take my car?'

'You won't need it,' Juanita said. 'The studios are in the next block. It's best to park your car here most of the time.'

Juanita led the way. We walked along the path and up a few steps, then she took out a key and opened one of the doors. It was very clean and bright inside, the white walls and marble floors offset by pretty peach curtains and soft furnishings. There was a large open room with two steps down from the sleeping area to the sitting room, a shower and toilet, and a tiny kitchen. A sliding glass door led out on to a sunny balcony.

'This is lovely,' I said. 'I wasn't expecting anything quite as nice as this.'

'We've put in a welcome pack so that you can make a cup of tea,' Juanita said. 'But if there's anything you need, just ask.'

'Thank you.' I smiled at her. If everyone was as nice as that around here, there would be no need for me to be lonely.

As she went out, I walked on to the balcony, sighing with contentment as I felt the warmth of the sun on my face. I could see the tennis courts and bowling green from my vantage point, and a swimming pool with a waterfall. It was going to be a restful holiday, I thought, and decided to unpack before I explored the complex.

I made friends with Juanita and other staff from the reception office and the sports centre. There were Americans, British, Danish and French as well as Spanish staying at the resort, and everyone mixed in together. Most days were spent lazing by the pool, sipping iced orange juice or sangria. At night I went to various discos and nightclubs with my new friends. It was a different world, and after a few days I felt much better. I had allowed those stupid phonecalls to get on my nerves, and that was silly. It must be someone who had read about me in the paper and decided to make my life a misery.

I rang Julie at the end of the second week.

'That's great, Aline,' Julie said when I told her I was having a wonderful time. 'I'm glad you're enjoying yourself . . .' She hesitated, as if reluctant to introduce a sour note, then added, 'Michael came to see me the other day.'

'Oh.' I was suddenly wary. 'What did he want?'

'He's been trying to ring you. Zena isn't too well.'

'Did he say what was wrong with her?'

'I gather she had a miscarriage.'

'I'm sorry,' I said. 'I suppose I ought to write.'

'He said not to. She doesn't want a fuss,' Julie went on uncertainly. 'I popped over to your flat the other day, to water the plants and check it out for you. A girl from downstairs said someone had been asking for you.'

I had an unpleasant prickling sensation at the back of my neck.

'Who was it?'

'She didn't know. She thought he was a friend of yours, so she told him where you were staying. I wondered if it might be Nick.'

'I gave Nick my address.' I frowned, then decided that I was making too much of it again. 'I don't suppose it was important. Were there any letters for me?'

'Nothing special,' Julie said. 'Anyway, everything is all right, so don't worry.'

'Thanks, Julie. You're welcome to come out if you want.'

'I wish I could, but we're busy at work just now. I'll see you when you get back.'

Replacing the receiver, I was thoughtful for a moment. The girl Julie had spoken to downstairs hadn't lived in the building long, so she wouldn't necessarily recognize my friends. It could have been almost anyone. My friends from college were scattered all over the place. They sent postcards every now and then, and it was just possible that one of them might have turned up out of the blue. It would be foolish to see something sinister in it. If I carried on this way I would soon be jumping at my own shadow.

Leaving the booth, I got into my car. It didn't matter. Juanita had invited me for a meal at her home, and I didn't want to be late. Besides, I was on holiday and I intended to make the most of it.

'This is very kind of you, Aline,' the woman said as she slid into the front passenger seat of my car. 'I've always wanted to visit the Alhambra but my husband hates anything like that – and I'm too nervous to go alone.'

A plumpish, fair-skinned woman, Janet Hendry was already beginning to show signs of burning on her arms and face, although she had only been in Spain for a few days. She was a rather timid person, completely dominated by her overbearing husband, and I couldn't help feeling sorry for her. The previous day when we were all sitting by the pool bar, he had crushed her tentative request to visit the ancient Moorish castle in Granada, and I had impetuously offered to take her there myself. I'd been once before, on a trip with my mother, but it was so beautiful that I didn't mind revisiting it.

'*Would* you take me?' Janet Hendry's eyes had lit up. 'Oh, I would be so grateful.'

We set out in the cool of early morning, before the roads were congested with heavy traffic. Even so, it was several hours before we caught our first glimpse of the magnificent palace on a hilly terrace outside Granada.

45

'Isn't it fantastic,' Janet breathed as she saw the domed roofs and exquisite plasterwork. 'They say it's one of the finest examples of Moorish architecture in Spain.'

'I'm sure it is,' I agreed. 'I always think the colouring is so rich – and all that marble.'

'It was built originally by the Moorish kings, wasn't it?' Janet asked. 'In the thirteenth century, I think.'

'It was their last stronghold. I can't remember all the details but I remember reading about the tears of Boabdil as he was turned out of paradise.'

'I don't know any of the history. Who was Boabdil?'

'The last Moorish King of Granada. He was dethroned by his father and taken prisoner by the Castilians a year or so later. I think he had to pay a tribute of some kind, then he returned to Granada to try and regain his throne. The city was besieged in fourteen something or other, despite tremendous resistance by the Moors, and he had to surrender to Ferdinand of Spain . . . But the guidebooks will tell you much more. I've forgotten most of it, I'm afraid.'

Janet looked at me with admiration. 'I think it's wonderful that you know so much. I wish I were more like you.'

I laughed and shook my head. 'I'm very ordinary.'

'Well, I certainly would never have got here if it hadn't been for you,' Janet said. 'When we leave I should like to buy you lunch somewhere, if you'll let me.'

'I should like that. Now, do you want to take the guided tour or just wander about yourself?'

'Oh, the guided tour. I shall miss half of it if not.'

'Do you mind if I wait for you in the Court of the Lions?' I asked. 'I've been on the tour and I would rather just wander about.'

'No, of course not.' Janet beamed at me. 'Will you wait for me by that wonderful fountain? I've seen a picture of it in a friend's guidebook – that's what made me want to come.'

'Yes, that's a good place to meet.'

I saw Janet off on her tour with several other eager sightseers, then wandered off alone. The gardens were a riot of flowers and fragrance, with oleanders, bougainvillaea, geraniums and lavender amongst others I could not name. Silver fir and maple gave shade to the walks; the sunshine in the open courts made the fountains sparkle with a rainbow of colour.

Occasionally, I caught the sound of voices as I passed other visitors, but most of the time I was alone. My footsteps echoed beneath the ancient arches as I walked slowly through the various courts and halls, lingering to admire the shimmering surface of the water as it reflected the intricate plasterwork of the royal apartments in the Myrtles Courtyard. I stayed longest in the harem gardens, wondering what it must have been like to live there when it was a Moorish palace, before the Spanish kings had made it their own.

What would it be like, I wondered, to be pampered and kept in luxury yet be a virtual prisoner, at the beck and call of a master? Of course the slave-concubines had had some influence on the lives of their masters. They were often well educated, skilled in the arts of singing, music, literature and science, and these skills were used to educate the children. It was possible in certain circumstances for some of the women to win eventual freedom, but what of those who didn't?

Perhaps it was fancy, but some of the atmosphere of those long ago days seemed to haunt me as I explored further.

Some time later I suddenly had the feeling that I was being followed. Halting, I heard the echo of another's footfall behind me. Glancing over my shoulder, I saw nothing, yet sensed that there was someone there.

'Janet,' I called. 'Is that you?'

My voice sounded hollow in the empty hall and I shivered. The palace was a maze of echoing passages and secret ways, and I began to feel nervous. Remembering the stories of Boabdil and the siege of the capital – the Moors were finally starved out, despite their desperate resistance – my imagination ran riot. The screams of the dying rang in my ears, and for a moment I could smell the cannon smoke and taste the bitterness of blood, reliving the stories of war, death and destruction.

A shadow haunted my mind, playing tricks on me, conjuring half-remembered dreams and secret fears of rape, physical attack and pain. I was listening for every sound, my breath rasping in my ears as I tried to find my way back to the sunny courtyard where I had arranged to meet Janet. I took a wrong turning, and found myself confronted by a locked door. For a moment I was paralysed by fear, fear of the unknown, creeping horror that pursued me through my dreams.

I couldn't move, then I took a deep breath and fought my fear. Just because I'd heard footsteps that seemed to follow mine, stopping when I stopped, it didn't mean that someone was pursuing me. Sounds were often deceptive, especially in a vast place like this. There were bound to be other people about; no doubt it had been an official keeping an eye on things, checking locked doors and areas forbidden to the public. Now my breathing was easier. I thought about my situation, working out where I'd gone wrong.

Retracing my steps, I could no longer hear the footsteps that had bothered me. How foolish I'd been! I laughed at myself as I emerged into the large, open courtyard called the Court of the Lions because of its magnificent fountain, which was supported by stone images of the king of the beasts. Janet was standing by the fountain, and I called her.

'Have I kept you waiting? I lost my way for a while.'

She turned to me with relief in her face. 'I was just beginning to wonder if I'd misunderstood you,' she said. 'Shall we go and have lunch now? My feet are killing me.'

'It's a tiring tour, isn't it?' I said sympathetically. 'I hope you found it worthwhile.'

'I've loved every minute of it, but I could do with a nice cup of tea and something to eat.'

'Let's get back to the car. We'll find somewhere to eat in Granada, and you might as well see the cathedral while you're here.'

Janet chattered on as we made our way to the car, stopping several times to take photographs, and begging me to pose for her in front of the palace. She took her time getting the exposure right. It was not until we were driving away that she said, 'There was a man taking pictures of you – at least, I think he was.'

'Taking pictures of me?' I stared at her. 'I didn't notice him.'

'He kept turning away every time you looked in his direction. Or I thought he did. Malcolm would say I was imagining it, but he *was* acting oddly. Perhaps I should have told you, but I couldn't believe it at first. I mean, it's rude, isn't it?'

'Perhaps he was just taking pictures of the Alhambra,' I said. 'It couldn't have been me he wanted to photograph.'

'No . . . I suppose not. You do hear of strange things sometimes, though, don't you? He might be a movie director looking for a new star or something. Suddenly he sees this beautiful woman and is haunted by her face until he finds out who she is . . .'

I laughed and shook my head. 'Very romantic, but I don't think so, Janet.'

'You're pretty enough,' Janet said. 'I wish I'd pointed him out now. He followed us all the way down to the car. I'm sure he did.'

Remembering the footsteps in the Alhambra, I felt my skin prickle with goose pimples. I'd almost convinced myself that I'd imagined the whole thing, but now I wondered. Without being vain, I knew I was attractive. It was possible that a man had decided to follow me. He might even have contrived to take a photo of me while I posed for Janet, but that was all there was to it. It was an isolated incident. It wouldn't happen again.

48

'He was probably just killing time,' I said to Janet. 'If he was on his own, he could have felt a bit lonely up there.'

'Yes.' Janet's face cleared. 'I expect that's it. I hate going to places like that on my own. That's why I would never have got there if it hadn't been for you. I can't tell you how grateful I am.'

'It was my pleasure,' I said, deciding to put the man in the Alhambra out of my mind.

And that's just what I did for the rest of the day, but when we got back to the apartment, something happened that brought it all back. I met Juanita as I was passing her office, and she called to me.

'Did you have a good day?' she asked. 'I told your friend where you were going when he rang this morning. He said he might try to catch up with you at the Alhambra.'

'My friend?' My spine tingled. 'Did he give his name, Juanita?'

She wrinkled her brow, looking puzzled. 'I think he just said he was a friend of yours. He knew you were staying here.'

Her expression became anxious. 'He seemed to know you so well . . .'

'Don't worry about it,' I said, 'but if he should ring again, ask his name.'

I was frowning as I let myself into my apartment. Someone had been inquiring for me at my flat at home; now the same thing had happened here; and the incident at the Alhambra . . . It was worrying. Yet it might all have a simple explanation. Nothing terrible had happened. I wouldn't let it get to me, but it was there at the back of my mind, making me uneasy.

I'd just emerged from the shower when the doorbell rang. I went to answer it, wrapped in a short towelling robe, my tanned legs and feet bare. Surprised, I could only stare at my visitor.

'Nick,' I managed at last. 'Was it you who telephoned earlier and asked for me?'

'No, I've only just arrived.'

'Oh . . . What made you decide to fly out here?'

'I told you we were doing a report on time-sharing,' he said, grinning as I moved back to let him in. 'I persuaded the programme director to let me do some advance research – so here I am.'

'How long have you got?'

I was pleased to see him. I would feel easier with Nick around.

'A couple of days before we start filming. I thought we might be able to spend some time together.'

49

'Why not? I'd arranged something for tomorrow but I can get out of it.'

'And this evening?'

'As it happens, I hadn't planned anything.'

'Then why don't I take you out to dinner?'

'I'd love it. Pour yourself a drink – and give me ten minutes.'

Because it was a studio apartment there was no separate bedroom, so I went into the bathroom to change. I was back in record time, dressed in a soft, floating dress of peach silk, a wide gold belt and sandals. Nick smiled at me appreciatively.

'That was quick!'

'I only need moisturizer out here.'

'You've got a terrific tan,' he agreed. 'And your hair is different. You've had it cut. It suits you.'

'It's easier to look after.'

'Where shall we go?' he asked as we left the apartment. 'Is there anywhere special you like?'

'There's a marvellous seafood restaurant in the marina at Marbella.'

'Sounds good.' He smiled at me. 'I'll drive and you can direct me.'

We parked in a side street and walked along the promenade of pink and grey paving stones. The sea was a deep turquoise in the warm evening sunshine, and the perfume of tropical flowers wafted on a light breeze. Red and pink hibiscus bushes bloomed in beds at the edge of the pavements, while swathes of trailing geraniums and a pretty blue flower cascaded from the balconies of sea-facing apartments and hotels. Marbella was just beginning to wake after drowsing in the heat of the day. Coloured lamps on restaurant tables enticed customers inside to the intimacy of quiet corners, others were eating and drinking at pavement tables, watching the constant flow of holiday-makers, while loud music issued from bars and nightclubs.

During the day everyone wore swimming costumes, shorts and tee-shirts, but during the evening the beautiful and the outrageous took over. The marina was popular with both tourists and local people looking for a night's entertainment, and the fashions on display were as varied as the personalities of their wearers. Expensive designer dresses mingled with torn jeans, green hair worn in Mohican style and lots of gold jewellery. There was a special atmosphere: cosmopolitan, exciting, slightly dangerous. A cocktail of Marbella life, to be sipped slowly and with pleasure.

We ate huge Mediterranean prawns that had been grilled over charcoal, peeling the skins and dipping the fish into a spicy pink sauce that had a faint taste of armagnac; freshly cooked mussels brought to the table in their shells; and a platter of sardines smoked to perfection and served on toasted squares of bread, all washed down with a bottle of well chilled Rioja and followed by ripe strawberries and ice cream.

We ate leisurely, talking and laughing, using our fingers and rinsing them in the lemon-scented water provided in little bowls. It was a meal to linger over, to savour as we savoured each other's company, the mood sensual and relaxed. A young Spaniard was moving amongst the tables, playing his guitar and singing romantic songs, his dark eyes passionate and soulful. He sang two songs for us, and Nick rewarded him with a thousand-peseta note.

It was late in the evening when we left the restaurant and wandered back to the car, pausing to look out over the sea. The water was a dark, midnight blue tinged with silver now, and the lights on the yachts bobbed and twinkled like fallen stars. The cafés throbbed with life, and there was the sound of music, laughter and tuneless singing as holiday-makers abandoned all inhibitions. An impromptu conga burst out from one bar, with boisterous youths shouting and grabbing passers-by as the dancers weaved their way around the marina. One boy tried to catch my hand, but Nick whisked me away, out of danger. I smiled at him.

'They're just having fun, but I'd rather stay clear of it,' I said.

Nick looked down at me, his eyes intensely blue. 'Can I see you tomorrow?'

'Of course.'

For a moment we looked at each other in silence, then he reached out and drew me close. We stood in the shadows of an olive tree, our lips meeting in a gentle, fleeting kiss.

We drove back to my apartment in a comfortable silence. Nick saw me to the door, kissed me briefly and left.

'I'll be here about one,' he called as he ran down the steps to his car.

'Thank you for tonight. It was lovely.'

He waved as he reached the bottom step. I smiled, then turned and went inside. I was still smiling as I undressed, a warm feeling of contentment spreading through me.

After the incident at the Alhambra and the phonecall Juanita had taken, I'd been feeling uneasy. Now Nick was here and everything would be different.

'Have you had lunch?' I asked as I opened the door. I smiled when Nick shook his head. 'Good. I was afraid you might have, and I've made us an avocado salad. It's waiting in the fridge.' I led the way out to the balcony, where the table was set for a meal. 'I thought we might as well have it out here.'

Nick was wearing pale grey cotton slacks and a short-sleeved shirt. He stood on the balcony looking down at the tennis courts, his eyes hidden behind dark glasses. I noticed a little pulse flicking in his neck.

'Do you play?' he asked. 'My racket is in the car. We could have a game later, if you like.'

'I'm not very good,' I said, pulling a wry face. 'I played at college, but I haven't since.'

'Perhaps you would rather swim?'

'Perhaps. Can I get you a drink?' I sensed a tenseness in him and my stomach muscles spasmed.

'Just orange juice, please.'

Nick followed me back inside as I went to the fridge. I brought a tray with a jug and two glasses to the sitting area. Nick had taken off his dark glasses and was looking at me intently. My feeling of nervousness grew, and I hesitated. Nick took the tray from me and set it down on the coffee table.

'I'm not really hungry yet,' he said, his voice husky. 'Shall we leave lunch for the moment?'

'Of course.' My pulse skipped as I looked into his eyes and saw the longing there. 'Have you been working this morning – on your research, I mean?' My voice died to a whisper as a nerve jumped in his throat and he made an involuntary move towards me. 'Nick . . .'

He reached for me, his lips silencing me with a kiss that was neither gentle nor fleeting but hungry and urgent. I stiffened for a moment, then pressed myself against him, my arms going round his neck, my fingers moving in his thick, pale hair. I inhaled the masculine scent of his body, a slight muskiness mixed with the freshness of soap, and felt that odd clutching sensation in my stomach again.

'Aline,' he murmured. 'I'm not very good at this waiting business. I want you. I want you very much. But . . .' He looked at me seriously. 'I don't want to frighten or lose – '

Smiling, I touched two fingers to his lips. 'You won't,' I whispered, my breath catching. 'I – I want you too, Nick. It's just that I'm afraid of disappointing you.'

'Darling Aline,' he breathed, taking my hand to lead me up the two steps towards the bedroom area. 'Whatever happens, you won't do that. If I can't make you happy, it's my fault. Just trust me. I shan't hurt you.'

'I know. I do trust you.'

I gazed up at him, still a little uncertain as he held my face between his hands and kissed my forehead, the tip of my nose and then my lips once more. I turned round, letting him unzip my dress, and trembled as he kissed the back of my neck, his hands caressing my bare arms. I was shy and nervous but excited too, his kisses making me quiver with anticipation. The dress slid down over my hips and I stepped out of it. Beneath it I was wearing only a pair of white cotton panties. I turned to face him, trying not to show my inexperience, my fear of somehow messing up a relationship I knew was important.

'You're so lovely,' Nick said, his eyes moving over me hungrily. 'You know I care for you, don't you, Aline?'

'Yes,' I whispered. 'Yes, I know.'

Nick unbuttoned his shirt as I pulled back the bedclothes. I lay with my eyes closed, waiting until he slipped in beside me, and jumped as I felt the burn of his naked flesh against mine. For a moment I was tense again, but Nick had anticipated my reaction and he lay still at my side until I relaxed once more and moved towards him. Only then did he begin to kiss and caress me.

At first I had to force myself to accept the touch of his hand. My instinctive reaction was to push it away, but I fought down the fears that made me want to close my legs against him. I went limp, emptying my mind and blocking out the memories that haunted me, and accepted the pleasure that Nick's caresses were beginning to give me.

'Just remember that we care for each other, Aline,' he murmured against my ear. 'All I want is to make you happy, darling.'

'Nick . . . you are . . . making me happy.'

Suddenly, I found I could move. My hands wandered over the muscled hardness of his back, stroking and caressing, delighting in my new freedom. He was so good to touch, and it was wonderful to be this close to someone. I breathed deeply, experiencing a new, wonderful lightness as my body came alive, responding to his touch. I gave a little cry of relief as I realized that I wasn't a freak after all. I could feel normal emotions.

'You make me so happy, Nick.'

'Aline . . . Aline,' he said, his mouth seeking mine with a new urgency. I want you so much . . . so much . . .'

It seemed as if my words had released him from restraint. I cried out as he drove into me, calling his name and feeling first pain and then exquisite pleasure as he moved within me. Eagerly, I lifted my hips to meet the thrust of his body, experiencing a new sensation that I knew was desire. My response brought a frenzied reply from him and a swift, shuddering ending to something that had promised so much. For me it was over too soon, leaving me aroused and wanting more, but as I pressed my face against his shoulder and clung to him, I hid my disappointment.

'You're lovely,' he murmured, nuzzling my neck with his nose.

'Was it all right for you?' I asked. 'Really all right?'

'Of course – wasn't it for you?'

'Yes. Fantastic,' I said quickly, not wanting to hurt him. 'I – I enjoyed it.'

'Funny little Aline,' he said, kissing me lightly on the mouth before getting out of bed. 'Why were you so worried? You were great.'

'Thank you.' I gave him the answer I knew he wanted. 'So were you.' He looked gratified, and I was glad I'd told a white lie. I didn't want to see his smile turn to annoyance or boredom.

'Mind if I take a shower before we eat?'

'Go ahead. I'll have one later.'

As he disappeared into the bathroom, I got out of bed and dressed. When he came back wearing one of my towels, our meal was on the patio table. His hair looked much darker wet; slicked down flat on top of his head it made him look different. I could smell the sweet fragrance of my favourite soap on his skin. He stretched and sighed with contentment, looking, I thought, rather too pleased with himself. I was irritated, despite telling myself that it was my own fault if I felt let down.

I hadn't told him what had happened on the marshes, or the way it had affected me afterwards, so how could I expect him to understand? What I needed now was a show of affection, a sign that what had happened between us was more than just sex.

Nick had told me that he cared for me, and he seemed satisfied with things as they were. If I was waiting for a declaration of love, it didn't come. I was a little disappointed; I wanted to feel that our relationship was more than a casual affair.

'Shall we have a game of tennis now?' Nick asked as I cleared the dishes. 'Or would you rather just swim and lie in the sun?'

'I'd rather swim – if that suits you.' I was a little stiff with him.

'Of course.' He got up and came towards me, a faint look of anxiety in his eyes. 'Is something wrong, darling? You're not angry with me for rushing you, are you?'

'No.' The moment of irritation had passed. It wasn't Nick's fault if I'd been late in responding. 'Of course not. I'm going to leave the washing-up. Let's go to the pool now.'

He smiled, kissing me on the tip of my nose. 'You're really special to me, Aline. I hope you know that.'

'You're special yourself,' I said, and kissed him back.

I was relaxed and smiling again now. Maybe it didn't matter that I hadn't experienced the same pleasure in our love-making as he had. He'd been gentle and thoughtful, and at least I hadn't laid there like a block of ice. It was bound to get better . . .

Chapter Five

I had been working hard all morning, trying to meet the deadline for the fortnightly auction catalogue, when the phone rang. Picking it up, I answered automatically, 'Silcott and Barrie. Can I help you?'

'You can meet me for lunch,' Nick said, and I felt a spurt of annoyance. It was just like him to ring out of the blue and expect me to drop everything.

I hadn't seen Nick for three weeks, and then we'd parted in anger as I felt that his attitude towards our relationship was just too casual. Nick was never around for more than a few days, breezing in and out of town when it suited him, which meant that we'd spend a couple of nights together every three weeks or so.

'I can't make lunch. The catalogue has to go to the printers this afternoon and I still have work to do.'

'I have to see you. I'm leaving first thing in the morning. Please, Aline.'

I hesitated, then said, 'Come over this evening for dinner.'

'I won't hold you up now. See you tonight.'

I replaced the receiver and frowned, wondering why I'd given in. This casual relationship wasn't what I wanted, but even after a year as lovers, Nick seemed incapable of making a commitment. Our last row had been over what he thought of as my old-fashioned ideas. I knew he wasn't keen on marriage, but I'd said he could at least move in with me, so that when he was around we would be together.

'We're fine this way,' he'd said, glaring at me. 'Why spoil it?'

'All I'm asking for is a little commitment.'

'You'd know about that, of course!'

There was a sarcastic note in his voice that hurt me. 'What's that supposed to mean?' I asked.

'Nothing . . . Just leave it.'

'You meant something.' My nails dug into the palms of my hands.

'Maybe I think you're the one who isn't ready for anything permanent.'

'More riddles! What are you getting at?'

56

'For heaven's sake, Aline, can't you ease up?'

'So now it's my fault. You're saying I'm the one who's wrong, aren't you?'

He refused to answer. Perhaps because in my heart I knew what he was hinting at, I lost my temper.

'Blame me,' I yelled. 'Your trouble is that you're not prepared to give anything. Two days of passion when you feel like it may suit you, but it's not enough for me.'

'You're asking me to chuck my job,' he yelled right back. 'Well, I'm not prepared to do that, Aline. Not the way things are.'

'Then go to hell!'

I was so angry that I walked off, leaving him standing in the park. He didn't try to stop me, and when he didn't ring, I assumed it was over. That hurt me, because despite our fights we'd been happy most of the time, and if I'd lost Nick, it would create a great void in my life. Feeling quite wretched, I had cried every night for a week, but just when I was beginning to get over it, he was back, expecting to take up where we'd left off. I didn't know what to think. I loved Nick but I wasn't sure what I meant to him. Did he really care, or was I just a convenience?

Maybe it *was* my fault. Things hadn't been as good as they might have been between us. I'd imagined that our love-making would improve as time went on, but it hadn't, for me. The trouble was, I couldn't talk about it. Instead, I faked my responses, pretending that everything was wonderful. I'd believed Nick was fooled, but now I had an uncomfortable feeling that he'd known all along.

I'd kept silent because I didn't want to hurt him, because I cared for Nick very much. We had a comfortable relationship, and we enjoyed the same things; that seemed to be enough for Nick, but it wasn't for me. I had this need, this longing to be deeply loved. Sometimes I was on the brink of telling Nick how I felt, but I was afraid of rejection.

I was afraid of being pushed away and told that big girls didn't need to be cuddled.

'Grow up, Aline, and leave your stepfather alone.'

No, it was better to pretend than to be hurt.

The crowds were impossible at lunchtime, and it was spitting with rain. I didn't manage to find everything I wanted for the meal that night. It meant that I would have to finish shopping after work, and that was a nuisance. Why on earth had I said I would cook?

Checking my watch, I saw that it was already a quarter-past one; I had to be back at the office by half-past. Unless I could grab a taxi soon . . . My attention was suddenly drawn to the large oil painting in the window of a gallery and I stood transfixed in the middle of the pavement. Surely I wasn't mistaken?

Lured by a fascination stronger than my desire to turn and run, I approached the window. The painting, large and important in a gilt frame that had one corner damaged, was of a windswept marsh, looking towards a church on the rise. I knew that scene so well – and the artist. Instinctively, I looked for and found Michael's familiar scrawl in the corner.

But he'd always said he would never sell that painting, not that one . . .

I backed away. Couldn't he have kept his word just once? He knew what that painting meant to me.

Making contact with something hard and unyielding in the centre of my back, I spun round, only to discover that I'd bumped into a man carrying a heavy picture frame.

'I'm so sorry,' I apologized hastily. 'I wasn't looking where I was going.'

I caught a glimpse of cold grey eyes and a startled face, but even as he began to speak, a taxi drew up at the kerb and its passengers stepped out. Abandoning any attempt at politeness, I ran for it.

It was past six when I got back to my flat that evening. I threw my clothes into the linen basket and had a quick shower. I was preparing a simple meal of fillet steak, jacket potatoes and salad, but I wanted to have everything ready when Nick arrived and even making the special salad dressing he liked took time. I was just about ready when the doorbell rang. I answered it, smiling despite everything, and saw Nick standing there wearing a light blue shirt, pale grey slacks and a worn leather flying jacket. My heart did a little flip; I'd missed him more than I wanted to admit. He was clutching a bottle of my favourite sparkling white wine, presumably as a peace offering.

'Hi,' I said, standing back for him to enter.

'Not too early, am I?'

'No, of course not.' I tried frowning at him, remembering I had a right to be annoyed. 'So where are you off to tomorrow? Another war? The overthrow of a government – or a royal tour?'

Nick relaxed, sensing that my mood wasn't too hostile. He knew me well enough by now to understand that I didn't enjoy arguments.

'The rain forest,' he said. 'It's a long trip this time. We're doing an exposé on the illegal clearing of primary forest. We're convinced it's being organized by big business. There's a lot of talk about how impossible it is to stop what's happening but – ' He caught himself and laughed. 'But I didn't come here to talk shop.'

Giving me the wine, he advanced into the sitting room and flopped down on the big old settee which took up most of the available space. It had come from the drawing room at Hazeling, where it had looked a normal size. In my flat it was huge, but I found it useful as a makeshift bed if one of my college friends dropped in unexpectedly and wanted to stay over. Nick loved it, and had been known to spend a Sunday afternoon stretched out dead to the world while the television played on. Sometimes when he came back from a hectic trip he seemed drained of energy, and it took him a while to unwind. Perhaps that was at the root of our trouble; we hadn't had a chance to get to know each other properly. Despite our long friendship, we were still almost strangers. Yet Nick seemed to belong in my flat. Seeing how relaxed he was now, some of the annoyance drained out of me.

'What did you want to talk about?' I asked, returning from putting the wine in the fridge. 'You were pretty insistent when you rang.'

'I had to see you.' Nick hesitated. 'I'm sorry. I should have rung you before, but I've been so busy I didn't get around to it.'

'You're always busy,' I said drily.

'That's just it. The job is so demandng, Aline. I wanted to – '

'Something's burning!' I cried. 'The steak! Back in a minute . . .'

I dashed into the kitchen. The meal was at a crucial stage and it was several minutes before I returned with the loaded plates. Nick had been flicking through some magazines, but he got up as soon as I came in.

'That looks good,' he said. 'Shall I open the wine?'

'Yes, please.' I sat down, glancing up at him and then away quickly. I knew that look in his eyes, but I didn't want to go to bed with him – at least, not until we'd sorted things out. I tried to keep the conversation on a light note. 'It's a pity you're leaving tomorrow. Julie's having a party in the evening and she would have loved you to come. She told me she hasn't seen you for ages.'

'That's right. I'm sorry I shan't be there.' Nick was standing by my chair and I sensed the tension in him, but refused to give him the lead he wanted. He poured the wine and sat down. 'The last thing I heard, she and Tony had had a fight – have they made it up?'

'Yes, at least provisionally. She was pretty miserable after he walked out on her. She said she wouldn't ever want to go through that again, but this party is to celebrate their getting together again.'

'I'll ring her before I go – and send some flowers,' Nick said.

'I've always liked Julie. Tony is a fool if he doesn't know how lucky he is.'

On that at least we were in perfect harmony.

As we ate, I was aware of Nick's mood. He had taken his lead from me, keeping the conversation to casual chat about various friends, but *that* look was in his eyes and it made me nervous. Our last quarrel had upset me, because it had been more than a lovers' tiff. We needed to sort things out in a rational manner not just to fall into bed the way we usually did.

After the meal was over, I cleared the table and Nick helped me stack the dishwasher. Then he put his arms around me, looking down into my face with a rueful smile.

'Friends?' he asked.

'Maybe,' I hedged. A part of me wanted to make up, but he always seemed to take everything for granted and I resented that. 'So what was so important that it couldn't wait?'

'I thought that when I get back from this trip we might take a holiday together somewhere. Perhaps Greece or . . .' His hand moved idily over my blouse, caressing the nipple of one breast with his thumb. His casual assumption that I wanted to make love made me angry again. I moved away, going to put a Phil Collins record on the turntable.

'This holiday – is it just a fun trip, or what?'

Nick frowned, obviously sensing my change of mood. His mouth went hard and his jawline tightened, and I knew we were on the verge of another row.

'Don't go all broody on me again. I'm trying to apologize, to make up for being so bloody-minded last time we met but – '

'But you don't want to move in with me. I'm OK for a fast – '

'Don't say it,' he warned. He looked angry. 'I've told you a thousand times that I care about you more than any woman I've ever known.'

'Why won't you commit yourself?' I countered, furious. 'What's wrong, Nick?' I was suddenly afraid as I asked, 'Is it me? Is it something about me that makes you – '

'Oh, for goodness sake,' he cried. 'It's the job, can't you see that? It's you I'm thinking of, Aline. As long as we keep it light, you're free to lead your own life, do your own thing. If we lived together, you would be spending so much time alone. If I didn't ring on the dot, you would be working yourself up into a temper and – '

'So your job is more important to you than me,' I said. 'Well, if that's the way you feel about it, you can leave now.'

'I didn't mean that. Why do you always jump on everything I say?'

'All you care about is sex.'

'If it was, I wouldn't hang around you.'

'Damn you!' Before I could stop myself, I had struck him across the face.

'If that's the way you want it, I might as well go,' he said bitterly.

'Go on then!' I stared at him miserably. 'I don't know why you bothered to come.'

Even while I yelled at him I was wondering why I was behaving like this – pushing him to the limit, destroying our relationship . . . What devil lurked in my subconscious that I couldn't accept Nick as he was – a little too casual perhaps, sometimes careless, but deep down a decent man? What was I looking for?

Nick had obviously had enough. He grabbed his jacket and left without speaking, slamming the door behind him. I watched him go. I refused to call him back or to give in to tears. If he didn't want more than a casual relationship, it was better to end it now. Yet even as I blamed Nick, I knew that it wasn't all his fault. I knew I hadn't allowed him to get really close to me. Always, even when we made love, I'd kept a barrier between us. There was this tightness inside me, a feeling of wanting to protect myself, that I didn't properly understand.

The telephone was ringing when I got back to the flat the next evening. Already regretting the quarrel with Nick, I snatched it up eagerly, but even as I did so there was a click at the other end. Frowning, I replaced the receiver.

Crossing to the sitting room window, I glanced out, half-expecting to see someone staring up at me. It was a dull evening, cool and damp with the rain still in the air. No one knew I even existed; they were all hurrying by, wanting to get back to their families and their televisions. I breathed a sigh of relief and then scolded myself for being stupid, worrying about nothing.

Those strange phonecalls had stopped after I went to Spain, so the caller just now had probably dialled the wrong number, I told myself. Or maybe it was Nick trying to get through from an airport somewhere. No, it wasn't likely to be him. That was all over, and deep down I knew I was to blame. I sighed, wishing it hadn't ended. I was going to miss him; my life would be as empty as it had been before we met. For a moment my throat tightened with emotion and I wanted to cry, but the hurt went too deep for tears. Nick had cared for me at the start, but if he'd really loved me, he wouldn't have walked out that way. *There must be something wrong with me, something that made me unlovable. Nick had cared at the start, but now he'd turned away.*

Feeling cold, I switched on the electric fire. It was summer but the evening was chilly. I walked into the bathroom, turned on the taps, poured my favourite Anais Anais oil into the water and began to undress.

It would be good to spend the evening with Julie and Tony. Julie always made me feel better, and I needed to relax. I was too tense, and it wasn't just the row with Nick. Thinking about it, I realized that the chance sighting of Michael's painting had really upset me and it had been hovering at the back of my mind ever since.

Why had Michael decided to sell it when he had promised he wouldn't? It held so many memories. I could remember clearly the day it had been painted: the day before my life had begun to fall apart.

Memories from the past crowded in on me, forcing their way into my mind . . . Michael's eyes looking at me reproachfully . . . my mother scolding . . . I didn't want to think about any of this! It was over and done with. I hadn't spoken to Michael since our quarrel, and I didn't want to. I was never going back to Hazeling while he and Zena lived there.

Forcing myself to think of something else, I concentrated on the situation at Silcott and Barrie. I still enjoyed my job, but it looked as though I might soon have to look for a new one; Mr Silcott was finding the competition more and more difficult to withstand. I'd typed a letter for him to the bank late that afternoon, and I knew that unless he got the loan he needed, he might have to sell up. It would be a pity, not because I needed a job, but because I liked working for Mr Silcott. I had learned a lot over the past three years and I wanted to build on my experience.

Of course, I could offer to loan Mr Silcott some money, or I might even ask him if he would consider taking me in as a junior partner . . . I sat up in the bath, excited at the idea. It would entail considerable investment, but surely I could manage to find the money?

It would mean talking to my trustees, though, and that included Michael. In another six months I would be twenty-five and come into my inheritance. I knew that I would be wealthy. Judging from the amount of income my trust fund generated, I would have capital of five or six hundred thousand pounds – I didn't know exactly and I wasn't bothered. I'd always felt guilty about the money, as though I wasn't really entitled to it. If my father had lived long enough to enjoy the money himself, I might not have felt so strange about it. However, if I wanted a large sum of money to invest, it meant that I would have to talk it over with Michael. So I had come full circle.

I put it out of my mind for the moment and, closing my eyes and relaxing in the scented water, tried to get into a party mood.

By the time I'd finished my bath, I was feeling better. The tensions inside me receded as I slipped into a black leather mini skirt and a new leopard-print silk shirt. Julie's parties were always worth dressing up for, so I added a pair of extravagant gold earrings.

Glancing in the mirror, I was pleased with the result. My heavy dark hair had grown out of the very short cut I'd had the previous year. Soon I would be able to braid it into a French plait, but for now I simply tucked it behind my ears. A light dusting of powder eye-shadow, bright peach lipstick and a swish of blusher and I was ready.

The doorbell rang and I picked up my bag and went out. What was the matter with me? Why was I on edge tonight? I'd thought I was over all that. I *was* over it, I decided as I took the lift down to the waiting taxi. It was just seeing that picture so suddenly. *Why* had Michael sold it?

The party was already noisy when I arrived. Julie's windows were open and the latest offering from Yazz was blaring out into the street. How Julie managed to hear the doorbell above the din, I didn't know, but seconds after I rang she was there, grinning at me in delight.

'Aline!' she kissed my cheek. 'I wasn't sure if you were coming . . .' She peered out into the street, brushing back a lock of flyaway blonde hair. 'Is Nick with you?'

'No. Something came up and he's off, as usual.' I didn't mention the quarrel. It was a party, and I was going to enjoy myself and forget about Nick.

'Oh, well . . .' Julie smiled and shrugged her shoulders. 'That's Nick for you.'

'He said he hoped to be around next time.' I thrust a bottle of Martini extra dry at her, hoping to change the subject. 'You like that, don't you?'

'Love it.' Julie drew me inside. 'You look terrific, Aline. Where did you get that shirt?'

'An Italian boutique in George Street . . .' I smiled. 'How's Tony – did he get that order he was after?'

Julie pulled a face. 'Don't ask. It's a sore point.'

Tony designed knitwear and was pretty good at it, but he'd found it difficult to get his business off the ground. His designs weren't cheap to produce, and the orders came in in ones and twos instead of the bulk he needed to employ expert knitters. Julie helped to support him. She earned twice as much as he did, and that was the cause of quite a few rows between them.

'Is he here? You haven't had another row, have you?'

'Only a little one,' Julie admitted. 'It's the same one, of course. I want a baby but we can't afford it.'

'It will come right in time,' I said, rather lamely I thought. 'Tony's good at what he does and he loves you.'

'Yes,' Julie admitted with a sigh. 'I know I'm lucky – but sometimes . . .'

I followed her through the sitting room. Someone had changed the record, and the softer tones of Elaine Paige greeted us.

'I like this one,' I said. ' "Love Hurts". It's one of my favourites.'

'Tony's a big fan, too – but why does she always sing about betrayal?' Julie gave me a wry look. 'Have a drink, Aline. Tony!' She beckoned him across the room. 'Aline's here.'

He advanced towards us, beaming a welcome and carrying a couple of glasses. As he reached us, Julie was called to settle an argument between some of her guests.

'Bubbly?' I raised my brows as I tasted the wine. 'Who's won the pools then?'

'Nothing is too good for the woman who supported Julie all through my absence,' he murmured sotto voce. 'I don't know what she would have done without you. Besides, we're celebrating.'

'It's great you're back together again,' I said, knowing that it was what Julie wanted, despite her moans. 'How's business?'

'It's picking up. I'm hoping to take on a workshop in a converted garage in the King's Road soon, and maybe a full-time worker. That should please Julie – her sitting room won't be full of bits of wool then.'

'I don't suppose she minds that. Is everything all right with you two now?'

'Great. Keep your fingers crossed!'

We laughed together. Julie's temper could flare without warning and their rows were always stormy, yet I knew that they were a team despite their frequent quarrels. I sipped my champagne and we talked about various things, including the precarious state of the property market and the fantastic summer the country was enjoying. Then the doorbell rang and Julie went to answer it.

'Did she say anything to you about us?' Tony looked anxious.

'Not much – just that you'd had a bit of a tiff earlier.'

'You'd think I'd learn, wouldn't you?' he said ruefully. He ran his fingers through short brown hair. 'I just can't accept that Julie has to keep me. Don't tell her, but I've managed to get tickets for *Aspects of Love* for her birthday. I thought perhaps you and . . .' His words trailed away as Julie returned with a man in tow. 'Well, that's a surprise. I never thought he would come. Excuse me,' he apologized as he left me, 'I have to say hello. You know everyone, don't you?'

'Yes. I'll have a word with Rita and Tim.'

Rita was Julie's younger sister. Taller and darker than Julie, she was a trainee beautician at a large London store. Tim, her latest boyfriend, was something in computers. He was staring at her adoringly from behind gilt-rimmed spectacles.

'Grab something to eat before it all goes,' Tony advised, and moved off to meet his guest.

As I went to join Rita, I took a closer look at the outstandingly good-looking new arrival. For a moment I thought I'd seen him somewhere else, though I had no idea where. Tall, smartly dressed in a blue silk suit that was a little too formal for this kind of party, he had very dark, almost black hair, thick straight brows and grey eyes. He turned towards me for an instant and seemed to frown as he realized I was staring at him. Feeling embarrassed, I dropped my gaze and moved on to speak to Julie's sister. The look in the stranger's eyes hadn't been particularly friendly. Deliberately, I turned my back on him as I talked to Tim and Rita for several minutes. Then, as I was hungry, I decided to take Tony's advice.

I helped myself to sausages on sticks, tiny cheese and bacon rolls, celery and crusty bread and joined a group of friends by the window. Soon we were having a political discussion. It was all good-natured, but the atmosphere suddenly changed as a woman called Ronnie joined us. She worked at the same clinic as Julie, as an administrator; I knew her well and wasn't surprised when she jumped straight into the conversation.

'We shall never get the economy straight until someone brings in a stringent taxation system. No one should be allowed to amass so much wealth that it becomes indecent . . .'

Dressed in a rather mannish dark suit with no collar and no embellishments of any kind, Ronnie relied on her perfect make-up for the startling effect she created; her lipstick was a dark, plummy purple and her skin a dead white against the black of her short straight hair. She was always outspoken and her left-wing tendencies were well known.

'It's been tried before,' I said. 'If you take away the incentive, you lose your top management and – '

'So what?' Ronnie was derisive. 'The mess most of them have made of the country recently, we could do without them. Besides, I wasn't talking about earned income so much as inherited wealth . . .'

Her eyes were contemptuous, and now I knew *I* was the target. Despite my own misgivings, I was forced to defend myself.

'So you think parents shouldn't be able to pass on money they've worked for all their lives?' I asked, keeping my tone light.

'Over and above a certain amount, no,' Ronnie said, and looked at me challengingly. 'By the way, how's your stepfather?'

Her direct thrust made me gasp. Ronnie was one of the few people who knew about the quarrel with Michael. I'd liked her when we first met, and had made the mistake of mentioning his marriage to Zena. It was only in the last year or so that Ronnie's attitude towards me had changed. I'd learned to my cost that she could be a real bitch. Staring at her, I wondered just why she was so antagonistic these days. Was it that she resented the fact that I was going to inherit a great deal of money – or was it because she had taken more than a passing fancy to Nick at one of Julie's parties?

As I considered my next move, someone else took over the argument.

'That's rather short-sighted, isn't it?' A man's voice spoke from behind me. 'Personally, I think stringent taxation encourages people to evade it by any means possible. If inherited wealth were punished too severely, business would suffer. Farmers wouldn't be able to pass on their land to their sons and – '

'Land should belong to the people collectively,' Ronnie said. 'If everyone had to rent, it would solve the problem and improve efficiency.'

'Surely events in Eastern Europe have shown you that that system doesn't work?' The voice lost none of its reasonableness. 'I've worked hard for what I've got and I'd fight to protect it. I'll pay my taxes, but if they became ridiculous, I'd leave the country . . .'

'Your lot always do,' Ronnie rejoined in a sarcastic manner.

'I'm not sure what you mean by "my lot". I've used the past few years to take advantage of business opportunities . . .'

'What about the disabled, the old and the poor? They're the ones who have suffered . . . Or perhaps you don't care about them?'

Steady grey eyes met fierce blue ones, and I watched, fascinated by the battle between a man I'd never seen until a few minutes before, and the champion of many a previous argument. Ronnie seldom backed down.

'Whether I care or not isn't the point,' he said, looking straight at her.

'I could give away everything I possess and it wouldn't even begin to solve the problem. There are always going to be people who are disadvantaged. What we have to do is to make sure they're protected. While I don't pretend to claim that we've got it right, I think you should take a look at what's happening in the rest of the world before you condemn your own country. It might not be as bad as you imagine.'

The atmosphere was electric. I waited breathlessly, expecting Ronnie to go for the jugular, but to my surprise she seemed disconcerted.

Ronnie's eyes narrowed and a faint flush stained her cheeks. She got to her feet, saying that she needed a drink.

'Well done,' I murmured as Ronnie walked off. 'Not many of us get the better of her. She doesn't often run out of answers.'

'That type doesn't.' Something flickered in the grey eyes, then he looked amused. 'I hope I haven't upset her – or you. I did rather barge in on your argument, and you were doing pretty well yourself.'

'I'm no match for Ronnie,' I said, wondering again just what I'd done to annoy her. 'She's a member of a left-wing action group and she does quite a bit of debating. I was expressing a personal view. I'm not very political; I'm not even sure what I think about inherited wealth. I just think you have to be careful, or you might end up destroying what this country is all about.'

'And that is?'

'Oh, I don't know – maybe the right to make something out of your life . . .' I frowned as his face reflected amusement. 'Now you're laughing at me.'

'At the indignant look in your eyes, not you,' he said. 'As a matter of fact, I happen to agree with every word.' He held out his hand. 'I'm Piers Drayton. We met briefly yesterday, but you wouldn't remember.'

'We met . . .' Suddenly, I recalled the man I'd bumped into outside the gallery. 'Oh – that was you. No wonder I had the feeling I'd seen you somewhere before. I'm afraid I was very rude, rushing off like that. I was in such a hurry.'

'As long as I didn't hurt you. You walked right into the frame I was carrying.'

'It was my fault.' I took the hand he offered, feeling the cool strength of his grip. He had very powerful hands. 'Aline Marlowe,' I murmured. I had a tingling sensation, almost like touching a live wire. 'Have you known Tony and Julie long?'

'I met Tony a few weeks back, when I returned from America. The delightful Julie I met for the first time this evening.'

'She is great, isn't she? We were at college together. They called us the Siamese twins.'

'Because you were always together?'

I nodded, and his eyes lit with humour. There was something slightly unsettling about the way he looked at me then, yet I found him very attractive. I sensed that he was a man of deep passions, which he endeavoured to keep hidden.

'You said you had been in America,' I said. 'Do you live there?'

'I spent some months there setting up a business. I'm based in London now, though as a child I lived in Cornwall. Our cottage was isolated and I seldom got into town. Consequently, I couldn't wait to escape.' He looked at me, his eyebrows raised. 'And what should I know about you, Aline?'

'I'm not sure – what do you want to know?' He had made an instant physical impact on me, but I was still smarting from the debacle with Nick. 'I work as an appraiser at the Silcott and Barrie auction rooms. Have you heard of them?'

'I bought a picture there a few weeks ago.' He smiled as he saw he had intrigued me. 'Art is my business. I have a gallery in London and another in New York.'

'Piers Drayton . . . Of course! I remember now. It was your gallery . . .' I caught back the question that rose to my lips. I didn't want to get into a discussion about Michael's picture. I was trying to put it out of my mind. 'I've heard of you, I think. You have quite a reputation for picking new young artists.'

'I do my best,' he said, seeming amused. 'Do you like modern art?'

'Not when it's a few blobs of paint that look as if they've been thrown on to the canvas and sells for hundreds of pounds.'

'So you're one of those are you?' His brows went up. 'I can see you need to be – '

'And what are you two up to?' Tony asked, putting his arms about my waist. 'This is a party, you know. Circulate, darlings. I didn't invite you here to monopolize the prettiest girl in the place, Piers.'

'Yes, I'd better have a word with Keith and Joan,' I said, a little relieved at the interruption. 'And then I'd like to ring for a taxi, Tony. I don't want to be late. We've got a busy day at the auction tomorrow.'

'Don't bother about the taxi,' Piers Drayton said. 'I've got my car. I'll drive you home, if you like.'

I looked into his eyes and felt my stomach muscles clench. Instinct told me that this man was unlike anyone else I knew. For all sorts of reasons, I was wary about being drawn into a new relationship, yet I found him exciting.

'I'd like that,' I said. 'But are you sure you don't want to stay on? I was thinking of leaving soon.'

'That's fine,' Piers replied. 'As a matter of fact I'm going out of London for a few days myself. There's some business I have to take care of. I could do with an early night.'

Chapter Six

The girl was alone, alone in the vastness of the desolate marsh. It was dark and a mist was falling, a mist so thick and wet that it had soaked into her thin dress, making it cling to her breasts and thighs, accentuating the fact that she was naked beneath the flimsy garment. She was running, plunging blindly through the mud and the treacherous pools that could bring death to the unwary. Her hair hung in damp strings about her pale face and stuck to her lips as she gasped for breath, and her eyes were dark with terror as she glanced back over her shoulder. A scream escaped her, rising in a shrill crescendo as she sensed the nearness of the thing – the shadowy, creeping horror that pursued her . . .

I awoke with a start and lay in the darkness, my heart thudding. I'd had one of my dreams again, the first for months. It was exactly the same as the nightmares that had haunted me at intervals since I was a child of eleven. Vivid, terrifying, it portrayed the same scene over and over again – a scene of which I had no real memory, but one that I knew must have taken place.

My nightdress was soaking wet and so were the sheets. I'd forgotten to close the curtains, and the moon was shining directly on to my face. That was, perhaps, the cause of my nightmare. I remembered having had bad dreams at Hazeling when the moon was full and my curtains had been left wide open. I'd woken screaming and Michael had come in, holding me in his arms while I sobbed. And then Mother had arrived . . .

Dismissing the painful memory, I wondered what had brought on the dream. As a child I'd been nervous, but now I thought of myself as a level-headed woman; I lived alone and I wasn't afraid of the dark any more. Something had got to me, stirring up old fears and memories – but what? Probably seeing that painting of the marshes of Blakeney, I decided as I got up and went to close the curtains. Glancing out of the window, I saw a drunk swaying unsteadily on the pavement opposite. He cast an empty wine bottle into the gutter, then he staggered his way down the street. I turned away with a feeling of revulsion.

For me it was incomprehensible – and yet there must have been something, some turning point that had led to that poor man becoming the wreck he was now. Something had once happened to him, just as something had once happened to me . . . something so awful that I couldn't remember it years later. But I knew that it had changed me. Before the incident on the marshes I'd been a normal, happy girl of eleven. Afterwards, nothing had been the same.

Feeling cold and shivery, I went into the bathroom and ran a hot bath. I lay in the water, forcing myself to forget the dream. There was no point in looking back; it could only make things worse. It still hurt to think about Michael, and I would never, ever forgive him for the way he had married so soon after Mother's death, but I wasn't going to let it make me bitter. The past was gone and the future was mine, to shape as I liked.

I relaxed a little as I let my thoughts drift towards Piers Drayton. He was intriguing. There was something very intense about him; it gave him an added attraction, a hint of danger that I found exciting.

'Will you have dinner with me if I ring you when I get back?' he'd asked as he delivered me home after the party.

'Why not?' I'd replied, hoping that he wouldn't guess how interested I was. 'Thanks again for bringing me home.'

'My pleasure.' His eyes had held mine. 'I hope we're going to be good friends, Aline.'

He'd lingered a moment longer, then turned away to leave as I inserted my key in the lock. Alone in the flat, I'd thought about him as I prepared for bed. He was attractive, thirtyish perhaps, with an air of confidence that made me think he was very sure of what he wanted out of life. I'd decided that I liked him a lot.

Now, soaking in the perfumed bathwater, I wondered what it would be like to be kissed by Piers. Then I sat up and reached for the soap, surprised at myself.

Surely it was too soon? The row with Nick had upset me, and it was difficult to believe that the relationship had ended. It had been a special relationship and I had still cared deeply for Nick. But it was over . . .

The bathwater grew cold as I deliberately hardened my heart against Nick. If he had loved me, he would have moved in with me. Surely it wasn't too much to ask? All I'd wanted was reassurance, a sign that he did love me.

I grabbed the towel and sighed. Not that it mattered how I felt about either of them. Nick had already walked out on me and Piers Drayton would probably never get in touch . . .

★

71

The telephone rang just as I was about to leave the flat. I hesitated, my hand on the door, then went out without answering it. Let it ring. If I delayed I would miss the bus, and it was going to be another busy day at the saleroom.

I was a few minutes late at the saleroom, and I got on with typing the monthly accounts straight away. They were up on the previous month, after all. Mr Silcott had been running an advertisement in the evening papers, and business was actually picking up. If he could just manage to get that loan and hang on, the tide might turn in his favour.

I'd just finished the accounts when the telephone rang.

'Silcott and Barrie. Can I help you?'

'Aline.' Julie's voice came over the line. 'Sorry to bother you at work. I tried ringing this morning, but you didn't answer.'

'What time was that?' Julie told me, and I thought back. 'I'd left by then. You didn't ring about half an hour earlier, did you?'

'No.' Julie hesitated. 'Do you think we could meet for lunch?'

'Yes, I should think so. What's wrong?'

'We've had another row.'

'You haven't split up again?'

'No – but there's another problem. I'll tell you later.'

'I have to go now,' I said as I saw Mr Silcott at the door of my office. 'About one then.'

Replacing the receiver, I turned to face my employer. He smiled at me and glanced at the paperwork on my desk approvingly.

'I see you've finished the accounts. Good work, Aline.'

'Thank you.'

I saw the anxiety he was trying to subdue and wished I could do or say something that would help, yet I hesitated to speak. If I made my offer to buy into the business he might resent my interference.

'No calls for me this morning?'

'Not yet.'

'Well, I'll be in my office if I'm wanted.'

The restaurant was crowded but we managed to find a table in the corner. We both ordered quiche and salad with freshly baked herb bread and a glass of white wine. When the waiter retreated, I looked at my friend's miserable face.

'So what was the row about this time? Not the same old one?'

'No, not this time.' Julie smiled wryly. 'I've been left some money by an aunt. Not a huge amount, but enough to make a difference.'

'So what's the problem?'

'Tony wants me to invest the money in that workroom of his and I – '

'You want to use it to have a baby?' I felt for her as she nodded, knowing how much she wanted a child. 'If you're asking me what you should do, I can't tell you, Julie. But, love, if I were you, I'd think very carefully. Would you really want a baby if it meant that you might lose Tony? He isn't ready for it yet. You do know that, don't you?'

'Yes, I suppose I do.' Julie sighed and shrugged her shoulders. 'I find it so much easier dealing with other people's problems. I know it makes sense. Tony needs the money . . .' She toyed with her quiche.

I watched her, remembering and sympathizing. Even at college Julie had always had this dream of having children when she found the right man. Several men had wanted to marry her, but Tony was the only one she had cared about.

'Is this going to affect your relationship with him?'

'I shan't let it. I'm having a moan, that's all.' Julie grinned suddenly. 'That's enough of me and my problems. So tell me, what's Piers Drayton like? Tony met him through another friend – a business contact, actually. He never expected him to come to the party; it was just a casual invitation. He's very attractive, isn't he?'

'Yes, he's good looking,' I said thoughtfully. 'So Tony doesn't know him very well then?'

Julie's eyes sparkled. 'He's a bit of a dark horse really.'

'What do you mean?'

'I'm not sure . . .' She seemed puzzled now, wrinkling her brow. 'Ronnie was hinting at something, but you know what she is. I'm afraid I didn't take much notice.'

'She might have been in a mood because he won their argument,' I said, frowning as I wondered again if Ronnie had turned against me because she was interested in Nick. But I wasn't sure that she was. It would explain her dislike of me though. 'Are you having a pudding?'

Julie glanced towards the array of gateaux and creamy desserts, and groaned. 'Better not,' she said reluctantly. 'I can't afford to put on weight.'

I settled down that evening to watch television with a tray on my lap. The weekend stretched long and empty before me, and I sighed as I wriggled my toes in the fluffy rug in front of the settee. Julie and Tony were going to her parents for a couple of days, and most of my other friends were either on holiday or deeply involved with their current men . . . Which led me back to the problem of Piers Drayton. What was I going to do if he phoned?

The telephone shrilled as if in reply to my thoughts. But Piers had said he was going out of town, so it couldn't be him. I snatched it up, feeling nervous. 'Aline Marlowe speaking.'

For a moment there was silence, then I could hear the sound of harsh breathing. I slammed it down, more annoyed than frightened. Someone had definitely been on the line this time. I stared at the phone, then unplugged it.

'Now play games, whoever you are,' I muttered.

I wasn't going to be intimidated by some freak who thought this kind of thing was amusing!

I tossed and turned, waking from another disturbing dream. Not one of my nightmares this time, but memories I would rather not relive. They filled my mind as I lay watching the first rays of a rosy dawn steal through the window. I'd been dreaming of the day Michael, my mother and I had picnicked by a stream. I was five years old and I'd been stung on my bottom by a bee.

I could remember screaming with pain. The sting was still in my flesh. Michael had pulled it out with my mother's eyebrow tweezers, and then bathed the wound with cool water from the river. His hands had been gentle and soothing, but I'd gone on crying, refusing to be comforted. He'd started to tease me, kissing my bottom and pretending to bite chunks out of it until my tears turned to laughter. For some reason Mother had got very cross with us both.

'For goodness sake stop crying and causing such a fuss, Aline,' she'd snapped. 'And you're encouraging her, Michael. All this excitement will make her sick. Leave her alone now.'

'You're too hard on her,' Michael had said, his tone gentle and appeasing. 'She's just a baby, Sheila, and that sting must have been damned painful.'

'Then stop rubbing it and let her rest.'

Michael had gone very quiet then. Neither he or Mother had spoken much for the remainder of the day, though Michael had winked at me behind her back. I'd thought my mother was just being cross and I'd been sulky with her for a day or two after that. It hadn't occurred to me to question the undercurrent of tension I'd felt between them. Not until several years later did I become aware of what was causing it . . .

I glanced at the phone, which I'd left unplugged. Why was I thinking about Michael so often these days? It was almost as if he was trying to reach me . . . Yet why should he? Dismissing the idea as ridiculous, I pulled the covers over my head and went back to sleep.

*

74

I had always loved the day before sale day. Helping to put the lot numbers on the various items of furniture, pictures and glass wasn't part of my job. I'd started to do it when we were short-handed, and I enjoyed it so much that it had somehow become a part of my routine. That Tuesday morning, I was given the job of checking the smalls – about two hundred lots of china, glass and oddments that were set out on a long trestle table in the middle of the saleroom. Studying my list, I rechecked before going to Mr Silcott.

'I can't find the Dresden mirror,' I said. 'It's down here as lot number 198, but it isn't on the table.'

'It must still be in the store room,' he said, taking a key from his pocket and handing it to me. 'I know it's there, Aline. I saw it myself the other day. It's rather nice, about twelve inches high and bordered with cherubs and china flowers. Could you see if you can find it?'

'Of course.' I smiled at him and took the key. Leaving the bustle of the saleroom, I went through to the private area at the back.

I switched on the light just inside the store room and looked around with interest. It was beginning to burst at the seams with items already booked in for next month's sale. There were pictures stacked against the walls, small items of furniture – the bigger ones were in an outside warehouse – china and bric-a-brac. Valuable things like silver and jewellery were stored in the safe in Mr Silcott's own office.

The missing mirror was on a shelf, tucked out of sight behind a Derby tea service. Picking it up, I turned to leave, then my gaze fell on a small landscape. Something about it seemed familiar, and I stopped to look closer. It was another of Michael's paintings. Why was he selling paintings he'd kept for years? He'd always made a decent living from the watercolours he sold to tourists in the summer at a little shop in Blakeney, though they would never make him wealthy. I suspected that Zena had thought she would be rich when she married him, and sometimes wondered if that was why Zena had chosen a man so much older than herself.

Perhaps I ought to get in touch again. I felt guilty about the quarrel. At the time I'd been overwrought, but now I'd begun to think I might have been a little unfair to both Zena and my stepfather.

Yet as I left the store room, I deliberately blocked it from my mind once more. I had work to do. I finished lotting the smalls, ticking them all before going back to my own office. It was almost lunchtime, and I was hungry.

The telephone rang just as I was putting on my jacket. I picked it up, my nerves jangling as they did whenever the phone rang these days.

'Silcott and Barrie. Can I help you?'

'May I speak to Aline Marlowe please?'

'Speaking,' I said, feeling a tingle of excitement.

'Aline, this is Piers Drayton. I hope you don't mind my ringing you at your office, but I tried to get you last night and again this morning.'

'I've had some trouble with my phone,' I told him. 'No, I don't mind you ringing here. But you only just caught me. I was about to leave for lunch.'

'If I were free I'd join you,' he said. 'Unfortunately, I have an appointment. I was wondering about dinner this evening . . . if you're free.'

'Yes . . .' I hesitated for a moment. 'Yes, I am.'

'Good. I'll pick you up at seven-thirty, then.'

'Fine. I'll look forward to that.'

Excitement brought a glow to my eyes as I dressed that evening. On a whirlwind shopping trip at lunchtime, I'd bought a new dress. It was black, short and clinging, and I felt good in it. Somehow I hadn't wanted to wear anything I'd worn with Nick. It was a new beginning.

I couldn't wait to see Piers. The afternoon had seemed to drag on for ever. Now as I glanced at my reflection again, I decided the dress needed something. I chose a gold and pearl link chain Julie had given me for my eighteenth birthday. I had more expensive jewellery that had come from my mother, but it had painful memories and I seldom wore it.

Just as I was putting on my shoes, the phone rang. Steeling myself, I went to answer it. Julie's voice said, 'I just wanted to tell you that I've talked it over with Tony and he's going ahead with the workroom.'

'That's great, Julie.' I heard the doorbell. 'I'm going to have to ring you tomorrow. There's someone at the door.'

'Is it someone nice?'

'I'll tell you tomorrow.'

I flew to the door, my heart pounding. Piers stood there, looking fantastic in a loose-fitting dark suit with a cream silk shirt and tie, and I had a feeling that he'd chosen his outfit carefully. The way he was looking at me made me breathless.

'You are even more beautiful than I remembered.'

Nick would never have complimented me like that. Piers was different: sophisticated, cool, and yet with a hint of something hidden . . .

76

'Are you coming in for a drink before we go?'

'I'll come in,' he said, 'but I'm driving so I'd better leave the wine for later. I'll just watch you . . . '

'I'm almost ready,' I said, feeling an urge to run my fingers through his thick straight hair. 'I've just got to pick up my jacket.' He moved towards me, and I ached for him to take me in his arms. When he didn't it was almost a physical pain. 'Sit down if you like.'

I went through to the bedroom to fetch my white tuxedo. When I came back, he was standing by the pine dresser, looking at my collection of records. I stood watching him for a moment, trying to see the room as he must, for the first time. Apart from the sofa from Hazeling, it was a hotchpotch of secondhand furniture that I'd picked up from the saleroom and unusual trinkets that had caught my eye when browsing at market stalls. An Indian carved hardwood stand, a string of brightly coloured ethnic beads draped round a plastic hand made in the fifties, a Chinese fan and, of course, my collection of old records . . . What would he make of them? He seemed fascinated, picking things up to look at them closely, as if he wanted to know more about me.

Piers turned and smiled as he saw me watching him. 'I like your flat,' he said, as if to reassure me. 'It's like you – very distinctive and individual. Full of surprises.'

'I think that's the nicest compliment anyone's ever paid me,' I said.

Piers moved towards me, taking my jacket to place it around my shoulders. The firm touch of his hands sent a delicious tremor down my spine. Our eyes met, and for a moment I sensed the tension inside him. I caught the scent of an expensive cologne I didn't know but immediately liked – it matched his personality. In an instant that hint of unease had gone and he was once more the cool sophisticate who intrigued me, slightly aloof but exciting. His eyes were almost hypnotic. I wanted him to kiss me, but he moved away.

'Shall we go? I've booked a table for eight-fifteen at Boulestin. I hope that's all right?'

'I've never been there,' I said, 'but I've always wanted to.'

Piers was obviously pleased with my answer.

'I'm glad you like the idea. I find it a rather special place, but until I saw your flat I wondered if it would be trendy enough for you.'

'Now you know I'm just an old stick in the mud.'

'Now I know that everything I sensed when I first saw you wasn't just imagination,' he said, being infuriatingly mysterious. I questioned with my eyes but he shook his head and laughed. 'Leave me some secrets,' he said. 'Just for a while.'

'I'm not sure that's fair after such a provocative remark,' I teased. 'But I'll let you off, for now.'

Piers took my arm and we went out into the street. I was surprised his car wasn't the one he'd been driving when he brought me home from Julie's. That was a practical estate, used mainly for his business, I suspected. The car waiting for me that evening was a Rolls-Royce Silver Shadow. It must have been about eight years old but it was immaculate, its leather upholstery still like new. Piers opened the door for me, making sure I was comfortable before closing it.

'I feel like a princess,' I said. 'What a wonderful car.'

'I'm rather fond of it,' he admitted. 'I prefer the shape to the newer ones; that's why I don't change it. Besides, a car like this is almost a friend.'

Everything he said was making me more sure that he was a man I could like. Stop lying! I told myself silently. Liking had nothing to do with what I felt for Piers Drayton. Every touch, every look, every movement made me more aware of the ache inside me. I had never felt quite like this before, even with Nick at the beginning.

The restaurant was in the heart of Covent Garden. Immediately, I was drawn by its atmosphere of richness and charm that belonged to gentler days, and I felt very privileged as a hovering waiter gave me the royal treatment.

Uncharacteristically, I asked Piers to choose for me. He didn't raise a brow but I had the feeling that he was pleased because I had deferred to him. It suited my mood. This was a night for being looked after, for being made to feel very feminine, protected, cherished . . . loved. Yes, love wasn't too strong a word to use, even though we'd only just met. Perhaps I was on the rebound from my affair with Nick, but I was enjoying the way Piers made me feel that I was important to him. It was a new experience. His attitude was so – I couldn't put it into words – almost possessive? The word surprised me, and yet I saw that it was correct. Remembering what he'd said earlier about his car, I realized he would be the same over anything he prized: possessive . . . Yes, it was a good word to describe him.

'You were looking at a picture when we first met,' he said, breaking into my thoughts. 'It seemed to have mesmerized you. Was there any particular reason?'

I was tempted to tell him exactly why that particular painting had upset me, but it was too soon, and it wasn't the kind of thing I could talk about in a restaurant. Besides, my feelings on the subject were still too muddled, too confused to put into words.

I smiled and shook my head. 'I thought I recognized the scene,' I said. 'It was somewhere on the Norfolk coast, wasn't it?'

'Blakeney,' he replied. 'Painted by a local man, I believe. I wasn't there when it was brought in. We've got it on sale or return, I think.'

'I see.' My eyes slid away and I felt guilty. Why hadn't I told him the truth? He had sensed something hidden, and because of it he had slightly withdrawn from me. I changed the subject. 'Did you have a good weekend?'

'Not really.' He pulled a wry face. 'I drove all the way up to Glasgow to look at some pictures that turned out to be fakes.'

His eyes had turned cold and distant. I had a feeling that he too had lied, though why was a mystery.

'I'm sorry,' I said. 'I spent my time shopping, but I couldn't find anything I wanted.'

'Then we both wasted our – ' He broke off as the waiter approached. 'Here comes our champagne,' he said, and he was smiling again. 'We do have something to celebrate, don't we, Aline?'

My stomach lurched and I felt the desire flare inside me. What was it about him that had this odd effect on me? 'I do hope so, Piers,' I said, my breath catching. 'I do hope so . . .'

'That was the most delicious meal.' I sighed with content as Piers stopped the car. 'You are coming in for a coffee, aren't you?'

He glanced at his watch. 'I want to, Aline, but I have a plane to catch first thing in the morning.'

'You're going away?'

The disappointment must have shown in my face, because a smile flickered at the corner of his mouth. 'A big auction in New York. I really have to go.'

'OK.' I tried not to sound as if it mattered. 'How long will you be away?'

'Five . . . six days.' He shrugged back his sleeve and glanced at his watch again. 'Maybe one coffee then.'

'Sure? If you have to . . .'

He placed a finger against my lips and I felt desire stir once more. This need to be close to him was overwhelming, turning me weak inside. 'One coffee,' he said, and smiled.

Locking the car, he followed me into the apartment building. The gentle whirring of the lift was the only sound as we stood silently, our eyes saying it all. Whatever it was between us was so strong that it was almost tangible. At the entrance to my flat, he took the key from me and opened the door. It was an automatic action, as if he were used to commanding every situation. I threw my jacket on the settee and went into the kitchen. When I came back, Piers had selected a record and the soft music was playing in the background. We looked at each other, both hesitating before the inevitable kiss, then he took a step towards me. The phone began to ring. For a moment I ignored it, then picked it up.

'Hello,' I said, still looking up at Piers. The expression in his eyes was making me feel shaky.

'Bitch,' the ugly spiteful voice said. 'I'd like to . . .' The words were filthy, threatening and frightening.

Piers took one look at my white face and grabbed the receiver. He listened for a moment, a nerve flicking in his cheek, then he replaced the receiver and unplugged the phone.

'How long has this been going on?'

'That's the first one like that. I've had a few odd ones recently – silences and then heavy breathing. That's the worst.'

'We'll leave it like that for tonight,' he said. 'First thing in the morning I'll see about getting your calls intercepted. It may be best if you go ex-directory.'

'In the morning . . .' I stared at him, my head whirling. 'I thought you had a plane to catch?'

'That can wait,' he muttered. 'I'll get to the auction somehow. You don't think I would leave you now, Aline?'

The need to be in his arms was almost a compulsion. I moved towards him. 'I don't think I could bear it if you did,' I said.

'Oh, Piers,' I whispered as he reached for me. 'I – I think I love you.'

'Then you'd better make up your mind pretty damned quick,' he said huskily. 'Because I know how I feel about you, and once I have I hold.'

'Piers. Piers darling. I think you should know about my life.'

'Not now,' he muttered. 'We'll talk later.'

I nodded, drawn by a stronger will than my own. I wanted to feel his lips on mine, possessing me. It had been there between us from the very beginning, this unseen bond, hidden, suppressed but undeniable. Maybe it was too soon. We knew nothing about each other, but it was too late for caution. Nothing could have stopped us now.

As soon as his lips touched mine, I felt a desperate hunger. My arms went round his neck, my fingers venturing into that thick dark hair. His arms surrounded me; he lifted me up and his hands caressed me through the soft material of my dress, making me tremble. I kissed his earlobe, biting it gently and inhaling the spicy scent of his aftershave.

'You smell good enough to eat,' I murmured.

'Feel free,' he said, and laid me on the bed. I tingled as he gazed down at me, his eyes serious. 'I'm not rushing you, Aline?'

'No.' I shook my head. It was as if I had been waiting all my life for this moment, as if it were predestined. Taking his hand, I held it against my cheek, then turned to kiss the palm. 'I've been wanting this all evening.'

He bent to kiss me, his lips gentle and searching. 'I meant to take it one step at a time,' he said smiling wryly. 'So much for self control.'

'It feels like years since we met,' I whispered, gazing up at him. 'It's so strange, but I felt that I knew you as soon as we met – though we never have met before, have we?'

He shook his head and touched my cheek, his eyes dark with an intense passion.

'Aline, darling . . .'

All at once, we couldn't wait to get out of our clothes. Piers groaned in frustration as he pulled at the knot in his tie. I laughed, tugging at my zip as it stuck halfway down, but at last we were free of them. I lay looking at him, shy now as I wondered what he would think of me, longing to be the most beautiful, the most perfect of women for him. He reached out to touch my hair.

'You're so beautiful,' he said. 'I knew you were for me the moment I saw you. You belong to me. Don't you feel it?'

The power of his eyes was mesmerizing, draining me of any will to resist. He was right: I did belong to him. I'd known it from our first meeting. My body felt as if it was no longer mine, and there was no stiffness, no awkwardness as I lay looking up at him, my eyes misty with love.

'Yes, Piers,' I murmured. 'I belong to you.'

He drew me to him. The heat of his flesh against mine was like a torch lighting a flame inside me. In the grip of a feverish excitement, I groaned, pressing closer to him, wanting him so badly that I was shaking. His mouth crushed mine, demanding so much, but not more than I was willing to give.

That first frantic coupling was something that neither of us could control; hot, desperate and swift, slaking a mutual need. It was a recognition of something deep inside us – loneliness, a meeting of souls, lust . . . I'd never experienced anything like it before. It was desperate, primeval, tearing; as much, I sensed, for Piers as for me. Afterwards, we were both exhausted.

I lay with my eyes closed, a tear trickling down my cheek. Piers bent over me, his face concerned as he smoothed it away, then kissed my eyelids.

'Did I hurt you?'

'No.' I opened my eyes and looked at him. 'If you did, I wanted it that way.'

'Yes,' he said, lying back on the pillow beside me. 'I know.'

We were silent, both thinking our own thoughts. We lay without touching but in perfect harmony. Perhaps we slept. I wasn't sure. It was some time before I was aware of his hand stroking my thigh. I turned towards him. We kissed, slowly, lingeringly. This time we wanted to touch and taste, to savour, the passion mounting between us little by little until it flamed once more.

I cried his name as he entered me, gasping, melting with pleasure as my head turned from side to side on the pillow and I arched beneath him, straining to meet the thrust of his body. I was panting, moaning, lost in the sheer delight of this new experience. I hadn't known it could be this good. Piers had somehow released me from bonds of my own making. For the first time I let go of whatever it was that had held me chained. I cried afterwards as I hid my face in the curling black hairs on Piers' chest.

He stroked my head, his fingers moving comfortingly at the back of my neck. 'Sleep now,' he said. 'We'll talk tomorrow.'

'Piers,' I murmured, lifting my head to look at him in the half-light. 'Yes?'

'I just wanted to say thank you.'

He smiled. Of course he didn't understand. How could he?

Chapter Seven

I awoke refreshed, to find Piers standing by the bed with a breakfast tray. To my surprise he had washed, shaved and dressed in a casual black sweater and jeans. He laughed as he saw the question in my eyes.

'My cases were in the car,' he said. 'I've been awake for hours, sleepyhead.'

He poured steaming hot coffee into two cups. 'Milk, one sugar please,' I said, glancing at the toast, grilled bacon and scrambled eggs. 'Am I going to get this every morning? Or is it just to show me what you expect?'

'If you always sleep in this long, I'll be getting the breakfast. I need very little sleep. Too much nervous energy, I suppose. Normally, I've run a couple of miles by now.'

I glanced at the clock. It was only a quarter to seven. 'A fitness freak,' I groaned. 'Just my luck!'

'Don't worry, darling,' he murmured, his tone matching mine. 'It only hurts for the first three months; after that you won't feel a thing.'

'I'll probably be dead,' I said, but it was hard to keep the smile from my face. I felt so good: really alive and bubbling over with happiness. Just the thought of being with Piers in three months' time was enough to make me want to shout for joy.

'You look even better in the mornings,' Piers said, bending down to kiss me lightly on the lips.

'You taste of toothpaste and soap,' I replied. 'And I need a shower.'

'After you've eaten,' he insisted, his grip on my arm restraining me.

I felt the strength in his powerful hands and realized that I would be the loser in any physical tussle. Piers was in any case a large-boned, athletic man, and his dedication to exercise had made him lean and fit.

I smiled submissively. 'Just a piece of toast then. I hardly ever eat breakfast.'

'I can see I'm going to have to teach you how to take care of yourself,' he said. 'I want you to keep that beautiful body just as it is.' As I blushed, his expression became serious. 'I've been through to Telecom, Aline. They're going to intercept all your calls for two weeks, and after that you'll have a new number and it will be ex-directory.'

'You move fast,' I said, relieved. 'Thank you, Piers.'

'No man is going to do that to you while I'm around.' His mouth was grim and he seemed almost affronted, as if he had taken it as a personal insult.

'It certainly wasn't funny last night,' I said, shuddering. 'I doubt if I'd have slept at all if you hadn't been here. I'll be all right now, though.' I looked at him thoughtfully. 'Will you be able to catch a later plane? Would it get you there in time for the auction?'

'I could . . . but I'm not going.'

'I'll be fine now, Piers. It was just the shock.'

He gazed down at me, his expression unreadable. 'I made some more calls while I was about it. One of my colleagues will bid for the pictures we want. I've cancelled all my appointments for the next three weeks.'

'You have? Why?'

Piers' eyes were glinting with amusement as he saw my expression. He moved one finger over the back of my hand, tantalizing me.

'Why, Piers?'

'I've been planning our schedule while you were sleeping, darling,' he said at last.

'Oh?' My eyes opened wide. I knew that he was teasing me and I made a murmur of protest. 'Tell me then!'

He smiled provocatively. 'I thought we would get married on Saturday. That should give you time to invite anyone who matters to you, buy a dress, get your hair done or whatever you think necessary. Then I thought we'd take a couple of weeks in the Bahamas . . .'

I felt as if all the breath had been knocked out of me. He couldn't mean it. 'You're joking, aren't you?'

'Am I?' His brows arched. 'I thought we'd made up our minds about each other last night.'

'Yes, but . . .'

'But what?' He looked at me intently and the protest died on my tongue. 'You've decided it was all a mistake? You don't love me and you don't want to marry me?'

'I do love you and – I do want to marry you.' I was shocked to hear my own voice. Had I actually said that?

'Then what's the problem?'

I felt as if I was riding on a merry-go-round, whirling so fast that I couldn't think properly. I'd had all those arguments with Nick because he wouldn't commit himself, and here was Piers almost demanding that I marry him before we'd known each other five minutes. There was something so magnetic about this man's personality that I was being

84

swept out of control. It was frightening but also very exciting. I knew I ought to come up with a hundred reasons why I shouldn't marry in such haste, but I couldn't think of a single one. Piers had made me happier than I'd ever been. I wanted to be with him, and I was afraid that if I didn't seize my chance now it would disappear and I might miss something wonderful. Piers' eyes were hypnotic, dominating, and they drained me of willpower.

'There isn't a problem,' I said at last. Suddenly I was laughing. 'It's utterly mad! People don't do these things. They take time to get to know one another and – '

'It's more fun this way.' Piers seemed to relax, and I realized that he had been waiting tensely for my reaction. It reassured me to know that he wasn't quite as cool as he seemed at first glance. 'Besides, I think we jumped quite a few stages last night, don't you?'

'Yes.' I was still shell-shocked by the speed at which it had all happened. Piers leaned towards me, that amused glint in his eyes once more, supremely confident as he kissed me. I was seized by a mood of recklessness. 'Let's do it,' I cried, flinging my arms around his neck. 'It's insane, ridiculous, crazy, but I love it!'

'I love you,' he said. 'You belong to me, Aline. Always remember that, whatever happens.'

Whatever happens? I wondered what he meant, but as we fell back on to the pillows together, the thought was lost in surging desire. The worst that could happen was that we might one day fall out of love with each other; but somehow that possibility seemed very remote.

'You are quite, quite mad,' Julie cried when I rang her. 'But I think it's the most romantic thing I've ever heard.'

'You will come, won't you?' I said. 'You and Tony?'

'Of course. I wouldn't miss it for anything, and Tony will be thrilled. What did your family say?'

'Nothing. I haven't told anyone at Hazeling.' I hadn't even told Piers about my family yet. I knew I ought to have done so at the beginning; now it was too difficult.

'Surely you'll invite them to the wedding?' Julie sounded very surprised.

'I've tried ringing a couple of times recently and no one was there. I think they must have gone away. Besides, I'm not sure I want them to come.'

'Of course. I wasn't criticizing, just thinking of you.'

'I know. I'll have to ring them sometime. Now, I want to tell you what we've arranged. We're having a register-office ceremony with a special licence, and then a celebration lunch at Langan's.'

'Piers must have considerable influence to arrange that at short notice,' Julie said drily. There was a hint of disapproval in her tone as she asked, 'Have you thought about what Nick will say when he gets back?'

'Nick isn't interested. We had a row and he walked out. It's over.'

'Can't you contact him? I think you should, Aline.'

'It's impossible. He's at a secret location in South America. Even if I tried, no one would be able to reach him for days. Besides, he would only say he wasn't interested.'

I wished Julie wouldn't go on about Nick. It was confusing and painful to think about him. My decision was made, and nothing could change it. I was going to marry Piers.

'I think he might have rather more to say than that.' Julie sounded awkward, as though she was afraid of interfering. 'He'll probably ring you when he gets back and expect things to be as they were. You know what Nick is, Aline. He doesn't seem to care much, but I know he thinks the world of you.'

'He certainly didn't *seem* bothered when he walked out. His job means more to him than anything or anyone else.'

'I can't believe that.' Julie hesitated. 'Don't you think you should wait for a while? I mean, you don't know Piers very well, do you?'

'I know as much as I need to know.' My reply was sharp, defensive. Perhaps I was being hasty, but she didn't understand. I didn't really understand it myself; I just knew that something deep inside me had responded to Piers. 'I'm in love with him, Julie. I didn't plan it, it just happened.'

'It usually does,' Julie said, laughing as she gave in. 'I know when I'm beaten. You've made up your mind, so I'll shut up. As long as you're happy . . .'

'I am happy, Julie.'

'Then so am I,' she said. 'I'll see you on Saturday.'

Putting the receiver back, I hesitated, then picked it up and dialled the number for Hazeling. Perhaps Julie was right: I ought at least to let Zena and Michael know I was getting married. The phone rang several times but again no one answered. Perhaps I'd scribble a few words to Zena before the weekend.

Frowning, I stared at the telephone. I could ring Nick's office . . . But what was the point? It was impossible to leave the message I wanted to give Nick. I would get in touch with him when he came home and explain.

*

I went into the saleroom office that Friday afternoon to clear out my desk and make sure that the temp I'd engaged to take my place was settling in. Mr Silcott was going to appoint a new appraiser himself. He had been disappointed that I was leaving.

'You were getting on so well,' he said. 'I shall miss you, Aline.'

I felt a bit guilty about letting him down, but Piers didn't want me to work. At least I'd found Tracy to do the accounts and some typing.

'Are you sure you've got the hang of the filing system?' I asked.

'I'm not quite sure about the sheets that come in from the saleroom. How do I know what belongs to which customer?'

I explained that buyers had a prefix of BY and vendors VE so that it was easy to see whether we were billing or paying out.

'It sounds a bit complicated.'

'You'll soon get used to it,' I said. 'Don't forget that there's a buyer's and a seller's commission.'

'I'm not sure I'll ever get this right.'

'Of course you will – ' I broke off as the buzzer sounded from Mr Silcott's office and Tracy answered it.

'He wants to see you before you leave.'

'I'll pop in now. Is there anything else you need to know?'

'No, I don't think so.' Tracy giggled. 'It's so romantic, you meeting a stranger, falling in love and marrying all in a week. It sounds like something out of a movie.'

'Yes, I suppose it does.'

Going through to Mr Silcott's office, I thought it was true that I really knew hardly anything about the man I was about to marry. How could I hope to explain the feeling inside me, which, if I was honest, was almost a compulsion? But I did not want to fight it – I was in love with Piers.

Mr Silcott had a bottle of wine waiting. He handed me a large, heavy parcel, smiling broadly as I exclaimed over the expensive canteen of King's Pattern cutlery.

'Everyone contributed, Aline. You're a popular girl. We shall all miss you.'

'I didn't expect . . . Thank you. I've enjoyed working for you.'

He looked pleased. 'I'm glad about that. You're very good at your job, and if you should ever want to come back . . .'

'Thank you,' I whispered. 'But I don't expect to work in future. Piers likes to travel and – '

'Of course.' He nodded cheerfully. 'But the offer's there.'

Hesitating, he cleared his throat. 'I got the loan I was after, Aline. I thought you would like to know that.'

'That's wonderful,' I said, pleased for him. With all the excitement, I'd forgotten Mr Silcott's problems. It was just as well that I hadn't mentioned my interest in buying into the firm. 'I'm glad you told me.'

We chatted for a few minutes longer and then I left. I felt that he had seemed slightly concerned for me, as if he thought I might regret my impulsive decision to marry. Again, I felt the niggle of doubt. Was I being foolish? Most people would probably think so, but then, how could anyone else know how happy Piers had made me?

Arriving at my apartment building, I saw him waiting for me. We were taking Julie and Tony out to dinner that evening. I'd said he should be having a stag night, but he wasn't interested.

'That's the last thing I want,' he'd said. 'I prefer it this way – unless you want to go out with some of your friends?'

'No, of course not,' I assured him. 'I love you, Piers. I don't need anyone else.'

As I saw the way his face lit up when he saw me coming, my doubts fled. What did I know about him? I knew that I loved him and he loved me. That was enough.

For my wedding I wore a pale lemon Louis Feraud suit and a white filigree lace vest. I'd managed to find a pair of satin shoes that matched the colour of my suit, and after some deliberation, I decided to buy a very expensive hat. It was a white straw plate that sat on my head at an angle, with a spray of yellow silk roses beneath the brim. The roses framed my face, providing that special touch I'd been looking for.

Julie stayed overnight at my flat to keep me company on the eve of my wedding. When she saw the hat, she exclaimed in delight.

'It's the sort of thing the Princess of Wales wears,' she said. 'You look gorgeous in it, Aline.'

'I've never worn hats, but I wanted something different. It cost an arm and a leg, but I think it was worth it.'

'You look beautiful.' Julie was misty-eyed.

'Thank you.' The fluttering sensation in my stomach eased a little. 'I'm so nervous.'

'You're not having second thoughts, Aline? Because if you are . . .'

I shook my head. 'No. I feel a little breathless, but it's all right. This is what I want.'

Julie nodded. 'We'd better go,' was all she said, though I sensed she was uneasy and I believed she thought I was making a mistake. 'The taxi is waiting.'

I wished I could tell her why I had to marry Piers, but I couldn't find the words. So I simply smiled and picked up the posy of white roses and freesias he had sent that morning. 'Let's go then,' I said.

Piers was waiting outside the register office with the handful of friends we'd invited. I saw a couple of faces that were new to me. As Piers introduced them as Mark Davies and Roger Best, I got the impression that they were colleagues of his rather than close personal friends. Piers had no family. His parents had died when he was quite young and he'd been brought up by his maternal grandparents. He had told me about his childhood one evening and I'd had the feeling that it had been pretty wretched, so I hadn't asked too many questions. He would tell me when he was ready, just as I would tell him about Michael and Zena when the time was right.

The ceremony was over so quickly that I could hardly believe we were married. I felt a pang of regret for the lace dress, church bells and bridesmaids I'd dispensed with, but it vanished as Piers took me in his arms to kiss me. Then we were out in the street, with the sun on our faces and the noise of the traffic in our ears. The unreal atmosphere of that brief ceremony vanished, and then Julie was throwing confetti and rice. She hugged me and kissed Piers on the cheek as she congratulated us.

'Be happy, you crazy, wonderful pair,' she said, blinking hard. 'Damn it! I think I'm going to cry, and it took me ages to get my mascara on this morning.'

'You look lovely,' Tony said, squeezing my hand. 'We both wish you and Piers lots of luck.'

'Thank you.' I smiled, feeling emotional at their show of affection.

Everyone piled into the cars Piers had ordered to take us to the restaurant. Alone for a few minutes, he took my hand in his.

'Happy, darling?'

'Very.' I smiled as he touched my cheek. 'I love you.'

'That's good, because I'm rather fond of you, Mrs Drayton.'

'Mrs Drayton,' I repeated. 'That sounds nice.'

He reached for me, grimacing as my hat got in the way. 'It's very fetching, but I want to kiss you.'

The hat was removed, and the kiss went on and on until we were nearly at the restaurant. Tissues, fresh lipstick and a mirror came hastily into play, and we arrived looking more or less respectable to meet our guests. After that things became a little hazy.

Probably we all drank too much champagne, though afterwards I remembered only my first glass. It was just such a wonderful party. The tables had all been grouped together with vases of pink roses and white cloths; the food was delicious, the wine ambrosial and the company superb. We never stopped laughing the whole time. I was sure that the other customers must have thought we were all drunk or crazy, but perhaps they realized it was just a very special occasion. I knew that I didn't need the champagne. I was intoxicated with happiness.

I'd given Julie the spare key to my flat. Rita was looking for a place of her own, and I'd arranged for her to take over the lease. It had all been a terrific rush, but I'd told Julie her sister could move in when she liked.

'I'm not going back today,' I explained. 'My cases are at Piers' flat in Belgravia. We're going there first, and then to the airport in the morning.'

'Are you sure you don't mind?' Julie asked. 'What about when you come back?'

'I'll collect what I need, and Rita can have the rest of my stuff if she wants it,' I said. 'We can decide then. Just tell her to make herself at home for now.'

'Thanks,' Julie said, and hugged me. 'Rita could never have afforded all that furniture.'

'All my junk, you mean,' I joked. 'Seriously, Julie, it will be easier for me, I would have had to let the flat go anyway. I'm not sure where we'll be living, but it won't be there.'

'Surely you'll be based in London?' Julie looked at me in surprise and some alarm.

'We haven't had time to discuss it yet.' There was so much we hadn't had time to discuss. It had all been such a rush, and we'd spent more time making love than talking. Piers had told me not to worry about anything, and in the end I'd just left it all to him. He seemed to prefer it that way.

Lunch was over at last, and everyone emerged into the street to look for taxis. We all hugged and kissed. I thanked Tony and Julie for the extravagant presents they had given us: for me a pretty simulated pearl cocktail watch, for Piers a Waterman's pen.

'We thought something personal,' Julie said rather awkwardly. 'You've both had your own homes . . .'

I nodded and thanked her again. All our friends had had similar thoughts. No one had bought a joint present. I wondered if it was because no one had got around to thinking of us as a couple yet, or if they didn't expect the marriage to last. It was a sobering thought and I dismissed it at once. I was Mrs Piers Drayton, and very happy about it. Taxis arrived and we dispersed amongst laughter and more confetti. I waved to Tony and Julie as the car drew away.

'Thank God that's over,' Piers murmured, loosening his tie. 'It was a necessary evil, but . . .'

I felt a little hurt on my friends' behalf. They had all been so generous and affectionate towards us.

'Didn't you enjoy the party?'

'Naturally, darling. But I'd rather be alone with you. The important thing is that we're going to be together from now on, isn't it?'

'Yes.' Something in his manner was puzzling. His eyes narrowed and I knew he was waiting for me to respond more positively. 'Yes, of course it is,' I murmured.

A dark bronzed mirror ran the entire length of Piers' sitting room, reflecting the rather spartan decor and giving warmth to what might otherwise have been a cold room, its stark white walls broken only by one splash of colour in a picture that turbulently combined reds, purples and blues. On the gleaming wooden floors were shaggy white rugs, black leather and tubular steel chairs and a large coffee table made out of a heavy slab of black marble supported by a gilt scroll. There were no books, no plants, no photographs, not even a television in sight.

I'd seen Pier's flat for the first time when we took my cases over a couple of days before the wedding.

'I had it done by a very avant-garde interior designer,' Piers said as he saw the shock it had given me. 'It suited me because it was easy, but you can do whatever you like with it, Aline.'

'It's startling at first glance,' I said thoughtfully. 'But I rather like it. With a few personal touches it could be perfect.'

Piers smiled. 'It's up to you, darling. We could even move if you hate it.'

I was exploring further as he spoke. The kitchen had an expensive space-age look, its black and white decor almost an extension of the living area, but here there were copper pans, jugs and greenery; also a friendly clutter of cooking utensils and spice racks, coffee jars and a well-stocked wine rack. I had the feeling that Piers spent time there, and I knew that he liked to cook. The bathroom was a sumptuous extravaganza of burgundy and gold-plated taps, softened by several large pots of trailing ferns. The spare room was a pleasant blend of green and beige with a huge mahogany armoire and had a traditional feel, and the main bedroom was very masculine, its black, gold and brown decor a little austere for my taste. But it had long french windows that opened out on to a paved and enclosed area with tubs of flowering plants and a charming little pool.

'Oh, how lovely,' I cried. 'Are there fish in the pool?'

'Yes.' Piers watched me with an indulgent smile as I opened the window and went out. 'It was the garden area that really appealed to me when I bought the place. It's really a conservatory.'

I gazed up at the arched dome of glass, feeling the warmth of the late afternoon sun, then turned to look at him. 'It's lovely, Piers. All of it.'

'Then you can be happy here?' He sounded anxious. 'We'll be in London most of the time . . .'

I moved towards him, gazing earnestly up into his face. 'Don't you know, Piers?' I whispered. 'Don't you know that it's you I want? Wherever you are, I'll be happy.'

A wry smile had touched his mouth as he reached for me. 'I'll remind you of that one day,' he murmured. And then everything had been forgotten as he kissed me.

I was surprised when I walked in after our wedding. Piers had filled the room with flowers, so many of them that I felt I was walking into a garden. As I saw what he had done to please me, the doubts I'd had in the taxi fled.

We flew first-class from Gatwick to Nassau. It was a nine-hour flight, but Piers had ordered champagne and the hostess served us with a special meal. It was all part of the fantastic dream I seemed to be living in. I had to keep touching the smooth gold of my wedding ring to make sure it was real.

Piers had bought me a magnificent emerald and diamond ring. 'Just because we were never actually engaged, it doesn't mean you can't have a ring,' he'd said as he slipped it on my finger. 'I hope you like emeralds. I chose it because emeralds were once believed to protect the wearer from evil.'

It was a large square dark green stone surrounded by twelve pure white diamonds. 'I love it,' I said, smiling up at him. 'But there was no need to buy me something this extravagant, Piers.'

'I wanted you to have it,' he said. 'Everything I have is yours. Isn't that what marriage is all about – sharing?'

'Yes, of course, but this must have cost a fortune.'

'I hope you're not going to be the sort of wife who nags about money.'

It was said lightly, but I felt that he wasn't jesting.

'Of course not, Piers. It's just that I keep wondering what I've done to deserve all this.'

His answer was to make love to me with an exquisite tenderness. I climaxed swiftly, crying his name again and again at the intense pleasure he gave me.

'Oh, Piers. Piers darling,' I whispered. 'I never knew I could be this happy.'

'I love you, Aline,' he murmured. 'Never leave me, my darling. Swear it! Swear you'll never leave me. I need you so much.'

At that moment he seemed so intense, almost desperate. It only made me love him more.

'I'll never leave you,' I had vowed, burying my face in his chest. 'I'll never leave you. I promise, darling.'

We stayed at a hotel right on the silver, powdery sand of Cable Beach, spending the long, hot days swimming, sailing, windsurfing or just lying in the sun and talking. We ate delicious Polynesian-style meals or succulent shellfish at the hotel bars; sometimes we strolled along the beach to a restaurant where they served superb French food. Piers took me shopping in Bay Street straw market, and to the expensive stores in the centre of Nassau that catered for Americans, buying me clothes, shoes, bags and jewellery. My protests counted for nothing. Whenever I said that something was too expensive, he laughed and said that I had to get used to being the wife of a wealthy man.

Sometimes I nearly confessed the secret of my imminent inheritance, but Piers so obviously enjoyed spending his money on me, I didn't want to take the edge off his pleasure.

Nor did I ask questions about his past. Sometimes we would talk about the gallery, or we would discuss music and books we liked, films we had seen. Piers like factual programmes, biographies and classical works; I preferred novels and drama, but we agreed to differ. Neither of us demanded too much. It seemed best that way, and each new discovery was exciting. I was too happy to rush our relationship; I didn't want anything to intrude into the little paradise we had found.

The days passed in a whirl of excitement. We took a trip to look at coral reefs from a glass-bottomed boat, visited the underwater observatory and the botanical gardens, and picnicked on Paradise Island on a beach with white sand overlooking Pirates Cove. At night we went to a disco or walked hand in hand at the edge of the water, stopping occasionally to kiss.

Piers seemed to have limitless energy and was seldom satisfied just to laze around. Sometimes, when I wanted to lie in the sun, he would get restless and go off for a run along the beach, returning an hour or more later. Only when that extra energy had been consumed did he seem to relax.

Once the stronghold of pirates, Nassau was an enchanting mixture of old, graceful colonial buildings, bustling markets and lively modern restaurants. We explored it eagerly, strolling through the streets to gaze at pink-washed walls and old guns, their barrels pitted and polished by countless years, reminding all who saw them of an age gone by.

Piers took dozens of photographs of me by the harbour when the fishing boats had come in with their rich harvest, on rocky outcrops and sandy beaches or beneath waving palms. Everywhere there was brilliant colour, and fields of exotic plants that dazzled the eyes. I adored the flowers, and Piers bought me masses of scented blooms from the market. I wore them in my hair when we went dancing or to the casino.

Two days before the end of our holiday, we decided to go deep-sea fishing. At first we caught only a few small fish, but then Piers' line began to reel out madly, and the owner of the boat got very excited.

'You got a big one there, man,' he said. 'You watch what you doing now, or he gonna break your line.'

Piers nodded, his eyes bright with excitement. He reeled in furiously, the rod buckling and bending with the strain of whatever was on the end of his line. The sweat stood out on his brow as he fought to hold the catch.

I watched, fascinated and yet frightened by the battle between man and fish. Whatever was in the water was refusing to give in – and so was Piers. I'd always sensed that he was a strong-willed man, but this contest revealed something more.

Piers' line went out again and again, the force of the creature trapped on his hook dragging the boat behind it as it struggled to escape. Again and again Paul reeled in, determined to win.

'Maybe not marlin, maybe big shark,' the boat owner said, looking doubtful as the struggle went on for too long. The tension was strange and alarming. 'Maybe too big. Best let go now.'

Piers ignored him. I could see veins bulging at his temples as he fought to bring in his catch. It was very hot. The sea reflected the glare into my eyes, and it was no longer fun to watch. I was frightened by Piers' expression. It was as if he would rather die than give in.

'Let it go, Piers,' I begged. 'Let it go now.'

I might not have spoken, for all the notice he took of me. I looked at the boat owner in desperation, digging my nails into the palms of my hand, mutely begging him to do something. He nodded, moving swiftly towards the side of the boat. With a deft jerk of his hand, he cut through the line. For a moment longer the water boiled and thrashed, then we all saw the long, dark shape as a huge shark rose to the surface and then plunged deep into the ocean.

'What the hell did you do that for?' Piers asked, furious. 'I nearly had him.'

'You see that, man,' the boat owner cried. 'Maybe thirty, forty feet. You lucky he don't take you down with him.'

'Oh, Piers,' I said, trembling. 'It could have killed you. I was frightened.'

He stared at me, his eyes still angry. 'Don't be a fool, Aline. I was never in any danger. That's why I'm strapped into this belt.'

The thick leather belt was attached to a steel frame bolted to the floor of the boat, but as I stared in silence at my husband, who had suddenly become a stranger, the boat owner pointed to the link that held the belt: it had begun to open slightly. Without his action, the pleasure trip could have ended in disaster. Piers' eyes narrowed as he saw it, then he frowned.

'It looks as if I owe you an apology,' he said. 'I'll pay for any damage, of course.'

Suddenly I felt angry. Piers seemed so unlike the man I'd fallen in love with. 'Is that all you can say?' I cried. 'He just saved your life, Piers!'

'Don't interfere, Aline,' he said, unbuckling the belt. 'I'm going below for a drink.' His eyes were cold as he looked at me.

Watching as he went down into the small cabin, I felt my throat tighten.

The desert was vast, empty and lonely, stretching away into the distance, undulating with ridged dunes that seemed endless. The girl could feel the hot sand burning her feet. She was naked, and the heat of the sun scorched her pale skin. Her throat was so dry that she felt as if she were choking, and she whimpered, begging for water, as she ran, stumbling, near exhaustion, yet knowing that she had to go on. She was searching for someone . . . a man . . . a man she loved. She knew that he was in great danger. If she didn't find him he would die, and so would she. He was somewhere out there in that vast wilderness. She had to find him. She had to! Despairingly, she cried his name . . .

★

I awoke to find Piers bending over me, his hand on my shoulder. My skin was damp with sweat and I felt thirsty. I sat up, wiping the salty droplets from my eyes.

'You were having a nightmare,' Piers said, looking anxious. 'You must have had too much sun. I'm going to ring for a doctor.'

I laid my hand on his arm. 'Please don't, Piers. I'm not ill. I do sometimes have strange dreams, then I wake up drenched with sweat. It's nothing, honestly.'

He gazed at me doubtfully. 'How long have you been having them, Aline?'

'For years – since I was a child. They're always the same – I'm being pursued by something I can't see, something evil – but this one was different. I was looking for you – your life was in danger. I knew that I had to find you or we would both die.'

'Then this one was my fault.' Piers looked at me, his eyes dark with regret. 'Because of what happened on the boat.' He took my hand and held it to his face. 'Forgive me, darling. I didn't mean to hurt you. You must believe me. I usually manage to exercise control, but . . .'

He was so intense that it made me anxious. I smiled and turned my lips to kiss his hand. 'You've apologized so many times already, Piers. It was nothing.'

'It was my stupid pride,' he said. 'I don't know what gets into me sometimes, Aline. It's as if I can't give in. I know I'm being stubborn, but something inside me won't let go. I'm like a terrier after a rat – and sometimes I end up having to be dug out of a hole.' A rueful smile flickered about his mouth. 'So now you know what kind of man you've married.'

'Yes, I know – and I love you.' I jumped out of bed as he tried to kiss me. 'I need a shower first.' At the door of the bathroom, I turned to look back. 'Of course you could always share it with me.'

Piers shook his head. 'I need some exercise. We don't want any more little incidents, do we?'

'What do you mean?'

Piers shook his head. 'Nothing. Take your shower, darling. I shan't be long.'

Chapter Eight

'And what are you going to do today?' Piers asked, bending over to kiss me. He tasted of peppermint and his hair was still wet from the shower. 'Or were you planning to stay in bed all day?'

'Just because you've been for a run round the block doesn't make you a paragon of virtue,' I said teasingly. 'I'm going to get up now, cook your breakfast and then take a shower. After that I shall probably ring Julie's sister – you remember I let Rita move in before we went away – and I need to collect some things from the flat. Can I borrow your estate?'

'We're going to have to get you your own car,' he said thoughtfully. 'I do need the estate this morning. You can take the Rolls, or I'll run you over and pick you up at lunchtime. Will that give you long enough?'

'It sounds fine,' I said, throwing back the covers. 'I'll get the breakfast now.'

'Have your shower,' he said, his eyes sparkling with gentle mockery. 'I can't have you slaving over a hot stove before you've had time to wake up.'

We had been home a couple of days now, but he was still being very attentive, even a little overprotective of me. If anyone else had attempted to fuss over me the way Piers did, I would probably have thrown a screaming fit, but I enjoyed being babied by my adoring husband. It seemed he couldn't do enough to make up for the way he'd behaved on that boat. I'd decided that in my anxiety I'd made too much of it. Piers had simply been annoyed because he felt a bit foolish. It was natural enough.

When I emerged from the bathroom wearing a pair of white cotton jeans and a bright yellow silk shirt Piers had bought me on the last day of our honeymoon, he was just finishing a phonecall.

'I didn't hear it ring.'

'It was just a business call,' he said. 'Nothing you need bother about.' But there was something evasive about the way his eyes slid away from mine.

'I didn't get a chance to cook the eggs,' he said. 'How do you want yours – scrambled or boiled?'

97

'Just toast and honey,' I replied. 'Why don't I make you an omelette?'

'Since you insist.' He grinned at me, and I felt that familiar spasm of desire. 'I do have another call to make.'

He was already dialling as I went into the kitchen. I heard him speak to someone, then he walked into the bedroom, taking the phone with him.

'So what's it like being married then?' Julie's sister asked as she carried two mugs of coffee into the sitting room. Rita had soon made the flat her own. The walls were plastered with posters of pop stars and hunky men. 'As good as you expected?'

'Better. I'm so happy, Rita. I've never felt like this in my life.'

'Let's hope it lasts,' Rita said, a note of bitterness in her voice. 'In my experience the honeymoon period soon loses its appeal.'

I saw the pinched look about her mouth and felt sorry for her. 'You sound as if you've had a rough time.'

'Before Tim, I'd had several bad experiences. Most men are rats, aren't they?'

'But you're happy enough with Tim, aren't you?'

'He's OK . . .' She got up and started fiddling with her hair in front of the mirror. 'What do you want for your furniture, Aline? I'm not sure I can pay you now, but when – '

'I don't want anything,' I told her. 'I'll take the things I'm fond of, and you can keep the rest. It's only junk anyway. It wouldn't fetch much if I sold it.'

'You're lying through your teeth, but thanks. I'm not exactly flush at the moment. I haven't been in my new job long. Speaking of which . . .' She glanced at her watch. 'I'll have to go or I'll be late.'

'Don't let me delay you,' I said. 'I've brought some boxes and it won't take long to pack the things I want. They're only oddments.'

'I'll be off then.' Rita picked up her jacket. 'Thanks again, Aline.'

'It's nothing.' I smiled at her. 'Glad to be of help.'

After Rita had gone, I began to pack what I wanted into cardboard boxes; my large collection of old records, LPs and cassettes took a lot of sorting out. I would probably never play some of the 78s. Piers' taste was more classical, and I could imagine his reaction if I put on a few of these, which were admittedly a little corny. Discovering the copy of 'Blue Suede Shoes' that Nick had given me, I felt a pricking behind my eyes, then quickly hid the damned thing under the others.

The records packed, I collected a few sentimental bits and pieces: a book Michael had bought me, some china from Hazeling, and a leather writing case that had been my mother's. I was concentrating on my work when the phone rang behind me. For a moment I hesitated, remembering all those odd calls, then I realized that Piers had had the number changed. It would be someone for Rita. I picked it up.

'Hello,' I said. 'Rita is out just now but if you'd like to leave a message . . .'

There was a moment's silence and then a click as the receiver was replaced at the other end. I frowned, looking at it in dismay. It couldn't be one of *those* calls. No one but Julie knew the number – and Rita and her friends, of course. Perhaps it had been someone for Rita, thinking they'd misdialled when they heard my voice. I shrugged and started opening cupboards, taking out the things I wanted and packing them. It didn't really matter. In an hour or so I would be leaving the flat for good.

I'd been working for some time when the doorbell rang. I glanced at my watch. Surely it couldn't be Piers already!

'Now this won't do,' I said, opening the door and laughing. The words froze on my lips as I saw who was standing there. 'Nick, what are you. . . ?'

'So you are here then.'

His eyes looked very much like blue diamonds. I didn't remember ever seeing Nick like this. He'd always seemed to take things so easily; even when we'd quarrelled he had been more irritated than angry. Or so I'd thought, but now I was seeing a different Nick Winters. Watching his hands clench at his sides, I had the feeling that he was itching to wring my neck. Obviously, he'd discovered I was married and he was every bit as furious as Julie had predicted. I was overwhelmed with guilt. Julie was right, I should have left him a personal message somehow. He'd been told by a third party and he was very angry. I wished that I'd made that phonecall after all.

'How did you know I was here?' I looked at him, and then I understood. 'It was you on the phone earlier, wasn't it? You wouldn't answer me . . .'

'Tracy – the temp at the saleroom – said you were coming back this week,' he muttered. 'She gave me the new number, so I've been ringing the flat on the off chance of catching you here.' He glanced at the boxes. 'I see I was only just in time. You little two-timer! It was going on behind my back all the time.' He was furious, and I was shaken as I realized how much I must have hurt him.

'It wasn't like that.' I held out my hand in supplication. 'Please believe me, Nick. I met Piers at Julie's party and I fell in love with him. He asked me to marry him a few days later and – and I did.'

Nick was breathing hard, his hands clenched at his sides. 'He asked you . . . You hardly knew him, yet you said yes. We'd been together for months.'

'I'm sorry, Nick.' I felt wretched and so guilty. It was very painful to see his distress. I just hadn't understood that he felt this deeply. I'd thought that because he wouldn't move in with me, he didn't really care; now I saw that I was wrong. 'I – I didn't want to hurt you. I thought it was over . . .'

'Over!' His voice was sharp with scorn, his expression one of disbelief. 'I *was* angry when I walked out of here, but we've had rows before. You know I always come back.'

'Nick . . .' I felt close to tears and my throat was tight. 'It all happened so quickly. I . . .'

'And you didn't even have the decency to tell me!'

'I didn't know how to reach you. But I should have left a message or written to you. I'm sorry.' My excuses sounded inadequate even to my own ears and I dropped my eyes in shame. Nick had deserved better. There was no way I could explain to him that I'd hardly known what I was doing myself, that I'd been driven by something that defied reason.

'And you wanted a commitment from me.'

His sarcasm brought flaming colour to my cheeks. 'You didn't really love me,' I said in my own defence. 'You never said . . .' My words died into a whisper as I saw his expression.

'You're a woman, not a child,' he cried bitterly. 'I didn't think you needed to be told. For God's sake, what did you think it was all about?'

'Sex.'

'Don't be a bloody fool! I can get that anywhere. We had something special. In time it would have worked out. I thought you needed time, Aline.'

'But you never said . . .' I choked on the emotion rising in my throat.

'If you weren't forever putting yourself down, you wouldn't need to be told.' Nick stared at me, anger mixed with sadness. 'I don't know what happened to you, but whatever it was it must have been pretty bad.'

'Of course, it would be my fault.' I lashed out in my pain and saw the sympathy die from his face.

'I can't win with you, can I? I'd like to shake some sense into you,

Aline,' he said. 'But I won't – you aren't worth it. No woman is worth the bother – you're all the same, selfish little cats who can't be trusted once a man's back is turned.'

'Nick, that isn't fair . . .'

I stood immobile, not daring to breathe or speak as he walked to the door and flung it open. Then the colour drained from my face. Piers was outside in the hall, his hand raised to ring the bell. For a moment the two men looked at each other, and it was difficult to say which one of them was the more surprised.

'What's going on?' Piers asked, his eyes moving to my white face. 'What is it, Aline?' He was alert, tense, ready to defend me.

I shook my head, still feeling wretched. Nick looked back at me, his mouth twisted in a travesty of a smile.

'I take it this is the lucky man, Aline,' he said. 'I wish you both luck!'

He pushed past Piers and went on down the hallway. The clatter of his footsteps on the stone stairs was still echoing in my head as Piers entered and closed the door with a little snap.

'I think you'd better tell me what that was all about,' he said grimly.

'Nick was . . . I . . .' My mouth went dry and I swallowed hard, still feeling stunned by Nick's outburst. If he cared that much, why hadn't he made it clear? Why just walk out the way he had? If I'd known . . . But would it have made any difference? Piers was staring at me, and the look in his eyes made me nervous. 'Piers – '

'You were lovers, am I right?'

'Please don't . . .' I wilted under his anger. 'It's over, Piers.'

'He didn't seem to think so. When did you last see him?'

Piers' face was so cold, so accusing. I dug my nails into the palms of my hand. 'I – I can't remember. A few weeks ago.'

'A few weeks!' A tiny nerve jumped in Piers' throat. 'You were sleeping with him right up until . . .'

'No!' I cried, unable to bear the look of disgust in his eyes. 'We hadn't – not for a while. I didn't see him that often.'

His mouth took on a smile of disbelief. 'I can't believe that, Aline.'

'But you must!' I moved towards him in desperation. 'It wasn't the same with Nick,' I finished lamely as I saw he was unconvinced. 'I tried to tell you that night, but you said we knew all we needed to know about each other.'

'I knew there must have been others,' he said, turning away. 'But I didn't expect you to be in the middle of an affair.'

'I wasn't,' I cried. 'It was over. Please believe me.'

'I hate liars,' he said.

'I love you, Piers. You have to believe me. Why else would I marry you when I hardly knew you?'

He stared at me in silence, that nerve flicking in his throat. 'I don't know, Aline. I don't know.'

'There must have been other women in your life,' I muttered defensively. 'I certainly wasn't the first.'

'No one for five years,' he said, his mouth twisting wryly. 'You may find that hard to accept . . .'

'No,' I said. 'I'm not into sleeping around either, Piers. Before you . . .' I faltered as his expression hardened. 'I had an unpleasant experience at college. It didn't last long. Since then there's been no one but Nick – not in that way.'

'I wish you could convince me.' Piers glanced at the boxes I'd been packing before Nick arrived. 'Have you got everything you want?'

'Yes.' I looked at him doubtfully, feeling miserable. 'Are you sure you want me to come back with you?'

'Don't be ridiculous,' he said. 'You're my wife. I told you, once I have I don't let go.'

Julie was wearing black velvet trousers and a low-necked top when she opened the door. She looked preoccupied and her hair was straggling about her face in lank wisps, but her smokey grey eyes lit up with pleasure when she saw me standing outside.

'You do look brown,' she exclaimed. 'Gorgeous tan! Come on in. The place is a tip, but Tony's been working on some new designs.' She led me into the sitting room. 'Sit down – if you can find a space.'

The room was piled high with bits of wool, patterns, cut-outs of suede and leather raffia. I noticed a pretty waistcoat with appliqué sequins and lace.

'This is wonderful, Julie. I love it.'

'Tony has been selling quite a lot recently,'

'So the workshop looks like paying off?'

'Yes, I suppose it does.' Julie grinned. 'It's all right, I don't need another lecture. We've decided to give it two years, then take a fresh look at how the business stands.'

'I'm glad you've settled it at last,' I said.

'I'll make some coffee and you can tell me all about the Bahamas. Do have a look at Tony's new patterns and tell me what you think.'

Returning with a tray a few minutes later, she gave me a thoughtful look. 'So, are you going to tell me about it?'

'Does it show that much?' I grimaced as she nodded. 'Nick came over to the flat while I was picking up my things. He was as upset as you said he would be. We quarrelled, and then Piers arrived – '

'You hadn't told him about Nick?' Julie's lips pursed in a silent whistle. 'Did you have a row?'

'Not exactly. Piers – Piers just went cold on me. He's being very polite and distant at the moment.'

'When did all this happen?'

'A couple of days ago.'

'Have you tried talking about it?'

'He says there's nothing to talk about.' I remembered Piers' reaction when I'd tried to put my arms around him the previous night. 'He doesn't come to bed until he's sure I'm asleep. Sometimes he just gets up and goes out without a word, and doesn't come back for hours. He says he has to work.' I breathed deeply. 'I don't know what to do, Julie. He was so loving until . . . And now he acts as if we're strangers.'

'Give him time.' Julie's smile was understanding. 'It must have been quite a shock. I expect his pride's hurt. You know what men are.'

'But there's nothing for him to be upset about. It *was* over, even though Nick doesn't seem to think so.' I laughed shakily. 'I don't think I'm very good at the psychological side of relationships. I love Piers so much, I couldn't bear it if our marriage has gone wrong already . . .'

'Don't be an idiot,' Julie told me. 'Piers is crazy about you. He senses a rival in Nick, and you can't blame him. He just needs a little while to sort this out in his own mind.'

I reached for the bag I'd brought with me. 'I didn't intend telling you any of this; I just came over for a visit. I brought back a few things for you and Tony – a special tee-shirt and a necklace for you; just beads and shells and stuff like that for Tony. Things he might use in his designs.'

'Great!' Julie cried as she pulled out the tee-shirt and then tipped the collection of oddments on to the table. 'Oh, these are wonderful. I can almost smell the tang of the sea. Tony will be thrilled.' Her smile dimmed as she looked at me. 'Don't worry, love. Piers will come round. You'll see.'

I nodded, forcing a smile. 'Of course you're right. I expect it's just a lovers' tiff.'

'You're late.' Piers' eyes stabbed at me as I walked in. 'I've booked a table at Odin's for eight this evening. I was beginning to think I might have to cancel.'

'I went over to see Julie,' I said, staring at him uneasily. 'You can ring her to check if you like.'

'Don't be ridiculous.' His tone flayed me. 'I'm not doubting your word.'

'Aren't you?' Suddenly I was angry. My head went up and I looked straight at him. 'I've apologized enough, Piers. I admit I should have told you about Nick from the beginning, but I wasn't sure that we – it didn't seem important, and then it was just too difficult. Besides I'm not the first woman in your life.'

'There's been no one since Helena . . . I told you.' His eyes flicked away from mine. 'This is getting us nowhere.'

'Helena?' He hadn't mentioned her name before. I felt a flicker of jealousy. 'She must have been important if it took you five years to forget her.'

'Stop trying to pick an argument, Aline.'

'I'm not, I just want you to understand about Nick, that's all.'

'It doesn't matter now. It's over.'

'If it's over, why are you behaving like this?'

'Like what?' His eyes had all the warmth of a refrigerator. 'I thought I was being perfectly civilized.'

'Oh yes, you are!' I yelled, stung to anger. 'So damned civilized that it's like living with a stranger. OK, I made a mistake. So what? I'd rather you lost your temper. I can't stand men who sulk. It's so childish.'

'I'm sorry to disappoint you, Aline. I don't go in for all this macho caveman stuff. I dislike all forms of violence. Control is everything.'

'Damn you!' I shouted, and ran into the bathroom. 'Damn you – damn the whole bloody lot of you!'

I began to rip off my clothes, discarding them in a heap on the floor. Angry tears were forming, but I wiped them away with the back of my hand. Turning on the shower, I stepped under the water, trying to control my emotions. I wasn't going to cry, but it hurt so much.

The water was cascading over me. I lifted my face, welcoming the coolness, my eyes closed as I fought the misery inside me. Then I was aware of movement. My eyes flew open as Piers pulled back the sliding door of the shower and came in with me, fully clothed apart from his shoes. I stared at him, tasting the salt of tears on my lips, then he reached out and took me in his arms. I could feel the imprint of his shirt buttons in my flesh as he held me against him.

'Is this what you want?' he muttered, as he began to kiss me – first my throat, then my breasts, working down to my navel. 'Yes, I'm angry Aline. So angry that I wanted to kill him – and you! Is that what you wanted to hear?'

I trembled as his flicking tongue set the desire churning inside me, and my fingers moved in his hair. 'Piers . . . Piers darling,' I whispered, as he half-lifted me and my legs curled around him. 'I love you. I love you so much.'

'You'd better,' he murmured feverishly, his mouth against my throat. 'I was so jealous, Aline. So damned jealous.'

'You needn't be,' I whispered, melting against him. 'He didn't mean anything to me. No one has meant as much to me before – '

His mouth silenced me. The water had soaked into his clothes, and his hair was plastered to his head. I reached up to turn off the tap, but he gripped my wrist, his strong fingers paralysing me.

'Leave it,' he muttered, his voice grating.

I laughed as he ripped the buttons off his shirt, then I was pulling impatiently at the buckle of his belt, hindering as much as I helped in my eagerness. Between us we stripped off his clothes, leaving them in a sodden mass in the shower tray. Piers was licking at my wet breasts, sucking the nipples, biting gently as I moaned with pleasure and slid my hands down over his stomach to the hot, pulsating hardness of his penis. I began to massage and stroke it, moving my hand back and forth in a slow, sensuous rhythm. He sucked in his breath, shuddering as I knelt before him and took it into my mouth, using the same lazy, caressing movements and then flicking at the sensitive tip with my tongue until he groaned aloud.

Then I was in his arms. He lifted me, and held me pinned against the wall of the shower as he thrust into me, the water still trickling over us, taking our breath away. I moaned feverishly, panting and crying his name as the unbearable pleasure mounted inside me and I gripped my legs around him. And then it was suddenly over. I bent my head, kissing the dark wet hair, crying.

'Piers, I love you. I love you,' I whispered, and it was a prayer for forgiveness.

'Do you?' he asked, looking at me searchingly.

'You must know I do.'

'We'd better get dressed. I've booked the table for eight.' His voice was emotionless, as if what had just happened between us had no meaning.

I placed the plate of grilled bacon, sausages and mushrooms on the table in front of Piers. He glanced at it and then at my coffee cup.

'Aren't you eating?'

'I'm not hungry. I'll just have coffee this morning.'

'You should take up running in the morning,' he said. 'You would have an appetite then.'

'I'll be hungry by lunch time,' I replied, forcing a lightness I didn't feel into my voice. 'Will you be home?'

'No. I have an appointment.' He glanced at his watch. 'I'm going to the gallery this morning. Would you like to come?'

'Yes.' I was surprised and pleased. It was the first time he'd asked me to go with him. 'Yes, I'd like that very much, Piers. I'd love to see your gallery.'

He pushed away his plate, the food half-eaten. 'I'd better take a quick shower.'

While Piers was in the bathroom, I stacked the dishes and changed into a cream silk blouse and soft jersey skirt. Just as I was buttoning my shirt, the telephone rang. I could still hear the water running, so I answered, though I thought it was probably for Piers.

'Hello, Aline Drayton speaking. Can I help you?'

There was a brief silence, then a woman's voice said, 'Aline, is that you? It's Zena. I had to ring you . . . Michael's not well. He's had a heart attack.'

'Zena,' I gasped, feeling stunned. 'When – how bad is it?'

'Nearly a month ago now.' Zena hesitated. 'He's better than he was but I'm still worried about him. I did ring you soon after it happened, but I was out of breath and you slammed the phone down on me before I could say anything. I should have rung again but I was too upset.'

'I was having peculiar calls. I'm sorry about that.'

'What happened?'

'Oh, Piers sorted it out. It's not important. I did write to say I was getting married – presumably you got my letter.'

'Yes. I should have answered – I'm sorry, Aline. It's just that I've been out of my mind with worry.' She drew a deep breath. 'Besides, Michael said I wasn't to bother you, but I know he wants to see you. It broke his heart when you walked out that night.'

'What makes you think that?'

'I know him, Aline. He's my husband.'

'Yes.'

'Oh, I know you blame me for everything.'

'Don't let's quarrel, Zena.'

'I know you've resented me from the start.'

'My mother had been dead for three months when he married you. That hurt me, Zena. It's not you I resent, it's the fact that he thought so little of her he could just go out and get married again.'

106

'We fell in love,' Zena cried. 'Is that such a terrible crime?'

'Perhaps not,' I replied, 'but my mother was ill. I can't forgive Michael for leaving her to be with you. I saw you together months before she died.'

'You see it all from her side,' Zena said, and there was anger in her voice now. 'Don't you ever wonder how it must have been for Michael? He was miserable for years before – '

'I don't want to hear this, Zena.'

'No, of course you don't,' she said. 'Your precious mother was a saint, wasn't she?'

The receiver at the other end went down with a bang. I felt angry and resentful as the memories came pouring back – painful memories I'd tried to bury deep in my subconscious. Zena had stirred them up with a vengeance. I was still staring at the phone when Piers walked in from the bathroom, a towel round his neck. He looked at me, his brows rising.

'Who was that?'

I lifted my stunned gaze to his face, 'It was Zena – my stepfather's wife. She rang to say he was ill.'

His eyes narrowed as he looked at me, and his words sounded measured as if he was being careful to avoid another argument. 'Your stepfather? More surprises, Aline. Why haven't I heard about him before?'

I felt the colour burn in my cheeks. 'Don't look at me like that, Piers. I didn't tell you because . . . because I quarrelled with him – both of them – some time ago. I haven't been back to Hazeling since.'

'Hazeling . . . Hazeling Manor?' Piers spoke hesitantly, his face impassive. I could imagine him working it all out. 'The picture of Blakeney – you're Michael Courteney's stepdaughter! Good God! Why didn't you tell me?'

'I didn't think think it mattered.' I felt guilty. Piers' expression wasn't so much surprised as annoyed. 'I was going to tell you . . .'

'When it suited you,' he said, his tone cutting. 'I wonder just how many more little secrets you have in store for me.'

'Please, Piers, don't be like this with me. I'm sorry I didn't tell you, but don't be so – so suspicious all the time.'

His expression changed. 'Something happened five years ago . . .' His voice died to a choked whisper. 'It doesn't matter.'

'Please, Piers,' I begged. I sensed that whatever had caused that look *did* matter. 'Talk to me. Don't shut me out.'

'There was someone special to me,' he said, and it was as if the words were dragged out of him. 'She lied to me and we quarrelled. She walked out . . .' Piers' eyes were bleak as he looked at me.

'Go on,' I said. 'I want to understand.'

'It was raining,' he went on. 'Helena was furious. She drove off in a temper and . . .'

'And?' I prompted as he stopped.

He looked into my eyes then, and I caught a glimpse of his turmoil. 'Her car went off the road into a tree. They said she must have died almost instantly . . . I blamed myself for her death.'

I remembered the urgency in his voice when he'd begged me never to leave him, and I felt I understood. I went to him, sliding my arms about his waist and laying my head against his chest.

'Piers darling.' I looked up at him, the tears pricking my eyes. 'Thank you for telling me. I'm so sorry about Helena; it must have hurt you so much. But it isn't going to happen again. I shan't leave you. I love you.'

He glanced down at me, doubt in his face. 'Do you, Aline?'

'Yes, very much. I'm sorry I didn't tell you about my family. Will you forgive me?'

'There's nothing to forgive, is there?' He smiled at last and I felt relief. 'Are you going down to Hazeling?'

'I think I should.'

'If your stepfather is ill . . .' He shrugged his shoulders.

'Don't make me feel guilty about it,' I said. 'Zena has already done that.'

'Well, it's up to you,' he replied. 'If you're ready, it's time we left.'

As we went down to the car, I realized it was time Piers and I really talked about ourselves. Neither of us had asked questions, perhaps because we had both been hurt. Now I sensed that there were things that needed to be discussed.

Piers' gallery was on the corner of a little arcade of shops not far from Bond Street. He dropped me off and went to park his car, leaving me to look in the windows of the various antique and jewellery shops in the arcade. Many of them had displays of expensive diamonds and precious stones, but there were others with pretty, old-fashioned pieces at more reasonable prices. I remembered that Julie's birthday was approaching and I thought that I might buy her a brooch. The shop adjacent to Piers' gallery had several, and a large selection of Victorian love-jewellery, including pendants and brooches, and a double-heart diamond ring.

'I'm sorry to keep you waiting,' Piers said as he joined me. 'I just missed one space and I had to drive around looking for another.'

'You were lucky to find anything at all.'

He glanced at the window display. 'Seen anything you would like?'

I pointed to a large gold and pearl brooch. 'I was thinking of that for Julie's birthday, but it isn't for a week or two yet. I might pop into the saleroom and see if they've had anything in this month.'

'Nothing you want yourself?' I shook my head. 'We'll go in then. I'll introduce you to my staff, then you can wander around while I make a few calls.'

'Don't worry about me. I can amuse myself for as long as it takes. I'm looking forward to seeing your pictures.'

We went inside the gallery, and I looked about me with interest. The dark brown carpet was soft and springy beneath my feet. The walls were parchment colour and the lighting was soft and inviting. In the reception area there was a mahogany desk and a chair with a ribbon design carved into the back. From my experience in the auction house, I thought the chair was probably Hepplewhite or Chippendale. Other similar chairs stood about the large rectangular room, placed so that customers could view the pictures at their ease.

'Aline, this is my manager, Mathew Williams – and his assistant, Gillian Hastings.'

Gillian Hastings was about twenty and very pretty, with pale blonde hair and a fantastic figure. I saw a gleam of something in her eyes that suggested an interest in her employer. He'd told me that there had been no one in his life since Helena was killed, but I found that difficult to believe. Piers was a passionate man. He would need a very strong reason to live like a monk for all that time.

Crushing the flicker of jealousy Gillian had aroused, I shook hands, exchanging a few words of polite conversation before I moved away to look at the pictures.

'The next floor is for modern art,' Piers said. 'Why not start there and leave these for last?'

Obediently, I went to the spiral staircase at the other end of the room and climbed to the floor above. Walking very slowly, I looked at the various paintings on offer, trying to understand what some of them were about. While some of them were self-explanatory, others baffled me. One seemed to be never ending circles, the colour intensifying as they became smaller and smaller, until the dot in the middle was a dark crimson. I glanced at the title and the price.

'Energy Source,' I read. 'Six thousand pounds.'

Standing back, I studied it for several minutes. Gradually, the rings seemed to vibrate, taking on a life of their own, and I could suddenly see what the artist was getting at. It was rather like the light and heat given off by the sun. I could almost see it shimmering in a golden haze.

I walked the length of the gallery, looking at the names of the artists, some of whom were known to me through the saleroom: Michael Kidner, Bridget Riley, Bryan Wynter, Alan Davie – all artists whose work was selling well these days. I stopped in front of one paintings, by an artist I didn't know, studying it in bewilderment. It seemed to me to be a muddle of squares, stripes, dots and circles. Priced at eight thousand pounds, it was less than many of the others, but it had no appeal for me. I preferred the paintings downstairs.

I went back down, starting at the far end, away from the reception area, where I could see that Piers was still on the phone. Here, the pictures were much more to my liking. I gazed at a collection by the Norfolk artists J. F. Herring senior and J. F. Herring junior – farmyard scenes, country cottages and horses, and still reasonably priced. A little further on, I stopped to admire a group of paintings by Thomas Bush Hardy. Scenes of Venice and Ships off Calais Harbour, I read on the little placard underneath. There were paintings by Sickert, Fredrick William Watts, Landseer, Fragonard and a dozen others, some just listed as being of the English school. I thought there must be pictures here to suit all tastes and most pockets. Seeing the gallery made me realize just how successful Piers was in his chosen profession; it gave me an insight into the character of the man I'd married.

On the wall behind the desk was a picture I found particularly pleasing. I stood gazing at it for a long time, fascinated. Piers smiled as he joined me.

'You seem to have found the best picture we have at the moment,' he murmured. 'That's a Constable.'

I laughed and nodded. 'I did recognize his work,' I said. 'I must confess I like the Herrings and Thomas Bush Hardy collections much more than those upstairs – though I quite like the one called "Energy Source".'

'I'll make a modern art fan of you yet,' he replied, amused. 'In my opinion, that's one of the best. It's by a new young artist I've started to buy. Within a few years he'll be selling for five-figure sums.'

'Do you often buy the work of unknown artists?'

'All the time – that's the fun and the challenge of this business. In New York I concentrate on the top end of the market. I doubt if there's ever anything under fifty thousand dollars in stock, but here I like to mix it up a little. The prices start at about a hundred and fifty pounds, I think. When you get a Constable, of course, it's rather different.'

'Naturally.' I laughed. 'I won't even ask.'

'If it were for sale, I'd tell you, but at the moment it's being considered.' Piers smiled as I arched my eyebrows. 'It doesn't belong to the gallery. We're handling the sale for an important customer, and we're waiting for the results of a special auction at Sotheby's, then we shall know what the market is doing.'

'I suppose that's the best way of gauging the present situation.'

'All kinds of things are causing fluctuations in the fine art market, high interest rates being one of them. Trends come and go and estimates aren't always reliable – as you know. Modern art was on the crest of a wave in the late sixties, then it dipped as tastes swung back towards the traditional. I think it may be about to take off again.'

'Doesn't it worry you that something you buy now could become unfashionable and drop in price?'

'It happens. You develop an instinct.' He frowned slightly. 'I sold my first picture when I was nineteen, with a little help from someone I knew. Bill was a good friend to me right up until the day he died. He taught me the basics of the business, and I've gone on from there.'

'Who was Bill?' I asked. He'd never mentioned him before and I was curious. Until now I hadn't wanted to know too much about the past, but it was time to ask questions.

'Oh, just a friend. Someone I met when I first came to London as a youngster. I was on my own and he took me in, gave me a place to stay and helped me to sort myself out.'

'Was he a dealer?'

'It was in his blood. He bought anything he could sell.'

'You must have missed him when he died.'

'Yes, I did. It was a heart attack. Some yobbos attacked him when he was walking home one night with a pocket full of cash. I found him dying . . .' A strange emotion flickered in Piers' eyes. 'There was nothing I could do. Bill was fond of his whisky, but he knew a good picture. I owe him a lot.' He looked at me and I sensed that he wanted to change the subject. 'But you must know something about modern art yourself. Michael Courteney is a talented artist.'

'Yes. I can recognize his work, and I learned a lot at the saleroom, but I wouldn't claim to be an authority.' I drew in my breath. 'There's something I have to settle with Michael.'

'When did you want to go down?'

'If you agree, I'll ring Zena and we'll drive down this weekend.'

Chapter Nine

It was a lovely day for the drive down to Norfolk; the sun was warm without being too hot and the sky was almost free of clouds. We stopped in Norwich for lunch. Piers said it was only the second time he'd been there, but I knew it well from my childhood visits. It was a beautiful place, still retaining a great deal of its medieval charm in winding cobbled side streets and old, half-timbered buildings. Even after leaving Norwich we still had some way to go, much of it through narrow country lanes that seemed to twist interminably, past small secret villages of crumbling red brick, flint and pebble-dashed walls, fairytale cottages and old gardens flourishing behind high hedges, in parts almost untouched by the progress of the twentieth century. It was the countryside I'd been bred into, and it brought back many memories of picnics and sunny Sundays.

The Rolls purred softly as Piers drove along the narrow country roads. After a while he glanced at me. I'd been silent for some time, occupied with my thoughts.

'Did Zena tell you exactly what was wrong with Michael now?'

'Zena's worried because he's refusing to rest after the heart attack,' I replied. 'When I rang to say we were coming down, she said that he was out painting at the Point. That's the long bank of sand and shingle out beyond the saltmarshes and the sea channel at Blakeney. It's a wildlife area now.'

Lying between Sheringham and Wells-next-the-Sea, Blakeney had once been a busy commercial port, but for some years the estuary had been silted up, and only small pleasure craft could now negotiate the narrow channel. In summer there were often groups of tourists on the broad quay or wandering on the walkways across the marshes, but in winter it could be completely deserted.

'He said he was feeling better and was going to take the boat out. She's worried about what could happen if he has another attack.'

'Then if it happened out at the point, presumably he would die before anyone found him,' Piers said. 'It's rather foolish of him to go there alone.'

'Yes,' I agreed. 'It does seem reckless. It's so lonely and deserted for most of the time.'

I thought about the long bank of sand and shingle with the North Sea pounding the far shore, and then the stretches of saltmarsh, which provided feeding grounds for so many birds. Wild, desolate, even a little frightening in its isolation. Anyone suffering a heart attack out there wouldn't stand much chance of survival, and I wondered why Michael was willing to risk his life when there were so many other safer places of interest he could choose to paint. It was odd that Michael should have been in my thoughts so often these past weeks . . . Could it have been a kind of telepathy? Was it my fault that he was ill? Yet if he had cared, he could have got in touch with me. I refused to let myself feel guilty. I was still angry with him – or was I?

Glancing out of the window, I caught sight of the sea in the distance, through breaks in the woodland, and a windmill stood on the horizon, its wooden sails churning in a strong breeze. The pure, silent beauty of the scenery made me sad and a little sigh escaped me. Michael's uncaring behaviour had hurt me, but deep down I was worried about him. Piers shot me an inquiring look.

'Something bothering you?'

'I was just thinking about Michael – and my mother . . .'

'You've never mentioned your mother before.'

'She died more than three years ago, after a painful illness.' It was still difficult for me to talk about and the words came out stiffly. 'Michael married again soon afterwards. That's why we quarrelled.'

Piers nodded, his brows raised. 'Cancer?' he asked. I nodded. 'You were fond of her, weren't you?'

'Yes . . . She wasn't an easy person to know or love, but I did love her very much.'

'Is that why you didn't want to come here?'

'It's part of it – but there are other reasons. Too many memories, I suppose.' I sighed and looked at him. 'How old were you when your mother died, Piers?'

He was silent for a moment. 'I never knew her,' he said, a strange, intense expression in his eyes. 'Why do you ask?'

I shook my head. 'I just wondered, that's all. You never talk about your family either.'

'My mother died soon after I was born.' His face was bleak, his gaze fixed on the road ahead. 'She had some sort of tumour, I think. When they discovered it, it was too late to operate. Or that's what I was told. My father disappeared soon afterwards, leaving me with my

113

grandparents. He died abroad somewhere. I never knew much about him. My grandparents both died within weeks of each other when I was in my teens. Since then I've been pretty much on my own. If I don't talk about my family, it's because there's nothing to say.'

There was a touch of bitterness in his voice. I looked at him curiously. 'You weren't happy as a child, were you, Piers?'

'What makes you say that?' His profile was grim and for a moment I thought he was going to ignore the question. 'As a matter of fact, it was hell,' he said at last. 'My grandparents hated me. He was fond of hitting me with his belt and she – she was an old bitch.'

'I'm sorry. I shouldn't have asked.'

'You have every right to ask.' His hands clenched the steering wheel and the knuckles turned white. 'It was all a long time ago. None of it matters any more.'

If none of it mattered, why was he so tense? I'd learnt that Piers was skilful at controlling the emotions he didn't want to reveal, but he couldn't control the little pulse flicking in his cheek. There was a lot more I would have liked to ask, but Piers obviously didn't want to talk about his family, so I left it at that and we lapsed into silence again.

'Is it much further?' he asked about twenty minutes later.

'We're nearly there. Another couple of miles.' I arched my shoulders and rubbed the back of my neck.

He glanced at me with concern. 'Are you tired?'

'I have a bit of a headache, that's all.'

I couldn't explain, but with every minute that passed, the sense of dread was growing inside me.

Nothing could be seen of Hazeling Manor from the road, except the faded brick gateposts flanked by a boundary of thick trees. There was a track between an archway of ancient elms, then the land opened out with paddocks on either side. Now it was possible to see the house up ahead for the first time, and I wondered what Piers would think of it.

It wasn't large by country-house standards, but even after all this time away it still seemed beautiful and impressive enough to make me catch my breath when I saw it again. I knew from family history that it had been built in the fifteenth century, its deeply sloping thatched roof overhanging the half-timbered walls of plaster and blackened beams. The lower brickwork had been left to mellow over the years and was not tarted up with whitewash, and the leaded windows had the opaque look of old glass.

The car passed through a pair of tall wrought-iron gates, and now we could see the house in all its glory. It stood at the end of a short gravel drive edged by lawns broken by beds of roses and the occasional evergreen. As always, I was struck by its timeless, undisturbed air that made me feel I'd stepped back into the world of fifty years ago. I held my breath, realizing that I'd been afraid – afraid that Zena would have made changes; but from the outside at least, it was the same.

'It's beautiful,' Piers said, and whistled softly. 'I had no idea Hazeling was like this. How old is the house?'

I realized that he had wanted to see the house. His interest in it was more than that of a casual visitor.

'It was built in fourteen something,' I said, a quiet note of pride in my voice now. 'Bits have been added and restored, of course, but it's basically as it was in the beginning. It's been in my father's family for generations, and he passed it on to me. If I have a child, it goes to him or her. It's a kind of trust. Only the direct bloodline can inherit, and I can't sell it. It's a bit of a white elephant in a way . . .' I looked at him and grinned. 'It's haunted, of course, and there's a curse on whoever dares to live here.'

His smile faded. 'Haunted by ghosts or memories, Aline?'

'Both,' I said, my mouth going dry. Was I that easy for him to read?

'Are you sure you want to go in?'

I looked towards the house again. A curtain moved at an upstairs window, and I knew that someone was watching for our arrival.

'They're expecting us,' I said. 'I can't run away from it any longer, Piers. Besides, there's something I have to sort out with Michael.'

As Piers unloaded our bags from the car, I got out and waited, unwilling to go up to the front door alone. I could smell the stocks and roses from the overcrowded, old-fashioned beds, their scent heavy and almost overpowering. The sound of bees droning and the melodious song of a storm-cock from the branches of a flowering cherry stirred memories of childhood, tying my stomach in knots. I swallowed nervously, telling myself not to be a fool.

As we approached the porch, I was searching for the key I hadn't used in years. Then I realized I should ring the bell. But before I could do so, the door was opened. Michael stood just inside, looking at me, his soft brown eyes reproachful and faintly accusing. His look threw me off balance and my eyes searched his face for signs of his illness.

Michael wasn't quite as tall as Piers. His hair was a lightish brown streaked with grey and worn longer than I remembered. He was dressed in an old cashmere sweater and a pair of faded cords which I'd seen many times before and should have been thrown out long ago. Yet even in his disreputable old clothes, he was an attractive man, his smile full of warmth and charm as he held out his hand to Piers. I was relieved that the changes were not as alarming as I'd feared. There was an air of weariness about him, but otherwise he was the same.

'So this is your husband, Aline,' he said as they shook hands. 'I'm pleased to meet you at last, Piers – though of course we have spoken about the picture on the telephone. Don't stand there on the doorstep, Aline. This is your home. Come in, come in.' His hands took mine, and feeling them tremble, I realized that he too was nervous. 'We're both so pleased you've come, my dear. Zena's been cooking and cleaning all morning.'

'How are you, Michael?'

'Oh, not too bad. You look wonderful, Aline, but then you always do. I hope you're going to stay for a while?'

His smile dimmed as I moved away without answering him. As I saw his expression, I was sorry. I hadn't meant to hurt him, but I was confused. A part of me longed to reach out to him, to throw my arms around him and tell him that I loved him, but something held me back. I wasn't sure if I was still angry with him, or afraid of rejection.

We were in the large, airy hall, which had several rooms leading off of it, and a central wooden stairway, half-covered with a once rich red and gold carpet that had begun to fade. The walls were papered in a green regency stripe, which was new, but everything else was as I remembered it. There were paintings everywhere, clustered in every available space: landscapes, seascapes, drawings of birds and seals, and a few portraits.

'You certainly have a wealth of pictures,' Piers said, looking around with interest.

'Some of them are family pictures,' Michael said. 'But most of them are mine, I'm afraid.'

'Why afraid?' Piers asked. 'We've had a lot of interest in the picture you left with us. In my opinion you have considerable talent.'

'Interest but no buyers.' Michael's smile was wry.

'It's early days.' Piers' eyes went to a picture in an alcove. 'While I'm here, I'd be interested in looking at anything else you might be thinking of selling.'

'My stuff won't suit you,' Michael said. 'I've only done a few oils. I'm mainly a watercolour artist. I sell enough wildlife drawings and local scenes to keep us going during the summer.'

'Then why – ' I began, breaking off as someone came to the top of the stairs. Looking up, I saw her.

Zena was very beautiful – tall, slender and dressed in a simple linen skirt and silk blouse, she managed to look as if she'd stepped out of the pages of a fashion magazine. Her blonde hair was swept back into a knot at the nape of her neck, setting off the pale perfection of her face. She seemed nervous, and I noticed the shadows beneath her dark blue, almost violet eyes. Zena was motionless as we walked up the stairs, taking a few steps towards us at the last moment. I thought her movements were stiff and jerky like a marionette, and I wondered why she was so on edge.

'I'd begun to think you weren't coming,' she said. 'I expected you for lunch.' Her resentful gaze was trained on me.

Beside me, Piers made an involuntary movement. I glanced at him, but his expression was unreadable, telling me nothing. He appeared to be concentrating on the paintings.

'I'm sorry,' I said awkwardly. 'I can't have made myself clear when I rang. I thought I said we would be here in time for tea.'

'Zena always gets herself in a state when anyone's coming,' Michael said with a shrug. 'I told her a light meal would do if you did arrive for lunch – but she wouldn't listen. She was cooking for hours, all for nothing.'

Zena blinked, looking as if he'd slapped her, and I sensed that she was close to tears. Her hands were trembling, though she seemed to be making an effort to compose herself. I thought that perhaps she and Michael had quarrelled earlier in the day. Some of my antagonism faded.

'I'm sorry it was all such a rush for you, but you shouldn't have gone to so much trouble, Zena,' I said, trying to be friendly.

Zena stared at me, her mouth compressed. The atmosphere grew tense, but when she spoke, her words were conciliatory.

'I'm glad you've come, Aline. You don't know how glad . . . Perhaps Michael will listen to you. He certainly won't listen to me.'

'For God's sake, don't start, Zena,' Michael said with a tired sigh. 'Aline doesn't want to hear this.'

She looked at him, her eyes bright with unshed tears, then she turned away without answering. 'I've put you in the room you asked for, Aline.'

'Thank you.'

I thought it best not to comment as Zena led the way along the landing, one wall of which was massed with pictures. Zena stopped in front of the door right at the end of the hall, and turned to look at me.

'Well, here we are then. I hope everything's all right. I'd like a word with you in private before you talk to Michael, Aline.'

'Then I'll come down to the kitchen in a few minutes.'

As she turned away, I opened the bedroom door and went in, with mixed feelings. It was years since I'd been in this particular room, but it was just as I remembered it: dominated by the old four-poster bed with its dark mahogany posts fluted and decorated in wheat-ear designs, its dark crimson velvet canopy, and curtains tied with twisted gold ropes.

'This is nice,' Piers said, looking interested. 'Was it always yours?'

I glanced around, feeling the welcoming aura of the room enfold me. The deep pile carpet had a dark blue ground with a pattern of gold scrolls, and the window curtains were of silk in a shade that matched the bedropes, with tassels and ties of a deeper bronze. A large serpentine-fronted mahogany chest stood in one corner, and two big armoires against the wall flanked an oval gilt-framed mirror with ribbon-and-bow carving. In the window was a lady's writing desk and an elegant elbow chair. Bachelor's chests with brass handles stood at both sides of the bed, and there was a pair of Tiffany lamps with delicate glass shades.

I turned to Piers with a smile, and knew that I had made the right decision. 'It was my mother's room when she first came here as a bride. She moved into another room when she married Michael. I think she wanted to keep her memories intact. Since then it has never been used.'

'It's very beautiful,' he said. 'And obviously special to you.'

'The bathroom is through here, if you want to freshen up before tea.' I took off my jacket and checked my hair in the mirror. 'Are you all right if I go down to the kitchen now? I'd better see what Zena wants.'

'Of course.' Piers was about to say something then checked himself. 'I'll be fine looking at all these paintings. I've already spotted a couple of good pictures. I'm going to enjoy this visit.' I caught a note of satisfaction in his voice. He glanced at his watch. 'I'll give you twenty minutes before I come down. Is that long enough?'

'Plenty,' I said wryly. 'Zena and I aren't the best of friends.'

'Be nice to her, Aline. You're the one with all the cards, and she seems to be in a bit of a state.'

I stared at him, a little hurt by his tone. 'What do you mean, I'm the one with all the cards?'

'Well, it is your house, isn't it?'

'Yes, but it's her home. I've never tried to deny that she has a right to do as she likes.'

Piers moved towards me, taking me in his arms. 'I wasn't accusing you of anything, my darling. I know you're upset about coming down here, and I understand why. But if you quarrel with Zena again, it will only rebound on you. It's you I'm thinking of, Aline.'

I let him kiss me, but I didn't respond with my usual enthusiasm. Why should he take Zena's side when he'd just met her for the first time? In that instant, I realized that they hadn't been introduced, nor had they spoken directly to each other. The social niceties had been forgotten in the heat of the moment.

I was thoughtful as I went downstairs. Zena was only a few years older than I and very beautiful. She'd made an instant impression on Piers – or he wouldn't have felt sympathy for her. I suppressed a flicker of jealousy. I'd always hated any woman who was so possessive of her husband that she threw a fit everytime he looked at another woman. I was not going to join their ranks. As I approached the kitchen, I heard voices coming from inside and hesitated, wondering whether to go in or turn back.

'I'm warning you, Zena. If Aline is upset, I'm going to be angry.'

'Aline! It's always Aline with you, isn't it?' Zena cried. 'Sometimes I wonder why you married me when you're so – '

I went into the kitchen quickly, not wanting to hear any more of this particular conversation. Zena shut up at once, her cheeks flushing as she turned to look at me, and I saw anger and jealousy in her eyes, but also a kind of hopelessness.

'I'm sorry,' I said, aware that I'd intruded. 'I should have waited for a while before I came down.'

'It doesn't matter,' Michael said, his face tight and strained. 'You've probably saved us from having another row.'

'You started it,' Zena snapped. 'He's afraid I've got you down here to ask for money, Aline.'

'And have you?' I inquired calmly. 'Don't worry, Zena, I haven't come to throw you out.' I looked at Michael. The money was something I could cope with; emotions were more difficult. 'Zena asked me to come because she's worried about you – but I would have had to contact you soon. I know we have to talk about money when the trust ends.'

'We've lived off you long enough, Aline. I've told Zena that we don't need to live in this huge house. If I sell enough paintings, we should be able to buy a cottage in Blakeney ourselves.'

'So that's why . . .' I frowned. 'I wondered why you'd offered that painting to Piers' gallery. You did promise me you would never sell it.'

'I'm sorry, Aline.' His face was grave. 'I didn't think I had a choice.'

'Oh, Michael, you must have known I would be in touch sooner or later.'

'Should I have known?' Michael's voice was reproachful now. 'When you left that night, you swore you wanted nothing more to do with me.'

I flushed. Once, he'd been my adored father and he'd meant everything to me; that time had gone, and I wondered why it hurt so much to see his wounded look.

'I was upset,' I said. 'But you ought to have known that I wouldn't dream of throwing you out when the trust ends. I don't want to live here, and you know I can't sell it. It makes sense for you to stay on here.'

'We can't afford to,' Zena said. 'Not without the income from . . .' She dried up as Michael glared at her.

'I do realize that, Zena. That's why I have to talk to Michael.' I transferred my gaze back to Michael. 'Perhaps after tea?'

'I still think it would be better if we moved out,' he said, annoyed with his wife. 'Now that you're married you may change your mind about living here. Piers may have something to say about it.'

'Did somebody want me?'

Piers walked in, smiling, his brows raised as he glanced my way. 'Everything all right, darling?'

'Yes fine,' I said, my eyes flicking to Zena. 'If we send the men off to the drawing room, I can help you with the tea.'

'We can take a hint, can't we?' Piers grinned at Michael. 'Perhaps you'd like to tell me about a few of these pictures.'

As they went off together, Zena glanced at me, her face still flushed. 'Michael won't tell you, but he's in debt. There was a flood at his studio during the storms last winter and he'd neglected to renew his insurance premium. He lost a lot of last summer's work – and he hasn't been feeling well for months, so he hasn't been able to work much. This house costs a fortune to run, you know.'

'Yes, I know,' I said. 'While my mother was alive her own trust fund covered it, but that died with her. I knew Michael couldn't afford to live here without the income from my trust; that's why I signed most of it over to him. Don't worry, Zena. We'll sort something out. I can't expect you to pay for the upkeep of Hazeling.'

Zena's eyes were challenging. 'Supposing he dies? What happens to me?'

'Dies?' It was the first time I'd really considered it. 'Is it that serious?'

'Michael has angina, Aline. He's having treatment for it, of course, and it seems to work, but the attacks are frightening and very painful –

and one of them could prove fatal. The doctor warned him to take better care of himself, but he won't listen. Sometimes he goes out on the marshes for ten or fourteen hours at a stretch. He's shivering with cold when he gets back, and he starts coughing the minute he lights a cigarette. I've begged him to give them up, but he only smiles and says I'd be better off if he were dead.'

'He should stop smoking,' I agreed. 'But I don't see what I can do about it, Zena. If he won't listen to you, why should he listen to me?'

'Don't you know?' Her mouth twisted with bitterness. 'It's you he really cares about. It broke his heart when you walked out that night.'

'What do you mean?' My stomach tightened into a warning knot. 'You're his wife and he loves you. I'm only his stepdaughter. He wasn't really in love with my mother,' I added. 'They'd been having rows for years . . .'

Zena laughed harshly. 'Most of them were over you.'

'Over me?' I stared at her, beginning to feel a little sick. The look on Zena's face was disturbing, perhaps because it was more hysterical than spiteful. 'That's ridiculous – why should they quarrel over me?'

Zena's was breathing hard. She was close to losing control and I sensed that this outburst had been building for a long time. 'For the same reason as we quarrel over you. Michael is obsessed with you; he always was. All those paintings of you that he never shows to anyone . . .'

'Obsessed?' Zena was treading on dangerous ground now. 'That – that's not true, Zena. Michael was fond of me when I was a child, but as I grew up we drew apart. There was always a distance between us.'

'If he kept his distance, it was because he was afraid of what might happen if he didn't.'

A tense silence followed Zena's statement and I closed my eyes, feeling queasy. Zena was voicing the secret fears I'd tried to suppress for so many years. Drawing a deep breath, I turned on her, anger blazing.

'Shut up, will you? I refuse to listen to this. I won't hear it, Zena.'

For a moment she seemed as if she would continue the argument, then she turned away to switch on the kettle. For a few minutes she worked in silence, struggling with her emotions, then with her back still towards me, she said, 'I'm sorry. I shouldn't have said that. I'm just jealous because he thinks so much of you.'

I knew what that apology must have cost her, and my anger died. 'He's my stepfather, Zena,' I said. 'He was fond of me when I was a child, that's all.'

'If you say so, Aline.' Zena picked up the tray. She appeared docile and compliant, but neither of us was fooled. The argument had merely been postponed. 'Shall we take this in now?'

The drawing room was familiar, though shabbier than I'd remembered it; the curtains were beginning to fade at the windows. Zena had made very few changes, merely bringing in a sofa from one of the unused rooms to replace the one I'd taken to London. I sank into one of the deep armchairs, letting my gaze travel round the room. From my experience at the saleroom, I knew – the Hepplewhite cabinet, for instance – that some of the things I'd always taken for granted were valuable antiques, though there was also a comfortable clutter acquired over the years. I wondered if Michael had had the insurance updated. I'd left everything like that to him, but it would have to be discussed now.

After tea, I suggested to Zena that Piers might like to see the gardens. Zena seemed startled, but Piers stood up and agreed with alacrity, and they went off together, giving me the opportunity to be alone with Michael. He studied me thoughtfully.

'Would you like a sherry. Aline?'

I shook my head as he got up and poured himself a small brandy from a crystal decanter on the sideboard.

'Should you be drinking that?' I asked, as he came back to stand in front of the fireplace.

As always, the fire had been laid but not lit in the large, old-fashioned grate, even though it was still summer. The rooms at Hazeling were big and had high ceilings, and it could be chilly in the evenings, even after a warm day. I remembered toasting crumpets over that fire on winter evenings.

'Zena's had a go at you already, then,' Michael said, as he stood the empty glass on the marble mantel. 'She's been like a cat on hot bricks these past three weeks. I feel as if she's expecting me to drop dead at any minute.'

'She's worried about you,' I said. 'That's only natural, isn't it? She is your wife.'

'Yes.' He frowned. 'You don't have to remind me, Aline. I know I'm responsible for Zena's unhappiness – and yours, for a time.'

I flushed and dropped my eyes as he looked at me. 'Perhaps I was at fault too,' I said in a low voice. 'I was very upset.'

'I should have waited,' he said, sounding tired. 'It was too soon after Sheila's death. I ought to have considered your feelings, Aline. I'm sorry.'

He looked so weary and dispirited that I found myself apologizing. 'I – I know you and mother hadn't been happy for a long time . . .'

'No,' he said. Looking up, I caught an expression of grief on his face. 'Not for a very long time.'

'Was – was it. . . ?' The question died on my lips. I couldn't ask him about that day on the marshes, the day that had changed everything. I wanted to, but the words just wouldn't come.

'Was it my fault? Is that what you meant?' Michael asked. I let him draw his own conclusions from my silence. It was easier than pursuing something I found too painful. 'Most of it, I think. You accused me of being unfaithful to your mother, Aline, and I can't deny it. But there were reasons. Sheila and I . . . We hadn't been sleeping together. Even before her illness, that side of our marriage was long over. It was never very satisfactory on either side. Without being disloyal, that was more Sheila's fault than mine.'

'I see.' I turned and walked to the french windows to look out. Piers and Zena were walking towards the shrubberies. They appeared to be deep in conversation. 'Then I suppose I can't blame you for going to another woman. It just seemed so heartless to marry that soon after Mother died. Can you understand my feelings, Michael?' I faced him again, wanting to see his reaction.

He nodded. His hand shook as he played with the empty brandy glass. His whole body was tense.

'Believe me, I didn't mean to hurt you, Aline. That was the last thing I wanted. It just seemed the sensible thing to do at the time. Zena wanted to get married and I . . .' His voice trailed away as if he found it impossible to explain his innermost feelings. 'Well, I thought it best.'

'I'm sorry I quarrelled with Zena that night,' I said. 'It was silly of me to behave so childishly because she'd broken Mother's favourite vase.'

'It was an accident, Aline. She didn't do it on purpose, believe me. Zena appreciates beautiful things. She would never do something like that out of spite.'

'I believe you.' I smiled at him. It was painful to see him looking so tired, and it touched something deep inside me. I remembered the friend of my early years, the man I'd adored before the doubts began to creep in. 'The vase was just the touchpaper, I suppose. I was too angry to know what I was saying.'

'Yes.' Michael relaxed as he saw my smile. 'I understood why you just exploded like that. You'd been through a difficult time, with your mother's death and . . .'

'My affair with a married man?' I laughed as I saw the flash of relief in his eyes. 'That stopped hurting long ago, Michael. It was awkward, miserable – and my own fault. I knew he was married.'

'It was your first serious affair, wasn't it?'

'Yes.' I hesitated. If only I could find the courage to open up to him, to tell him the truth. 'You know why, of course.'

'I've wondered if – ' Michael broke off as Piers and Zena came back into the room. They were laughing and Zena looked happier than she had all afternoon.

I wished they'd taken just a little longer over their walk. Michael and I had hardly begun to say what was on our minds, but I'd felt that we were getting somewhere. However, we still hadn't discussed the future of Hazeling.

'I've decided we're all going out to dinner this evening,' Piers announced. 'Zena tells me there's a good hotel in Blakeney.'

'I told him I was going to cook, but he insisted,' Zena said as she saw Michael's frown. 'There's no arguing with Piers.'

'Why should you spend hours slaving over a stove when we can go out?' Piers asked, then turned to Michael with a winning smile. 'Do you think I could persuade you to show me what you have at your studio?'

'We could stroll over and have a look, if you like,' Michael offered reluctantly. 'It's a converted barn at the back of the house.'

'So Zena told me.' Piers glanced at me. 'Are you coming with us, darling?'

'No, I don't think so. If we're going out this evening, I'd rather have a warm bath and wash my hair.'

'I'll see you later then.' Piers bent to kiss my cheek.

Catching sight of Zena, I was surprised to see a sudden blaze of jealousy in her eyes. It was gone in an instant, and I might have thought I'd imagined it, but I could see from the look on Michael's face that he had noticed it too.

As I walked upstairs, I wondered about that look. I knew that Zena resented me, but that didn't explain her acute jealousy. Putting it out of my mind, I ran my bath. I was looking forward to a long, relaxing soak in the warm water. I felt tired, a little sleepy.

Chapter Ten

The child woke suddenly, a ripple of excitement running through her as she suddenly remembered it was her birthday! She had always loved the specialness of birthdays. Unlike Christmas, which everyone shared, a birthday was just for one person. And she just knew that this one was going to be the best, the very best. She was even being allowed a day off school.

A pile of presents had been placed on the table beside her bed while she slept. She knew who had tip-toed in so as not to wake her, and she smiled, a warm happy glow spreading inside her. She knew without even looking at the labels which parcel was from him. The smart black and silver paper with satin ribbon stood out from the others.

She tore the wrappings from books, games and a new sweater, deliberately leaving the best until last. Then she picked up Michael's gift, slowly untied the bow and lifted the paper, taking care not to spoil it.

Savouring the moment, she counted to ten before opening the pale grey velvet box. Inside was a delicate oval gold locket on a fancy chain. The locket itself was engraved with birds. It was just what she wanted. She had mentioned it to Michael when they were all shopping for her school clothes in Norwich, and he had remembered.

With a squeal of delight, she jumped out of bed and ran into her parents' room. The smell of bacon frying told her that her mother had already gone downstairs to prepare their breakfast, but Michael was lying with his eyes closed, seemingly asleep. Carefully lifting the covers so as not to disturb him, she climbed in beside him and snuggled up to him as she done so often in the past.

For a moment in his sleep he stirred, and his arm moved across her thin, childish form as she pressed closer, nuzzling his neck as she tried to control her giggles. He woke suddenly, a look of alarm in his eyes as he saw her.

'What are you doing, Aline?' he demanded, his breathing ragged and harsh.

'I came to say thank you,' she said, startled by his reaction.

'You should have waited until I came down to breakfast.' His reply was sharp and angry. 'Get out of this bed now and don't sneak up on me again.'

*

I woke from my daydream to discover that the bathwater was getting cold.

The pictures were still vivid in my mind and the memory was painful. I'd been too young to understand at the time, but now I realized just why he had been so harsh with me, and the realization made me wonder again just what had happened on the marshes that day. Had I been sexually assaulted, as my school friend had asserted? And if so, had it been Michael who had attacked me?

The police inspector had suspected Michael of the attack, but nothing had come of it – perhaps for lack of evidence. And my mother had suspected there might be something in it. All those slaps and warnings about behaving like a young lady had been given for a purpose. I'd believed that she blamed me for whatever had happened, that I had somehow brought it on myself, and it had made me feel guilty. That guilt had stayed with me for years. It lingered even now in my mind. Was Zena right, was it because of me that my mother and Michael had become estranged? I wished that I could remember the attack; it would be so much better if I knew the truth. For years I'd been haunted by my doubts and fears. I hadn't wanted to believe that Michael could hurt me that way, and yet . . . and yet there were men who preyed on young children.

'No! No, I won't believe it. I won't think about it,' I cried aloud.

I towelled myself furiously, rubbing at my skin as if I could wipe out the memories by punishing myself. It wasn't possible. Michael wouldn't do that! He couldn't . . . could he? I was surprised at how much it hurt me even now. For years I'd suppressed all my emotions, all my feelings towards him, but now that he was ill and Zena had said he might die, I realized that I still cared.

Sitting in front of my dressing-table mirror, I scrutinized my white face. Surely if Michael had attacked me I would have known? I frowned as I began to braid my hair into a french plait. It was too horrible to contemplate. I tried to put it out of my mind, to think about something else.

It was then that I became aware of the music. It was very faint and it seemed to come from somewhere above me. It had an odd tinkling sound, rather like a child's musical box. I listened, trying to make out the tune.

' "Greensleeves . . ." ' I murmured. ' "Who but my Lady Green-sleeves . . ." '

I wondered where the sound was coming from, then the door opened and I glanced over my shoulder as Piers came in. I jumped up and ran to greet him.

'I've missed you,' I said, slipping my arms about his waist and lifting my face for his kiss. 'Do you like my hair? I've managed to plait it at last.'

He looked at me with an odd intensity that made me uncomfortable.

'It suits you – but you always look beautiful, Aline.'

'Thank you.' I heard the music begin again. 'Listen – that music. It's "Greensleeves", isn't it? Where is it coming from?'

Piers listened. 'Is there a room above here?'

'I had a playroom in the attic once, but it hasn't been used in years – as far as I know.'

'Perhaps Zena uses it.' Piers loosened his tie and walked towards the bathroom.

'She must be fond of that tune to play it over and over again.'

He shrugged his shoulders. 'She's just sentimental, I suppose.'

'Perhaps,' I said, still puzzled. 'Or the musical box has a special meaning for her.'

Piers didn't answer. He had gone into the bathroom, so perhaps he hadn't heard me.

That night, I awoke with a start. For a moment I thought I must have been having a nightmare, but I couldn't remember anything. The curtains were thick and there was hardly any light in the room. Beside me, the bed was cold and empty.

'Piers,' I whispered. 'Piers, where are you?'

There was no answer, so I switched on the light. He wasn't in the bedroom or the adjoining bathroom. I glanced at my watch. It was only a quarter-past three – far too early for him to have gone out for a run. Perhaps he'd been restless and had gone down to make himself a drink. Resisting the temptation to get up and look for him, I switched off the light and closed my eyes. For a moment I felt a sharp prick of suspicion, but I knew I was being ridiculous to imagine that Piers might be with Zena just because he had paid her some attention at dinner. Michael had been in a mood all evening and had hardly spoken, and I could tell Piers felt sorry for Zena, who was obviously unhappy.

Lying there in the dark, I gradually became aware of a sound. It was like a muffled weeping, and it came from above – from the same direction as the music I'd heard that afternoon. It was odd the way sound carried in old houses, I thought. After a minute or so the weeping stopped, but now someone was walking above me . . . Then there was silence. I listened for a little longer, but there was only the normal creaking of old timbers.

I was just dropping off to sleep when the door opened very softly and Piers tip-toed towards the bed. I reached for the light switch and he blinked in the sudden glare. He was wearing a short black satin dressing robe but his legs were bare, his feet thrust into leather mules.

'Why are you awake?' he asked, frowning. 'Did you have a bad dream?'

I considered telling him about the sound of weeping, then changed my mind. He looked annoyed, which warned me not to make too much of his absence. Whatever he'd been doing, he clearly wasn't prepared to discuss it, and nor was I. Piers had such a temper when roused that I didn't want him to think I was nagging, so I said the first thing that came into my head.

'No, not a dream. Something woke me and I wondered where you were. I was just lying here thinking it must be at least three hours since we made love.'

'Feeling deprived, huh,' he murmured against my ear as he slipped into bed and put his arms around me. 'We'll have to see what we can do about that.'

I glanced at Zena across the breakfast table. She didn't appear to have spent the night crying; her make-up was immaculate, as were her clothes. Her dress was a simple sheath that hugged her body, but it looked expensive, and I couldn't help thinking that for all her complaining, Michael did not keep her short of money.

'Can I help you with anything this morning?' I asked, as Zena began to stack the dishes.

Zena smiled at me. 'How thoughtful you are. No, I can manage thanks. It's just a traditional Sunday lunch today.'

'If you're sure,' I said. 'I think I shall take a walk in the gardens.'

'That's a good idea, darling,' Piers said. 'After lunch we could go for a drive to Sheringham or Cromer, if you like.'

'I was hoping for another little talk with Aline,' Michael said hesitantly. 'There's some business we should discuss.'

'Later this morning, perhaps?' I glanced at my husband as I rose from the table. 'Are you coming for a walk?'

'I've already taken my exercise,' he replied. 'I'd like to go through some of those paintings again with Michael before lunch, if you don't mind, darling. I've had an idea.'

'Of course I don't mind. It's a long time since I've been down. I can amuse myself in the garden,' I said. 'I'll be back in an hour or so then, Michael.'

128

'I'll be waiting,' he promised, that anxious look in his eyes again.

Piers was frowning. I sensed that he wasn't too pleased about the little talk I'd promised Michael, though I couldn't see why. That was, after all, the reason we had come down, and the future of Hazeling had to be settled.

I went out of the front door, stopping to test the air before deciding which way to walk. It was the beginning of September now, but the weather was still remarkably good. Maybe there was something in all the talk about global warming, or perhaps it was just a stream of warm air from the Gulf.

The garden had an old-fashioned charm, with rambling roses climbing everywhere and big round laurel bushes. Delphiniums, asters and dahlias still flowered in the deep borders. There were clusters of pinks, snapdragons and the silvery seedpods of honesty. I thought that I might ask Zena if I could take some honesty back to London with me. I could, of course, just pick them, but I was only a guest, even though it was my house. It was Zena's right to be mistress of her own home . . . Remembering the sound of weeping in the night, I knew it could only have been Zena, and I wondered if I had in some way contributed to her grief.

At the end of the large garden was a crumbling brick wall with a gate. Beyond it was a dense wood. Michael had once built me a tree house there, but that was before . . . My swing had gone. Mother had had it taken down to prevent me sneaking away to play out of sight of the house – just after that afternoon when Mother had come looking for me and I'd heard an odd scraping noise from the other side of the wall. Someone had been there, climbing the wall, and then Mother had come . . .

'You're too big for swings anyway,' she'd said when I'd looked at her with reproachful eyes. 'It's time you learned to behave like a young lady.'

My mother's words were ringing in my ears. How those thoughtless words had hurt, making me withdraw more and more into my own little world. It was years before I stopped thinking of myself as wicked.

At the gate, I hesitated. Should I go into the wood or stay in the garden? Glancing at my watch, I saw that it was time to go back, or Michael would think I'd changed my mind. I began to retrace my steps towards the house. As I did so, I saw my stepfather coming towards me. He was smiling, dressed as usual in old trousers and a brown cardigan with patches on the elbows. Seeing him swept me back to my childhood, to the early days, and I felt a lump in my throat.

'I was wondering if you might be here,' he said. 'You always loved the woods. We don't want you getting lost, do we?'

'I'm not allowed to play in the woods,' I said, the words out of my mouth before I could stop them. 'Don't you remember?'

An expression of pain flickered in his eyes. 'Do you think I could forget, Aline?' he asked quietly. 'Do you think I haven't wished a thousand times that I could turn back the clock, that it had never happened?'

I gasped in dismay, staring at him, my eyes widening with horror. 'Then it was you,' I whispered. 'Oh no! Oh, my God, no!'

For a moment he seemed too stunned to answer, his face blanching. 'You thought . . .' He choked on the words, clutching at his chest. 'Aline,' he cried just before he keeled over. 'Help me . . .'

The rest of that day was a blur. Somehow I managed to support Michael as far as the terrace at the back of the house, and then Piers and Zena were suddenly there.

'Let me have him,' Piers commanded. 'Zena, telephone the doctor.'

Piers lifted the sick man in his arms. I'd always known he was strong, but even I was surprised at the ease with which he carried Michael inside and laid him on a large sofa in the drawing room. Michael's eyes were closed. He seemed barely conscious, and there was a slight blueness about his mouth.

'His pills,' Piers muttered, as Zena came back from her telephone call. 'Slip one under his tongue.'

She felt in Michael's trouser pocket, her hands shaking as she tried to open the little silver pill box. Seeing that she was incapable of doing it, I took it from her and shook out a capsule.

'Is this right?'

Zena nodded and I pressed it between Michael's clenched lips, forcing them open enough to place the tiny pill under his tongue.

'He's going to die, isn't he?' There was a note of hysteria in Zena's voice as she looked at Piers.

Seeing her fear, I realized that Zena did love Michael. I had wondered if she cared more for the house and the money she had expected him to inherit, but now I saw that despite all their difficulties, she cared very deeply.

'Don't panic,' Piers said sharply. 'He will probably come out of it now he has the medication.'

'I didn't know about the pills,' I said, feeling guilty as I looked down

130

at Michael's face. Piers had known but I hadn't. I ought to have known! 'He asked me to help but I didn't know . . .'

'Not your fault.'

The words were slurred and difficult to understand, but I heard them, a surge of relief flooding through me as I saw Michael's eyelids flutter. The pill was working; we'd acted in time. I turned away, retreating to the window as the tears threatened.

'Is that the doctor?'

Zena's words pulled me together. A car was braking outside in the drive.

'I'll let him in,' I said.

The doctor advised that Michael should be hospitalized for a few days, just to be on the safe side, and he was taken away in an ambulance, an oxygen mask over his face. I watched from a distance as they carried him out on a chair, Zena holding his hand as she walked beside him.

'Would you like us to come to the hospital with you?' I asked, but she shook her head.

'I'll ring for a taxi to bring me back,' she replied. 'I may stay overnight.'

'We'll probably drive back to London this afternoon,' Piers said. 'Aline has her old key, so we can see that everywhere is locked up before we go.'

She nodded, but was too distracted to hear what he was saying. After the ambulance had gone, Piers looked at me, his expression grim.

'What brought that on?' he asked.

'We had an argument.' I got up and went to the sideboard to pour myself a small brandy. 'I feel awful about it.'

'What was the quarrel about?'

My hand shook as I lifted the glass to my lips. 'I don't want to talk about it, Piers. We were discussing something that happened a long time ago.'

'Something you can't tell me?' His tone had become brittle and I knew that he was angry.

'Please don't have one of your moods, Piers. I can't take it at the moment.'

'I wasn't aware that I had moods.'

I stared at him, puzzled by his expression. He usually hid his feelings so well, but this time he couldn't quite manage it. He was jealous – jealous of Michael! His reaction when he'd found out about my affair with Nick had shown me what he was capable of – but he couldn't suspect that there was anything going on between Michael and me. Unless . . .

'What's wrong?' I asked. 'What has Zena been saying to you?'

'Leave Zena out of this,' he muttered. 'I don't need anyone to tell me that you have a thing for Michael. It's there in your eyes every time you look at him – and it's just as obvious that the feeling is mutual.'

'Piers!' I cried, horrified. 'You can't mean that. It's horrible – almost incestuous. He's my stepfather.'

'You wouldn't be the first to have a crush on your own stepfather,' Piers said harshly. 'I'm sure it happens in a good many families.'

'But it isn't true,' I said, my voice dying to a whisper as the world seemed to whirl around me. 'Michael was my father. I loved him – but not in the way you mean. That's my worst nightmare . . .'

Something flickered in Piers' eyes. 'What do you mean?'

I shook my head. 'Don't ask. Please, Piers. I can't talk about it now.'

He stared at me, his expression angry and accusing. Unable to bear it, I turned and ran from the room.

I was packing when Piers walked into the bedroom. He caught my arm, and swung me round to face him. As his fingers bit into the soft flesh of my upper arm, I was very aware of the strength in his hands.

'You're hurting me.'

'You can't just run out on me like that,' he said. 'I want to know what you and Michael were talking about before he was taken ill. I have a right to know, Aline.'

'Yes, I suppose you do. We were talking about something that happened when I was eleven . . .' I drew a deep breath, forcing myself to speak. 'I can't remember anything about it. I only know that I went out on the marshes with Michael to look for something and – and when I woke up I was in hospital. A policeman kept asking me what had happened, but my mind was a complete blank. I didn't know what he meant, but he kept on until I was frightened and in tears. Then the nurse made him go away.'

The little purple vein was standing out at Piers' temple. He seemed tense, uncertain. When he spoke, his words were careful, 'You think you were attacked by Michael, is that what you're saying?'

'I – I don't know,' I whispered. 'I don't know what happened that day. My mother would never talk about it, but a friend told me . . . She said that I had been indecently assaulted. I looked up the words in the dictionary . . .'

Piers stared at me hard, his expression unreadable. 'Do you think that's what happened? Do you think you were raped?'

I felt the blood drain from my face. Put baldly like that, it sounded so horrible. The words were pushed out of me painfully and I heard myself rambling as I tried to unravel my confusion. 'No – I don't know. I've never been sure. I can't bear to think about it, to think that Michael might have . . . I know my mother thought he might . . . Once when I was a child he – '

'He what?' Piers' eyes lit up with sudden anger. 'Are you telling me that he molested you? The bastard!'

'No,' I begged, frightened by his fierceness. 'Nothing happened. Michael – I was cuddling him and he had an erection. He made me get out of bed. I didn't understand. I was upset because he was cross with me.'

'When did this happen?' Piers' eyes bored into me. 'Tell me, Aline.'

'It was my birthday. I was eleven . . . The day before the attack on the marshes . . .'

Piers moved away from me abruptly. He looked out of the window, his back towards me. 'Did he ever try to touch you after that?'

'No.' I hesitated, remembering all the times when I was older and had seen a certain expression in Michael's eyes and wondered. 'I don't know if . . . I can't be certain that Michael had anything to do with what happened on the marshes.'

'But you've suspected it?' He swung round to look at me, his face sharp with tension. 'So why did you come down here? Why have anything to do with him?'

'I've never been sure . . .' The words sounded unconvincing even to my own ears. How could I explain my feelings for Michael when I didn't understand them myself? 'I've tried not to think about it, Piers. I don't want to believe that he . . . Besides, there's Hazeling to consider. It's Michael's home – and Zena's. They can't afford to live here unless I pay for the upkeep. I have to draw up a new trust fund on my birthday so that – '

'Why?' Piers was angry again. 'It's your house, Aline. You could tell them to leave.'

'I couldn't,' I said. I was wishing that I hadn't told Piers anything. 'There's Zena to consider as well. I thought you liked her.'

His eyes were cold as he looked at me. 'What made you think that?'

I shrugged, unable to explain my instincts. I'd noticed a kind of intimacy between them that seemed odd in two people who had only just met. 'Just little things.'

'I felt sorry for her,' he said. 'She seemed so unhappy. I can understand why now – but you come first, Aline. I had no idea Michael had abused you as a child. Can't you see how I feel? You're my wife. You belong to me. I thought you understood how much I care for you.'

'Piers I'm not *sure* about Michael . . . I don't want to think about it,' I said. Piers' face darkened. 'Oh, Piers of course I know you love me. Don't let's quarrel over this. Michael was trying to tell me something before he collapsed. It may be that I've been mistaken all these years. Besides, even if it were true, it was a long time ago . . .' I faltered as I saw the warning glint in his eyes. 'I don't want to live at Hazeling, Piers. I'm not allowed to sell it, so – '

'We could use it for weekends,' he said. 'I rather like Hazeling, Aline. I think you should consider every possibility before you decide what to do.'

'Yes, I suppose I should.' I looked at him pleadingly. 'Can we leave it for now?'

He hesitated, then nodded and drew me into his arms. 'Of course. It's your house, Aline. Your money. You must do as you please – just as long as you give it some thought.'

'You mustn't think badly of Michael because of what I've told you,' I said, looking up at him. 'As far as I know, he has never done anything to harm me. I don't remember anything, Piers; just that Michael changed towards me after that day and I never knew why.'

To my relief, he nodded. 'You're probably right, Aline. If he was cross with you when you crept into his bed as you said, he might have been trying to protect you, to control an urge he saw as shameful.'

'Then can we just forget it?' I relaxed as he smiled. 'Thank you,' I said, and reached up to kiss him. 'Let's leave now, shall we?'

'Finish your packing,' Piers said. 'I've persuaded Michael to have an exhibition and there are some pictures ready to take back with me. I shan't be long . . .'

A quarrel had been averted, but I had a feeling that Piers was still angry, though pretending not to be. I finished packing and then took the cases downstairs. There was no sign of Piers. I went out and checked the car. There were some paintings in the car, but he was nowhere around. He had left the car unlocked and gone off somewhere. I called and then went back into the house, thinking that he must be in the kitchen. It was very odd but he had simply disappeared. I checked my watch then put the kettle on and made myself a cup of instant coffee. I drank it, washed my cup and went back outside to wait, after locking the house.

It was a long time before Piers returned. He just came strolling up to the car and smiled at me rather absently as he got in. He seemed withdrawn and quiet, and I noticed that his hair was damp as though he had been sweating.

'Where have you been?' I asked. 'I was beginning to worry. You've been gone a couple of hours.'

Piers looked at his watch and frowned. 'Is it that long? I was walking, thinking. I'm sorry if you were worried, darling. I had something on my mind and I didn't realize the time.' He smiled and kissed my cheek. 'Are you ready to leave?'

It was as if he'd forgotten all about our argument, as if it had never happened.

'Yes, I'm ready,' I said. 'Let's go home.'

I rang Zena a week or so later. 'How is Michael now?' I asked, fiddling with the telephone lead. 'What did the doctor at the hospital say?'

'It wasn't as bad this time,' Zena said. 'Just a minor attack. He'll be all right if he takes things easy for a while. If he's sensible.'

'He hasn't been out on the marshes again?'

'He went out yesterday, but most of the time he's working in his studio, from memory. Sometimes I think he's utterly mad. His work is an obsession.'

'He's trying to get enough done for that exhibition Piers talked him into.'

'Yes, I know.' Zena sounded angry about it. 'Why can't he be content to show what he's already done? He never thinks of me, Aline. What am I going to do if anything happens to him?'

'Perhaps he needs to work,' I said. 'Perhaps it's his way of providing for you if – '

'You think I married him for the money, don't you?'

'No. No, I don't think that, Zena. I know you love him. So what's the problem? Is there anything I can do? If it's about Hazeling, I'm sure we can work something out.'

'I don't want to leave,' she said, 'but that isn't it. Not really.'

'Do you want to tell me?'

'No, I don't think so. I have to go now, Aline. I think I heard Michael come in.'

I replaced the receiver thoughtfully. Piers had taken a fancy to Hazeling, but I couldn't ask Michael and Zena to leave; yet I didn't want another quarrel with Piers.

He had seemed different since our return from Hazeling, quieter and

135

more distant. Most of the time he was my loving husband, but sometimes he would get up and leave the flat without saying a word. When he came back he simply said he'd been for a walk. His moods disturbed me, though I wasn't sure why.

I tried to put the problem out of my mind. If I left it long enough it might solve itself.

Chapter Eleven

Piers came out of the bathroom and glanced at the suitcase lying open on the bed.

'Is there anything else you want?' I asked. 'I've packed a change of everything and your overnight shaving kit.'

He shook his head. 'It feels strange having someone to pack for me. You've made a good job of it, Aline.' He looked at me thoughtfully. 'I still wish you were coming to New York with me.'

Piers was going to New York because a painting he had bought was alleged to have been stolen.

'You know there wasn't another seat,' I said, not quite meeting his eyes. 'It would mean you'd have had to catch a later flight. Besides, as you said, it's only going to be a quick trip. I'll come another time, when we can stay for a few days.'

I put my arms about his waist. Three weeks had passed since our visit to Hazeling and his strange mood had passed. 'Don't worry about it, darling. I'm going to miss you, but it's better if I don't come this time.'

For a few days now, I'd suspected that I might be pregnant. I'd forgotten to take my pills a couple of times when I was on honeymoon and I thought it might have happened then. I was a little nervous of telling Piers, though I was thrilled at the idea. I wanted a large family, having known the loneliness of being an only child myself. I was tempted to tell Piers that I'd been sick that morning, but it didn't seem the right moment to shock him with the news that he might be going to be a father.

He was watching me closely. 'It wouldn't be much fun for you,' he said after a moment. 'But I still hate to leave you.'

There was something peculiar about the way he was looking at me. It was almost speculative, as though he was wondering if he could trust me. Remembering his display of jealousy at Hazeling, I felt uneasy. He'd been so angry and then he'd just gone off for two hours, and his behaviour had been odd – almost too controlled – when he came back. Was he still jealous of Michael and pretending not to be?

I lifted my face for his kiss, which was possessive and demanding. 'Take care, Piers. Remember I love you.'

'Do you?' he said.

I stared at him uncertainly. *Was* he wondering if he could trust me? 'You don't mean that, Piers? You can't doubt that I love you?'

The look died out of his eyes and he laughed. 'The ramblings of a jealous husband, darling. Forget it.' He raised his eyebrows. 'What shall I bring you back? How about a mink coat?'

'Bring me a fake fur, if you like,' I said. 'Not the real thing. I wouldn't wear fur, Piers.'

He bent to kiss me on the lips. 'Just as you like, Aline.'

'Piers . . .' I hesitated, wanting to tell him my secret, then the telephone began to ring.

He swore under his breath. 'What did you want to say?'

'Nothing important. Answer that, darling. I expect it's for you.'

Still frowning, he turned to pick up the receiver. 'Piers Drayton speaking . . . Aline? Yes, she's here.' He held it out to me. 'It's Julie for you.'

'Thanks.' I took it from him.

'I have to go,' Piers said.

I nodded, watching as he zipped the case. 'Julie? It's nice to hear from you.' I blew a kiss to Piers as he picked up his jacket and walked out, mouthing the words 'Bye, darling.' As the door closed behind him, I felt a pang of regret.

'Did you hear what I said, Aline? Tony has got a huge order for his knitwear. It's a chain of new boutiques and they're crazy about his stuff. They want him to design a whole new line for them.'

'That's wonderful, Julie. I'm so pleased for Tony and you.' I stared at the door, wishing Julie hadn't rung just as Piers was leaving. 'We could have lunch together if you're free. Piers had to dash off to the States. It wasn't worthwhile my going. Besides, I had my reasons. Look, Julie, I'll see you later. I must go now.'

I put the phone down and ran to the door, wrenching it open. I could hear the lift whirring and I knew it was too late: Piers had gone.

After lunch, I walked a part of the way back to the clinic with Julie. Julie looked at me thoughtfully, her eyes serious.

'You're a bit quiet, Aline. Is there something on your mind?'

'Does it show that much?' I smiled. 'I'm not sure but I think I may be pregnant.'

'Aline! That's great,' Julie cried, hugging me. 'I'm really pleased for you. What does Piers say?'

Knowing how much Julie wanted a baby herself, I'd thought the news might upset her. Now I saw that she was a little envious but accepting.

'I haven't told Piers yet.' I hesitated. 'I'm not sure how he'll feel about it.'

Julie stared at me for a moment. 'You have discussed the possibility of having a baby?' She whistled as I shook my head. 'Does he think you're on the pill?'

'I forgot to take it a couple of times on our honeymoon.'

'It happens.' Julie looked at me in concern. 'How do you feel about it? Are you ready for a child?'

'Yes . . . Yes, I think I am,' I said. 'I could have waited another year or so, but I've always wanted a big family and I wouldn't want to leave it too long for the first one.'

'I'm happy for you; I really am.' Julie glanced at her watch. Now there was a slight note of envy in her voice. 'I must dash.'

As Julie ran across the road, I stood hesitating at the kerb, trying to make up my mind what to do. The thought of an empty flat wasn't inviting. Perhaps I would go shopping . . . or window shopping for baby clothes, just in case.

Back at the flat later that afternoon, I collected the post. There was just one letter for Piers: a white envelope with curious blue printing on it. I laid it on the hall table just as the phone began to ring.

'Hello, Aline Drayton here.' My heart was beating rapidly as I hoped for the impossible. Piers could not have arrived in New York yet. There was a slight, almost imperceptible silence before the caller spoke, but it was enough to set my nerves tingling.

'Aline,' Nick said, and my heart did a little flip. 'I'm in town for a few days, sorting a few things out. I wondered if we might meet for lunch or coffee or something.'

'Nick . . .' I took a deep breath, waiting for my pulses to steady. 'I'm not sure that's a good idea.'

'Look,' he said quickly, as if he was afraid that I would put the phone down on him. 'I lost my temper the last time we met. I'm sorry, Aline. I've been wanting to apologize.'

'It's not that I'm angry with you,' I said, feeling awkward. 'You had a right to be upset.'

'But you want me to get the hell out of your life, is that it?'

'Piers tends to get jealous.'

'Then don't tell him.' Nick's voice sounded odd. 'I do need to see you, Aline. There's something I think you ought to know.'

'What do you mean?'

'I can't tell you on the phone. Meet me for lunch tomorrow, please?'

It would be madness to agree and yet I felt that I owed Nick something. I had treated him badly. I hesitated and was lost. 'OK – where and when?'

'Thanks, Aline. One o'clock at Odette's – that's Regent's Park. Do you know it?'

'Yes,' I answered, wondering what on earth I was doing. 'It's nice there. One o'clock then . . .'

I sat staring at the phone for several minutes after I'd replaced the receiver. If Piers discovered that I'd agreed to have lunch with Nick . . . For a moment I felt frightened, then caught myself. This was ridiculous. Nick was still a friend. Surely I could have lunch with a friend without risking a row with my husband . . . couldn't I?

As it turned out, the lunch with Nick never materialized. It was half-past seven in the evening when my telephone rang again. I was deep in the paperback I was reading – a big, absorbing historical that had won the prize for Romantic Novel of the Year – and I answered absent-mindedly, my mind still caught up with the intriguing twists and turns of the plot.

'Aline.' Michael's voice sent an unexpected shiver down my spine. 'I'm sorry to ring you at this hour but – '

I heard the note of near panic in his voice and was suddenly alert. 'What's wrong?'

'It's Zena,' he said. 'She has just tried to kill herself.'

'She what?' I cried, startled. 'You can't mean that!'

'She had the bottle of sleeping tablets in her hand when I came in. I managed to grab them before she could swallow any, but then she had hysterics and fled upstairs to the attic. She's locked herself in and I can't get her to come out. I – I just don't know what to do, Aline.'

'Do you want me to come down?'

He hesitated. 'I'd be very grateful. I don't feel up to coping with this alone.'

'I'll leave in about half an hour,' I said. 'I must make a couple of telephone calls, then I'll drive straight down. Don't panic, Michael. She will come out when she's ready.'

I telephoned Julie to tell her where I was going, and asked her to cancel my appointment with Nick.

'If Piers should ring you, tell him it was an emergency, will you, please.'

'Of course,' Julie said, sounding worried. 'Take care, Aline. Ring me when you get back.'

The drive down to Hazeling was a nightmare. All the time I was aware that it might be too late when I got there, that Zena would somehow have managed to end her life – and that I was in some way responsible. I'd known Zena was getting herself in a state over Michael's health and the future, but instead of reassuring her, I'd dithered over making the decision that had always been inevitable. Hazeling was a big house. There was nothing to stop Piers and me using a part of it for weekends whenever we wanted to. We could even have it divided up so that we didn't have to intrude on each other. If that was all Zena was worried about, I could set her mind at rest.

At last I saw the turning for the manor. It was dark now and I'd been using the headlights for some time. As I swung into the narrow gateway, I thought I saw the outline of a man's body in the shadows of the trees, but in an instant it was gone and I couldn't be sure. I was too concerned about Zena to think about it much. Even if someone was there, it was probably only a villager on a late-night walk. I could see the house now, almost every window blazing with light. Braking hard, I switched off the engine and jumped out even as Michael appeared in the open doorway.

'Aline,' he cried, hurrying towards me. 'Thank you for coming. I know I shouldn't have asked but . . .'

'Don't be silly,' I said. 'I know Piers would have come with me if he'd been at home. I just hope I can be of some use.'

'Zena's still in the attic,' he said. 'I can hear her moving about, but she won't answer me when I speak to her.'

'Well, I'll do what I can.'

He reached for my hand, pressing it gratefully. 'I feel better just knowing you're here, my dear.'

I removed my hand from his grasp. 'I came for Zena's sake.'

Michael dropped his eyes. 'I didn't imagine you had come for mine.'

There was bitterness in his voice, and I knew he was thinking of my accusation just before his last heart attack, and I hesitated. I desperately wanted to ask him the things I needed to know, but this wasn't the time.

'Has Zena said anything to you? Told you what's wrong?' I asked as he led the way inside.

'She won't speak to me at all. I blame myself for this, of course. I should have seen the signs. She's been preoccupied ever since – ' He broke off, avoiding my eyes as I looked at him.

'Since we came down?' I followed him through the hall and up the back stairs to the landing. He paused there for a moment, looking at me thoughtfully.

'It's been going on for a couple of months now.' His eyes were evasive, reflective. 'The truth is, I should never have married her, Aline. I'm too old for her and – and there are other problems . . .'

'What kind of problems?'

He shook his head. 'Perhaps we should talk about this later.'

I felt that there was something I ought to know, but he wasn't going to tell me. 'Perhaps I'd better go up to the attic alone.'

'Yes,' he agreed. 'Tell her that I'm not angry. All I want is for her to come out and be sensible.'

'Why don't you wait downstairs?'

He hesitated. 'Yes – that might be best. Be careful, Aline. She was in quite a state earlier.'

'Don't worry, I'm only going to talk to her. I can't force her to come out if she doesn't want to.'

He nodded, looked at me as if he wanted to say more, then turned and went downstairs. I waited until I was sure he'd gone, then I climbed the stairs to the tiny landing above. I knocked at the door, feeling awkward and not knowing how to begin. What did *I* know of Zena's problems? It was presumptuous of me to try to intervene between husband and wife, and yet I had to try. Michael was in no state to deal with his wife's hysterics. I just wished I understood what was going on.

'Zena, it's Aline. May I come in?'

There was silence; I waited and then knocked again, listening intently. This time I heard a slight movement the other side.

'Zena, I know you're upset, but I think we ought to talk. You know staying up there won't do any good, don't you?'

'Why should you care?' Zena's voice was low and petulant, like a sulky child's. 'You've got everything you want, haven't you? Why should you care about me?'

'Look, if this is about Hazeling, we can work something out. This is your home even if – well, don't worry about it. I was thinking we could divide the house. Piers and I can use one wing for weekends, and you can live in the main part, just as you do now. We can have a separate kitchen put in and – '

'It isn't about the house,' she said. 'You just don't understand, do you?'

'No, I don't, Zena,' I replied. 'But I'm willing to listen. Please open the door. Overdosing on sleeping pills won't help anyone. If you're worried about Michael, this is about the worst thing you could do. If you really care for him, don't do this to him.'

'Of course I care. I love him.'

There was silence for a moment, then I heard the sound of a key turning in the lock. Zena opened the door and stood just inside, an odd, defensive expression in her eyes. She came out and locked the door behind her, and slipped the key into her pocket. Then she turned to look at me.

'If Michael dies,' she said in a cold, brittle voice. 'You'll be his murderer, Aline, not me.'

She swung on her heel and walked down the stairs, leaving me staring after her.

For a moment I was too stunned to react, then I ran after Zena, catching her just as she reached the door of her bedroom. I took hold of her arm, and she swung round to face me, her eyes blazing.

'He doesn't love me,' Zena said fiercely. 'It's you he's always loved – why else would he paint all those pictures? I was just someone who happened to be around when he needed a shoulder to cry on.'

'What did you mean just now – about it being my fault Michael is ill?'

'Exactly what I said.' Her mouth twisted with bitterness. 'I don't know what you and Michael quarrelled over when you were down here last time, but it almost destroyed him. He told me he wished he could die, and that if it were not for the insurance, he would take his own life.'

'Insurance. . . ?' I frowned. 'Oh, you mean they wouldn't pay up if they thought it was suicide. But I can't believe he would – '

'Can't you?' Zena looked at me as if she hated me, and I was shocked by the intensity of her emotion. 'Ask him then. If you think I'm lying, ask him why he's trying to work himself to death.'

As I stared at her, unable to think what to say, she opened the door of her room and glanced back. 'Tell Michael I shan't do it again,' she said. 'Ask him to leave me alone for a while.'

Zena closed the door with a little snap and I turned away. If what

Zena had said was true . . . I took a deep breath, knowing that the time had come for asking the questions I'd avoided for so long. I had to know the truth now.

When I went into the drawing room, Michael was sitting in a high-backed chair, his head leaning against the worn leather wing, his eyes closed. His face looked so drawn that I paused, afraid of disturbing him, but even as I hesitated on the threshold, he seemed to become aware of my presence. He opened his eyes and smiled wearily.

'She's in her room,' I said. 'She asked me to tell you that she won't do it again.'

'I expect it was my fault,' he said. 'I know I haven't been easy to live with recently. I've also been unfair to her.'

'She says you're working too hard.'

'Painting is never work to me. Zena could never understand how much it means. And sometimes it's the only way I have of forgetting . . .'

He got up and went to the sideboard and poured himself a brandy from a decanter on a large silver tray. A wry smile touched his mouth as he saw my frown. 'Medicinal,' he said, raising the decanter again. 'Can I get you one?'

'A small one,' I said, and he looked amused. 'I could do with something on medicinal grounds myself. It was quite a shock when you rang earlier.'

'Yes.' His smile faded. 'I ought not to have phoned you, but Zena has no one of her own and I felt I couldn't cope alone. I'm sorry, Aline.'

'Don't apologize,' I muttered, feeling stifled by my stupid desire to weep. What was happening to me? Why was I getting so emotional these days? I'd thought I'd conquered all that ages ago. 'What I should like to know is why Zena is so unhappy that she tried to take her own life.'

'If she really did,' he said, and sighed as I looked puzzled. 'She must have heard me come in, and she was just standing there with the pills in her hand. She probably wanted me to find her. It could have been just another of her tantrums. She's rather prone to them when she can't get her own way.' I was silently disapproving and he shrugged. 'If that sounds callous, I'm sorry.'

'Neither of you seems very happy.'

'The marriage was a mistake.' Michael hesitated. 'Part of the problem is that Zena wants children, and we can't have them. It's physically impossible for her – and it seems I'm too old to adopt.'

'Too old? That's ridiculous!'

'Well, it's the official reason . . .' He looked away. 'Though I've wondered if there are others they're not giving.' His shoulders were stiff and I sensed the tension in him.

My throat went dry as I realized what he was getting at, and I couldn't speak.

He turned to face me. 'Yes, Aline,' he said. 'You weren't the only one to suspect me. The police questioned me after you were attacked. For a while they thought I might have done it – and that sort of thing lingers. I suppose it's on file somewhere, although in the end they seemed to accept my story, probably because you hadn't been raped and they didn't quite know what to make of it.'

'I hadn't. . . ?' For a moment the room seemed to spin crazily and I sat down in the nearest chair, feeling sick and dizzy.

Michael stared at me, looking shocked. 'You didn't know?' he said. 'You thought. . . ? All these years, you've thought. . . ?'

I gazed up at him as the room began to steady and my vision cleared. His face was white and stricken, just as it had been before he collapsed in the garden. I saw him reach for his pill box and pop one under his tongue. When I spoke, it was as if my voice came from a distance and had little to do with me, 'All Mother would tell me was that something bad had happened to me, and that because of it I wasn't to go out on the marshes alone with you any more.'

'My God! How could she?' He stared at me in horror. 'How could Sheila do that to you? To both of us!'

'Please,' I whispered, my heart thumping. 'I have to know – please tell me what really happened that day.'

His eyes were bleak. 'I wish I knew, Aline. I can tell you what happened before and after the attack, but I didn't see it. I wasn't there at the actual – '

'Tell me as much as you know. Please.'

He nodded, his eyes dark with sympathy as he looked at me. His colour had come back and his breathing was easier. 'We'd been on the marshes the day before. It was the day I painted that scene you've always . . .' He nodded to himself. 'So that's why you asked me not to sell.'

'Yes. It was always special to me – but go on. I remember we went looking for your palette knife, but nothing more.'

'We looked for it for half an hour or so, but we couldn't find it. I started to paint again and you kept on searching. I called to you, telling you not to bother, but you wouldn't give up. You kept saying it was

145

there somewhere.' Michael frowned, a flicker of pain in his eyes. 'I told you not to wander off on your own, but I suppose you didn't listen. I'd become engrossed in my work and when I glanced up you weren't there . . .' He paused, and I saw the guilt in his eyes.

'Is this too much for you?' I asked, concerned.

He shook his head. 'No. I'm all right now. I should have told you long ago, but every time I tried to get near you, Sheila . . . She blamed me, you know. And of course it was my fault. I was supposed to be looking after you. I've always blamed myself.'

'What happened then?' I asked, my eyes stinging as I heard the sadness in his voice and I began to understand that he too had suffered.

'I should have come looking for you at once.' His face reflected remembered grief. 'If I had . . . But there was a special light over the sea that day and I wanted to capture it. I was sure you would come back when you were ready. You'd never been afraid of the marshes, and I thought you were sensible enough not to get into trouble. What I hadn't reckoned with was . . .' He choked on the words and I waited until he recovered. 'It must have been an hour later that I began to get worried. I packed my painting things and started walking in the direction I thought you'd taken, calling your name . . . It was another hour before I found you. You were lying face down in a patch of sand, unconscious, your eyes closed. Your – your clothing had been torn and you were a mass of bruises, but the doctors said that you hadn't been interfered with sexually, though there was blood on your legs and that was everyone's instant assumption. At first I thought you were dead . . .' Michael looked at me then and I saw the horror in his face. 'In that instant I would have killed the bastard who – '

'Oh, Michael!' I caught back a sob. For years I'd lived in the shadow of my fears, and they were groundless. The sheer relief of it made me weak. 'It wasn't your fault. It wasn't your – ' And then I was crying and the words came bubbling out as I tasted the salt on my lips. 'I thought I was wicked and that you didn't love me any more. Mother said I was a naughty girl and that I wasn't to show my knickers and . . .'

I was sobbing as Michael took me into his arms, his large, thin hands stroking my hair. 'Hush now, my darling. I was the only one to blame. I should have looked after you. You did nothing wrong. Sheila was so upset and angry that she reacted badly. Try to understand; she became overprotective and scolded you too much, but it was only because she was frightened. She loved you so much. You could have died that day. It isn't surprising she was reluctant to let you out alone after that.'

'Oh, Michael.' I wept into his shoulder, feeling weak and shaky as the emotion drained out of me. A cloud had lifted and I was dizzy with relief. I could admit my love for my stepfather and not feel guilty or ashamed. 'I remembered you picking me up in your arms afterwards, then nothing more until I woke up in hospital.'

'You remembered me picking you up?' He drew back to look at me. 'But you said – you told the police you remembered nothing.'

'They frightened me,' I said. 'I was bewildered and confused. He – the policeman – looked so stern and I couldn't remember anything between you telling me not to stray and then you picking me up and saying that it was all right now. I didn't want you to get into trouble, so I just said I couldn't remember anything at all. The worst thing was that afterwards you seemed to turn against me.'

'Oh, my darling, that you should believe that,' he cried, then I felt him stiffen. He gave a startled cry and looked towards the door. My eyes followed the direction his had taken, and I drew away from him as I saw Zena, standing there, her face cold and tight with jealousy.

'Charming,' she said. 'I came to apologize, but I see I've wasted my time.'

'Don't go, Zena!' Michael cried, as she turned away. 'It isn't what you think. Aline was upset and I – '

'You rushed to comfort her, of course,' she said bitterly. 'Naturally, I wouldn't expect anything else. You've always had a – '

'Zena,' he warned. 'Don't be ridiculous. Aline is my stepdaughter.'

'Yes, that did make things awkward for you, didn't it?' she said. 'Don't think I don't know. You married me because you couldn't have her. You're obsessed with her. You always have been.'

'Zena! That's enough,' Michael cried, his face white and guilty as his eyes met mine and then slid away. 'That's enough!'

'I'm sorry,' I said, and the cloud that had lifted so briefly came down again at Zena's accusation. 'I wanted to help, but I seem to have made things worse.'

Zena had quietened. She stared at me in silence, and the measure of her inward struggle showed in her strained expression. Then she suddenly seemed to crumble, her shoulders sagging as she began to cry. Michael went to take her in his arms. She clung to him and I heard her choked apology.

Taking the opportunity to escape, I went upstairs to the room I'd shared with Piers. It was far too late to drive back to London. Besides, I was in a state of shock and I wanted to think. I needed to assimilate what Michael had told me about the incident on the marshes – and about my mother.

I'd been attacked but I hadn't been raped. Why hadn't someone told me before? All those years, all those nightmares . . .

I went down to the kitchen soon after eight the next morning. Zena was already there, and I caught the delicious aroma of fresh coffee.

'There you are,' Zena said, smiling as if the arguments of the previous evening had never existed. 'I was about to bring up a tray. I thought you weren't an early riser.'

'I'm not as a rule, but I want to get back to London.' I noticed that she was wearing a bright red and black knitted suit. She certainly had a flair for clothes, and plenty of them.

'Of course.' Zena frowned, her eyes dropping. 'I want to apologize for yesterday, Aline. Michael should never have asked you to come. I wouldn't have killed myself. I was just feeling so depressed . . .'

'If there's anything I can do?'

She shook her head, flushing. 'Michael says we should have a place of our own, and perhaps he's right.'

'Let's wait until the end of the trust, shall we? Perhaps we can sort something out. I'd like you to stay on here – if it's what you both want.'

She smiled slightly, looking a bit shamefaced. 'I'd like that – if Michael agrees.'

'Just give him time to think it over. I'm sure he'll see the sense of it. Hazeling needs someone to love it – and I think you do love it, don't you, Zena?'

Zena nodded and gave an awkward laugh. 'That's what Michael doesn't understand. It isn't just that it's a big house – I love the sense of generations having lived here . . .' She blushed as I smiled. 'It was my first real home. My parents were in the forces, and as a child I was dragged all over the world. When I met Michael I was living in a bedsit. Coming here was like entering paradise. It's such a wonderful house, it would be hard to leave now.'

'Well, don't worry about it,' I said. 'Let's try to be friends, Zena, for Michael's sake.'

She looked half-ashamed. 'It wasn't just the house or the money; there are other problems. I do love him, you know.'

'Yes, I've sensed that, Zena. I'm glad he has you. I'm afraid he's very ill. He seems so tired.'

'That's why I want him to rest more. But I've promised not to nag so much. It's his life. If he wants to paint . . .'

'Painting always has been his life,' I said. 'But he should think of you, too. I'll talk to him about the house before I go – and the trust. I'm not sure how much my capital will be, but it's bound to be far more than I need. I'm going to transfer a part of it into Michael's name, and then you will have an income for life if – well, if the worst happens.'

A deep flush swept up her neck into her cheeks. 'You're so generous, Aline. I feel awful after – '

'Well don't,' I said. 'We've both been awful to each other. I said some pretty rotten things to you the night I stormed out. Michael is my father, Zena. We – I misunderstood something that happened a long time ago, and we've grown apart, but I haven't forgotten how kind and gentle he was to me when I needed him. I'm doing this for him – and for his wife.' I smiled at Zena, willing her to understand.

'He might not accept,' Zena said.

'I think he will now,' I replied, and shook my head as she looked curious. 'Oh, there's no big secret, Zena. It's just that we understand things a little better now.'

Piers telephoned me at the flat later that day. 'I'm sorry I didn't ring last night,' he said. 'We had a three-hour delay on the flight and it would have been two in the morning in London by the time I got to a phone. I didn't want to wake you.'

'That was thoughtful of you,' I said, feeling a flood of relief. I didn't want to have to explain my trip to Hazeling over the phone; Piers might not understand. I would tell him when he came home, of course. 'How are things at your end? Can you sort it out?'

'It's just a matter of signing some forms. Everything was documented, so the authorities are satisfied with our handling of the affair. Unfortunately, that still means we lose the painting.'

'Aren't you insured for that sort of thing, Piers?'

'If it had come through an auction, we could have sued for the money, but this was a private purchase. I'm afraid it's down to experience. It will teach me to check more carefully next time, but it's not the end of the world. My main concern is that I had to leave you behind.'

'I miss you, darling,' I assured him. 'But it's OK. When will you be home?'

'A couple of days should finish it.' He hesitated. 'What are you going to do?'

'I'm planning a surprise for you when you get back.'

'What sort of a surprise?'

'If I tell you, it won't be, will it?'

He laughed, and the sound set me aching for the touch of his lips. 'No,

I suppose I'll just have to wait. Take care of yourself, Aline. I wish you were here.'

'So do I – you don't know how much. I love you, Piers. Come home soon, please.'

'Two days at most, but I'll ring you tomorrow.'

'Good. I can't wait.'

The room seemed achingly empty after I'd replaced the handset. I sat staring into space for a moment, then jumped up, smiling as I made up my mind. Piers had told me to do what I liked with the flat, but so far I hadn't rearranged anything. Before he returned from New York, I meant to transform the sitting room. I knew exactly what I wanted to do, but first I had to go shopping.

Chapter Twelve

Pushing back the damp hair from my forehead, I let my eyes travel round the room with satisfaction. It had taken me the whole of one day to paint the walls, but the soft shade of yellowish-beige had transformed the atmosphere of the room exactly as I'd hoped, and was a perfect background for the bronzed mirror. With the dark crimson of the Turkoman rugs I'd bought and the heavy bronze velvet curtains, the change was startling. Several green plants in various copper or pottery jardinières gave it a softer, lived-in feeling. I was delighted: Piers' credit card had done us proud. Bright, multicoloured cushions, books, records and oddments that I'd brought with me but left unpacked until now added the finishing touches. And, to my relief, Piers' picture blended in well.

I was heading for the bathroom and a much-needed shower when the street doorbell rang. For a moment I was tempted to ignore the bell, but whoever was there was persistent. I pressed the intercom button.

'Who is it?'

'Delivery of flowers for Mrs Aline Drayton.'

'Flowers . . .' Piers must have arranged for them before he left. 'Come on up,' I said. 'I'm pressing the release now.' Moving away, I glanced at my untidy appearance in the mirror. I was wearing my oldest jeans and sweatshirt, and my face was smeared with dirt.

When I opened the door all I could see was the huge bouquet of flowers, then the man carrying them poked his head out from behind. I caught my breath as I saw it was Nick.

'They aren't from me,' he said, before I could open my mouth. 'They had just been delivered downstairs so I offered to bring them up.'

'You used them to get up here under false pretences,' I said, frowning. 'Why didn't you just say it was you, Nick?'

'I thought you might refuse to see me. You cancelled our lunch date.'

'But Julie told you why,' I said, still vaguely uneasy as I stood back to let him enter. 'It was an emergency.'

Nick laid the flowers on the hall table. 'I thought you were giving me the brush-off.'

'I suppose it did look like that, but it wasn't true. I really did have to leave town in a hurry, and I wasn't certain when I would be back.'

He smiled his lazy smile. 'Sure, I believe you.'

'It's true, Nick.' I looked at the card with the flowers. They were from Michael.

'OK.' He looked at me, his smile fading. 'Julie said Piers was away for a few days – are you alone?'

'Yes. Why?' I asked warily. 'What do you want, Nick?'

He must have sensed my unease because he said, 'Don't look so nervous. Surely we can still talk to each other, Aline. Is there any chance of a cup of coffee?'

'I was just going to take a shower. I've been painting all day and I'm exhausted.' I grimaced at my paint-stained hands. 'I must look a sight.'

'You look beautiful,' he said, and glanced round. 'And you've done a great job. I'll have to hire you to do my place over. So no coffee, huh?' He looked so like a puppy pleading to be forgiven for some misdemeanour that I gave in.

'Just one quick one then,' I said with a reluctant laugh. 'Come on into the kitchen – and bring the flowers, will you?'

'Yes, ma'am.' He gave a mocking salute and followed me into the kitchen. 'So how's life?' he asked, perching on one of the high stools.

'Good,' I said. I switched on the percolator and took matching mugs from a shelf. 'I'm very happy. How are you, Nick?'

'Getting old and decrepit.' He sat watching me as I moved about the kitchen. Glancing at him, I saw the longing in his eyes and turned away, confused. 'I'm thinking of giving up my wild decadent ways and settling down.'

'What would you do? You'd get bored in a month.'

He shrugged, his eyes hidden by thick dark lashes. It was surprising that a man with hair as light as his should have such dark eyelashes, I thought, then gave myself a mental scolding.

'Maybe, but I've got a few ideas to try out. If the worst happens I can always work for a regional TV station.'

'I can't see you reporting the local agricultural show,' I said, turning as the coffee machine began to make little plopping noises. 'Cream or milk?'

'Black, two sugars.' He cocked an eyebrow. 'You haven't forgotten already?'

Blushing at the reminder of our former intimacy, I found a vase for the roses and carnations Michael had sent me to say thank you for going down to Hazeling, and left the card on the table.

'So,' I said as Nick began to sip his coffee, 'what was it you wanted to tell me?'

Nick was uncharacteristically hesitant. 'I'm not sure how to put this, Aline. It concerns Piers . . .'

'Piers?' I echoed, staring at him in surprise. 'I didn't think you knew him.'

'I don't, not personally.' His expression was grim as he went on, 'There was just something about the name – it triggered something in my mind. I'm like that, Aline. If I've worked on a story, the details stay buried in my subconscious forever.'

'So?' I waited for him to come to the point, the hairs on the back of my neck beginning to prickle. 'What about Piers?'

'You aren't going to like this, Aline, but you have to know . . .'

'Well, tell me then.'

'I worked on a story five years ago.' Nick paused, and I dug my nails into the palms of my hands. 'I went down to the reference library and got it all out. A woman was killed in a car accident – '

'Her name was Helena,' I said, relieved. For a moment I'd thought it was going to be something else. 'She was engaged to Piers but they quarrelled and she broke it off, then she went off in a temper and drove her car into a tree. I know. He told me about it.'

Nick's eyes narrowed until they almost closed. I thought he looked like a cat that was about to devour a saucer of cream. 'The thing is . . .' He paused for effect. 'The police were never sure that it was an accident.'

'What do you mean?' Then the implications of what Nick was saying hit me and I was furiously angry.

'She was rich, Aline, and she had just drawn a large sum of cash – money that was never found.' As I drew breath, ready for the onslaught, he went on quickly, seemingly determined that I should hear it all. 'One of the tyres on her car was almost bald. The police found a perfectly good tyre in the boot of – '

I didn't let him finish. 'Get out, Nick. I won't listen to any more of this slander.' I was hurt and disappointed. 'I can't believe you would do this,' I said. 'Not you, Nick.'

He stood up, looking at me unhappily. 'I suppose you hate me now, but no matter what you think, Aline, I am your friend. If you ever need me, I'll be around.'

I was so furious I didn't know what I was saying. 'Then you'll wait until Hell freezes over!'

'The police never closed the file,' he said as he turned away. 'I'm sorry, Aline. I thought you should know.'

'Get out before I throw something!'

Nick didn't say anything else. Perhaps he knew it would have been pointless, as I wouldn't have listened. I was angry that he should be jealous and mean-spirited enough to insinuate something so awful about Piers. I stood staring after Nick until I heard the door slam, and the spell broke. When I remembered how upset Piers had been when he'd told me about Helena, I felt disgusted with Nick. He had dug up as much dirt as he could to try and make Piers sound like . . . like a murderer. How could Nick say such terrible things? Was he trying to hurt me? He couldn't really believe that Piers had been responsible for Helena's accident.

Still upset by his behaviour, I swept the coffee mugs into the kitchen sink and went through to the bathroom. I needed my shower.

The warm water was refreshing. I let it cascade over me, soaking my hair and my skin, and enjoyed the sharp, invigorating fragrance of the gel Piers liked so much. It evoked the scent of his body and helped me to calm down. I was not going to let Nick upset me. I was looking forward to an early night and the new paperback I'd bought.

I wrapped myself in a large white towel, and walked into the bedroom. Piers' case and various packages were lying on the bed. My heart jerked. Piers was home! 'Piers!' I cried, running across the hall to the living room. 'Are you there?'

The kitchen door was open. He was standing by the table, looking at Michael's card. He was frowning as he turned to look at me, and my heart sank as I saw his face.

'Michael sent me some flowers,' I said, sensing an outburst and trying to diffuse the situation. 'I didn't hear you come in, darling. I wasn't expecting you home until tomorrow.'

'Obviously.' The sarcasm in his voice was like a whiplash. ' "To my dearest Aline," ' he read. ' "With my sincere thanks for listening and being so understanding. Love, Michael." '

'Yes, wasn't that nice of him. I needed a shower and the – the flowers came just as – ' I averted my gaze as his eyes flicked towards the used coffee cups. 'Rita popped in and I haven't had time to wash the mugs.'

'Don't lie to me, Aline. I told you once before, I hate liars.' His look was razor-sharp. 'Michael has been here, hasn't he?'

'No. I promise you that isn't true.' I took a chance. If he guessed the truth he would be even angrier than he was already. 'I went down to Hazeling the day you left for New York . . .'

'You what?' That pulse was beating at his temple. 'I think you had better explain.'

154

I felt my cheeks getting hot under his scrutiny. 'Zena tried to kill herself. Michael took the pills away from her but she locked herself in the attic and he didn't know what to do.'

'So he came running to you?' Piers frowned but some of the ice had left his eyes. 'Why didn't you tell me on the phone?'

'I didn't think it was important, Piers,' I lied, not quite meeting his eyes. I'd hoped to avoid a row by picking the right moment to tell him, but now I realized my mistake. 'Anyway, it's all over now. Zena has calmed down and I think we've sorted it all out.'

'What do you mean by that?'

'I'm going to settle some money on Michael when the trust ends on my birthday. I'll be in control of my inheritance then so . . .' I dried up as I saw his frown. 'It wasn't him on the marshes that day,' I said hastily, thinking I understood the reason for Piers' annoyance. 'We finally talked about the attack and he told me what happened. I wasn't sexually abused; I was bruised and hurt but that's all. You can't imagine the relief.'

'And you believed him? Just like that?'

'What do you – Michael wouldn't lie, Piers.' I was on the defensive again.

For a moment he seemed as if he wanted to argue, then he shrugged, and I felt the moment of danger was passed.

'Well, you know how you feel about him, Aline. If it makes you happy to believe he's innocent, I'm not going to quarrel with you. But I would rather you didn't go running off to Hazeling every time Michael calls.'

I took a deep breath. 'It was an emergency.'

'So you say.' He looked down at me. 'As for this settlement, I should think about it if I were you – but that's your affair, not mine.'

'Don't be angry about it, Piers,' I said, gazing up at him pleadingly. 'After all, the money can't mean anything to you, can it?'

He hesitated for a moment. 'I'm not exactly flush with it at the moment, but it's your inheritance, Aline. My problems are only temporary.'

'Oh dear,' I said, feeling guilty. 'I've just spent a few hundred on that credit card you got me.'

Piers' smile was wry as he came to take me in his arms. 'A few hundred is neither here nor there, Aline. You're my wife. I expect to pay your bills.' He looked down at me for a moment and then he crushed me against him. I felt a shudder run through his body as he brought his lips down to mine. 'I'm a jealous brute, my darling. When I saw that card I thought – '

155

'You didn't think, you just got angry,' I said, smiling up at him. Thank goodness he'd dropped the subject of the coffee mugs! If he ever found out that Nick had been here in the kitchen, I dreaded to think what he might imagine. 'Michael is my stepfather, Piers. I feel I owe him and Zena something – but I love you. You mean everything to me.'

'Do I?' Piers' eyes clouded as he looked down at me. 'I'd like to believe that, Aline.'

'But you must,' I cried. 'It hurts me so much when you doubt me.'

'I'm sorry, darling,' he said, stroking my cheek with one finger. Piers had big hands, the fingers long and square at the tips. His touch made me tremble, and he frowned. 'You're not afraid of me, are you? I know I can be cruel when I'm angry. I strike out without thinking, but it's only because I'm so jealous. I don't want anyone else in your life. I want all of you.'

'But you have all of me,' I said, ignoring his question. Sometimes his moods frightened me, but nothing would have made me admit it. 'Don't let's quarrel any – ' I got no further. His mouth was crushing mine in a bruising, demanding kiss. My body swayed into his and he swept me up in his arms and carried me into the bedroom.

'I want you so much,' he muttered. 'I don't think I could stand it if you left me.'

'Don't, Piers,' I whispered, my lips feverish against his throat. 'I want only you.'

It was a long, long time later that we lay sprawled lazily on the bed, drinking coffee and relaxing in a languorous aftermath, and I turned to Piers. 'Did you really think I had a thing for Michael?'

'Forget it,' Piers said. 'It was said to hurt you, because I was jealous.'

'I – I was always fond of him as a child. It spoilt things when I thought . . . But he's explained all that.'

'Just what did he say?' Piers seemed more curious than angry now. 'So he didn't see any sign of this attacker then?'

'No. He must have gone by the time Michael arrived.'

'If he was ever there and not a figment of your stepfather's imagination.'

'You can't mean that, Piers.' I was anxious again. He seemed determined to turn me against my stepfather. 'Why should Michael lie now?'

'Because of the money.' I shook my head. 'Or because he's afraid of how you would react to the truth. His feelings towards you are not those of a father for his daughter – that much I know.'

I was sitting on the side of the bed, my face turned away from him. 'I can't accept that, Piers. I'm uncomfortable with it.'

'It's still true, Aline. I'm not the only one who thinks it. Why do you imagine Zena is so jealous of you?'

'It's because of Michael,' I admitted reluctantly. 'But that doesn't mean he . . .'

'But you've always suspected it, haven't you?'

I nodded once, unable to deny it but loath to agree. 'I even thought it might be him making those strange phonecalls – not the one you answered, I'm satisfied that that was just a crank – but the first calls were different. More personal.'

'There you are then.'

'But now I realize I was wrong,' I said, my conviction growing even as he looked doubtful. 'No, Piers, I'm sure it couldn't have been Michael. I'm *sure* of it.'

Piers thought for a moment. 'The calls frightened you so much because the man seemed to know all about you?'

'When it first happened, yes. It was uncanny, the way he knew the details. He – he knew about the marshes. He asked me if I remembered.'

'Doesn't that make it more likely to have been Michael?'

'No, I don't think so.' I twisted the sheet between my fingers, wishing I hadn't brought the subject up. 'I've been thinking it over recently. Anyone could have read that old report. It was in all the papers.'

'Yes,' Piers agreed at last. His expression was strange, and when he spoke his words chilled me. 'The calls could have been made by the man who attacked you.'

My mouth went dry and my heart began to thump. 'I thought so at the time – but surely he wouldn't have dared?'

I felt cold and very threatened. Why was Piers doing this to me? He must know the effect it would have.

'He might have been following your life with interest, Aline. If he attacked you, there must have been some reason for it, don't you think?' As I gazed at Piers and tried to make sense of what he was saying, he seemed to warm to his theme, almost as though he was trying to force me to some conclusion. 'Perhaps you saw something you shouldn't have done. Perhaps this man has lived with the fear that you might one day remember everything. It might even be that having let you live, he feels that your life belongs to him.'

My skin crawled with fear as my imagination took over. The idea of the man who had attacked and almost killed me continuing to watch me from a distance was terrifying. I could imagine him following me, spying on me . . . plotting to kill me.

'Piers, don't. You're scaring me.'

I was trembling and I felt sick. Piers lay quietly at my side, then he stirred. 'I'm sorry, darling.' He reached out and touched my hand. 'Let's talk about something else. Open the presents I brought you.'

I looked at the parcels we'd taken off the bed and put on the floor. 'Which one is for me?'

'They're all for you,' he said, laughing. 'I don't see any more wives round here, do you?' He leaned over, lifting the duvet to peer under the bed. 'Unless she's under here . . .'

'Oh, Piers.' I giggled with relief as he tossed me a bulky parcel, relieved that his mood had passed. 'You spoil me.'

Opening the bag, I drew out a beautiful pale grey simulated fur coat. The Italian designer label told me a donation had been made to wildlife conservation. It was a fake, but so gorgeously soft and silky that no one could want the real thing.

'Put it on,' Piers said, his tone gentle now. 'The girl in the shop told me she would rather have a coat like that than a dozen furs. Apparently it's the in thing. She thought it was my idea, but I told her you were the one who had a conscience, and she said you obviously had both taste and compassion, and I was lucky to get you. As it happens, I agree with her.'

'Flatterer!' I slipped the coat on, holding it around my shoulders to parade barefooted about the bedroom as if I were on a catwalk. Then I went back to Piers and bent to kiss him. 'Thank you, darling. It's lovely.'

'Open this now.' He handed me a long slim package. 'You don't have any objections to diamond or emerald mines, do you?'

Opening the box, I stared in amazement at the magnificent bracelet. It was platinum with large emeralds set in squares of pure white diamonds. 'This must have cost a fortune,' I said, remembering what he'd said about not being flush with money just now. 'You shouldn't have . . .' I saw the warning flash in his eyes and checked myself. 'It's gorgeous! I love it, and no, I don't have a conscience about diamond mines . . .' I smiled as Piers drew me to him. 'Maybe you should go away more often – and I don't mean because of the presents.'

'Because of this then?' he asked, his tongue flicking delicately at my breasts, his hands caressing my back; I was still naked beneath the coat. 'Or this?' His voice was husky as he rolled me on to the bed and trapped me with his body.

'Let me at least take off the coat,' I whispered, but he covered my mouth with his own, his hand moving down to part my legs.

With a shock of pain and pleasure, I gasped as he drove into me, with a shudder I responded to his savage thrusting. The bracelet slipped from my fingers to the floor, my nails dug into his back and I moaned. I murmured his name over and over again. It went on and on, and all I could hear was the harsh sound of Piers' breathing and my own cries of pleasure.

I awoke to find Piers at the bedside with a tray of tea. He was wearing the comfortable old grey jersey tracksuit he used for his early-morning runs, and I realized he'd already taken his regular exercise. I pulled a face at him as he opened the curtains, and blinked in the sudden brightness.

'Why are you so disgustingly fit and healthy first thing in the morning?' I groaned. 'I need at least an hour to come alive.'

I was feeling a little queasy in the mornings, though the symptoms seemed to have eased considerably. I'd been too busy to visit my doctor over the past few days, but I would have to find the time soon. Perhaps I'd been putting it off because I was already certain in my own mind? Perhaps I did not want to tell Piers?

'You should take up jogging,' Piers said with a grin. 'You're wasting half your life in that bed – or perhaps waste is the wrong word.'

I saw a certain look in his eyes and threw a pillow at him. 'Sometimes I could hit you!'

'Feel free, darling.' He handed me a cup of tea. 'So what are you going to do today?'

'I've no idea – any suggestions?'

'Well, there's a sale of paintings at Sotheby's I want to view this morning. You could come with me if you like, then we could have lunch somewhere.'

'I'd like that.'

Dressing quickly in the new Escada suit and silk shirt Piers had bought me just before he went to America, I went through to the living room. Piers was standing by the window, frowning. I saw he had opened all the letters that had come for him while he was away, including the one with the distinctive blue print. He looked annoyed, and I thought perhaps he didn't like the changes I'd made.

'We can put it back the way it was if you don't like it, darling,' I said. 'It's only a coat of paint.'

He blinked and looked at me. 'The room is fine, Aline. Much

better . . .' His frown deepened. 'Michael was on the phone just now. He's got some paintings together for the exhibition and he wants us to go down this weekend.'

'Oh.' I looked at him warily, but his frown cleared.

'I told him we would drive down on Friday evening. Is that all right with you?'

'Yes, of course. I've invited Tony and Julie for dinner on Thursday, but we've nothing on for the weekend.'

'You've invited . . .' Piers looked annoyed. 'I wish you'd told me earlier, Aline. I've arranged to view a house sale up north on Wednesday and Thursday. I thought you might come with me.'

'I suppose I could put them off.'

'No, don't bother,' he said. 'I might be back in time. If not, you'll have to make my excuses.' He glanced at his watch. 'Now I'd better take my shower, or we'll be late.'

We spent just over an hour at Sotheby's, looking at pictures Piers was interested in buying. I found it fascinating to watch him at work. He seldom even glanced at the catalogue, his keen eyes picking out immediately those that appealed to him. Quite often they were not the ones that caught my attention, and some were in an appalling condition. He smiled as he saw me looking doubtfully at a canvas he had marked with a tick on his list.

'Don't you like it, Aline?'

'It needs cleaning,' I said. 'I can't judge it as it is.'

'It hasn't been treated well,' he agreed, 'and I may get it for a reasonable price, but there's no real damage. It's a Morland. In this condition I may be able to buy it for under five hundred. I acquired my first Morland for twenty pounds almost eleven years ago.'

'You must have handled so many pictures,' I said. 'How do you remember them all?'

'I don't – that one was special for me.' He shook his head as I looked inquiring. 'It was when I was just beginning to make something of my life . . . to shake off the past.'

'What do you mean, Piers?'

'It doesn't matter.' His eyes darkened for a moment and he seemed lost in his thoughts, then he shrugged and marked his list. 'I've finished here. Do you mind if we call at the gallery before lunch?'

'No, of course not,' I said.

I presumed he had been thinking about the way his friend Bill had died. I wished I knew how to reach him when he was in this mood, but

160

he was seldom willing to talk of the past – and I sensed that there was something more he hadn't told me.

While Piers was in the gallery, I passed the time browsing round a small antique shop nearby. I was looking for a present for him, but I wasn't sure what he would like. I'd noticed that when he did buy himself something it was always of the best quality. His suits were custom-made, as were his shoes. Most of his shirts and ties were silk, but he preferred cotton socks and underwear. He already owned more than sufficient of everything. His watch – which kept perfect time – was solid eighteen-carat gold. He wore no other jewellery. He drank sparingly and hated cigarettes. All of which made finding a present for him particularly difficult.

I was no nearer to solving my problem half an hour later. There were several pieces of silver that I found attractive, but nothing that I thought would appeal particularly to Piers. Discovering an antique silver baby's rattle, I lingered over it, then decided to wait until I was certain about my pregnancy. I left the shop without buying anything when I saw Piers emerge from the gallery.

He noticed I was empty-handed. 'Nothing you fancied?'

'Not really. How did you get on?'

'They hadn't bought much,' he said, and frowned. 'But there's a call in Hampstead this afternoon. Would you like to come with me? I understand it's an elderly woman who was several pictures to sell. She asked if a woman could go, so it would help me if you came. I think she may be a bit on the nervous side.'

'Would it really be a help to you?' I was pleased to think that I could do something for him. 'I'd love that, Piers.'

I felt very happy as we lunched at L'Escargot and then drove out to Hampstead.

Piers' call was at a big house set in large, overgrown gardens near the edge of the Heath. Surrounded by wrought-iron railings with spikes on top, it was sheltered from view by tall trees and thick holly bushes. There was an intercom on the gate, and another on the door. The big iron gates opened, then locked themselves automatically after the car entered. It seemed that the owner was more than a little nervous.

Mrs Pearson was in her late sixties, a tall, upright woman with neat grey hair and expensive but rather old-fashioned clothes. Her hands were wrinkled and swollen with arthritis, but she was wearing several rings with huge diamonds and a gold and turquoise bracelet that might have been Victorian. As she let us in, she smiled and apologized for all the security.

161

'You must think it odd,' she said, shaking hands, 'but since my husband died, I've been afraid of intruders.'

Glancing around the room into which she led us, I understood the reason for her precautions. It was full of antiques of every kind: gilt clocks under glass domes, two marquetry longcase clocks in the drawing room and another in the hall through which we'd passed; large porcelain figures and groups that could have been Chelsea or Derby and were worth a lot of money, huge Chinese vases, cabinets crowded with silver and little gold snuff boxes, as well as the paintings, which were clustered on all the walls.

'My husband was a keen collector,' Mrs Pearson explained with a sad, sweet smile. 'He just went on and on buying, and as he never sold anything, I'm afraid the collection rather took us over.'

'You have some beautiful things,' I said. 'It must be very expensive to insure all this.'

'Oh, I gave up trying to insure everything years ago,' she said. 'I couldn't possibly afford it. That's why I've decided to sell a few bits and pieces, Mrs Drayton. I was recommended to your husband by a friend . . .' She glanced at Piers, frowning. 'Will you take a glass of sherry, or a cup of coffee first, Mr Drayton?'

'Coffee for me – if it's no trouble.' He glanced at me and I nodded.

'Yes, please.' I looked hesitantly at Mrs Pearson.

'Would you mind if I wandered round the room a little? I'm interested in antiques and I'd like to look at some of your treasures, if I may.'

'Please do,' the old lady said. 'My husband liked to show his things to visitors. If you've time, I'll take you over the house later. Perhaps your husband could give me some advice about the things I want to sell.' She looked at Piers again, that slight frown in her eyes. 'I keep thinking that we've met before, Mr Drayton, but I can't imagine where.'

Piers turned, studying her with sudden intentness. His eyes narrowed and it seemed to me he was uneasy. Then he dismissed the suggestion. 'I'm sure I would have remembered. I have a good memory for faces. Perhaps we bumped into one another at an auction once.'

I had a feeling that he was lying. But if he had remembered the old lady, why didn't he just say so?

'It would have been many years ago, when Bob was alive,' she said. 'Forgive me, it's probably just my memory playing tricks again. I'll get our coffee.'

Piers glanced at me as she went out. 'I don't think she has any idea what all this stuff is worth,' he said. 'She really needs professional

162

advice, but I'll do what I can. It means we may have to spend more time here than I'd planned. You won't be bored, will you?'

'She's a dear,' I said. 'And I'm fascinated by all these wonderful things. Just look at those snuff boxes, Piers. Even one of those would fetch several hundred in an auction.'

He glanced at the collection in the antique vitrine. 'I'm not an expert, but I think you're right.'

I nodded. *'Have* you met her before?'

I saw a flicker of annoyance in his eyes, but then it was gone and I thought I might have imagined it.

'I shouldn't think so for a moment.' He moved away to study a painting on the wall.

Mrs Pearson returned with a tray, and poured coffee into delicate porcelain cups.

'I was just saying you need an expert opinion on the antiques, too.' Piers accepted his coffee, perching on the edge of a gilt-framed sofa. 'These collections are worth a small fortune.'

'Oh, I expect so,' she said, unsurprised. 'I couldn't sell anything from the house. Bob wouldn't like it. No, it's the stuff in the sheds I want to clear. I'm not sure if you will want any of the pictures, Mr Drayton. There are about twenty or so stored there, I think.'

'I'll certainly have a look for you. And I'll give you my opinion of what you could get at auction for anything else you might want to dispose of.'

She smiled and stood up. 'Shall we go then? I'll lead the way; it's right through the house and down at the back of the garden, I'm afraid.' She glanced at my shoes, which were high-heeled. 'The paths are a bit overgrown, my dear.'

'Don't worry,' I reassured her. She was a very pleasant person and I'd taken an immediate liking to her. 'I'm looking forward to seeing the pictures, Mrs Pearson.'

'Oh, do call me Phyllis,' she said.

'Wasn't she great?' I asked Piers as we drove through the big iron gates an hour or so later. 'And all that stuff in the shed! It should bring her in a lot of money, don't you think?'

'The paintings alone are worth in the region of twenty to thirty thousand pounds,' he replied. 'I didn't tell her, because I want to work my figures out and give it to her in writing.'

'I could see she was shocked when you told her that bronze figure was probably worth several thousand pounds.'

'That figure of a hunter?' He nodded thoughtfully. 'It's probably Italian, sixteenth or seventeenth century. I would expect it to make at least six thousand at auction, but it could fetch twice as much on a good day.'

I agreed with him. If anything, it would make more. 'I hope she gets a good auction house in to value her things.'

'Why didn't you tell her about Mr Silcott?' Piers glanced at me. 'I should have thought it was just his sort of thing – a good mixture of bric-a-brac and some decent pieces.'

'Do you think I should have suggested it? I didn't like to volunteer in case she thought I was being pushy.'

'She liked you. I'm sure she would be grateful for your help.' He smiled at my diffidence. 'Why don't you give her a ring tomorrow and ask if she would like you to make an appointment for her?'

'Yes, I will,' I said. 'It can't do any harm, can it?'

Piers left on his buying trip without me. I hadn't believed he would go when it came to it, and I was a little upset; but he said it would probably have been boring for me anyway and I wasn't to worry.

'It's your first dinner party at the flat,' he said. 'You can't cancel it. I'm just sorry I won't be around.'

'You couldn't manage to get back in time?'

'Well, I might,' he said, kissing my cheek in an off-hand way. 'But don't count on it.'

I had a feeling that he didn't want to be there for the party, and I resented it. He might have made an effort, for my sake. I had a suspicion that he wasn't keen on becoming too intimate with my friends, but then I dismissed it as being ridiculous.

After Piers left, I felt a bit down, but I started to prepare for the next evening and my spirits lifted. It would have been nicer if Piers had been around, but I wasn't going to let it get to me.

Rather than have just the three of us, I'd invited Rita and Tim to make the numbers up a little. Julie raised her eyebrows when she realized Piers wasn't going to be present, but she didn't comment.

She followed me into the kitchen while the others were talking in the sitting-room. 'I had a call from Nick the other day,' she said.

'Don't talk to me about him.' I banged down a copper-bottomed pan. 'Do you know what he had the effrontery to tell me?'

Julie nodded, her eyes serious.

'He knows you're angry with him, Aline. He just thought you ought to be told, in case there was something in it. You hardly knew Piers when you married him . . .'

164

I flushed with annoyance. 'But it's so ridiculous, Julie. Piers had already told me about Helena. It upset him so much that it was years before he could think of starting another serious relationship. I mean – why should Piers want to . . . It was a disgusting thing to imply!'

'Well, of course there was never any proof that it wasn't a straightforward accident,' Julie admitted, obviously torn between Nick and me. I was a little annoyed that she should take his side and said so, which made my friend spring to Nick's defence. 'Nick might have allowed his jealousy to colour his conclusions, but he was concerned about you, Aline. And he has grounds for questioning the accident –the police couldn't get anywhere in their investigation.'

'Surely you don't think there's anything in it?'

Julie looked uncomfortable. 'No, of course I don't, Aline. It was just that . . . Forget it. Nick was following his reporter's instincts, that's all.'

'Go on,' I said, glaring at her. 'You're thinking something, so you might as well come out with it.'

'It was just what Ronnie said at the party.' Julie avoided my eyes. 'She was annoyed after their argument and she said Piers Drayton was a dangerous man to have as an enemy. She made quite a point of it.'

'What was that supposed to mean?'

'I've no idea,' Julie said, flicking a strand of hair out of her eyes. 'Sour grapes, I should think. Forget it, Aline. I wish I hadn't brought the subject up. It was only that Nick seemed so concerned about you . . .' She broke off and looked at me unhappily.

'Nick is jealous,' I said, realizing that I'd come close to having a row with my best friend. 'I'm afraid I did treat him badly. But I thought it was over.'

'I did try to warn you.'

'Yes, I know. It was just such a rush. Piers wanted to get married at once and I – and I couldn't help myself.' I knew that sounded peculiar, but it was true.

'No regrets?'

'None. Piers is a wonderful husband, Julie. He spoils me all the time. Really, I couldn't be happier.'

'Then take no notice of me or Nick,' Julie said, looking contrite. 'I'm sorry, Aline. One of the first rules of being a counsellor is not to force your advice on friends. It's just that, well, I see so much unhappiness at the clinic.'

'You weren't pushing your advice.' I smiled at her. 'We both need a sounding board now and again. Nick's attitude upset me, that's all. Let's forget it.'

'Good idea. That fish smells delicious. Is it a new recipe?'

'It's one of Piers',' I said. 'When he's home he does most of the cooking.'

'Now that is something.' Julie laughed, clearly relieved that a quarrel had been avoided. 'All Tony can do is burn the toast!'

I fiddled with the twisted leather belt at my waist. 'Anyway, I'm determined to make the marriage work.' Julie looked at me, sensing something, and I nodded. 'I went to the doctor this morning and it's confirmed – I'm pregnant.'

'Oh, Aline,' Julie cried, hugging me. 'That's wonderful! Have you told Piers yet?'

I shook my head. 'I wanted to be sure. I'm going to tell him when he gets back.'

Chapter Thirteen

'How was it then?' Piers asked as he kissed me. It was a proper kiss this time, not the off-hand peck I'd received before he left. 'I'm sorry I couldn't get back in time for your little party, darling, but something came up and I had to take a detour.'

I let that pass.

'Did you buy some interesting paintings?'

He shook his head. 'No, unfortunately it turned out to be a waste of time – but that's something you learn to live with in this business.'

Why did I have the feeling that the whole trip had been merely a way of avoiding the party, and that Piers had been punishing me for not consulting him in the first place?

I held my breath and crossed my fingers behind my back. 'I've got something to tell you, Piers. I hope you'll be pleased . . .'

'You've rung Mrs Pearson and she says she wants to sell the pictures?' He looked amused as I shook my head. 'Well, it's obviously exciting. Don't keep me in suspense.'

'I – we're having a baby . . .' I faltered as I saw the shock in his face. There was a pause. 'You're not pleased. You think it's too soon, don't you?'

For a moment he stared at me in silence, his expression unreadable, and I felt a terrible disappointment. He didn't want the child. There was a flicker of something in his eyes that told me he wasn't ready to be a father, a look almost of rejection – of revulsion. I blinked hard, feeling the sting of tears. Then Piers suddenly moved. He swept me up in a fierce hug, holding me so tightly that it was difficult to breathe, and when he spoke his voice caught with emotion.

'I can't believe it,' he choked. 'My God! A child! I hadn't expected – you didn't say anything, Aline.' He drew back, looking into my face. 'You do mean it, don't you? It's certain?'

'It's certain,' I whispered. 'You don't mind, Piers? I know it's quick but – '

'Mind?' he said in a hoarse voice. 'I'm stunned, breathless, in total shock – but very grateful, darling. I can't tell you what this means to me. I just hope you don't resent the idea of being a mother so soon.'

'I love it,' I said, laughing now as I saw that his initial reaction had been misleading. 'I was afraid you might not.'

'Then you can stop worrying. I'm delighted.' He kissed me gently, looking down into my face. 'Surely you know that all I want is your happiness.'

'Oh, Piers,' I whispered as I moved back into his arms. 'I do love you so much.'

'And I love you,' he said.

He had given me the reassurance I'd wanted, and his kiss was warm, strong and as passionate as ever, and yet deep within me there was still a small nagging worry that something was not quite as it should be. I felt uneasy, but I didn't know why.

For a moment I wasn't sure what had woken me. Then I realized that the bed was cold and empty beside me. Piers wasn't there. I switched on the bedside lamp, slipped on a soft satin robe, and went through to the sitting room. It was empty. Obviously, he had gone out, but it was only two o'clock in the morning. Surely he couldn't have gone for a run at this hour? I knew he liked to exercise, but this didn't make sense.

I didn't want to go back to bed, so I went into the kitchen and made myself a coffee, then I curled up on the sofa with a book. These odd disappearances of Piers' worried me, and I was determined to find out what was behind them. It was almost five when Piers came in. I heard his key in the lock and went to meet him. He looked put out to find me waiting for him, though his voice was gentle as he said, 'What's wrong, darling? Couldn't you sleep?'

'I woke up and you weren't there.' I studied his face; his expression was unreadable. 'I was worried about you, Piers. Are – are you angry with me?'

'Don't be silly, Aline.' He walked through to the kitchen and filled the kettle. 'I just went for a run, that's all. I like to exercise when I need to think about something.'

'What is so important that you have to get up in the middle of the night?'

'Business problems – nothing for you to worry about.'

'Don't shut me out, Piers. If something is worrying you, I would like to know.'

For a moment his eyes were angry, then he nodded. 'Things aren't going so well with the American gallery. I may have to close it, but I'm not sure yet.'

'Can I help? I could get an advance on my trust . . .'

'I prefer to sort this out myself.' Piers turned away. 'Tea or coffee?'

'Tea, please. Piers, I'd like to help.'

'No!' He was frowning as he looked at me. 'Just forget it, Aline. You insisted on knowing why I needed some exercise, so I told you. Don't make a thing out of it. For heaven's sake, don't nag. I can't stand women who nag. I had enough of that when I was a child. She just wouldn't leave me alone. She wouldn't stop nagging me.'

'Do you mean your grandmother?'

'The old bitch never stopped nagging.'

I was shocked by the hatred in his voice. I'd known that Piers' childhood had been unhappy, but this was something more. I sensed that I was on very dangerous ground and I went to lay my hand on his arm.

'I'm sorry. I didn't mean to nag . . . I love you, Piers. I was just worried about you.'

For a moment he was silent and I saw that his hands were clenched into tight fists, then he took me in his arms, holding me pressed against him.

'I'm the one who should be sorry,' he said into my neck. 'You're not her. I don't mean to hurt you. Forgive me. It's just that sometimes I need time to myself, Aline; especially when I'm uptight. It – the pressure builds up inside me and I have to fight it. The only way I can do that is by using up all that excess energy. I'm sorry if you feel shut out, but it's the only way I can cope.'

Looking up at him, I caught fear in his eyes. It was only there for a moment, then the shutters came down and he was smiling again. He released me and went to make the tea.

'My financial difficulties are temporary, darling. Believe me, there's nothing for you to worry about. Besides, I don't want you upset – not now the baby is on the way.'

'And you're really pleased about the baby?'

'Of course,' he said, but his eyes didn't meet mine.

'I so want you to be pleased about it, Piers,' I said.

'Yes, I know.' His voice was tender, caressing.

I stared at him. Feeling suddenly cold, I shivered, and Piers looked at me in concern.

'Go back to bed, darling,' he said. 'I'll bring the tea in on a tray – and stop worrying. Everything is going to be fine. I've got it all worked out now. I know exactly what I have to do.'

*

169

'It was so kind of you to come yourself,' Phyllis Pearson said, taking my hand. Hers trembled a little, and I thought how frail she was, though she did her best to hide it. 'And this is that nice Mr Silcott you told me about?'

'Aline insisted I had a look myself,' Mr Silcott said, shaking the hand she offered. 'And I was of course delighted to oblige. I'll make a preliminary estimate of what I think your goods will fetch at auction, and if you're agreeable, we'll discuss terms. I think we can reduce our normal commission since you're a friend of Aline's.'

'How sweet of you,' Phyllis said, tucking her arm through mine and leaning on me as we walked out to the shed. 'Shall we have a look then?'

Taking a key from her pocket, she unlocked the shed door. Mr Silcott followed her in and I walked behind, noticing many of the smaller items I'd missed on my first visit. Besides the bronze hunter and the pictures, there were several occasional tables and two sets of chairs – one late Victorian with thick, heavy legs, the other Regency and inlaid with brass. I saw copper jugs and kettles that had turned black from disuse, American wall clocks, a roll-top desk, pewter inkwells and platters, and at least six wooden writing boxes. There were also many boxes stuffed with bits and pieces that I knew would do well in the saleroom.

'It's going to take me at least two hours to list everything,' Mr Silcott said. 'Why don't you go back to the house, Mrs Pearson? I'll lock up and bring you the key before I leave.'

'What a good idea,' she said, smiling at me. 'Shall we go and have a cup of tea, my dear?'

'I'd like that,' I said, glancing at my former employer. 'If you're sure you can manage alone?'

'Leave it to me,' he said. 'We can't have you tiring yourself out, can we?'

I laughed and shook my head, blushing. Phyllis looked at me curiously as we walked back to the house.

'I'm pregnant,' I told her, too happy to keep it to myself. 'Mr Silcott heard me telling a friend at the saleroom before we came here.'

'That's wonderful. Your husband must be so pleased.'

'Yes, I think he is.'

'Such a pleasant man,' Phyllis said. 'I've been puzzling over it ever since you came to see me last time. I'm sure I have met Mr Drayton before; I felt I recognized him almost at once, but the name doesn't ring a bell. Silly me. I expect I'm getting old and forgetful.'

'Perhaps you've seen him in the street or in a restaurant. It's strange how the memory plays tricks on you, isn't it?'

'It was his eyes,' Phyllis murmured, half to herself. 'Something about his eyes . . . Oh, what a nuisance. I'm sure I shall remember in the end. I usually do. Anyway, please tell him he can pick up the pictures whenever he likes.'

'You're quite sure?'

'Perfectly,' Phyllis said as we went into the house. 'Now, we're going to have our tea and a chat – and then I'd like to give you a present, if I may.'

'Oh no,' I said, blushing. 'There's no need. You mustn't feel obliged because I asked Mr Silcott to come. He was pleased to have the chance.'

'Nonsense, my dear,' the older woman said in a scolding tone. 'That's business and nothing to do with it. I want to give you something for the baby. It's a christening robe – very old and very precious to me. It's been in my family for years; but I have no children of my own, so now I'd like you to have it.'

'It's very kind of you,' I said. I was honoured by the offer of such a personal gift. 'I should love to have it.'

'And you will visit me now and then? I know you must be busy but perhaps. . . ?' She looked so anxious and somehow vulnerable that I was touched. She was obviously lonely and I was drawn to her.

'Of course I will,' I said.

'A christening robe?' Piers' eyes were amused as he looked at Phyllis Pearson's gift. 'Be careful, darling, or she'll be expecting you to visit her regularly.'

'I wouldn't mind,' I said. 'She's lonely and very sweet – and this is beautiful, almost an antique, I should think.' I spread out the delicate robe of old cream silk with its petticoats and trimmings of ivory lace for him to appreciate.

'Very pretty. It's up to you what you do, Aline. Just make time for me.'

'Of course I will.' I looked at him, sensing that he was only half joking. He was such a possessive man, but surely he didn't want to cut me off from anyone who might be a friend? 'Phyllis asked me to tell you she was satisfied with the estimate you gave her. You can collect the pictures whenever you're ready.'

'That's something,' he said, seeming pleased. 'So it wasn't a complete waste of time then. Keep up the good work, Aline. I wouldn't mind a few of the better pictures in the house.'

'Piers! I couldn't use our friendship to persuade her to sell something she would rather keep.'

'Did I say you should?' He frowned at me. 'I don't know why you had to go back there with Silcott.'

'You know how nervous she is.' I hesitated, looking at him unhappily. 'She still thinks she knows you – are you sure you've never met her?'

'For heaven's sake!' he ejaculated. 'I've told you once that I've never seen her before. Can't you take my word for it?'

His face had gone cold and his eyes were like flint as he stared at me. I recoiled and turned away, hiding my hurt. I knew that these sudden moods of his never lasted long, but I still couldn't get used to them.

'I was only asking,' I said in a muffled voice.

For a moment there was silence, then I felt Piers' hands on my shoulders. His lips touched the back of my neck, sending little ripples down my spine. I turned and he drew me close, kissing me with a satisfying intensity.

'Forgive me,' he whispered. 'Sometimes this devil inside me gets out of hand. I'd do anything rather than hurt you. You must believe me.'

Sensing a hint of desperation, I reached up to touch his cheek. 'Something is wrong, Piers. Can't you tell me?'

He seemed to hesitate, and I felt that he wanted to speak, then he changed his mind and the moment passed. 'Maybe I'm just tired. I think I might like to go away for a short break when we get back from Hazeling. What do you think?'

'It sounds wonderful,' I murmured, kissing his eyelids. I loved him so much. Nothing must come between us. Whatever brought that bleak look to Piers' eyes belonged to the past. It must not be allowed to destroy us. 'I love you, Piers. We'll do whatever you want, darling.'

'We'll go then,' he said, nuzzling my neck. 'I'll book up somewhere as soon as we get back.' He was breathing heavily. 'I don't have any appointments this afternoon, do you?'

'No, Piers,' I said. 'None at all.'

It was getting dark when we drove through the gates of Hazeling. As the car lights swung in an arc, they illuminated the figure of a man. For a moment he was caught in the spotlight, then he melted away.

'Who do you think that was? There was someone lurking in the hedges the night I came down alone, too.'

'We'd better tell Michael about it,' Piers said. 'There are some valuable things at Hazeling. One or two of the family pictures are genuine Impressionists. I doubt if you've got them insured for anywhere near their present value, and it would be silly to lose them.'

There were no lights at any of the windows as we drove up to the front door, and Piers had to leave the car lamps on until I reached the door and rang the bell. As we waited for someone to answer, I looked at Piers in concern.

'That's odd,' I said. 'I thought they were expecting us. You told Michael what time we would be here, didn't you?'

'We're half an hour early,' he said, checking his watch. 'What a nuisance. Do you have your key?'

'Yes.' I began to search in my bag, but as I did so we saw the flash of headlights and then a battered maroon Volvo estate drew up behind Piers' car. 'Oh, here's Michael now.'

Michael hurried towards us, and I caught the look of annoyance on his face before he smiled. 'Isn't Zena in? She didn't say she was going out this evening. If I'd known I would have been here to meet you myself.'

'She probably just popped out to meet a friend,' I said, without thinking.

'Zena doesn't have many friends,' Michael replied. 'Not the kind she just pops out to see, anyway.'

He took a key from his pocket and opened the door, calling to Zena and switching on the lights as he went. It was obvious that no one was at home. There was a strong scent of lavender polish everywhere and Zena had even arranged fresh flowers in the hall and drawing room, so she was expecting us.

'I'm sorry about this,' Michael said. 'It just isn't like her to go off without letting me know.'

'It doesn't matter,' I assured him. 'I'll just go up and take off my coat, then I'll make us all a cup of tea, shall I?'

Zena had prepared our room. There were roses and freesias in a bowl on the dressing table and fresh towels in the bathroom. She had gone to a lot of trouble. It seemed rather odd of her to be out when we arrived.

Taking off my coat, I went to look out at the gardens. It was dark but there was a light shining from one of the downstairs windows, and I caught sight of a shadow in the shrubberies. I couldn't be sure, but I believed it was Zena making her way hurriedly towards the back of the house. I turned away from the window and opened my bag to take out my lipstick.

It was at least ten minutes before I went downstairs. At the bottom I turned left and went through the small sitting room into the back hallway, pausing as I noticed that a picture had gone from the alcove under the stairs – a portrait of a pretty young woman, done in oils, and probably French late nineteenth-century. I must remember to ask Michael about it sometime, I thought. As I approached the kitchen, I heard raised voices, and stopped. Michael sounded angry.

'Stop lying to me, Zena. You've been out to meet him, haven't you?'

'I just went for a walk,' Zena answered, her voice low and sullen. 'You're imagining things, as usual.'

'If you want your freedom, say so.' Michael sounded calmer now. 'Why bother telling lies . . .'

'I promise you, I only went for a walk. I haven't been meeting anyone. You never believe me, do you? Oh, it's just not worth trying.'

Suddenly the door opened and Zena came rushing into the hall. For a moment she checked herself, staring at me, her face wet with tears.

'It's all your fault,' she said bitterly. 'Why did you have to arrive early?'

'Zena . . .' I stared at her, bewildered by the unprovoked attack. 'I don't know what you mean.'

'Oh, go to hell!' Zena screamed, pushing past me to go running up the back stairs.

'What's wrong?' I asked, as Michael came out of the kitchen. 'Why is Zena so upset?'

'It's my fault.' Michael sighed. 'I lost my temper and she got upset again. I just don't seem to be able to understand her these days.'

As I heard the weary note in his voice, I was concerned. He looked so ill. 'Would you like me to talk to her?'

He shrugged. 'I can't cope, Aline,' he said. 'I just don't know what she wants. I've offered her her freedom . . .'

'Perhaps all she wants is to be assured of your love,' I said. 'You do love her, don't you?'

'Yes, of course,' he said, looking at me in a helpless way. 'She's my wife, and I want to do what's best for her.'

'Let me talk to her,' I said, and he nodded.

I smiled to reassure him and turned away. Michael was ill and not up to dealing with his wife's unhappiness. Walking slowly upstairs, I was thoughtful. The man's shadow in the hedge . . . could that have been someone Zena was meeting? Zena had denied it vehemently, but was she telling the truth?

I went to Zena's room and knocked on the door. There was no answer, so I turned the handle and peeped inside. Zena wasn't there. Suddenly I knew she would be in the attic. It was her refuge, the place she escaped to when she wanted to cry. I hesitated. Perhaps I ought to respect Zena's privacy; and yet I had the feeling that she needed help. The back stairs led to a part of the house that was seldom used. The top landing gave access only to the attics, which I hadn't been in for years. I went up the three stairs that had been put in when I was a child and knocked at the door of my old playroom, 'May I come in, Zena?'

For a moment there was silence. 'It isn't locked,' she said. 'Come in if you want.'

I opened the door and stood on the threshold, half afraid to intrude. The first attic room was large, and painted white, with thick dark wooden beams overhead. There were two dormer windows with tiny leaded panes, just as I remembered, but everything else had changed. It was no longer my playroom. This was obviously the one part of the house Zena had made her own. Pretty velvet curtains were draped at the windows, matching the rust-coloured carpet on the floor. Everywhere there was evidence that this was Zena's private place, with books, flowers and sewing materials. Yet as I began to take in the details, I realized that it was much more than just a pleasant place to sew.

There were dolls everywhere: French fashion dolls in eighteenth-century clothes, Spanish dolls with lace dresses and mantillas, wooden dolls with painted clogs and Dutch faces, and valuable antique dolls with porcelain heads that might be Bru or Jumeau, if those I'd seen in the auction were a guide. A large old wooden rocking horse with a worn yellow leather saddle and a moth-eaten mane occupied the centre of the floor, a battered teddy astride its back. Train sets and building bricks were placed here and there, and at each setting there was a group of dolls arranged as if at play. Dolls sat in the Windsor chair by the window, and at the scaled-down writing desk. A large wax-faced doll with pale blonde hair, red lips, and period costume was pushing an old-fashioned pram; another smaller doll in a bride's dress was bending over a cot; others were apparently playing with a toy cooker, a post-office counter and a shop. It was a world peopled entirely by dolls – a fantasy, a playground, an agonized cry from the heart.

Slowly Zena turned towards me. There were tears on her cheeks. She was cradling a doll dressed in the clothes of a human baby, a wistful expression, like a clown's, pulling down the corner of her mouth. I watched from the doorway as she rocked the doll, soothing it, kissing its painted china face as tenderly as a mother with her newborn babe.

'Susie was crying,' she said in a high, childish voice. 'She doesn't like to be left alone too long. Poor little Susie. Does your tummy ache, then?'

175

There was something terribly sad in that grief-filled and despairing little scene. 'Zena,' I said. 'Michael didn't mean to be angry with you. He's sorry if he upset you just now.'

'He's always sorry,' she muttered. 'But he doesn't care. He doesn't know how I feel.'

'Perhaps you should tell him,' I suggested. I felt uncomfortable at witnessing so much grief and wondered if it had been such a good idea to follow Zena.

Zena began to sing the tune I'd heard coming from the attic on my last visit, its melody haunting and strange on her lips. ' "Greensleeves was my delight . . ." La, la, la . . ."Who but my Lady Greensleeves. . ." ' Her voice was high and quavery.

'Oh, Zena, what's wrong? Is there anything I can do?'

Zena looked at me then, her eyes bleak. 'Have you any idea what it's like to want a child so much that it hurts? Sometimes I go shopping and I pretend I'm pregnant. I buy toys and clothes . . . But you couldn't know.' Her voice broke. 'Go away, Aline. I'm going to bath Susie and put her to bed, then I'll come down.'

'But she's a doll, Zena,' I said.

Zena turned on me, her eyes blazing. 'She's my baby,' she cried. 'The only one I'll ever have. I can't have a child and they won't let me adopt because – because my husband was once suspected of attacking a child.' There was hatred in her eyes as she looked at me. 'Because you couldn't do as you were told.'

I recoiled at her fury, and then I understood. In her misery, Zena was blaming me for her unhappiness. Shocked, I stumbled from the attic and made my way downstairs.

I didn't say anything to either Michael or Piers about the dolls, or Zena's accusation. The scene I'd witnessed in the attic was too personal. Besides, I didn't really understand it.

I wasn't sure if Michael knew about his wife's obsession with her dolls. He must have known that she collected them, of course, but so did many women. Did he realize that Zena was using them as a substitute for the child she wanted so much? I didn't think so, but it wasn't my place to tell him. Zena would resent any such interference.

When I went into the drawing room, Piers and Michael were examining a painting and talking about the exhibition. They looked up to ask if Zena was all right, and I nodded, forcing myself to smile.

'She just needs some time to herself,' I told them. 'She'll be down soon. If you want coffee or something to eat, I can get it.'

176

'I wouldn't say no to a cup of tea,' Michael said, smiling at me. 'But I'm not hungry. Get yourself and Piers something. I know Zena stocked the fridge this morning.'

'Why don't I make us omelettes?' Piers offered.

We sat down to eat as Zena came in. She didn't look as if she had been crying. Her make-up and hair were immaculate, as was the silk blouse she was wearing. She looked at me and smiled, and it was as if the scene in the attic had never been.

'I'm glad Piers has made himself useful,' she commented. 'You found the wine I bought. Good. I got it specially for you, Aline, because I know you like it.'

'That was kind of you,' I said. 'Would you like half of my omelette? I haven't touched it yet.'

'No. I'll just have a sandwich,' she replied. 'We don't often eat at night, and I had tea with Michael earlier.' She glanced at Piers. 'He went into Blakeney to fetch some paintings he'd left at a shop on sale or return. Do you think there are enough for the exhibition yet?'

'More than enough,' Piers said with enthusiasm. 'I like some of the latest canvases. Only a couple of weeks to go! I was telling Michael just now that I think we're going to have a big success with it. I'm taking Aline away for a few days next week – perhaps to Greece if we can find a vacancy – but we'll be back in time for the exhibition, of course.'

'How lovely,' she said. 'I wanted Michael to go away this summer, but he said he couldn't spare the time.'

I had the feeling that she was hoping to be invited to accompany us, and I turned to Piers, half willing him to suggest it, but he made a quick, angry movement of denial.

'It's a treat for Aline,' he said. 'We may not get away much next year.' He paused for a moment and I knew what he was going to say. I tried to find the words to stop him, but my lips were numb and I could only stare in dismay as he went on. 'Congratulate me, Zena. I'm going to be a father.'

Zena was looking at me, so Piers couldn't see the sudden flash of anger in her eyes. For a moment there was such jealousy in her that I turned cold, feeling a chill run down my spine. I sensed that Zena was on the verge of hysterics, but she battled for control and then she was smiling – a false, lying smile that hid her inner feelings from Piers . . . but not from me. She congratulated Piers, then she turned to me once more.

'How wonderful, Aline,' she said. 'You must be so excited. Now you really do have everything you want, don't you?'

You have everything and I have nothing! Her eyes screamed, even though no one but me could read them.

At that moment I felt that Zena hated me.

'Yes.' I stared into those empty yet threatening eyes and was suddenly afraid. 'Yes, I suppose I do.'

I lay awake, staring into the darkness, listening to the music box playing that tune over and over, then I covered my ears with my hands. Zena was in the attic again, alone in her make-believe world. I knew how much Piers' announcement had hurt her, and I imagined her pain as she kept winding the musical box.

'Alas my love . . .' Haunting and unmistakable, the music filtered through the silent house, accompanied by Zena's sobbing, and I knew she was lying on the floor above us.

I couldn't bear the sound of weeping any longer. Piers was asleep beside me. Lifting the covers gently, I got out of bed and slipped on my robe and soft-soled mules, then tip-toed to the door.

I made my way to the back stairs. Perhaps Zena ought to see a doctor, yet I was reluctant to suggest it. She would think it was interference, and perhaps after all there was no real harm in it. Many women collected dolls; there was a thriving market for the old ones. I could understand the fascination, though I couldn't share it. Perhaps it was only a hobby of Zena's . . . Perhaps I'd made too much of it.

I crept up the stairs to the attic and knocked. There was no answer. I tried the door but it was locked. I called again, pressing my ear to the door, but I could hear nothing. Zena must have gone back to bed. I turned and went back downstairs. There was a light on in the kitchen. I hesitated, then I heard the sound of voices. Zena and Michael were talking.

'Go back to bed, Michael. I'm perfectly all right.'

'But you're not,' he said. 'I'm sorry if I upset you earlier.'

'It wasn't that.'

'Oh, my dear,' he said, sounding anxious now. 'I thought you were getting over . . .'

I turned and walked away, not wanting to listen to their private conversation.

'Piers has told me the good news,' Michael said the next morning, kissing my cheek. I caught a quickly concealed flash of anxiety in his eyes. 'Does Zena know?'

'Yes. Piers told her last night.'

'I see.' Michael nodded. 'So that was it. She didn't tell me, but I knew she was upset about something. Well, it can't be helped. She had to know sometime, I suppose. She went out early this morning. I expect she wanted a few hours to herself.'

'Has she seen a doctor, Michael?'

'What do you mean?' He was annoyed with me. 'She had all the tests after the miscarriage. It's quite definite that she can't have a child.'

'I meant about her emotional state. I think she could be heading for a mental breakdown.'

'Surely it's not that bad? I know she can be a bit touchy sometimes, but . . .'

'I think it's more than that.'

'It's my fault, of course. If . . .' He sighed, looking unhappy.

'Do you think it would help if I saw the adoption people and told them you had nothing to do with what happened to me?'

'I very much doubt it, my dear.' Michael smiled and touched my hand just as Piers walked in.

He looked excited, as though he had just discovered something. 'That little painting in the alcove at the top of the stairs – I think it's a Renoir.'

Glancing at Michael, my lips twitched. 'Oh, Piers,' I cried, beginning to giggle. 'I didn't think it would fool you . . .'

'What do you mean?' A look of annoyance came into his eyes.

I laughed outright, overcome with mirth. 'It's one of Michael's. He copied it from an original years ago. If you look closely, you'll see that one of the girls is me.'

'Don't laugh at me!'

My laughter died. 'I wasn't laughing at you,' I said. 'You're not the first to think that.'

'Piers couldn't see it properly,' Michael soothed. 'From a distance it does look a bit like a Renoir, but if Piers really looked at it he wouldn't be fooled for a moment.'

'Of course not,' I said, feeling chastened. Piers was still angry but trying not to show it. I should have remembered that he hated to be embarrassed or made a fool of; the incident on the fishing boat had taught me that. 'I'm sorry, darling.'

'Just don't laugh at me,' he muttered.

'I ought to burn that picture,' Michael said. 'Though of course it is signed by me.' He smiled at Piers. 'You know, I'm warming to the prospect of that show at your gallery.'

'Good. I don't think you realize your own potential.'

Piers' expression had lightened. 'I thought we might take a drive into Sheringham and have lunch,' he said. 'Would you and Zena like to come, do you think?'

'Zena's out,' I said, uneasy as I saw his expression. He still hadn't forgiven me for laughing at his mistake. 'But I'd like to go. What about you, Michael?'

'I'm going out to the Point this morning,' Michael said. 'Perhaps you would both like to come with me in the boat?'

Piers glanced at me. 'How do you feel about that, darling? We could have lunch in Blakeney instead.'

'I'd love it,' I cried. 'It's ages since I've been out to the Point.'

'Put something warm on then,' Michael advised. 'The sun is shining now, but you know it can be cold on the sea.'

The tide was high. Michael helped me into the boat, and Piers climbed in after us. A stiff breeze was blowing as Michael negotiated the narrow channel to the long stretch of shingle. The ferries often landed their passengers at Pinchers Creek, but Michael took the longer voyage round the sand bars at Far Point, so that we could catch a glimpse of the seal colonies.

'We had several common seal pups in July,' Michael told us. 'But the greys usually begin pupping this month. If we're lucky we might see one or two.'

We were lucky. There was a small colony on the sandbanks and it was possible to see the soft white fur of the young as they lay beside their mothers.

'Are the seals recovering from that virus now?' I asked.

'Everyone has their own opinion on that,' Michael said. 'But I would say there has been a very slight improvement.'

Looking up at the blue sky, I watched the gulls circling and wheeling overhead, their cries echoing in that wild, beautiful place. I looked back towards the saltmarshes, their seemingly endless vastness stretching into the distance towards Blakeney. The village rose to a crest in a haze of autumn sunshine, the church towering above everything else. Around us the sea had a gentle swell, the waves topped with yellow-tinged foam. It was a scene from a picture postcard . . . the scene Michael had painted long ago.

A cloud passed across the sky, obscuring the sun, and it was cold for a moment. My flesh was all goose pimples. Had someone walked across my grave?

Michael was sitting alone in the drawing room when Piers and I returned that evening. We had left him after lunch in Blakeney and driven into Sheringham, and spent the afternoon wandering around its streets and shops. There were not as many people milling round the quaint clock tower in the centre of the town as there were during the height of the holiday season, but it was still busy. We had scones with raspberry jam and cream for tea at a pleasant restaurant, and then drove back through little winding lanes, past cottages that looked as if they had sprung from a child's storybook, weathervanes shaped like cockerals or foxes, stretches of unspoilt coastline and wooded ridges of stunning beauty, taking time to enjoy the scenery. It was quite late and getting dark when we got back to Hazeling.

As we went into the drawing room, Michael looked up, obviously worried about something.

'What's wrong?' I asked.

'Zena hasn't come home yet,' he said. 'It isn't like her to go out for the whole day like this.'

'Perhaps she just felt like having a day out,' I suggested.

'But she might have said something. It's thoughtless and rude of her to go off like that when you've come down for the weekend.'

'I don't see why she should bother about us,' I said, feeling that I ought to make an excuse for Zena. 'After all, we've been out all day, too.'

'That isn't the – ' Michael broke off as he heard the front door bang. 'That sounds as if . . .' He got to his feet and went out into the hall.

I looked at Piers. 'Do you think. . . ?'

He shook his head. 'No. Better leave them to it.'

Even as I began to reply, Zena came into the room. She was carrying several shopping bags, and I could see by the labels that she must have been into Norwich.

'I'm sorry to be so late,' Zena said. 'I decided I needed some new clothes – and I wanted to buy a present for the baby, Aline.' She pulled out a huge teddy bear and held it out to me.

'It's lovely, Zena,' I said. 'But you shouldn't have spent your money on – '

'I've bought lots of baby clothes for you,' she said brightly. 'I'll give them to you later.'

Michael had come in behind her. He looked at the teddy bear and then at Zena's face, and his eyes darkened with grief.

'For God's sake, Zena,' he said. 'Aline's baby won't be born for ages yet. Besides, she may not like what you've bought.'

I frowned at him as Zena's face began to crumple. How could he be so insensitive? It had cost Zena to accept the fact that I was pregnant; buying the baby clothes had been a kind of release for her.

She stared at him, her eyes brimming with tears. For a moment I thought Zena would scream or strike out at him, but then she turned without a word and ran from the room. He stood looking after her, his face stricken.

'Damn,' he said softly. 'I'm a stupid fool.'

He moved as if to go after her, but Piers caught his arm. 'Let her go,' he said. 'You'll only make things worse.'

Michael's face was torn by indecision. As he stood hesitating, I looked at him and saw the mute appeal in his eyes.

'You were right,' he said. 'She's worse than I thought. What am I to do, Aline?'

'I'll go after her,' I said. 'She needs to cry and she's frightened of upsetting you.'

I knew that Zena would be in the attic. The door was unlocked. I knocked and then went in. A small light was burning and in the dim glow the dolls looked strange and eerie, their waxen images almost alive, their eyes watchful and waiting. These were the guardians of Zena's private world and I was an intruder, and I could almost feel their hostility.

The atmosphere in the attic was unpleasant, but I was unable to leave. Zena's grief at her inability to have a child was natural enough, but her obsession was not, and it was very powerful. I was afraid for her. How long had this withdrawal into her world of dolls been going on?

I felt the hairs on the back of my neck prickle as Zena glided into the light. She had the baby doll Susie in her arms, and she was singing softly, singing the tune that had now become so familiar. She turned, smiling, as I entered.

'I knew you would come,' she said. 'I knew it would be you.'

Her voice sounded strange, as if she was close to hysteria.

'I wanted to thank you for the teddy and the clothes,' I said. 'It was kind of you to buy them for me.'

'Susie was crying,' Zena said. 'She doesn't like me to be away all day.'

For a moment I almost believed her, almost believed that the painted face and stiff limbs were alive and breathing, and then I snapped out of it.

'Susie is a doll.' I moved towards Zena and laid my hand on her arm, then I tugged the doll from her embrace. This obsession had to stop; it was unhealthy and dangerous. 'Susie is a pretty doll, that's all. You need help, Zena. You should talk to a doctor.'

182

Zena closed her eyes but I sensed her antagonism. 'Are you saying there's something wrong with me?'

'No, of course not. It's just that you've been under a strain. I want to help you, Zena. Believe me, I'm your friend.'

'Do you really want to help me?' Her breath expelled in a little hiss.

'You know I would do anything I could, Zena.'

Zena looked at me; the expression in her eyes sent a chill through me, and I knew she was on the verge of a mental breakdown.

'Would you give me your baby?' She laughed shrilly as she saw my instinctive recoil. 'Yours and Piers'. Would you do that, Aline?'

'You know that's out of the question,' I said, drawing a sharp breath. 'That wasn't what I meant.'

'Then you don't want to help me.' Zena's gaze narrowed, becoming menacing. She snatched the doll back from me. 'You're like Michael. He married me but he only cares about you. He's obsessed with you. When he makes love to me, it's you he wants. It's your name he cries when . . . It's your picture he paints over and over.'

'No!' I cried, shaking my head and backing away from her. 'No, Zena. You're just saying that to hurt me.'

Zena's eyes had a fixed look and she was breathing hard. 'He told me once that he couldn't stop thinking about you, wanting to touch you. He's always wanted you, even when you were a child.'

My head began to spin. Zena's voice went on and on, saying all the nightmare things I'd dreaded for so many years. Flashes of light streaked inside my head. I was eleven years old again and on the marshes. Someone was following me. I was terrified. I started to run, but he was running too and I knew he would catch me . . .

I felt so dizzy and ill. My chest was tight and the pain in my head was becoming unbearable. Zena's voice was coming from a long way away, and she laughed hysterically at something she'd said. Sickness churned inside me. I wanted to call out, to cry for help, but my lips were too stiff. With an effort, I staggered from the attic. Everything was going hazy.

I reached the top of the steep stairs leading down to the back hall and stopped to catch my breath. I felt so ill. My thoughts whirled, confusing the past and present. I was on the marshes again. I knew I had to run or he would catch me, and I was afraid of him. The lights were flashing in my head. I felt for the banister, trying to steady myself, and my slippery hands slid off the wood.

I swayed, crying Piers' name in desperation. And then, as if all the lights in the house had suddenly fused, everything went black. I missed my footing, catching the heel of my shoe as I tried to save myself. There was a sharp, strong smell of perfume or cologne, and something hit me in the middle of the back. I screamed as I pitched forward down the stairs. Pain shot through me and I screamed again, then my head struck against something hard, and an even deeper blackness enveloped me.

Chapter Fourteen

There was a time before I was fully conscious when I was aware of the voices – concerned, competent voices that spoke in controlled tones of blood transfusions, injections and pulse rates. And then there were the others, more disturbing, penetrating to the core of pain that lay beneath the cottonwool haze of the drugs they pumped into me.

'It wasn't me! I swear it.' A shrill, frightened, female cry. 'You have to believe me. She fell. She missed her footing when the lights fused, and she fell. It was an accident – why would I push her?'

'Out of jealous spite . . .' The man's voice was cold and accusing. 'Because she was carrying the child you couldn't have.'

'No! No, it's a lie,' the woman protested. 'I was nowhere near Aline. You have to believe me. She fell . . .'

Their voices faded, lost in the maze of hallucination that had me chasing wildly down the frightening avenues of a hall of mirrors and misshapen images. Strange, distorted faces leered at me, threatening and terrifying. There were other voices from the past, crowding in, clamouring to be heard: a child laughing in the sunshine until a bee stung her and the tears began . . . A woman scolding . . . A man's voice raised and angry, frightening the child with its ugliness.

'For goodness sake, Sheila! She's only a child. Don't look at me like that, as if I'm some kind of a monster. Do you really think I would do anything to harm her? She's my little girl. I love her. I love her. I love her . . .'

The voice went on and on, echoing in my head.

'I love you, Aline. Oh, God, I'll never forgive myself if . . .'

Piers' face was obscured by the mist. I peered at him, wanting to see him, wanting to tell him . . . I couldn't think. I couldn't remember what was so important. I tried to speak but my mouth felt slack and my tongue was swollen. The words would not come, and all I could move was one finger.

'It's all right, darling.' Piers took my hand in his. 'You've been very ill and they've been keeping you drugged to help with the pain, but you'll be fine now. The doctors say you'll be able to come home soon.'

'How. . . ?' I struggled to form the words but it was too much of an effort. The sentences took shape in my mind but slipped away before they could emerge from my mouth.

'Five days,' Piers said, stroking the back of my hand. 'You've been in hospital for five days. You fell down the stairs and hit your head. You were badly bruised but your back isn't broken. At first they thought there might be internal injuries, but you're fine. You're going to be as good as new very soon.'

Something was wrong. I knew there was something I had to ask, but I couldn't remember. The mists were returning and Piers' face was slipping away. It came to me then. The baby. What had happened to my baby? Why had I been so ill? Why had I needed all those blood transfusions? I had to ask. I had to know, but it was all fading, fading into the mist . . .

The voices came back with a vengeance, hammering at my consciousness, demanding to be let in.

A child was screaming, begging her attacker not to hurt her any more. She was in a panic as she ran across the saltmarshes, terrified of the man who pursued her. And then he caught her, and she heard the rasp of his breath against her ear as he pressed her down on the coarse grass. She inhaled the strong, salty tang of the sand beneath, tasting its grittiness on her tongue and her lips as the man bent over her and she looked into his face.

'I'm going to kill you,' he taunted. 'You laughed at me. No one laughs at me. They've all been laughing, but they won't laugh after this.'

She fought wildly, desperately, scratching and biting as she struggled against his superior strength. His eyes had a strange intentness that made her scream again and again for the help that never came. His hands closed around her throat, and she saw his face again through a curtain of pain, pain so all-consuming that she found it unbearable. Then the blackness came down, releasing her.

I was drifting away, back to the peace of forgetfulness. With memory came pain – and I did not want to feel such pain ever again. For one moment in my hallucinated dreams I had seen the face of my attacker. *I had seen him and known him, but I did not want to know him.*

'Aline, my darling. Please don't die. I love you so very much. I've always loved you – God forgive me.'

Michael's voice came from a great distance. I tried to open my eyes, struggling to penetrate the mists that surrounded me. Was it real this time, or merely another of my dreams?

Michael was bending over me, his cool hands smoothing my brow. I felt the touch of his lips on mine, light and caressing like a gentle breeze.

'If you die, it will be my fault,' he said. 'Aline, my darling, I can't bear it if you die. Forgive me . . . Forgive me . . .'

I heard the sound of weeping. Michael's deep, hurting sobs broke through the mists obscuring my mind and almost tore my heart from my body. My eyes flicked open. I moved my hand, reaching out to him, wanting to tell him it was all right, and then the mists came down again.

'That's very much better, Mrs Drayton.' The nurse smiled at me encouragingly as I swallowed lukewarm tea from an invalid's plastic cup. 'You did give us all a fright, you know. We thought you were getting better, then you developed that infection, but you're over it now. Another few days and you'll be going home to that nice husband of yours.'

'Piers . . .' I struggled to remember. 'Has he been to see me?'

The nurse laughed and shook her head as if I'd asked something very amusing. 'Only every single day since you were brought in. Devoted, that's what he's been – just look at all the flowers. All the other patients are green with envy.' She grinned at me. 'And some of the nurses.'

I gave her a weak smile. 'It looks like a funeral parlour,' I said, and stopped. 'I mean I can't remember him coming. I can't even remember what happened.'

'Don't you recall feeling faint and falling down the stairs?'

I tried to concentrate. 'Is that what happened? How long have I been here?'

'Nine days.'

I pressed a hand to my eyes. 'My head feels as if a horse had kicked it. Did I hit it when I fell?'

'Yes. You – you were badly bruised, but nothing was broken, though you cracked a couple of ribs.'

I sat up in bed, staring at her in alarm. 'My baby! What happened to my baby?'

The smile went out of the nurse's eyes and she looked away. I grabbed her hand as she turned to leave. 'Please, you have to tell me.'

The nurse brought her eyes round to meet mine, and I knew. My fingers fumbled for the nurse's. 'I've lost it, haven't I? Please tell me the truth.'

'Sister said she would talk to you,' the nurse said uneasily. 'I'm sorry, Mrs Drayton. Really I am.'

My grasp loosened and I lay back, fighting the tears. 'Does this mean I can never have another child?'

'Good gracious no!' The nurse sounded relieved. 'No, you mustn't think that, Mrs Drayton. You've had a miscarriage but there were no damaging internal injuries. The doctors think that you may have been losing the child before you fell, that it may have been the reason for your tumble.' Her clear eyes gazed into mine. 'Can't you remember what happened just before you fell? Were you dizzy or faint?'

'I – I don't know.' I closed my eyes as I struggled to remember, but it was just like the time I'd been attacked on the marshes. I couldn't remember anything. It was just as if the incident had been wiped from my memory, leaving a blank space – and that was frightening. 'We'd been out for a drive that afternoon. I was very happy . . .' I caught the sob in my throat. 'Everything seemed so wonderful.'

The nurse looked at me with sympathy. 'It will be again, Mrs Drayton. You're young and you obviously have a good marriage. You'll have another child.'

'But I wanted my baby,' I cried, as a great gaping wound opened in my heart, a wound I feared would never quite heal. 'I wanted this baby . . .'

'Shall I ask Sister to come – or your husband?'

I shook my head, turning my face to the pillow. 'Please leave me alone. I'll be all right.'

I had lost my child. Now I knew how Zena felt. I understood the emptiness and the aching misery that she had kept inside her for months. I could not remember what had happened before my accident, but the thought forced itself into my mind that it had had something to do with Zena . . .

I managed to smile when Piers came to see me later that day. He sat on the edge of the bed, leaning forward to kiss me, his eyes smoky with suppressed anxiety. I smelt the spicy tang of his aftershave. It was a new one, something he had never used before. I didn't know why, but I didn't like it.

'Are you really better now?'

'Yes, I think so.' I held his hand. 'They – they've told me . . .'

His fingers closed about mine. 'If I could change what happened, I

188

would,' he said. 'It hurts me too, Aline, but you mustn't let it break your heart. We'll have another child, I promise you. You'll be all right, darling.'

'What did happen?' I asked, as a picture of Zena's face suddenly flashed into my mind. 'Was it – was it something to do with Zena?'

'Why do you ask that?' He turned his head to look out of the window. 'Do you remember something?'

I wrinkled my brow as vague memories flickered in my mind, like a kaleidoscope, forming patterns and changing again before I could grasp them. 'I'm not sure. I seem to remember a quarrel . . .'

'There was a little quarrel between Michael and Zena. You went after her. I was in the kitchen when I heard you scream and the lights went out. Michael called out that he would mend the fuse, and when the lights came on I found you at the bottom of the stairs. I glanced up and saw Zena standing on the landing, looking as if she would faint, then Michael came rushing from the hallway and we phoned for the doctor.'

'Zena was at the top of the stairs? She was there?'

'You don't think that Zena. . . ?' He stopped, seeming horrified. 'Michael told me she desperately wants a child of her own.'

'Surely she couldn't be jealous or vindictive enough to – to push me down the stairs?'

'No. No, of course not.' Piers' eyes avoided mine. 'I'm sure she couldn't have done it, Aline. You missed your footing when the lights fused. It was just a very unfortunate circumstance that it should happen when you were at the top of the stairs.' His expression was awkward, almost embarrassed. 'I asked Michael about the wiring; I was angry and I'm afraid we had a row. I thought the wiring might be old, but he said it had all been renewed. It does seem strange that it should fuse like that, but I know nothing about fuses, I'm afraid. You don't remember anything – nothing at all?'

'I wish I could remember. I have a feeling that there was something . . .' I sighed and shook my head. 'I know it's no good. It was the same when I was attacked. It's as if my mind simply shuts out anything I can't bear to remember.'

'Don't worry about it, darling.' He stroked the back of my hand with one finger. 'It may be only temporary this time. The doctors seem to think you may get your memory back when you get over the shock. You've had a rough time.'

'They say I can come home soon.'

'We'll go home, and then I'll book that holiday.'

I was silent for a moment. 'Not just yet, Piers, if you don't mind. I'd like to go back to Hazeling for a while.'

'I don't mind,' he said, his eyes intent as he looked down at me. 'But I don't understand. I'd have thought you'd hate the place after what happened.'

I struggled to put my thoughts into words. 'I need to know what did happen, Piers. I don't know why, but I feel it's important. And I believe my best chance of jogging my memory is to go back. I know that may seem stupid . . .'

He gazed down at me for several minutes and I tried to guess what was in his mind, but it was impossible. It was odd how Piers could sometimes be so – so difficult to read. He was able to hide his feelings completely when he chose. He seemed to become aware of my scrutiny, and nodded his head as if he had reached a decision.

'No, it doesn't seem stupid,' he said at last. 'I can see the reasoning behind it. I just thought it might be painful for you, that's all.'

'Running away won't help, Piers. It never does.'

'No . . .' He sounded defensive. 'No. Fate has a way of catching you out if you try. Perhaps it's best to face up to it straight away.' He kissed the palm of my hand. 'I just don't want you to be unhappy.'

'I won't be,' I promised. 'As long as I have you, I can bear it. Be patient with me, darling. Just for a while.'

'Of course,' he said, and smiled. 'I love you, Aline. You do know that, don't you?'

'Yes,' I replied, but even as I did so, an inner voice was warning me to be careful. I withdrew my hand from his, lay back against the pillows and closed my eyes.

'Are you tired, darling?'

'Yes. Just a little.'

'Then I'll go and leave you to rest. Take care of yourself. It won't be long before you're well again.' He bent his head to kiss me. 'I can't wait for you to come home.'

'Nor can I,' I said, but I went cold inside as his lips touched mine. He noticed the small withdrawal, and there was an odd expression in his eyes, but it vanished in an instant. Frightened, I grabbed his hand as he turned away. 'I love you, Piers,' I said, as much to reassure myself as him. 'It will be all right, won't it?'

For a moment he hesitated, and then he smiled. 'Yes, of course,' he said.

After he had gone, I lay staring into space for a long time. I wasn't aware that I was crying until I tasted the salt on my lips. What was wrong with me? Why hadn't I responded to Piers' kiss? Why did I feel this curious coldness inside me when he said he loved me?

I had the feeling that it was something to do with my accident – something I'd seen or felt or remembered just before I fell . . . It was no use; there was a blackness in my mind, a curtain between me and the memory I so desperately wanted to recall. I only knew that I had to return to Hazeling. It was important for me to remember everything.

Nick sent me a get-well card. It had a big fat teddy bear with a bandage over one eye on the front. Inside he had written a brief message:

'Chin up, darling! We're all thinking of you. Love from Nick.'

He'd filled the rest of the space with kisses in red ink. The nurse wanted to pin it up with the others above my bed, but I hid it in my locker. It was typical of Nick to send a humorous card without thinking; he had meant to cheer me up, and the kisses were his way of telling me that he was still my friend. But I knew that if Piers saw it he would think the worst. He might even suspect that I was still seeing Nick. I couldn't cope with Piers' jealousy at the moment.

And yet I couldn't help wishing that Nick had come to see me.

Michael brought me a basket of fruit. He hovered at the bedside, looking at me anxiously.

'Are you really better now?'

'Yes, I think so.'

'Thank goodness for that. You gave us all a fright.'

'I'm sorry.'

'Can you remember what happened?'

I shook my head. 'No. Nothing at all.'

'I suppose you just missed your footing when the lights fused. It's my responsibility, I ought to have had the wiring checked. Some of it is probably faulty.'

But hadn't he told Piers it had been renewed recently? Why was he lying? Was it to protect Zena? The thought was so horrible that I shut it out at once. Zena couldn't have pushed me . . . could she?

'It might have happened anyway. You mustn't blame yourself.' I changed the subject. 'Did you visit me earlier, when I was still in a fever?'

His eyes avoided mine. 'Yes. A couple of times. Why?'

'Oh, no reason,' I said. 'I just wondered.'

'We were all very worried. Zena came once, but she hates hospitals.' He seemed awkward. 'Perhaps I ought to go.'

'No.' I smiled at him. It was strange but I could accept my love for him now. He was the father I'd never known, the friend of my childhood. My antagonism towards him had all gone, washed away by the tears he had wept for me. 'I'm glad you came, Michael. Please stay and talk to me for a while.'

'So you're going home tomorrow,' Julie said, depositing a huge bunch of flowers and a bag of Belgian fresh cream chocolates on my bed. She proceeded to munch the chocolates as we talked. 'Thank goodness for that. I wanted to come before, but I just couldn't get away. I'm very sorry about the baby.'

'Yes.' I blinked, forcing a weak smile. 'They tell me I'll be able to have another one in time. The doctor had a long chat with me yesterday. He said my body will take a while to heal so I mustn't be impatient, but eventually there's nothing to stop me getting pregnant.'

'I'm glad.' Julie squeezed my hand. 'Tony sent his love. And Mr Silcott rang me. He'd tried ringing the flat but no one was there. Apparently a Mrs Pearson wanted to see you. I told him about your fall and he was most concerned. He asked me to give you his best wishes. We're all rooting for you, Aline.'

'Thanks.'

'When are you coming back to London?'

'I'm not sure. Why – is something wrong?' There was something hidden in her expression. Unlike Piers, Julie was very bad at hiding her feelings.

'No . . .' Julie fiddled with the buttons on her jacket, a very smart knitted affair that I knew Tony had made for her. 'Piers said you wanted to stay at Hazeling. Do you think you should? I mean, you've never really been happy there, have you?'

'I feel I want to stay there for a while. I can't explain, Julie.'

'Well, just don't mope,' she said. 'And be careful coming down stairs in future.'

I saw that odd expression again and frowned. 'You don't think it was an accident, do you?'

'I – I don't know,' Julie said, still avoiding my eyes. She bit her lip, hesitating and then making up her mind. 'Have you made a will, Aline?'

'Yes, as a matter of fact I have,' I said. 'It was just after Zena told me that Michael was really ill. It made me realize . . .' I stared at Julie, suddenly understanding what she was getting at. 'Why do you ask?'

'I – Nick wondered if . . .'

'Nick!' I felt a surge of annoyance. 'Piers doesn't know about the will –

and he isn't the only beneficiary, so don't get any crazy ideas. I've left half of the money to Michael if I die before I can make a settlement on him. Besides, Piers didn't even know I was rich until after we were married.'

'Oh, he could have read about it in the paper. Didn't you tell me that there was an article in the local paper about your family after your mother died? Sometimes these things get picked up by the nationals. After all, Sheila did a lot of charity work and Michael is quite well known as a Norfolk artist.'

'Piers didn't even know I was Michael's stepdaughter. We had a row about it. He couldn't have known about the inheritance when he married me.'

Julie looked confounded, then contrite. 'I'm sorry, Aline. I shouldn't have said anything . . .' She took a deep breath. 'Who does know about the will?'

'No one,' I snapped. 'You're in it as well – so are you planning to bump me off now you know?'

We stared at each other, both angry, then Julie started to grin. 'I suppose it does sound a bit ridiculous when you say it out loud. It was just such a shock. Nick went mad. He wanted to come charging down here but I wouldn't let him.' The smile faded from her eyes. 'We thought for a while you might die. I do care about you, you know. We all do, Nick as well.'

'Yes, I do know.' I squeezed her hand. 'If anyone pushed me it wasn't for the money.'

'What do you mean?'

I explained about Zena, and Julie looked concerned. 'She sounds as if she is having a mental crisis. Most women suffer a certain amount of depression after a miscarriage – that's normal – but Zena is verging on a dangerous obsession. I think she needs psychiatric help.'

'She isn't crazy,' I said, a sudden chill bringing me out in goose pimples. 'But I do think she might be in trouble. She's so mixed up and unhappy.'

Julie nodded, her face thoughtful. 'But if she wants a baby so much herself, surely she wouldn't try to destroy yours? Isn't that the last thing a woman who desperately wanted a child would do? I mean, she might snatch the baby – but would she kill it? In most cases when a baby is snatched, we find that the woman responsible cares for the child as if it were her own.'

'Perhaps I turned dizzy and fell.' I shrugged. 'Anyway, let's talk about something else.'

We talked about Tony's business. He was doing well now and the orders were coming in almost faster than he could meet them. I was glad for him, and for Julie. It meant that she would be able to afford to take the time off work to have a baby.

'It seems as if you'll be able to give up work sooner than you planned,' I said. Julie nodded, looking guilty, and I shook my head. 'You can't avoid talking about babies for ever.'

'No, I suppose not,' Julie said. 'It will be all right, Aline. You'll have other children.'

'Yes,' I said in a low voice. 'We'll have others . . .'

After Julie had gone, I turned my face to the pillow and cried.

'Do you want to go upstairs?' Piers asked as we walked into the house. 'Are you tired?'

'No, not really.' I made myself smile at him. 'I've had enough of lying in bed. I would rather just wander round the house and garden. Don't worry about me, Piers. I'll potter about and read. If you need to go up to town for a while, I'll be all right here.'

He looked at me in silence and my eyes dropped. I knew that he was aware of the change in me, and I felt guilty. He had done nothing to deserve this coldness, but I couldn't help it. Every time he touched me, I had to steel myself not to pull away. My mind told me that he was still the man I'd fallen in love with, but I felt different. I no longer experienced that surge of fierce desire when he looked at me. Why? The miscarriage? The doctors had warned me that I might have an emotional crisis, that I might alternate between moods of guilt and deep depression, but I hadn't expected this numbness, this coldness inside me. It was as if I were only half alive. I prayed that it would go away in time, because otherwise my marriage would be in trouble.

Piers turned away, and I sensed he was hurt. 'I'll take your bag upstairs then,' he said, his voice cool and emotionless. 'If you're sure you don't mind, Aline, I may go back to town until the weekend,' he told me when he came down again.

One part of me wanted him to stay, but another was urging me to let him go. 'Of course I don't mind, darling,' I said. 'I'll probably come back with you next time. I just need a few days of peace and quiet.'

'Is that all?' he asked, and for a moment there was a flash of hope in his eyes.

I moved towards him, wanting it to be as it had been, needing to feel that warm glow inside. 'Yes, Piers. I'm sure I'll be ready in a few days,'

I whispered, but as he bent his head to kiss me, I had to fight to stop myself pulling away.

He looked into my eyes for a long moment, then drew back. 'Take care of yourself. Don't have any more accidents while I'm gone, will you?' I shook my head and he smiled. 'I'll be back this weekend then. Phone me if you need me.'

'I promise,' I said.

'Aline, if – ' Piers broke off as Zena came in.

'I thought I heard the car,' she said, looking at me nervously, her hands twitching at her skirt. 'How are you, Aline? I wanted to come to the hospital but those places always depress me. I visited once when you were still unconscious, but I hated to see you like that. Besides, I wasn't sure if you would want to see me.'

'Why shouldn't I?' I stared at her.

'Don't you remember? We had a bit of a quarrel that evening, just before you fell . . .' Her eyes darkened to that peculiar violet blue and I had the feeling that she was about to lie. 'You were annoyed with me for going off all day without letting anyone know where I was.'

'Was I?' I looked at her blankly. 'That doesn't ring any bells, I'm afraid.'

'You said you didn't feel well, that your head ached. If you'd told me you felt faint, I would have come with you, Aline.'

Her hands were trembling and she seemed afraid. Again, I wondered – could Zena have been so jealous, so vindictive, that she had pushed me down the stairs in the hope that I would lose my child?

'Would you?' I asked. 'I don't know whether you're telling me the truth or not. I don't even know if I fell or if I was pushed.'

'So you do blame me,' she croaked. 'They all think I did it. Your friends, Piers and – and Michael . . .' Her voice cracked and she turned suddenly and rushed from the room.

'Zena,' I cried, realizing too late that I'd let grief cloud my judgement. 'I'm sorry. I didn't mean that.'

I glanced at Piers, surprising a look of satisfaction in his eyes. It faded in a moment and I wondered if I'd imagined it.

'I shouldn't have said that,' I said, feeling guilty. 'It wasn't fair to accuse her.'

'You didn't,' Piers said. 'You merely stated a fact. If she took it personally . . .' He left the sentence unfinished, its implications clear. I realized that Zena was right: Piers did think she was to blame.

'I think perhaps I will go and lie down for a while,' I said, blinking back tears that made me feel weak and stupid.

As I walked upstairs, the tears began to slide down my cheeks. Zena was jealous of me. I'd always known that, but it was hard to believe that she could hate me so much.

The house was very quiet. Piers looked in before he left, but I pretended to be asleep, even when he kissed my cheek. I opened my eyes after he had gone, listening to the sound of his car as he drove away. Soon afterwards, Zena went out. I was alone in the house.

I was too restless to sleep and, after washing my face, I decided to go for a walk in the gardens. The emptiness of the house seemed to echo around me as I went downstairs. It was years since I'd been alone at Hazeling. I couldn't understand why Zena loved it so much. It was too big for modern living, and should have been turned into a convalescent home or a hotel long ago. The family trust was outdated and ridiculous. I wondered if there was any way of breaking it, and I decided to ring my solicitors as soon as possible. In a few months I would be twenty-five and the capital would be mine to do with as I pleased. I still had no idea how much it would be, though I knew it must be several hundred thousand pounds. *Enough to make someone want to kill me!* My attitude towards my inheritance had been to pretend that it wasn't there, but I supposed I ought to start making inquiries soon.

I'd dismissed Julie's fears as nonsensical, but now they haunted me. No one knew I'd made a will. Even if someone thought it likely, they had no way of knowing what was in it, and besides, I'd promised to give Michael his share of the money as soon as the trust ended. Zena knew that – so why should she want me dead? It was in her interest that I lived until my twenty-fifth birthday. Without a will, everything would have gone to my nearest relative. Michael wasn't a blood relation. He was not entitled to anything unless it was bequeathed to him. If I'd had brothers or sisters, nephews, nieces, uncles, aunts or children they would automatically have inherited a share, but I had no one. No one but Piers . . .

I felt suddenly chilled. Remembering Nick's insinuations and Julie's doubts, I wondered. Piers had always seemed so wealthy in his own right, surely he couldn't be so desperate for money that he would . . . *No!* I thrust the suspicion from my mind. It was unthinkable. I loved my husband and he loved me. He was generous with his money, buying me extravagant presents . . . all those flowers when I was in hospital . . . the honeymoon. And it was his child, too. Why would Piers want to kill his own child?

*

I changed my mind about a walk in the garden, and made my way up to the attic. What drew me there I did not know, unless it was a vain hope that it would trigger something in my memory.

The door was unlocked. Zena must have left it open for me. Why? Had she guessed I might go there? She would know how I felt, the emptiness that filled me. The loneliness that no one else could share. My hand trembled as I reached for the handle, and for a moment I could not find the strength to turn it. Then, breathing deeply, I went in.

Content in their own little world, the dolls were at work and play. I had the oddest sensation that their eyes turned towards me expectantly, that they had waited for me, just as they waited for Zena, waited to claim me into that twilight world at the edge of insanity.

I touched the dolls, tracing their waxen faces. My throat was tight with emotion as I moved between them, perceiving them as individuals. They were not just dolls, but characters in their own right, with lives of their own. I pushed the rocking horse into motion. Its comforting sound drew me back to early childhood, to a time of warmth and love. I understood now why Zena came here. I understood only too well the yearning and the grief: the desperate need to hold something, to cradle a child.

A deep sob shook my body. I'd lost my baby. I pressed my hands to my stomach, feeling the loss as if it were a physical pain.

I looked at Susie and wanted to hold her in my arms. Her eyes pleaded with me, and as I gazed at the painted face, I saw the red mouth open and heard a plaintive cry. It was the wail of a hungry child. Susie was crying for her mother. Zena was right – Susie didn't like to be left alone. She was asking to be held. She wanted to be loved.

I reached towards her and then stopped, shocked at what I was doing. Susie wasn't a child, she was a doll.

'No!' I cried, backing away. 'No, I won't.'

Turning, I ran from the attic.

Slipping on my coat, I went outside. The weeks in hospital had seen a change in the weather. It was now early November and I shivered as I felt the cold strike me. Frost had blackened the roses that still clung determinedly to their stems, and they looked forlorn and depressing. I walked, hands in pockets, eyes down. I could not remember ever having felt this unhappy before, even when I was sent away to boarding school. Tears were burning behind my eyes, and my chest ached. My world had crumbled, leaving me nothing. Yet I still had Piers and I would have another child . . .

'Aline.' Michael's voice startled me. 'It's cold today – should you be out?'

He had come from the direction of the converted barn that was his studio, and I knew he'd been working. He was wearing the faded green cords and the old sweater that he loved so much, and the sight of his familiar figure filled me with a sudden rush of emotion. Memories of my early childhood crowded into my mind and I ached for the comfort of his arms around me. He was my father, the only one I'd ever known, and like Susie, I needed so much to be loved.

'Michael . . .' I lifted my eyes to his pleadingly and my voice was that of a woebegone child. 'Oh, Michael, please help me.' I choked on a sob.

He hesitated for one breathless moment, then he reached out to draw me into his arms, his head coming down to rest against my hair. We stood like that for a few minutes, saying nothing. I felt him shudder and I lifted my face to look up at him. And then his lips touched mine, so gently that it was like the whisper of a butterfly's wing.

'My poor little love,' he said, and the words were a balm. 'I wouldn't have had it happen for the world.'

I closed my eyes, leaning my head against his shoulder as the tears slipped down my cheeks. I felt warm and comforted within the circle of his arms. It was as if the years had slipped away and there had never been that wide chasm between us. Yet as I looked up at him once more, I knew that it was not the same. Michael was gazing at me with the eyes of a lover. I knew then that I had not imagined that impassioned plea at my hospital bedside.

I waited for the surge of revulsion, but it did not come. I was a woman now, not a child, and I had learnt about desire. Looking up into his face, I felt only the warmth of his love, and the sadness of it. I knew too that I was safe with him; he would never expect or ask for a physical consummation of his love. He had lived with it, conquered it and long ago accepted that it could never be more than a hopeless passion. In that moment I knew without a shadow of a doubt that whatever had happened to me on the marshes when I was eleven years old, it had had nothing to do with his man. Perhaps his thoughts and feelings towards me had not always been pure, but he had suffered for his sin, if sin it was, and now nothing was left but the love.

He drew away from me and I saw that he was shaking. 'I shouldn't have kissed you,' he said, a look of shame in his eyes. 'Forgive me, Aline.'

'There's nothing to forgive,' I said. 'There never was, Michael.'

'Thank you, my darling,' he said, and smiled in understanding.

'Now, what are all these tears for?' He held my hand gently. 'To lose a baby is sad, but you can have another one. Zena isn't as lucky as you, Aline. Don't let this ruin your life – or your marriage.'

I heard the sadness in his voice. 'Zena thinks you blame her for my accident,' I said. 'You don't – do you?'

'I thought at first she might have had something to do with it,' he admitted with a sigh. 'But I've realized since that I was being unfair to her. I'm afraid I've been unfair to Zena too often, but from now on I'm going to try and make it up to her. When the exhibition is over I shall take her away for a holiday.'

'The exhibition . . .' I stared at him. 'I'd forgotten about that. When is it? Surely it should have been weeks ago?'

'We couldn't think about it while you were ill,' Michael said with a reproving look. 'Piers has been out of his mind with worry over you – to say nothing of his financial problems.'

'Financial . . . What do you mean?'

'He's had some serious losses at the gallery,' Michael explained. 'Bad debts and one thing and another affected his business for a while, but I shouldn't have told you. He didn't want you to know. He was in difficulty for a time but he's managed to sort it all out now, and there's no need to worry. He's sold some property and paid off his overdraft and – '

'But he never breathed a word,' I said. 'If I'd known . . .'

'Pride.' Michael smiled at me. 'You must know what a proud man he is, Aline. And very much in love with you. We had a row when you were in hospital. It was supposedly over the wiring but it had been brewing for a while. You do know how jealous he is?'

'Yes,' I said, worried. 'I – I think perhaps I should go home tomorrow.'

'I can't tell you what to do,' Michael said. 'But your memory is just as likely to return in London as here. Besides, what difference can it make? It was an accident, Aline. An unfortunate accident.'

'Yes,' I said. Michael had made me feel better. 'Yes, I'm sure you're right. I think I shall go back to town tomorrow. I'll ring Piers this evening and tell him.'

Chapter Fifteen

Zena was preparing the dinner when I went into the kitchen that evening. I watched in silence as she poured red wine over the pheasant and put the pan into the oven. She glanced at me and then carried on with chopping stalks off the asparagus spears, her back rigid.

'Could you stop for a while,' I said, as I saw that Zena meant to ignore me. 'I want to talk to you. I want to apologize . . .'

Zena paused with the knife in her hand, 'I don't see what we have to talk about,' she said angrily.

'I want to apologize if – if I seemed to accuse you this morning,' I said. 'I was upset and – '

Zena's face was pink and her eyes stabbed at me. 'You thought I'd pushed you out of spite,' she said. 'You thought I did it deliberately . . .'

'I thought you might have done,' I admitted, feeling ashamed. 'But now I realize how unfair I was. I've always had an active imagination and I'm afraid it got the better of me. I've accepted that it was an accident – and I'm sorry.'

Zena stared at me and I knew she was on the verge of another outburst, but she hesitated, and then her mouth tightened. 'I might be jealous of you, and I might say things I shouldn't, but I wouldn't kill your baby, Aline. Not your dear little . . .' Her voice caught on a sob and her shoulders shook with the force of her emotion.

My last doubts vanished as I saw her misery. 'I should have known that,' I said. 'I'm sorry, Zena. I've always tended to imagine things that aren't so. I remember as a little girl, I was always afraid of the evil I couldn't see. I used to have bad dreams . . .'

Making a visible effort, Zena pulled herself together and nodded her agreement. 'Yes, I know what you mean. When you lie in bed and hear the wind howling and it's dark outside, you start thinking of something so evil it isn't possible to picture it in your mind.' She frowned. 'But sometimes reality can be even worse than anything you can imagine.'

'What do you mean?'

'Just before you came in I was reading in the newspaper about a murder in London. It happened just a few days ago. An old woman was strangled.' A shiver went through Zena. 'She lived alone and she was terrified of intruders. She'd got all kinds of alarms and things on her gates, but it didn't do her any good. Someone killed her and ransacked the house. She had a lot of valuable antiques – a treasure house, the paper called it – and the thief took a collection of silver snuff boxes – '

Zena broke off as I gasped and sat down, my knees going weak. 'Did they say whereabouts in London?' I asked, feeling sick.

She shook the asparagus ends off the paper she'd been using and brushed it, then handed it to me. I read it swiftly, in horror. My fears were confirmed. My hands were trembling as I glanced up.

'I know her,' I said. 'Phyllis Pearson. Piers and I went there quite recently to buy some pictures from her. I took Mr Silcott to see her a few days later. She wanted to clear some things from her shed . . .'

'That's awful,' Zena said, concerned. 'You don't look well, Aline. Would you like some brandy?'

I shook my head. 'I'd love it, but I'd better not. The doctor at the hospital gave me some sleeping tablets, but he warned me not to drink alcohol.'

'I'll make a cup of tea then,' Zena said. 'You're shaking.'

'I can't believe it,' I whispered. 'How could anyone. . . ? She was so sweet, Zena. She – she gave me a beautiful christening gown for the baby – ' I choked and stopped.

'Oh Aline.' The tears rolled down Zena's cheeks. 'Some people are so wicked.'

We turned as Michael came into the kitchen. He looked alarmed, as if afraid that we had been quarrelling again. Zena wiped her eyes, looked half ashamed and then smiled.

'It's all right, we're not quarrelling,' she said, and explained about Phyllis Pearson.

Michael was shocked. 'The police will probably want to talk to you, Aline,' he said. As I registered alarm, he went on, 'Well, it sounds as if it was someone she knew – or someone she was expecting. It says here that she had opened the security locks on the gates to let in a visitor. You said she had decided to sell some of her things, Aline. And I should imagine whoever killed her had heard about the house being full of antiques, wouldn't you?'

The silence deepened and we gazed at one another in dismay. There was a sudden ringing from the oven and Zena jumped in fright, then hurried to adjust the temperature.

'That's awful if it's true,' I said. 'I feel responsible. I asked Mr Silcott to go there, but . . . *he* couldn't have talked about it.'

'No, of course not,' Michael agreed at once. 'I know Silcott. He wouldn't be involved in it, but someone who was brought in to take the things to the saleroom might have talked about it. You know how it happens, a few drinks at the pub and some careless chatter about the house you've been to that day. Someone overhears and then . . .' He shrugged his shoulders. 'That doesn't explain why she let them in, though.'

'She seemed to be so careful,' I recalled. 'Mind you, she had reason to be. There was a lot of stuff in that house.'

Zena blew her nose. 'There are some valuable things in this house, Aline. I often wonder if we'll come back one day and find there's been a burglary.'

'Well, we're insured,' I said. 'As long as no one gets hurt, that's all that matters. But I can't understand why they had to kill her.'

Michael glanced at the report again. 'Rather a brutal attack, too,' he said, his mouth twisting with distaste. 'That's strange . . .'

'What?' Zena and I spoke together.

'It says that there were far more valuable things left behind than were taken. Perhaps the motive wasn't theft, after all.'

'But what else could it have been?' Zena asked.

'I've no idea. Who knows what is in the mind of a murderer? I once read about a youth who murdered his friend because he laughed at him.'

'He must have been mad,' said Zena.

Something triggered my memory. It was a cold February day and the light over the sea was a curious grey . . . The child was walking on the marshes, looking down at the mud and grasses. Something caught her attention. It was an odd choking sound. She looked towards it and saw – The pictures were gone in an instant, but a chill crawled over my body. Michael stared at me.

'What's wrong, Aline?'

'Nothing.' I shook my head as he started forward in concern. 'I almost remembered something, but it's gone again. It has something to do with that youth laughing at his friend.'

'Was it something that happened on the marshes, Aline?' Michael was very tense as he waited for my answer.

'Yes.' I forced the word out. 'I remembered the light over the sea – that special light you told me about. It was a pearly grey, almost translucent. And yet there was just a hint of rose . . .'

'Go on,' Michael said. 'You've described it exactly. What happened then?'

'I – I heard an odd noise,' I said, and stopped. Michael looked at me expectantly. I shook my head. 'I don't know – that's all I remember.'

'Was it laughter?' Michael asked. 'Was someone laughing? Come on, Aline. Try.'

'No. I think he was . . .' I was trying but perhaps I was trying too hard. 'It's no good, I can't remember any more.'

'It doesn't matter.' His expression was thoughtful. 'It's a good sign, though. You've never got that close before, have you?'

'No,' I said, and smiled at him. 'It will be ironic if my memory of that day comes back now that it doesn't matter any longer, won't it?'

'Perhaps that's why. The mind works strangely, Aline. Perhaps it's *because* you're not upset any more about what happened all those years ago that it's starting to come back.'

'Yes,' I agreed. 'You might be right.' I glanced at my watch. 'I think I'll go and ring Piers now. I wonder if he has heard about poor Mrs Pearson.'

There was no reply to my call. I let the phone ring for some time but no one answered. Glancing at my watch, I saw that it was past seven. Piers should be home by now.

I dialled Julie's number. Tony answered.

'She's working late with a client tonight,' he said. 'How are you, Aline?'

'I'm fine, thanks. Well, I'm feeling a bit better this evening anyway.'

'That's good,' he said. 'I'll get Julie to ring you. She's been very concerned about you.'

'Yes, I know.' I hesitated. 'Have you seen Nick recently?'

'He was over to dinner a couple of weeks ago, just before he flew out to the Gulf.' Tony sounded a little odd. 'He wanted to come and see you, but he thought he might not be welcome.'

'Oh . . . It was probably best not, anyway.'

'I'll get Julie to call you then.'

'Yes. Thanks, Tony.'

I replaced the receiver. I felt empty at the loss of my child. It would take some getting over, but I had to try. Piers was a very physical man and he would not be patient for long with a lacklustre bed-mate. But still the image of my baby was lodged in my mind, where it rubbed and fretted like a stone in a shoe.

Shrugging off my mood, I tried ringing Piers again, but he still wasn't in. I went back to the kitchen. Dinner was almost ready. Zena had opened a bottle of wine. She offered it to me, looking annoyed with herself as I refused.

'Of course, I'd forgotten,' she said. 'You're not supposed to drink with those tablets you're taking. Sorry, Aline.'

'It doesn't matter,' I told her, as she began to put food on to a hostess trolley. 'What I'm really going to miss is my after-dinner brandy. I never used to bother until I was married, but it's become a habit with us. Piers laughs at me and says it's my favourite tipple, but it's his fault for getting me into a bad habit. Piers wasn't in,' I added, rather anxiously.

Zena glanced at the kitchen clock. 'It isn't that late,' she said. 'I rang him a couple of times when you were in hospital and he didn't get in until much later.'

'Piers went back to the flat while I was ill?'

'Yes.' Zena paused, straining the vegetables through a colander, her mind on what she was doing. 'He had business in town and sometimes he made two or three journeys a day. He looked so tired when he arrived a few days ago that I thought he was heading for a collapse. I told him he ought to take a break for a while, and he politely asked me to mind my own business.' She glanced at me then, her face flushed as if she thought I might resent the slight criticism. 'He was under a strain. He didn't lose his temper, he just sort of went cold on me . . . But perhaps that was understandable, he thought I'd pushed you down the stairs, Aline. I'm sure he did.'

'It was his child, too,' I reminded her, then cursed myself as Zena's eyes clouded. 'Don't let's talk about it any more. It was an accident.'

'I really am sorry about it,' Zena said.

'I know.' We were both stiff and sounding less than convincing. It was too painful for us both. I had to change the subject or we would lose what ground we had made. Zena was wearing an attractive cream linen coat dress with unusual black and gold buttons, and I lit on that with relief. 'I like your dress,' I said, determined to lighten the mood. 'Did you buy it locally?'

'In Norwich,' Zena replied with a smile. 'A friend of mine has her own dress shop and she gives me a discount. I can buy almost twice as much as I would otherwise be able to afford. Anne wants me to go into partnership with her because she thinks I have a flair for clothes, but of course I could never afford it.'

'How much would you need?'

'At least two hundred thousand pounds. She wants to open another shop, and her stock is expensive. Hardly anything sells for less than two hundred pounds.'

'I could lend you the money when the trust is wound up.'

Zena stared at me, her face flushed with pleasure. 'Would you really?'

'Of course. If it's what you want.'

She looked awkward. 'Michael might not agree.'

'It will be a business agreement between us,' I said. 'Besides, it would give you security for the future.'

'I'll have to talk to Anne – and Michael,' Zena said, looking excited. 'But it's something I've always wanted to do. I like clothes, and I'm good at making them. We might be able to have a line of our own . . .'

Her face had come alive for the first time since I'd known her. She looked pretty and happy, her eyes free of anxiety for once. I saw the woman she might have been, and I was sorry for all the months when we could have been getting to know each other instead of quarrelling. If I'd been around when she needed someone to talk to, she might never have become so obsessed with those dolls in the attic. More than anything, I wanted to make up for what I'd done to contribute to her unhappiness.

'I'm sure Michael will agree,' I told her. 'I can't touch the money for a couple of months, but . . .'

'It will take that long to find the right premises.' Zena looked at me, her eyes very bright. Obviously, she couldn't quite believe in my change of attitude towards her. 'You are sure about this?'

'Perfectly sure. Look at it as an investment, Zena. We'll do it properly through a solicitor, and when you start to make a profit you can pay a low rate of interest or give me a discount on my clothes – we'll work something out.'

'I don't know how to thank you.'

'You just have.' I smiled, feeling better. Perhaps our relationship was on the mend at last. 'Are we going to eat tonight, or what?'

Zena laughed then. 'Shall we take this through to the dining room? Michael was setting up the video. There's a good film on television at the same time as a documentary he wants to see.'

She wheeled the hostess trolley through the hall and into the dining room, and plugged it in to keep the food hot. We could hear the sound of the television in the small sitting room. Zena pulled a face at me.

'Men,' she said. 'I told him dinner was almost ready. If I don't go and drag him out of there, we'll be waiting all night.'

I looked out at the garden. All I wanted was peace between Zena and myself; I was tired of quarrelling. It was quite light despite the hour and

I saw the moon had appeared from behind some clouds. A movement in the shrubberies caught my eye, but just as I wondered if I'd imagined it or if there really was something out there, I heard a shrill scream. Forgetting the shadow, I rushed through to the sitting room – and stopped when I saw Zena kneeling on the floor beside Michael.

As Zena looked up at me, her eyes wide and fearful, I knew that, this time, there was nothing anyone could do. His face was twisted in an expression of agony and his lips bloodless, Michael was dead. On the floor his little pill box was open, its contents scattered far and wide.

'Oh no!' Zena whispered, and ran frantic fingers up his face. 'Michael, no! Please don't leave me. I can't bear it. I can't bear it.' She looked up at me, her eyes swimming with tears. 'Aline, what am I going to do? I loved him. I loved him so much . . .'

'Zena.' My throat tightened with emotion as I saw the extent of her grief, and remembering Michael's gentleness to me earlier that day, I felt tears sting my eyes. Pictures of the younger Michael came into my mind, memories of days when he had given me so much love, and I choked back a sob. 'I'm so sorry. So very sorry . . .'

I sank into a chair opposite the twisted face. It was too much all at once. Phyllis Pearson's murder had shocked and upset me, but I'd hardly known her. Michael's death was so much worse. I gazed at his face – so familiar, yet so unfamiliar in death – and felt a terrible loss. We had just begun to understand each other, he and I, and now he was gone. All those wasted years . . . I felt the tears trickle down my cheeks and I desperately wanted Piers. I wanted him to be with me.

Zena got to her feet, her face rigid. 'We have to ring for the doctor,' she said. 'I – I don't know quite what happens in these circumstances.' Her mouth trembled. 'Will they have to do an autopsy?'

'I don't know,' I said, taking a deep breath. I had to help her now; she was Michael's wife. All this was much worse for her. 'Perhaps it won't be necessary. Michael was very ill, after all.'

'Yes,' Zena said, drawing a sobbing breath. 'He knew it could happen at any time – that's why he was so desperate to get enough paintings done. He wanted to be sure I had some security for the future.'

'You will have,' I said quickly, wanting to reassure her. At least she need not be concerned about financial matters. 'Don't worry, Zena. I was going to give Michael half the money, but now I shall – ' I broke off as the door opened, my heart thumping as I remembered the shadow in the shrubberies. Had an intruder broken in? And then I was on my feet. 'Piers!' I cried. 'Oh, Piers. I'm so glad you've come!'

★

Piers took charge of the situation, telephoning the doctor and arranging all the things that Zena and I would have found so very painful. He had driven down after his meeting in town because he was worried about me, and I was so grateful that I clung to him, forgetting all the foolish ideas I'd had when I left the hospital. He smiled at me indulgently, kissing me on the lips, and I sensed his relief at my return to normality.

Michael's doctor arrived and confirmed that it had been another heart attack. He saw no need for an autopsy and signed the certificate at once. He said that he had been expecting it and that it was a mercy it had happened at home instead of on the marshes.

It was Piers who saw to all the funeral arrangements. Zena and I sat in the kitchen, drinking cup after cup of tea. The meal Zena had cooked was abandoned; no one wanted to eat. It was quite late before everything was finished and anyone could think of retiring to bed. After her initial shock, Zena was very calm and she even managed a little smile as we parted at the top of the stairs.

'Thank goodness you were here,' Zena said. 'I don't know how I would have managed if it hadn't been for you and Piers.'

'I'm glad I was here,' I replied. 'And I'm glad we can be friends at last. We *can* be friends, can't we, Zena?'

'Yes, of course,' she said. 'There's no reason for us to quarrel now, is there?' Her smile was very sad but perhaps genuine for the first time.

I smiled back, but said nothing as I watched her go into her own room. Piers was still downstairs, locking up, and I went into our room alone.

I'd held back my tears for Zena's sake, but now I was overcome by sobs and it was several minutes before I could control my grief; then at last I wiped my face and splashed it with cold water. Michael would not have approved. In his own way he had been a very proud man, a private man. I could almost hear his voice telling me not to cry. I was brushing my hair when Piers came in.

'You look very tired,' he said, coming to stand behind me, his hands on my shoulders. He massaged them for me and I felt the strength in his fingers. For a moment his hand lingered about my throat. His reflection in the mirror was distorted in the dim light and almost menacing. 'It's been a terrible strain for you, coming so soon after your own accident.'

'Yes, I am tired,' I said. 'I don't think I shall need one of my pills tonight.'

'The sleeping pills they gave you at the hospital?' Piers asked, and I nodded. 'I think I should take one, if I were you, darling. You're tired, but once you're in bed you will start to think, and then you'll toss and turn all night.'

'Perhaps you're right.' I waited as he went to the bathroom to fetch a glass of water. He handed me a pill and I swallowed it. 'Thank you, Piers. I'm so glad you came tonight. You must have known how much I needed you.'

'Must I?' He smiled as I discarded my clothes on the floor and slipped into bed, then he bent to kiss my forehead. 'Go to sleep, Aline, and don't worry. I'm here and everything will be all right now.' He was so gentle. So kind. It was so easy to do as he said.

The next few days were quiet and sad. Although not much was said, Zena and I were obviously both grieving for Michael. During those strange, flat days we reached out to one another, giving comfort where we could with a look or a smile but we respected each other's privacy.

Michael and Zena had not had many friends, but those who were closest either called or telephoned to say how sorry they were. After the announcement in the paper, letters from people who had bought and admired his work began to arrive by every post. It eased the pain a little to know how much pleasure his pictures had given; I don't think either Zena or I had realized how popular his pictures were. Michael had been a quiet, unassuming man who preferred to stay out of the limelight, but he was getting his share of it now.

'I should like to go ahead with the exhibition next week,' Piers said. 'The interest in Michael's work is inevitably going to be increased by what has happened.'

For a moment Zena looked as if she wanted to protest, but then she nodded. 'It's what Michael would have wanted,' she said, her expression defensive as she looked at me.

To me it sounded very much like cashing in on the publicity. Michael had built up quite a following over the years, and two or three of the Norfolk papers published obituaries praising his work. Nursing my grief at his death, I kept my opinions of the exhibition to myself. Michael's will was very simple: he had left everything he owned to his wife, and Zena was entitled to whatever she could get from the sale of his work.

Piers and I stayed at Hazeling until after the funeral, then drove back to London that afternoon. Zena had decided to close the house and drive to Norwich to stay with her friend Anne for a few days. She asked if she could stay with us at the flat while the exhibition was showing, and a little to my surprise, Piers readily agreed.

'I'm sure Aline would enjoy the company,' he said, glancing at me. 'Yes, of course,' I concurred. I could hardly say anything else; besides, I wanted to help her. Those dolls were still in the attic and I knew she still shut herself away now and then. I'd found her there earlier that morning, the baby doll in her arms. We'd looked at each other in silence, then she'd put the doll back in its cot and we'd gone downstairs together. I hadn't said a word but I felt that sooner she got away from Hazeling, the better, so I smiled and said, 'Come when you're ready.'

Zena gave me a grateful look and came to the door with us, waving until we were out of sight. I wondered what she would do after we'd gone. Would she go straight up to her strange little world in the attic?

Unforgivably, I forgot about Zena as the countryside slid past. I had been thinking that I needed something to do, something to fill the hours when Piers was at work. I had given up my job in the first place because Piers didn't want me to have a full-time occupation, but I wanted an interest. I liked clothes, but running a dress shop would not be the solution for me. I had been very interested in the work at Silcott and Barrie. I didn't want my old job back, but I thought I might do insurance valuations or perhaps research for a private collection – something I could fit in in my own time, which would convince Piers I was not neglecting our marriage.

Piers was in a good mood as we drove home. When we got in, he insisted that I put my feet up while he made a cup of tea. For some reason I felt a flicker of annoyance.

'I'm not an invalid, Piers,' I said, and perhaps my tone was a little sharp.

He looked at me, his face expressionless. 'I wasn't suggesting that you were. But you haven't been sleeping well, have you? Have you been having nightmares? You've never stopped having them since the attack happened, have you? And they've got worse since your fall, haven't they?'

'Yes,' I agreed reluctantly. 'Those tablets don't seem to help much. I keep having the same dream over and over again, and then I wake up.' I closed my eyes for a moment. Piers' concern made me feel nervous and on edge, and I wasn't sure why. It was natural for him to worry about me, and yet it would have been easier if he hadn't. 'I was just upset by Michael's death – '

'These dreams,' he interrupted. 'Do you actually see who is chasing you? What happens?'

'Please, Piers,' I said, and turned my head away. 'I would rather not talk about it.'

'But don't you see, the only way you're ever going to get it out of your mind is if you face up to what happened.'

'I know you're right but it's difficult . . .' My voice trailed to a whisper as I remembered something else. I glanced up at Piers. 'Did you read about Phyllis Pearson?'

He frowned, his mouth tight. 'I'd hoped you wouldn't hear about that just yet, Aline. Who told you? Was it Julie?'

'No. What made you think it might be Julie?'

'Well, she wrote to you at Hazeling, didn't she?'

'Yes, but she didn't mention Phyllis. I don't suppose she even realized that I knew her. She just wrote to say she was sorry about Michael. She wanted to come down, but she couldn't get the time off work.' Piers didn't say anything so I went on, 'It was in the paper. Zena showed it to me. She just thought it was a terrible murder. She had no idea I knew Phyllis. I was going to tell you about it – but then Michael died and that drove everything else from my mind. I've been so preoccupied with Zena.' I paused and added, 'She loved Michael, you know. I suppose I just forgot about poor Phyllis.'

'I wish Zena hadn't mentioned it. I knew it would upset you, and I didn't want that, darling. You've had enough to contend with.'

'Michael thought the police might want to talk to me.' I looked at him, feeling anxious. 'Have they said anything to you?'

'I made a statement about our visit there, but you were in hospital when it happened and could have nothing useful to add.' Piers turned away, loosening his tie as he headed for the kitchen. His voice came back to me, sounding muffled by distance. 'They think it must have been an opportunist. Just a few snuff boxes were taken, and most of them were recovered from a garden further down the road. Whoever did it could have had no idea of their value.'

I followed him into the kitchen, watching as he ran water into the kettle and switched it on. He glanced at me over his shoulder.

'Shall I make us an omelette, or would you rather go out for a meal, darling?'

'I'm not hungry,' I said. 'I think something light and then I'll have an early night.'

He came towards me, gazing down at me with a worried frown. Then he touched my cheek with his finger. I froze. We hadn't made love since I came out of hospital. I wanted it to happen soon, and yet I was jumpy every time he touched me.

'You're still not well, Aline,' he said. 'I know you think you're over it, but losing the baby and Michael dying like that – well, it has all been a strain for you. Don't worry about things. It will all come right in time.'

There was such gentleness in him then, such tenderness. I gazed into his face, wishing that I understood this man who was my husband. Now more than ever, I sensed a hidden grief in Piers, though he did his best to shut me off from whatever it was. I was overcome with a surge of love, and at that moment, I believed he needed me as much as I needed him. Perhaps it was this – this area of darkness in Piers which had drawn me to him and which linked us. Perhaps we both had our own shadows.

'Oh, Piers. You're so good to me,' I cried, a break in my voice. 'I couldn't bear it if we ever parted.'

'I love you,' Piers said, his voice becoming husky. 'Don't forget that, Aline. That's why I'm not going to rush you. You need a period of rest to recover, and you need some sleep. I think you should take two of your tablets tonight.'

'Two?' I was doubtful. 'Do you think that's a good idea?'

'One isn't enough to ensure you sleep,' he said, smiling at me. 'The doctor said you could increase the dose to two if you needed to.'

'Then I will,' I said. I squeezed his hand, feeling grateful for his care of me. He was my husband. I loved him. His moods were not important. 'Thank you, darling. I don't know what I would have done these last few days without you.'

The girl was alone in the vastness of the desolate marsh. It was dark and a mist was falling, a mist so thick and wet that it had soaked into her thin dress, making it cling to her breasts and thighs, accentuating the fact that she was naked beneath the flimsy garment. She was running, plunging blindly through the mud and the treacherous pools. Her hair hung about her face in damp strings, sticking to her lips and getting into her mouth as she gasped for breath. She was panting, stumbling in her terror as she ran. Somewhere just behind her was a man. Now he was catching her up. She could see his face and his cold, cold eyes. She screamed again and again, but it was no use. No one could hear her. The man had caught up with her. For a moment he stood looking at her, and then his hands reached for her, closing around her throat . . .

I awoke with a cry. It was the old dream but it had changed, becoming even more terrifying. Piers was bending over me, his face creased with worry. My nightdress was soaking wet and I was shivering with cold. I looked up at my husband, feeling limp and exhausted.

'It was the nightmare again. But this time it was different. I saw him this time, Piers. He tried to strangle me.'

'Who was it?' asked a tense, anxious Piers. 'Did you recognize his face?'

'I – ' A little sob broke from me. 'Oh, Piers, I can't bear it. It was Michael!' I covered my face in my hands as the tears came. 'I can't believe it. He told me that he found me after the attack, and he was so gentle when I was upset after I lost the baby.'

Piers' arms went round me. He rocked me to and fro as I wept, kissing my hair and murmuring words of comfort. 'It was just a dream, my darling,' he said. 'Just a dream . . .'

I looked up at him then. 'But it was the old nightmare, Piers – the one that has haunted me for years – and this time he – he tried to strangle me.'

'You've got it all muddled up in your mind,' Piers said in a soothing tone. 'Now you know why I didn't want to tell you about Phyllis Pearson. I was afraid this might happen.'

'Oh, Piers,' I said, feeling bewildered. What was happening to me? 'I don't know what to believe any more. I'm so mixed up. I get all kinds of pictures in my head, flashes of light and faces . . .' I stared at him in horror. 'Am I going mad? Am I having a nervous breakdown?'

He laughed and shook his head. 'Don't be silly, Aline. You're sane, but you've been ill and you're under a strain. As soon as the exhibition is over I'm going to take you away for a holiday.'

'Oh yes,' I clung to him. 'I do love you, Piers. I need you so much. So very much . . .'

'And I love you,' he murmured.

'Go back to sleep now, darling. I'm with you. Nothing can harm you now.'

Michael's exhibition was an instant success. The gallery sold twenty pictures on the very first day, some of them for prices Michael would never have believed possible. If the rest of the week was as good, Zena would have several thousand pounds to fall back on. She was very excited and seemed to have overcome her initial reluctance.

'I talked to Anne,' she told me at breakfast on the third day of the sale. 'She says I'll need about two hundred and twenty thousand pounds for an equal partnership. I'll probably be able to come up with twenty to thirty thousand myself. If you could lend me the rest, Aline . . .'

'I've already written to my solicitors about it, Zena,' I said. 'I've told them to advance you whatever you need at a low rate of interest. You need not start to repay until the business begins to make a profit. And I'd like to give you some money to help you buy your flat, if you wouldn't think I was being patronizing.'

'I'll be glad of any help. Bless you, Aline,' Zena cried. 'You're so generous.'

'I've always thought so,' Piers said, coming in from the hall. 'But what has she done now?'

'She's going to lend me the money I need for my business venture,' Zena said.

I thought Piers looked annoyed, probably because I hadn't discussed it with him first, but he made no comment so perhaps I'd imagined it.

'Congratulations, Zena. I wish you every success for your venture.' He paused for a moment, then looked at her inquiringly. 'Are you planning on staying at Hazeling now that . . . Wouldn't you be better based in Norwich?'

Zena nodded. 'Hazeling is far too big for me on my own,' she said. 'I couldn't cope with the house and the shops. No, I shall find myself a little flat in or just outside Norwich. After the exhibition ends, I'll go back to Hazeling and clear out my things.' She glanced at me, an odd expression in her eyes. 'I've decided to sell my dolls, Aline. Some of them are valuable. I think they could fetch quite a lot at auction.'

I knew there was considerably more behind her words than the sale of some dolls. She was telling me that she was going to try and put her obsession with having a child behind her and make a new life for herself.

'I'm glad,' I said, and smiled at her. 'I thought I might pop into the saleroom this morning, and I could have a word with Mr Silcott, if you like. He has special toy sales every now and then, and I might be able to get you a good rate on the commission.'

'Would you?' Zena was eager. 'I'm going to clear out Michael's studio while I'm down there, Aline. He painted a few portraits of you. Would you like to have them?'

I hesitated, glanced at Piers, then nodded. 'I'd like to see them, Zena. We're going away for a couple of weeks as soon as the exhibition is over, but I could pop down to Hazeling when we get back. I shall need to speak to the insurance people if the house is going to be left empty. We might have to have special locks or store some of the more valuable things.'

'I can see to all that for you, Aline,' Piers offered. 'Besides, I think we'll be spending weekends down there quite often. It would be a shame not to use it, wouldn't it?'

'Yes,' I said reluctantly. 'Yes, I suppose it would.'

Chapter Sixteen

'You look bloody awful,' Julie said as soon as she saw me. 'You've got shadows under your eyes and you've lost weight again.'

I laughed and shook my head. 'Thanks for the compliments. I came here to take you to lunch, and that's what I get!'

'Sorry, love.' Julie kissed my cheek, looking concerned. 'Let's go and have a really wicked lunch, and drown our sorrows.'

'Oh Julie! It's so good to see you again.'

Julie studied me with narrowed eyes. 'You weren't like this in the hospital, so what's happened?'

'Nothing. I'm fine, honestly.'

'Don't lie to me,' Julie said. 'I know you too well. That brave face you're putting on isn't going to fool me.'

I hesitated, not wanting to bother her with my foolish fears, but somehow it all came out. 'I suppose it was Michael dying like that – but I feel so awful most of the time. I get headaches and I can't sleep. When I do I have dreadful nightmares.' Now that I'd started, it was a relief to tell her. 'I keep dreaming that someone is trying to strangle me.'

Julie was silent for a moment, then she frowned, a puzzled expression in her eyes. 'This isn't like you.'

'Piers thinks its because of what happened to Mrs Pearson.'

'Is that the woman who tried to get in touch with you through the saleroom?'

'Yes, that's right,' I said, and explained about the murder. 'I was becoming quite friendly with her and it was such a terrible thing to happen. In a way I feel responsible.'

'Why on earth should you? You were in hospital when it happened.'

'Oh, I don't mean in that way,' I said. 'But whoever did it must have heard about the antiques because of the sale, don't you think?'

'Perhaps . . .' Julie pulled a face. 'But it could have happened for all sorts of reasons. You can't blame yourself, Aline.' She gave me a worried look. 'You're moping about this, and it isn't good for you. I think you should get out more. Visit friends or take a job – keep yourself busy.'

'As a matter of fact I've been thinking the same thing. I'll give Mr Silcott a ring later.'

'That's a good idea.' Julie squeezed my arm. 'Come on, let's have that lunch. Tony's got a massive order so we have to celebrate. The champagne is on me!'

I hesitated, knowing that I ought not to drink, then I thought, to hell with it, why shouldn't I have a drink for once? I would just have to go without my pills. They didn't seem to be doing me much good anyway.

After I left Julie, I decided to go shopping. The champagne combined with my friend's company had done me the world of good. I decided I was making too much of the dreams; they *were* only dreams, and I'd had them for years, so why bother about them now?

After trying on several suits and dresses, I had to admit that Julie was right: I was now a very slim size ten. I bought a black and white spotted Mondi skirt and jacket and a couple of blouses for the holiday Piers was planning, then left the shop.

As I stepped out into Bond Street, I almost bumped into someone. Startled, I gazed up into a pair of bright blue eyes.

'Nick!' I cried. 'I wasn't looking where I was going. Did I step on your toes?'

'No.' He smiled his lazy smile. 'Not that it would have mattered. There's hardly enough of you left to make an impression. You've been slimming again.'

'Don't *you* start. I've had all that from Julie. You're looking very pleased with yourself.' In my surprise at seeing him again, I forgot that we had parted in anger. 'Have you just arrived from somewhere – or are you on the verge of departing?'

He laughed, running his fingers through his pale hair with that self-deprecating air of his. 'Neither, I'm afraid. You see before you a respectable businessman. I've opened a little antique shop in Richmond. As a matter of fact, I went to an auction this morning. And you're right, I am feeling rather pleased. I bought something very special.'

'You? You've opened an antique shop. . . ?' I stared at him in amazement. 'I don't believe it. Why?'

'I've been thinking about it for a while,' he said, his eyes searching my face as if looking for approval. 'I told you I had a few ideas to try out.'

'Yes, you did.' I hesitated as I remembered other things he had said. 'I'm sorry if I was angry with you last time we met, Nick, but – '

'I was out of line?' He looked rueful. 'You don't have to tell me, Aline. I guess I put my foot in it once too often, huh?'

'I understood why . . .' I faltered. Common sense told me that I should stay away from Nick, but I found myself wanting to prolong our meeting. 'It was all just a silly misunderstanding. Will you forgive me?'

'I'm the one who should be asking that. How about a coffee just to show that there are no hard feelings?'

His tone was light and casual, but I sensed the underlying tension. 'Why not?' I said, laughing up at him. My love for Piers had been like a whirlwind sweeping me along in its path, too strong to be denied, but I'd missed the easy companionship I'd known with Nick. 'Yes, I'd like that, Nick.' He offered his arm and I slipped mine through it, feeling relaxed and happy. 'Where shall we go?'

The accidental meeting with Nick lifted my spirits. I was feeling much better when I got home and rang Mr Silcott. He was pleased I'd telephoned and said he would think about my offer of part-time work.

'I'm sure I can find something for you, Aline,' he said. 'By the way, did you know about Mrs Pearson?'

'Yes, I read the report in the paper. Have you heard any more recently?'

'As a matter of fact, I had a letter from her solicitor this morning. I think I may be asked to clear the house, once a distant cousin has taken what she wants.'

'There's no news on the – the murder then?'

'No. The police are puzzled at the motive,' he said. 'They seem to think it may have been a nutter.'

'Oh, do you think so?' I felt relieved. 'You don't think it was someone she let in, then?'

'It was definitely a break-in,' Mr Silcott replied. 'The papers got it wrong.'

'And yet nothing much was taken?'

'Probably got frightened after attacking her.'

'She was such a dear,' I said, a sob in my voice. 'I can't understand anyone wanting to hurt her.'

'There are some nasty characters around,' he said. 'Anyway, I must get on now. It was nice to hear from you, Aline. I'll be in touch.'

After Mr Silcott had rung off, I felt a weight had been lifted from my shoulders. Phyllis Pearson's murder had had nothing to do with my advising her to sell through Silcott and Barrie. It was simply a terrible tragedy.

217

I decided that it was time to start living again. The grief for Michael and my unborn child was still there inside me, but I owed it to Piers to try to forget.

As a way of showing Piers that I was determined to make a new start, I prepared a celebration meal. I made a starter of salmon and avocado salad followed by gammon with peaches. And I surpassed myself by producing a luscious syllabub. I felt very proud of my efforts as I heard Piers come in and I went to greet him with a kiss.

'I've made you a special dinner,' I said. He loosened his tie, went through to the sitting room and poured himself a brandy.

Piers was frowning and he didn't answer as he swallowed his drink. He didn't offer me one as he usually did in the evenings, and I knew he was in one of his black moods. I sensed a quarrel looming.

'Is something wrong, Piers?' I asked. 'Did you have a bad day?'

He turned slowly to look at me, and I waited for the storm. Something was wrong . . . Had Piers seen me with Nick? It was just possible. The gallery was not very far from where I'd bumped into him. Yet surely if he had, he would say something.

'Wrong?' Piers asked. I knew that he was angry, though his face had that blank expression he could assume at will. 'Should there be something wrong, Aline?'

His eyes were cold – so very cold.

Perhaps I should have mentioned that I'd bumped into Nick, but I hadn't wanted to precipitate a row. Now it was too late. If I tried to explain, he would only think I had something to hide. And after all, I couldn't be sure that was what had brought on his mood.

'No.' I turned away. I always hated it when Piers went cold on me. When he was angry, I could cope, but not when he was like this. 'No, I can't think of anything,' I lied.

'Then that's all right, isn't it?' Piers said. 'I'm going to take a shower and then I have to go out again. I shan't have time for dinner.'

'But I've made it specially for you . . .'

For a moment his eyelids flickered. 'Guilty conscience, Aline?' he asked, and then before I could answer, he went through to the bathroom.

Piers came in as I was pouring a cup of coffee the next morning. He was wearing his tracksuit and had obviously been for a run. In his hand were several letters, two of which he put down on the table in front of me, the others he took with him as he went into the bedroom. He hadn't spoken a word to me since he went out the previous evening.

'Piers.' I followed him to the bathroom door. 'Do you want anything to eat?'

'I'll have scrambled eggs on toast,' he said. He looked at me and then suddenly smiled. 'You look worn out, darling. Didn't you sleep last night?'

'Not much,' I admitted. 'At least, not at first – I didn't hear you come in.'

'I was quite late so I slept in the spare room. I didn't want to disturb you.'

'Oh.' I hesitated, looking at him uncertainly. Perhaps it would be better to tell him the truth and get it over. 'I meant to tell you, I ran into Nick Winters yesterday. He asked me to have coffee with him and I couldn't get out of it. You don't mind, do you?'

'Of course not, darling,' he said. 'I'm sorry if I was a bit abrupt last night. I had things to do and it was late when I got in. That's the only reason I slept alone. I wanted you to get some rest. These past few weeks have been difficult for you.' He paused for a moment. 'It will be better when we can get away. Today is the last day of the exhibition – are you coming in?'

'Yes, I think I will,' I said. 'Can I come with you?'

'Of course,' he said, seeming surprised that I should need to ask. 'Why ever not?'

'Oh, no reason.' Piers didn't seem to realize how upset I was by our quarrels; apparently he was able just to shrug them off. 'I'll get breakfast and then I'll change.'

'Oh, yes,' Piers said over his shoulder. 'I've left a couple of casual jackets on the bed in the spare room. I would like to have them cleaned for the holiday. Don't let me forget them, Aline.'

'No,' I said. 'We can drop them off as we go.'

I returned to the kitchen and filled the coffee machine, then went into the spare room. The jackets were lying on the bed. I picked them up and went through the pockets. There were only a couple of letters – one of them had distinctive blue printing on the envelope – and a handkerchief with some dark brown spots like dried blood, on it. Piers must have cut himself some time ago. I doubted it was worthwhile trying to wash the marks out, so I picked up the handkerchief, took it through to the kitchen and put it in the bin. Piers had plenty of spare ones.

I would take the jackets to Piers' favourite cleaners. He was very particular about his clothes. After we got back from the gallery, I would have to start thinking about what to pack for the holiday.

The Seychelles were paradise. For ten days we were lost in our own little world of soft, sandy beaches, palm trees, and tropical forest with its exotic flowers. There were tumbling waterfalls and little thatched bungalows set in a coconut grove on the slopes of a hillside. In the peaceful atmosphere, the tensions we had both felt at home melted away.

We walked hand in hand by the edge of the blue water, swam, made love and talked of the future. It seemed as if we had shed our cares along with the winter fogs, and it was just like it had been on our honeymoon. I was sleeping at last, and without the pills. It had been a conscious decision to leave them at home. Piers had been a little doubtful at first, but now he admitted I was right.

'You're so much better without them, darling,' he said. 'I can hardly believe the change in you. I don't mind telling you now, I was getting very worried.'

'You seemed so strange sometimes,' I said, testing our relationship. 'Almost as if you didn't like me any more.'

'Silly girl,' he said, and kissed me on the mouth. 'I thought *you* had gone off *me* for a while.'

'You don't think so now?' I asked, and he laughed.

'Not after last night!'

As he drew me down to kiss him, I thought how foolish all my doubts had been.

We ate in small Creole restaurants, not wanting the faster pace of the large hotels. It was a restful, peaceful time and we needed the break from a life that had been difficult for us both. We stayed on Mahé for the first few days, then island-hopped by way of a light aircraft, visiting Praslin, La Digue and Bird – a home for thousands upon thousands of sea birds.

Most of the time, though, we just lazed on the beach, enjoying the tranquillity of our surroundings. I'd never felt happier, I told Piers, as were walking in the moonlight by the water's edge.

'That's good,' he said, drawing me towards him. 'I want you to be happy, darling. Always. I'd do anything to protect you from harm. You know that, don't you?'

I was a little surprised at the intensity of his look, but I shouldn't have been. Piers was a passionate lover.

'I love you,' I whispered. 'If I lost you, I think I should die.'

220

For a moment there was a strange, sad expression in his eyes, then he drew me to him. 'You won't lose me, Aline,' he said. 'I'll always be there when you need me. I promise . . .'

Piers made love to me that night with a passion that set my body on fire. I climaxed over and over again, clinging to him and weeping for the sheer joy of it.

'Never leave me, Aline,' he murmured into my ear. 'I don't know what I might do if you did.' His hand enclosed my throat and lingered. I was aware of the strength in his hands. *If he chose, he could snap my neck without thinking twice.* 'I'll never leave you, Piers,' I said, and kissed his shoulder over and over again in order to blot out what I'd thought. 'You mustn't even think it. I love you. I'll always love you.'

'It's just that I couldn't let you go,' he said, and stroked my hair. 'I'm a fool, Aline. I know you love me. Go to sleep now.'

I slept for several hours, but Piers didn't. When I woke up, the bed beside me was cold and empty. I got up and pulled on my robe. Piers was standing outside the bungalow, watching the sunrise. I slid my arm about his waist, sensing his turmoil.

'What's wrong, darling?'

He glanced down at me, and I was shocked by the bleak expression in his eyes. Then he smiled and it vanished.

'I was just wishing that we could stay here forever.'

'But you enjoy your life so much, Piers. You can't mean it!'

'Can't I?' He laughed. 'No, of course I don't. Come on, I'm going for a swim. I'll race you to the water.'

We returned to the flat on a wet December day. Shivering, we turned up the heating, and Piers made coffee while I unpacked. He sorted through the letters and laid them on the kitchen table.

'Anything for me?' I asked.

'A few Christmas cards and some bills, by the look of it,' he said. He slit open a letter of his own and frowned as he glanced through it.

'Something wrong, darling?' I looked at him curiously.

'Nothing I can't take care of.' Piers folded a white envelope with blue writing which looked vaguely familiar and put it into his pocket. He was smiling now. 'Well, duty calls. I suppose I'd better show my face at the gallery, especially if we're going down to Hazeling this weekend.'

'Do we have to?' I pulled a face at him. 'I want to do some Christmas shopping. There are only a few days left.'

'We did promise Zena we would sort things out when we got back,' he reminded me. 'Anyway, I thought it would be nice to have a real old-fashioned Christmas at Hazeling. We could have a huge tree and holly all over the place. Wouldn't you like that, darling?'

He so obviously wanted me to be pleased that I agreed, though I would have preferred to stay in town. My memories of Hazeling were still a little raw, but I couldn't disappoint Piers.

'Yes, I suppose it would be nice,' I said. 'Shall we invite Julie and Tony to stay – and Zena, of course?'

He hesitated for a fraction of a second, then nodded. 'Why not make a party of it? After all, it's your birthday soon, isn't it?'

'February.' I grimaced. 'I'll be twenty-five.'

'Quite an old lady,' he said, grinning. 'You'll have your own money then. Have you decided what to do with it all?'

'I'm going to give some away, set up a trust for Hazeling and – I've no idea. What do you think I should do with it, Piers?'

He hesitated, then frowned and turned away. 'Don't ask me about investments,' he said. 'Get your lawyers to sort it out. But I'll do the inventory of the contents at Hazeling for you. Some of the pictures are rather special.'

'Thank you, darling,' I said. 'There was a pretty little picture in the alcove under the stairs, but it must have been moved because it wasn't there last time. I thought that might have been one of the ones you were talking about.'

'I can't say I remember it.' Piers had turned away. 'No doubt it will turn up.'

'Yes, I expect so.' I smiled. 'I think I'll do a little of that shopping, and I'll probably have lunch with Julie.'

'Do that,' Piers said. 'I'll see you this evening.'

After he'd gone, I rang Julie at the clinic and made arrangements to meet her for lunch. Then I went on a spree and by twelve o'clock I'd bought most of what I wanted. All that was left on the list was something for Zena and a special present for Piers.

I decided to leave the rest for another day and hailed a taxi. Julie arrived at the restaurant at almost the same moment.

'Did you have a good time?' Julie asked, her eyes running over with me with approval. 'That's much better. You look more like yourself.'

'I feel so much fitter,' I said. 'The holiday did me good.'

'Have you stopped having the dreams?' Julie asked.

I nodded. 'Yes, completely. I didn't have one while we were away.' I smothered a sigh, and Julie looked at me, her brows rising. 'Piers wants to spend Christmas at Hazeling.'

'And you're not very keen?'

'Not very.'

'You think the dreams might start again?'

'Yes, something like that.' I laughed self-consciously. 'I know it's stupid, Julie, but I can't help it.'

'Then tell Piers you don't want to go.'

'He's looking forward to it. He wants a real old-fashioned Christmas with all the trimmings.' I looked at her. 'We're going to ask Zena and you and Tony. You will come, won't you?'

'Oh, I wish I could,' Julie said. 'But I promised Tony's parents that we would go there. We haven't been for ages, so I can't go back on it now. I'm sorry, Aline.'

'Don't worry about it.' I shrugged my shoulders. 'You'll be able to come for my birthday party, won't you?'

'I wouldn't miss it for the world,' Julie said. 'Now what are we going to have? I fancy the skate in black butter and peppers. What about you?'

'I think I'll have the same,' I said. 'Do you want chips or the salad?'

'Salad,' Julie said, and then opened her bag. 'I almost forgot. I popped into the saleroom yesterday to look at some nineteenth-century fashion plates I want to buy for Tony, and Mr Silcott came over to talk to me. He asked me to give you this.' She took out a white envelope with my name on it but no address.

'What is it?'

'I've no idea. Someone gave it to him for you. He was going to post it, then he saw me and asked me if I would be seeing you soon.'

'I wonder what on earth . . .' I slit it open and extracted the piece of paper inside. It was an old newspaper cutting, rather yellowed and dog-eared. 'What is this, do you suppose?'

Julie looked at part of an advertisement for nylon stockings. 'Turn it over – it might be on the other side.'

I did as she suggested and gasped. 'It's about a murder . . . It happened years ago . . . An old woman was strangled . . .' The cutting fluttered to the table as I looked at Julie. 'This is sick. Who would do something like that? Who would send it to me?'

Julie looked at my white face and picked up the piece of newsprint. She read it quickly. 'It happened almost twelve years ago,' she said. 'It was a Mrs Edith Dodson. She was sixty-three and her husband had died after falling downstairs and breaking his back a few weeks previously. She lived alone and her grandson was away on holiday at the time. The police were puzzled by the murder as nothing was taken from the house and they couldn't discover a motive for the attack – which was rather brutal, by the sound of it. She was badly beaten before she was killed.'

'Oh, Julie,' I whispered, feeling slightly sick. 'It's just like Phyllis Pearson.'

'Yes,' she said grimly. 'It does sound a bit like it, I must admit.'

'Who could have sent it to me – and why?'

'I don't know.' Julie's mouth hardened with determination. 'But I intend to find out. I'll keep the cutting, if you don't mind, Aline. And I'll ask Mr Silcott exactly where he got it . . .'

I heard the telephone ringing as I reached the door of the flat. I snatched it up just in time. My nerves were still jangling from the shock of receiving that old newspaper cutting, and I was breathless from rushing to open the door.

'Hello,' I said. 'Aline Drayton here.'

'Aline, it's Zena.' There was a slight pause. 'I'm afraid I have some bad news for you.'

My heart jerked. 'What's wrong, Zena?'

'We've had a break-in at Hazeling.'

'Oh no!' I cried. 'When? Are you all right?'

'Sometime this morning. Everything was fine when I arrived last night. I left the house at eleven today to do some shopping in Blakeney, and when I came back someone had broken a window at the rear and got in.'

'Have they taken much?'

'No, I don't think so. Just a few pieces of silver, as far as I can see. A couple of decanters were smashed and one of Michael's paintings was damaged, but that's about all. The police seem to think it was probably youths messing around. The house has been empty for a couple of weeks, after all.'

'It could have been worse then,' I said relieved. 'Piers was right, we shall have to make an inventory and get someone in to see about security.'

'Well, I'm going to be here until after Christmas now,' Zena said. 'I've had the window seen to and a new safety catch.'

'Thank you for ringing me,' I said. 'We're coming down this weekend. Piers wants to spend Christmas there, so you won't be alone for long.'

'Oh, I'm not frightened,' Zena replied. 'I'm used to being here on my own. It will be nice to see you, though. We can have a traditional Christmas, if you're up to it.'

224

'I'm feeling much better,' I said. 'I think Michael would want us to make the most of your last Christmas at Hazeling, don't you?'

'Oh, don't say that.' She laughed. 'I hope you'll invite me to stay sometimes.'

'Of course. You know I didn't mean it like that.'

'I'll see you at the weekend, then.'

Piers took me out that evening. He said I would only brood if we stayed in, so we had a meal and then went dancing at Annabel's. I felt much better after drinking my share of the champagne, and I slept soundly. In the morning Piers said he had meetings all day, and I decided to finish my Christmas shopping.

I'd bought a video camera for Tony, and a fabulous cream Renzo suit with gold embroidery and medallions on the jacket for Julie. She would have a fit if she ever guessed what I'd paid for it, but that would remain a secret. I was in the mood for being extravagant. I wanted to buy something nice for Zena, and I didn't have a clue what to get Piers – unless I could find a good bronze . . . Something like that Italian hunter we had seen at Mrs Pearson's.

Remembering that Nick had opened an antique shop in Richmond, I rang for a taxi. I thought I might as well see if he had anything suitable in stock.

Nick's shop surprised me. I wasn't sure what I'd expected, but it certainly wasn't the period building I discovered down a side street after much searching. It was a Tudor house with the lower floor converted into business premises. Inside, the plaster walls had been partly covered with a greyish-green hessian between blackened oak beams. It was a perfect foil for the pewter platters and shining copper and brass that hung everywhere.

Just inside the door was a sixteenth-century oak hutch with linenfold panelling. Standing on it was a famille rose Chinese bowl filled with flowers. A little further inside I saw a beautiful early English dresser with brass handles, its shelves full of interesting bits and pieces. There were all kinds of chairs, occasional tables and a couple of desks, besides many smaller items. Nick had gone mostly for traditional English furniture, and the shop had warmth and appeal.

He came in from a door at the back, and smiled as he saw me. 'Aline, what a terrific surprise,' he said.

'I love the shop,' I congratulated him. 'I'd no idea you were so knowledgeable about antiques.'

'When you're waiting around for news stories to break, you have a lot of time to kill,' he said. 'I've spent many hours poring over magazines and reference books. I suppose I always thought I might do something like this one day.'

'You never mentioned it to me.'

'No,' Nick looked rueful. 'I didn't think I was ready . . . '

'So what changed your mind?'

Nick shrugged, ignoring my question. 'Were you just passing or did you come specially to see me?'

'I'm looking for a Christmas present,' I said, and then my eyes fell on a magnificent bronze statuette of a rearing horse. 'And it looks as if I might have found it.'

The statue was about twelve or fifteen inches high, exquisitely modelled, with every rippling muscle showing the strength and power of the stallion. I thought it beautiful and it was perfect for Piers. Nick saw the direction my gaze had taken and he smiled.

'Isn't he fantastic?' he said. 'It's nineteenth-century French, and too expensive, I'm afraid.'

'What do you call expensive? I don't really mind anyway. It's for Piers.'

The smile faded from Nick's face. 'I'm sorry, Aline. I can't sell it to you.'

'But why?' I stared at him. 'Isn't it for sale? It's just perfect for Piers, who has been so good to me.'

Nick's face was grim and reserved as he looked at me. 'I'm glad you have such faith in your husband. I'm not saying anything – but I won't sell you the horse.'

I stared at him for a few seconds longer, then went out of the shop, letting the door bang behind me. Outside in the bitter wind, I fought off my overpowering desire to weep.

I found another bronze horse in an arcade of shops near Old Bond Street. It wasn't quite as well modelled as the one in Nick's shop, but I wouldn't have gone back if he'd begged me to buy it. I was so angry with Nick, and I couldn't understand why he wouldn't sell me that bronze.

I bought a cameo brooch for Zena. It was fifteen-carat gold and depicted the Three Graces. The stone had a pale grey background – less common than the brown ones. I thought Zena would be pleased with it because the setting was distinctive. Before I left the shop, the assistant advised me to have a safety chain fitted.

226

'It's for a Christmas present,' I said. 'But I may bring it back later if she wants a chain fixed.'

'Those old catches are very unreliable,' the assistant said. 'It would be safer to have something done.'

I thanked him and left. It was only four o'clock but it was getting dark and I wanted to wrap my presents before Piers came home, so I hailed a taxi.

I let myself into the flat, went to put the kettle on and then rang Julie.

'Could we meet tomorrow?' I asked. 'I want to give you my presents. We're going down to Hazeling at the weekend and may not come back before Christmas.'

'I can't manage lunch,' Julie said. 'Come to the clinic at eleven and we'll have coffee in my office before I see my first client. I wanted to discuss something with you anyway. I might have some news for you.'

'What kind of news?'

'About that cutting,' she said. 'I rang Mr Silcott and I know where it came from – '

'Where?' I interrupted, my heart jerking.

'Mrs Pearson's cousin found it in her writing case with letters from Mr Silcott. There was no address on the envelope, just your name. She asked if you were anything to do with the saleroom and Mr Silcott agreed to pass it on. Neither of them had any idea what was inside.'

'Phyllis had put it in an envelope with my name on it?' I felt a flicker of unease and my skin crawled. 'That's uncanny, Julie. I mean why should she? It's almost as if she knew that she was going to die . . .'

'I've no idea why she did it,' Julie said. 'Look, you may not like this, but I've asked Nick to do some research on the murder – the old one, I mean. I think we need to know more about this.'

'No, I don't like it very much,' I said. 'I would rather just leave things as they are, Julie.'

'Are you sure? Aren't you interested to know why she wanted to show you that report?'

'No, I'm not. I'm not sure why, but it frightens me, Julie. Please don't meddle. You might end up getting more involved than you think.'

'All right,' she said. 'If the idea upsets you that much, I'll tell Nick not to bother.'

'Thanks.' I was relieved. 'I'll pop in about eleven tomorrow, then.'

As Julie rang off, I went into the kitchen and began to sort out the various cards and wrappings. I didn't want to think about the newspaper cutting . . . or Nick.

*

227

I'd just finished washing my hair the next morning, when the doorbell rang, and thinking Piers must have forgotten his key, I went to open it. Seeing Nick standing there, I gasped.

'Can I come in?' he asked.

'Piers will be back soon . . .'

'I'm delivering presents. Julie asked me to call because she's too busy.'

'I was going into her office to see her.' Reluctantly, I stood back to let him enter. 'Come in, then. Would you like a drink?'

'Coffee, if it's no trouble.' He smiled as I rubbed my hair and let it hang loose. 'I always did like to see you with wet hair. It's sexy.'

'Nick . . .' I saw the hunger in his face. 'Don't – you mustn't . . .'

His look reproached me. 'You don't just forget someone you've loved, Aline. Someone you still love . . .'

'I know.' I looked at him unhappily. 'I wouldn't blame you if you hated me, Nick.'

'But I don't,' he said. 'That's just the trouble.'

I turned away, hiding the uncertainty I was afraid he would see in my face. I was married to Piers. I had no right to feel anything for Nick except friendship. That's all it was, I told myself firmly.

Nick deposited several parcels on a chair, then followed me into the kitchen. He watched as I made coffee, his eyes following my every move. I was afraid that he could sense my unease so I went into the attack. 'Just why did you come?' I asked. 'Julie knew I was going in. The presents were an excuse, weren't they?'

'Yes.' His face was serious now. 'She told me you don't want me to investigate that old newspaper cutting.' He frowned as I nodded. 'Why, Aline? Surely you must realize it could be important?'

I avoided his gaze and poured the coffee into two mugs. 'I would rather you left it alone, Nick. No particular reason.'

He got up and moved towards me. I looked up, trembling. 'You never were very good at lying,' he said.

'Please, Nick,' I whispered, my mouth going dry. 'Please don't . . .'

For a moment he stared at me in silence, then a little groan broke from him and he reached out, pulling me into his arms. His kiss was gentle yet demanding, drawing an answering response. I clung to him, bewildered and shocked. Then I suddenly wrenched away, shaking my head.

'No, Nick. I can't – it's too late.'

228

'Why?' he demanded fiercely. 'Why won't you admit you made a mistake? He's not right for you. You know you're not happy.'

'Don't say it!' I cried, holding up a shaking hand to ward him off. 'Please Nick. Don't say any more. Just go. Please go now.'

'I'll go,' he said, and his eyes were angry. 'But one day you're going to wake up and realize I was right. I just hope for your sake it isn't too late.'

The tears were very near as I watched him leave. I heard the door slam and I hugged myself to stop the weakness spreading through my body. I had no right to feel like this. I'd made my choice. Piers was my husband and I loved him.

Julie looked at the parcels I'd given her, her eyes shining. She wanted to have a little feel to see if she could guess what was inside, but I made her promise not to.

'Spoilsport!' she said, pulling a face. 'It's something to wear. I bet it's something to wear.'

'Maybe,' I said, teasing. 'And maybe not. It could be a cushion.'

'You wouldn't dare!' Julie looked at me speculatively. 'Or would you? I don't think I'll give you yours unless you promise me it isn't a cushion.'

'There – and I thought that was just what you wanted.'

We both laughed, remembering past Christmases spent together and the fun we'd had. I looked at her with affection. Julie was so natural. I never had to wonder what was going on in her mind and I knew she was a true friend. No matter how busy she was, she would be there for me if I needed her.

'I wish you were coming down to Hazeling,' I said.

'I wish I were too. Never mind, we'll definitely celebrate your birthday in style. That's a promise, Aline.'

'Nick came round,' I said frowning. 'He brought your presents and a card from him. It's rather unusual. Victorian, with lots of lace and things. I left it in its box. If Piers saw it . . .'

'That's why I let him bring the parcels round.' Julie looked anxious. 'I knew he would come anyway. At least it gave him an excuse to be there.'

'Piers is so jealous,' I said. 'It frightens me sometimes. I think he might . . .'

'Might what?' Julie stared at me.

'Nothing,' I said hastily, my eyes not quite meeting hers. 'Oh Julie, I do wish you were coming for Christmas.'

Chapter Seventeen

The snow was falling in gentle flakes which melted against the windscreen as we drove down to Hazeling on the Friday afternoon, and the sky was heavy with the promise of more. It was getting dark by the time we arrived, but Zena had the porch light on and she opened the door almost as soon as we got there.

'Isn't it cold?' she cried, as we hurried inside. 'There's a fire in the drawing room. Why don't you go in while I make a cup of tea – unless you fancy something stronger?'

'I could do with a drink,' Piers said, groaning. 'I don't know what Aline has got in this suitcase of hers but it weighs a ton!'

'Surprises,' I said, and laughed as I followed Zena into the drawing room. Zena poured Piers a brandy and then looked inquiringly at me. I shook my head. 'Tea for me, please. Which decanters were broken?'

'Oh, only a couple of plain ones,' Zena said. 'Whoever did it was quite considerate. Even the painting they damaged was one Michael hated. He often said he ought to paint over it.'

'A considerate vandal?' I raised my brows. 'That must be a first, I should think.'

'Probably a couple of kids,' Piers speculated. 'They got scared and ran off with the first thing they could lay their hands on.'

'I don't think so,' I disagreed. 'Don't you remember that prowler we saw, Piers? I thought he was in the garden the night – well, I saw him again.'

'A prowler?' Zena shuddered. 'Don't say it, Aline. I'm glad you two are staying over Christmas. After that, I'll be able to move into my flat.'

'What about furniture?' I asked. 'Is there anything you want from Hazeling?'

'A few small things that Michael bought me – and I wouldn't mind my bedroom suite. I'm going to buy a new sofa and chairs.'

'Take what you like. But let me know, so that nothing goes down on the inventory that won't be here.'

'Oh, I don't want anything of value. A few of Michael's pictures . . . we must sort out his studio while you're here, Aline. Anything I don't want could go to auction – unless Piers wants them for the gallery, of course.'

'That reminds me,' he said, and took a cheque from his inside pocket. 'This is the result of the exhibition, Zena. I think you will be pleased.'

Zena glanced at the cheque and her face lit up. 'Forty thousand . . . It's more than I expected, Piers.'

A little message seemed to pass between them. I sensed something hidden, but in another moment the look in Zena's eyes had gone and I thought I must have imagined it.

'We've sold some more pictures since the exhibition closed, and I haven't charged the full commission I agreed with Michael. It's my little Christmas present to you, Zena,' Piers said.

'It's very generous of you.' Zena looked at me, her eyes bright. Then she blinked. 'Michael would have loved this. He wanted us all to be together at Christmas.'

'Oh, Zena . . .'

'I'm not upset,' she said. 'I'm just so pleased you're here and that we're friends, Aline.'

'So am I,' I said. 'I'm glad we came down now.'

'Then everything's OK.' Piers was looking benevolent. 'I want to make it a happy time, Zena. For you – and my wife. A Christmas to remember . . .'

'Yes, let's make it special,' Zena said. 'In memory of Michael.' She lifted her glass. 'To Michael – and to friendship.'

'To Michael,' Piers echoed. 'No more tears, Aline. No more nightmares . . . I want this to be perfect.' He glanced at Zena. 'Zena understands. She knows that you have to let the past go.'

For a moment I sensed tension in her as she looked at him, then it was gone. I might even have imagined it.

'Piers is right,' she said, smiling at me. 'Michael wouldn't want us to grieve for him. He would want us both to go on with our lives.'

'Yes,' I said. 'I'm sure you're right.'

Yet as I went upstairs a few minutes later, I had the feeling that Michael was very close. Somehow it comforted me.

Over the next few days Hazeling was transformed into a bower of holly, mistletoe and ivy. Between us, we trailed it down the banisters and over pictures, tying it with gold bows and having the greatest fun. Piers went off and came back with the tallest tree I'd ever seen. We had to get the step-ladder to dress the top, and Zena brought out boxes of trimmings that hadn't been used in years. Everyone got covered in dust and silver hairs from the old tinsel, but it made us laugh.

I hadn't enjoyed myself as much in years. It was like the Christmases of my childhood . . . before the incident on the marshes. And it was all due to Piers. He was determined that both Zena and I should enjoy ourselves. Parcels were hidden under the tree with great secrecy. Once I came upon Zena and Piers whispering together in the kitchen. They stopped when I entered and Zena looked guilty, but Piers laughed and whispered, 'Secrets.'

On Christmas Eve we all went to a carol service in the local church, and came home to a bowl of hot spicy punch, which we shared with a few friends Zena had invited back after the service. Then after a splendid lunch on Christmas Day – cooked by Piers, at his insistence – we opened the presents.

Zena was delighted with her brooch, and with the matching Gucci snakeskin bag and belt Piers had given her.

To me, Zena's present was a pretty peach silk blouse from her friend's shop. And for Piers there was a leather-bound desk diary.

As usual, Piers had bought me not one but half a dozen gifts. A huge bottle of Giorgio Red perfume and cologne; a Chanel silk scarf and leather bag with gilt chains; a Cartier belt; shoes by Kurt Geiger: red and very stylish; and a diamond brooch in the shape of a flower.

'Oh, Piers,' I cried. 'You always spoil me – and you have such perfect taste.'

'I enjoy spoiling you, darling. Anyway, look who's talking. That bronze was far too expensive.'

'I thought you might like it,' I said.

'It's beautiful, darling,' Piers murmured, and kissed me. 'Exactly right. And now I suggest someone makes the coffee. And who's going to volunteer for the washing-up?'

'Men!' Zena laughed. 'We might have known, Aline.'

It had been a perfect day, except that Michael wasn't there to share it. I knew Zena was missing him, despite her smiles, and that made me feel closer to her. We were more nearly friends now than we had ever been.

'I've been meaning to get round to this all week,' Zena said the next morning as we walked together to Michael's studio. 'I want to get off tomorrow or the next day at the very latest.'

She was wearing a very attractive red wool suit and a pale cream shirt with a mandarin collar, and she had pinned on the brooch I'd given her. I'd flung on jeans and an old sweatshirt, and I thought to myself that

Zena might regret wearing such good clothes for the job we had in mind.

'It shouldn't take long. Michael sent most of his pictures to the gallery for the exhibition, didn't he?'

'Oh, you'd be surprised at how much stuff he's got in here,' Zena said. 'He's been hoarding it for years. He would never sell anything he thought wasn't quite up to standard – and then there are the pictures of you.'

'Are there many?' I felt surprised as she nodded. 'I remember sitting for one when I was about ten. Michael said I was a terrible model because I couldn't sit still for more than five minutes.'

'He must have done them from memory then. He showed me two. But I always knew when he'd been painting you.' There was that jealous glint in her eyes again. 'One was of you when you were five or six. You were playing with a grey kitten.'

'That would be Sukie,' I said. 'What was the other one like?'

'It was of you on your eighteenth birthday. You were dressed in a Roman toga.'

'That was for my party – it was fancy dress. I remember Michael took some photographs. He probably used them for detail.'

'Perhaps, though he often painted from memory. He would come home and finish sketches he'd made on the marshes. His accuracy was amazing.'

Zena took a key from her pocket and unlocked the door. She switched on the light inside and then went to open the window blinds, letting the daylight flood in.

'That's better. We can see what we're doing now.'

I looked round the long, narrow studio. Zena was right: there were still a lot of paintings here. Michael's easel was by the window and there was an unfinished canvas on it. He had probably been working on it when I met him that last afternoon. It must have been the very last of his paintings. I went over to look at it, blushing as I saw it was of me. Although it wasn't finished, he had captured the sadness in my eyes. I turned away, feeling uncomfortable.

Zena was checking through the paintings stacked against the wall. 'This could take forever,' she said. 'I think we'll just look for your pictures and let Piers go through these in his own time. I'm sure he'll know what's saleable.'

'Yes,' I agreed. 'If you're not in a hurry to sell them, I think that might be best. Now where do we look, I wonder?'

'I think you'll find they're over there.' Zena pointed to something bulky covered by a large waterproof canvas. 'Michael always kept them separate. He wouldn't sell them, of course, so he kept them tucked away.'

'Can you help me pull the cover back?' I asked. 'It's very heavy.'

'I know. I couldn't manage it alone. That's why I haven't sorted them out before this.'

Together we pulled back the weighty tarpaulin, and I stared in amazement as I saw at least thirty or forty canvases. They were turned inwards so that it was impossible to see what was on them at first glance.

'There are rather a lot,' I said, feeling a fluttering sensation in my stomach. 'Shall we have a look?'

She nodded, her face pale. 'You start, Aline. I'll just watch, if you don't mind. Some of them are years old and they're bound to be dusty.'

I pulled back the first canvas. It was the picture of me in a Roman toga, done soon after my eighteenth birthday. I looked very proud and a little unapproachable. Michael's insight was disturbing. That was pretty much how I'd felt at the time. I studied the picture in silence then passed it back to Zena, who accepted it without comment. The second and third were of me as a child, done when I was still quite tiny. Some of them had damp spots on them as if they had got wet. I pointed it out to Zena and she nodded.

'It was the leak last winter. Michael was quite upset when some of his pictures were spoilt.'

I turned back to the stack of pictures. There was one of me standing on the beach, wearing a faded print dress, my feet bare and my hair straggling about my face; I was looking back towards the saltmarsh, a wistful expression on my face. I could only have been about twelve at the time, and seeing it made me uncomfortable. Michael had caught the anxious, uncertain look in my eyes. He had had an uncanny perception, at least as far as I was concerned. Suddenly, I wasn't sure that I wanted to see any more. I said as much to Zena.

'But you must,' Michael's widow said, her eyes hostile. 'I want you to know. I want you to see them for yourself.' The old resentful note was back in her voice and I had a sinking sensation inside as I realized that Zena's jealousy had not been laid to rest with Michael.

Feeling a sense of doom, I began to pull the canvases back and stand them against the wall side by side, and gradually I noticed that there was a definite change in the way I'd been portrayed. At first they were just pretty pictures of a child playing, but after that wistful portrait came others even more disturbing. Now there was an eroticism about the poses. In some I was naked, in others I wore the flimsiest of veils. In one

I had a mermaid's tail, in another I stood with my arms stretched high above my head as if I were reaching for the sky, my face sad. I was a child of nature, innocent, beautiful but enticing, my eyes holding a woman's knowledge. They were images from Michael's imagination, fevered dreams that had a terrible pathos about them. It was a strange, depraved record of a child growing into a sensuous woman. Yet I could see that they had all been done with love. An obsessive, forbidden passion, but undeniably love . . .

Zena was breathing fast. I could see that the pictures were having a terrible effect on her. She strode across the studio and began tearing at them, throwing them down carelessly, half sobbing with rage and grief as the evidence of Michael's unnatural obsession grew.

'That's enough!' I cried, feeling a tightness in my chest. 'Don't look at them any more, Zena. Come away. Let's leave them for today.'

Zena turned on me then, her eyes wild with pain. 'You didn't believe me,' she cried. 'You thought I was just being ridiculous, but I knew. I knew he was – ' A sob broke from her and she suddenly turned and ran from the studio, colliding with Piers as he came in.

'What's wrong?' he asked, surprised.

'Ask her! Ask your wife.' Zena pressed a shaking hand to her mouth and fled.

Piers came towards me. His eyes flicked to the paintings and he went very still. He picked one up and studied it. It showed me at about eleven years old. I was standing on the marshes, dressed in old jeans and a print shirt. I was laughing, my eyes bright and the wind in my hair. Something about it seemed to annoy Piers, though it was quite innocent.

For what seemed like an eternity, he stood staring at the pictures, not moving or speaking. Then he began to pick them up; he walked towards the door, carrying a bundle under his arm. I found I was able to move at last, and I ran after him, catching at his jacket sleeve.

'What are you going to do with them?'

His eyes were cold and distant as he stared through me. 'I'm going to burn them,' he said, sounding unnaturally calm and reasonable. 'What else would you expect me to do with such filth?'

Some of the pictures were erotic, but none of them were actually obscene or indecent, because they were not really of me. They were figments of Michael's imagination. He had used them as an outlet for feelings that he could not keep bottled up inside him. Some of them were rather funny, in a way – or they would have been if the whole thing hadn't been so sad. But I couldn't see why Piers was so upset by them, even those that were innocent; like the one of me laughing, which had seemed to upset him the most.

'Not all of them,' I pleaded. 'Not the ones of me as a small child.'

A nerve jumped in his cheek, but he showed no other emotion as he ignored me and walked outside and threw the canvases on a heap on the ground. I made a dive to retrieve the portrait I wanted, but Piers seized my arm, his fingers digging into my flesh as he swung me round to face him.

'Not that one,' I begged. 'Please, Piers.'

'All of them,' he said. 'Touch one and you will regret it, Aline. Believe me, you will wish you had listened.'

Something in his eyes stopped me. I was chilled by the quiet menace in his voice. He turned and walked back into the studio. Glancing at the portrait I wanted to keep, I was tempted to snatch it while his back was turned, but I was afraid – afraid of what he might do if I disobeyed him. I'd never known Piers to be this angry. He hadn't raised his voice once, but somehow it would have been less frightening if he had.

I watched in silence as the pile of canvases grew, willing him to relent and let me keep just one of the innocent portraits. So much work had gone into them, so many hours of Michael's life. Perhaps they *were* the sordid delusions of a man possessed by an unnatural desire, but he had loved me, and I knew with a deep inner certainty that Michael had paid over and over again for that desire. He had been driven back to his easel time and again by his obsession, but he had kept the pictures hidden, living in fear of discovery. I looked at Piers as he brought out a can of paraffin and began to splash it over the canvases.

'They were how Michael imagined me,' I whispered. 'I didn't pose for them.'

'Didn't you?' he asked. 'Do you expect me to believe that?'

His eyes blazed with jealousy and anger. I'd never seen him quite like this. It frightened me.

'But you must!'

I took a step towards him, and then jumped back as he threw a lighted match on to the heap and there was a whoosh as the blaze leaped up. Within seconds the pictures were alight, the paint cracking and spitting in the fierce heat as the canvases shrivelled and curled before my eyes.

For a moment I stood watching, the smoke blinding me and getting into my throat, making me choke. Then I turned away, tears burning behind my eyes. Piers was intent on his work as he ignored me and went back into the studio to make certain that not one portrait had escaped.

Walking back to the house, I saw Zena jump into her blue Datsun and heard the engine splutter as she almost choked it in her eagerness to get away. I waved to her to stop, beginning to run towards her, but she reversed swiftly and drove past me, her face white and tense.

I went into the house. I couldn't hold back my pent-up emotion any longer. My thoughts were confused, and I was torn between love for the man I'd known, revulsion at the evidence of his obsession and pity for the waste of it all. If only Piers' reaction had been different. We could have talked it over together and then forgotten it. The tears began to slide down my cheeks. I stood in the hall, shaking and sobbing as I gave way to the tide of grief. Then, as I heard Piers' footsteps on the doorstep, I fled upstairs.

I cried for a long time. Once, I thought I heard the sound of a car engine starting, but I couldn't be sure. I cried as if my heart were breaking – for myself, for Michael and for Zena. And then I slept.

When I woke at last it was dark. I switched on the light; my eyelids were stiff and swollen. The house felt cold and my throat was sore. Getting up, I glanced at the alarm clock beside the bed. It was past seven. I must have slept for hours. It was dinner-time.

Going into the bathroom, I splashed my face in cold water, combed by hair and put on some lipstick. Nothing could disguise my red eyes, but there was no point in pretending anyway.

Downstairs, it was quiet and dark. Switching on the lights as I walked, I tried the kitchen first. There was no sign of any preparation for dinner, but that was understandable. The house seemed big and empty and I was very conscious of being alone.

'Aline . . .'

Someone had called my name, yet I was sure there was no one in the house.

'Aline . . . Aline . . .' It was like the wind sighing in the trees and it came from the attics.

Zena must be up there.

I walked up the stairs, my heart beginning to beat erratically. I could feel a prickling sensation at the base of my neck and my mouth was dry. Now I could hear that tune . . . 'Greensleeves' . . .

Zena *was* in the attic. Why did she want me to go up there? I remembered the fall and my fingers curled into a tight fist. I took a deep breath to steady myself. It wasn't going to happen again.

At the door of the attic, I paused and knocked.

'Zena, are you there?'

Silence. I tried the handle. The door was not locked. It opened easily. I felt for the light switch, flooding the room with brilliance.

The dolls were all still there, busy in their world of make-believe. Zena had said she was going to sell them, but apparently she hadn't been able to bring herself to pack them up yet. They stared at me, their glass eyes seeming to follow me as I moved amongst them. There was no sign of Zena. I was alone in the house; no one had called my name.

A child's musical box was lying on the floor. I picked it up and opened it; the tinkling notes of the old tune sounded eerie in the stillness. Surely I'd heard them moments earlier . . . or was that imagination, too?'

A sudden gust of wind blew through the house, and the attic door slammed shut behind me. I jumped and, dropping the box, ran to the door. I pulled at the handle. The door wouldn't open. I was locked in!

'Zena!' I cried, rattling the handle in a panic. 'Don't play games with me, it isn't funny.'

There was no answer. I tugged at the door again, and it opened, almost throwing me off balance. It hadn't been locked at all, just stuck. Leaving the light on, I fled downstairs.

It took me a while to stop shaking, but at last I managed to pull myself together. Either I was imagining things or someone was playing games. I went to the cupboard under the stairs and looked for the torch Michael had kept there for emergencies. As I reached for it, my hand knocked against a wooden box, which fell to the ground, its lid opening. A shock went through me as I saw what was inside: a gun and several small boxes of ammunition, together with cleaning materials and loading instructions. The gun looked quite new and I wondered where it had come from; Michael must have bought it, I decided, replacing it beneath a pile of oddments.

I picked up the torch and closed the cupboard door. Then I began to search the house room by room, starting downstairs and working my way up.

For a moment I hesitated outside the room in which my mother had died, then I went in. It was exactly as it had been. Neither Michael nor Zena had changed a thing, though it had obviously been cleaned. There was nothing to frighten me here. Next I tried the guest rooms. They had a cold, impersonal look but held no ghosts.

I looked in my own room, then I tried Zena's bedroom. Most of her things were packed into boxes and suitcases, though a few clothes still lay strewn on the bed. Obviously Zena hadn't returned to the house.

No one was here. No one had called my name. It was the wind in the trees or an overactive imagination.

I walked back downstairs. It was understandable that Zena hadn't returned, but where was Piers? He must have finished burning the pictures long ago. Surely he wasn't still angry? As I reached the hall, I suddenly saw a white envelope propped up against the telephone on the hall table. I hadn't seen it when I came down the first time. Could I have missed it – or had that sudden gust of wind in the attic been caused by a door shutting?

My heart thumped as I opened the envelope and scanned the brief message. It was from Piers. He had gone up to town and would be back in three days' time. Just two lines, that was all. No explanation. No apology. No words of love.

Screwing the letter into a ball, I threw it into a corner, feeling hurt and angry.

He had no right to be jealous because of the paintings. I hadn't even known that most of them existed until Zena told me. Her distress was understandable, but not Piers' jealousy.

I returned to the kitchen, filled the kettle and looked inside the fridge. Should I wait for Zena or –

The wall telephone shrilled behind me and I jumped. I picked it up, expecting it to be Piers.

'Aline.' I was surprised to hear Zena's voice. 'Look, I'm sorry about this afternoon. I was upset and I took it out on you.'

'It was upsetting for all of us,' I assured her. 'I can hardly believe Michael did all those paintings. He must have been obsessed – there is no other word for it. I'm sorry, Zena. I don't know what else to say, except that I had no idea.'

'I don't blame you,' Zena said. 'Oh, I know I've said a lot of silly things, but I do know it wasn't your fault. Michael was ashamed of it. He did try to stop when we were first married, but he could never quite bring himself to destroy them, and when our marriage started to go wrong . . . well, he began again. It was as if he couldn't help himself.'

'I feel sorry for him,' I said. 'If I'd known years ago I should have been upset, but just before he died I felt that Michael had found peace within himself, Zena. I think he had conquered the lust and there was only love left at the end.'

'Yes, I know. He changed quite a bit when he was ill. Look, there's something important I want to tell you, something that has been playing on my mind. I ought to have told you before, but I thought you might be angry.'

'That sounds ominous. Say it, Zena. I'm listening.'

239

'I would rather say it to your face. I've done something rather stupid, but I want to make amends if I can. I have to meet someone, but I'll be back in about an hour. I'm only in Blakeney.'

'I'll cook dinner then,' I replied. 'It's just us. Piers has gone back to London. He was very angry. He didn't even tell me he was going.'

'Oh . . .' Zena hesitated. 'Well, I'll see you later.'

It was past eleven when I threw away the ruined jacket potatoes and ate a turkey sandwich alone in the kitchen. Zena had obviously changed her mind about coming back for dinner, she had probably decided to have a meal with the friend she was meeting. I wished she had phoned to let me know. It was a nuisance but not a tragedy. Leaving the dirty plates in the sink, I went up to bed.

I tossed and turned for over an hour, listening for Zena coming in. The wind had died down now and the house seemed very quiet. Missing the warmth of Piers' body beside me, I tried hugging a pillow, but it didn't help. I kept recalling that I'd believed someone was calling me earlier. It had been my imagination, of course, but it was unnerving – especially in a house as big and old as this one with its locked, empty rooms and shadowy corners. Perhaps it *was* haunted, as Piers had once suggested – though as far as I knew no one had ever seen a ghost – but it didn't have to be; the silence was bad enough. I wondered how Zena had stood it, being here alone so often when Michael was out.

At last, I got up and took one of my sleeping pills. I hesitated, then shook out another pill and took that, too. One was never enough, and I knew I wouldn't sleep without them.

The woman was alone, alone in the vastness of the marshes. It was strangely light, the sky white and translucent as the moon shed its mysterious light over the flat wasteland. The woman was terrified. She screamed as she ran, stumbling in her haste to escape her pursuer. She was wearing a blood-red suit and her silver hair was dangling down her back. Her face was very pale, her eyes dark with fear. She had lost her shoes and her feet were bare. She was running very fast, but the man was faster. He was catching up with her. Looking back over her shoulder, she screamed again and again.

Suddenly the picture changed and she was no longer on the marshes, but in Michael's studio. Her face was distorted like an image in the hall of mirrors; it loomed towards her, the flesh falling away to become a grinning skull.

'I told you,' she screamed. 'You didn't believe me but I told you . . .

I sat up in bed, wide awake and shivering. The nightmare was the worst

I'd ever known, but this time the woman had been Zena, not me. It was a few minutes before I could bring myself to move. The blood was pounding in my ears, echoing the thudding of my heart. My mouth felt like sawdust and my eyes were heavy. As I got out of bed, the room spun around me. I glanced at the clock. It was eleven o'clock in the morning; I'd slept for hours. Now I felt sluggish and it was difficult to force one foot in front of the other.

A shower did me good, but my head ached and I still felt drowsy. The sleeping pills had certainly knocked me out. I hadn't felt like this when I'd taken two in the past. Perhaps the doctor had increased the strength. I would ask Piers, since he'd phoned for the last prescription himself.

I dressed in a warm jumper and slacks, and went downstairs. The house felt very cold, and I concluded that the coke-fired boiler must have gone out. I'd banked it up the previous evening, but I wasn't very good at it, and I'd hoped Zena would have a go when she came in.

Going into the kitchen, I saw the plates I'd left the previous evening were still there. I filled the coffee machine and switched it on, then washed the dishes. Zena didn't seem to have been in the kitchen at all. Perhaps she was still sleeping. I decided to give her a call. I knew she wanted to finish her packing that morning, the removal men were coming the next day.

I ran upstairs and knocked on Zena's door. There was no reply. I was about to leave, thinking that Zena might still be asleep, but something made me change my mind. I turned the handle and went in. Everything was just as it had been the previous night, with Zena's clothes lying across the bed. It hadn't been slept in. Either Zena hadn't gone to bed or she hadn't come home all the previous night.

I went downstairs again, calling her name. There was no answer. Somehow I hadn't really expected there to be. Remembering my nightmare, I felt my stomach spasm with nerves. Then I took a hold of my imagination. Just because I'd had a bad dream . . . But it was odd that Zena had telephoned to say she would be back in an hour and then hadn't turned up.

I made some toast. As I worked, I wondered what to do. If I rang the police they would think I was neurotic. It was much too soon to panic. I decided to telephone Zena's friend Anne.

Her name was in the address book in the hall. She answered on the second ring. Feeling a little foolish, I asked if Zena was there.

'No, she's not coming until tomorrow,' Anne said. 'I thought she was at Hazeling with you.'

241

'We had a bit of an argument, but she rang to say she would be back last night.'

'But she didn't turn up?' Anne seemed to hesitate. 'I think there might be a man involved.'

'She did say she had to meet someone.'

'That's probably it, then. I ought not to tell you, but I know there was someone else a few months back. She was unhappy, and I think she even considered leaving Michael, but then it petered out. I don't think there was much in it. I'm sure it wasn't an affair . . . just someone she used to meet now and then. Perfectly innocent.'

I remembered the quarrel I'd overhead between Michael and Zena in the kitchen. Michael's instincts had been right. There had been someone else for a time, even though Zena had denied it.

'I'm glad I rang you. Thanks for explaining. I expect she'll be back soon.'

I replaced the receiver, hesitated, then picked it up again and rang Piers. There was no reply. Giving up, I sat down and ate my late and lonely breakfast.

Zena had not returned or phoned by two that afternoon. Despite what Anne had said, I was beginning to get anxious. Surely Zena wouldn't stay away this long without telephoning? She'd said she wanted to talk to me, to tell me something important. I knew Zena was inclined to sulk and to change her mind, but the removal people were coming in the morning and she still had quite a bit of packing.

At half-past two, I took the keys to Michael's old estate from the hall table and drove into Blakeney. I cruised along the quayside, looking for Zena's car, but there was no sign of it. I knew I was on a wild goose chase and it was ridiculous to think that because I'd dreamed about her being on the marshes, I would find her car there. But I persisted. It was a very cold day and, apart from an occasional passing car, the road at the edge of the saltmarshes was deserted. The marshes themselves looked forbidding and seemed endless as they stretched away towards the unseen sea. The channel was low, its water muddy and dirty-looking, and small sailing boats were beached in the mud beside the walkway. The cries of seabirds echoed eerily in the stillness of the afternoon.

I parked the car and got out. I began walking slowly, my hands tucked into my pockets, my eyes fixed intently on the dunes and the coarse grass of the saltmarshes, straining for any sign of life. The marshes were deserted, devoid of the tourists who flocked to explore their wild beauty in summertime. Behind me on the quay, people went about their daily business behind closed doors, but there was an almost frightening isolation about the marshes.

I realized that I ought to go back to Hazeling, and if Zena still hadn't returned, I should ring the police.

It took me less than twenty minutes to get home. Letting myself in, I called to Zena, but a quick search showed that no one was there. The house was empty, cold and unwelcoming. Taking a deep breath to steady myself, I dialled the number of the local police.

At first they seemed a little sceptical about my fears, but as I explained about the packing and Zena's phonecall, they began to take more notice. I gave the sergeant a brief description of Zena and what she had been wearing, and the colour and make of her car.

'I'm afraid I don't know the number,' I said apologetically. 'It had an X in it somewhere and a 6, I think.'

'Well, that should help, Mrs Drayton,' he said. 'Where can we contact you if we have anything to tell you?'

'I think I shall stay here for a day or two, just in case Zena comes back · or – '

'I shouldn't worry too much if I were you, madam,' he said cheerfully. 'Most of these cases of missing persons turn out to be a storm in a teacup. You did say she was upset when she left the house.'

'Yes,' I acknowledged. 'She was – but when she rang she apologized and said she would be back in an hour.'

'Well, there may have been an accident. We'll try that first and let you know if anything turns up.'

I thanked him and then dialled Piers' number. This time he answered on the first ring. He sounded very distant and cold as I explained that I was worried about Zena.

'She was upset,' he said. 'I expect she'll turn up soon.'

'I wish I could be sure of that, Piers.'

'Do you want me to come down, since you've finished sulking at last?' he said.

'Sulking!' I was indignant. 'I don't think you've got that quite right. I wasn't the one who went off in a temper.'

'You were the one who rushed off upstairs in a mood,' he said.

'I was crying. Seeing those paintings upset me, and then you seemed so angry. I didn't even know they existed until Zena told me.'

'Why did you want to keep them, then?'

'Only the ones of me as a child,' I said. 'They were quite innocent, Piers. Michael's obsession didn't start until much later.'

'You can't still feel anything for him after what you saw, Aline! They were disgusting.'

'They were only paintings from his imagination. Plenty of artists paint naked women.'

'Women yes, but not a child – and not my wife.'

'They were from his imagination, Piers,' I repeated. 'You must believe that.'

He was silent for a moment. 'Perhaps I do, now that I've had time to think.'

'Only perhaps?'

'Very well, I apologize for what I said. I was angry because you seemed to defend him.'

'I'm not defending what he did . . . I hated some of the pictures, Piers, but I can't quite forget the love Michael gave me when I was little – and I feel sorry for him.'

'Well, *you* feel sorry, if you like. I'm just glad he died when he did. If I'd known about the pictures I would have killed him.'

'Piers!' The hairs stood up on the back of my neck. My hand trembled and my knees felt weak. 'I know you're angry, but you don't really mean that.'

'Don't I?' He laughed unpleasantly. 'We shall never know, shall we?'

'Piers, don't say such things. It upsets me.'

'Perhaps that's not a bad idea. I told you once that I would never let you leave me.'

He sounded so strange that fear spiralled through me. Once, I had thought his possessiveness romantic, a sign of how much he loved and needed me, but now it seemed threatening and ugly.

'I thought you were just saying that . . .'

'Then you had better think again, darling,' he said. 'I usually mean what I say. I'll drive down tomorrow and pick you up.'

I swallowed hard, trying not to give myself away. I didn't want Piers to know that his threat had frightened and shocked me. It was just another of his moods. He was angry and he wanted to punish me. It would soon pass and he would be my loving husband again. I took a deep breath.

'Don't you think I should stay here for a while, in case Zena comes back?'

'She's quite capable of seeing to her own affairs. I'll pick you up tomorrow, Aline. Be packed and ready.'

Piers hung up on me. I sat staring at the receiver, feeling stunned.

He had been so harsh and cold. Surely he *couldn't* have meant what he had just said!

Chapter Eighteen

The police rang at nine that evening to say that they had checked all the accident reports and nothing had turned up.

'I should stop worrying, Mrs Drayton,' the sergeant said. 'She will probably turn up in a few days.'

'I've decided to return to London tomorrow,' I replied. 'Could you let me know there if anything does happen?'

'Yes, of course,' he said. 'Now you just get a good night's sleep, madam, and don't worry.'

'Yes, I will,' I said, but I knew I wouldn't.

As I turned towards the kitchen, the telephone rang. I picked it up eagerly, saying, 'Zena? Is that you?'

'She's not back then.' It was Anne's voice that came over the line. 'I thought I would just ring and check.'

'The police say they've no reports of any accidents. I was hoping she might have contacted you.'

'No. I would have let you know at once.' Anne was silent for a moment. 'I can't understand her. I know she can be moody but she usually keeps her word.'

'Well, perhaps she just changed her mind.'

'Perhaps. You'll ring me if you hear anything?'

'Yes, of course. I'm going home tomorrow. I'll give you my number, shall I?'

Anne took down the number, told me not to worry and rang off. The silence of the house enfolded me as I walked into the kitchen. Everyone was telling me not to worry, but I had an uneasy feeling that would not go away.

After my experience the previous night, I decided not to take a sleeping pill. Looking at the brandy decanter, I was tempted, but drinking was not a good idea when I was on my own.

I heated a mug of milk, hoping it would help, but I woke almost every hour and lay for ages, listening. The wind had got up again and the house had begun to make little creaking noises. It sounded as if someone was in the attic, but I was not going up there in the dark. My imagination was already working hard enough without a visit to the dolls.

Once, I got out of bed and went to Zena's room, just in case she had returned. The silence seemed to shriek at me and, shivering with cold, I ran back to my own room and locked the door behind me. Even if Piers didn't come to fetch me, I was leaving the next day. Nothing would persuade me to spend another night alone here!

I was up and dressed at seven-thirty when the telephone rang again. I snatched it up, my heart drumming.

'Mrs Drayton?' the voice asked. 'Sergeant Sandstone here. I'm afraid we have some bad news for you.'

'Zena,' I said, my heart stopping with fright. 'You've heard something?'

'We have discovered the body of a woman on the beach at Cley,' he said. 'From your description – and the description of her clothes – it would seem that we have found your stepmother . . .'

'Oh no!' I cried, going cold. 'What happened to her?'

The beach at Cley lay beyond a wide stretch of saltmarsh which was protected from the sea by a high ridge of shingle. It was possible to walk right out to the Point from Cley beach, but it was a long way and only the most hardy attempted it. In winter the beach was deserted. What on earth had Zena been doing there?

'She was found face down at the edge of the sea. At first glance she appeared to have drowned, but her clothes were torn and she seemed to have put up a fight . . .'

'You mean she was murdered?' I felt sick and dizzy with the horror of it. 'She wasn't strangled, was she?'

'What makes you ask that, Mrs Drayton?'

'I don't know . . .' I was trembling now. 'I just wondered – I had a dream . . .'

'No, as far as I've heard, she wasn't strangled,' he said. 'She appears to have been held with her face down in the water. She is badly bruised and it isn't a pleasant sight, Mrs Drayton, but we do need an identification. If there's anyone else. . . ?'

'No,' I said. Zena murdered! It was mind-numbing, horrible. 'I'll come. Just tell me where to go, please.'

I wrote down the address. My fingers were stiff and clumsy as I dropped the receiver. Emotion closed my throat, and my eyes burned. It was difficult to breathe and for a moment I couldn't think properly. Should I let Anne know or ring her later, when I was sure? In my heart I already knew that the woman the police had found was Zena, but I couldn't bring myself to tell Anne just yet.

Zena had been found murdered, her face bruised in the fight for her life. It was so awful that I could hardly take it in. I had to get out of the house. I couldn't stand the silence a second longer.

Running upstairs to collect my coat, bag and Michael's car keys, I remembered just in time that Piers was coming down. It took a moment to scribble a note for him, and then I was out of the house and on my way. Every movement I made was automatic. My mind kept going round and round in circles as I drove. Zena had said she was going to meet someone – who? She had been in Blakeney when she telephoned; what was her body doing on the beach at Cley?

At the police mortuary it took me just one look to make the identification. I nodded and turned away, gasping as the sickness rose in my throat. Zena's face and body were discoloured, and it was even more distressing than I'd expected. The young policewoman took my arm and led me through to a waiting-room. She looked at me sympathetically.

'It's never very pleasant, but that was worse than most. Would you like a cup of tea?'

'Yes, please,' I said. My hands were shaking. I was close to hysterics but I breathed deeply, forcing myself to calm down. Giving way to my emotions would help no one. 'What happens now?'

'We would like you to identify some personal items, just to see if anything is missing. Her shoes were found some distance away . . .'

'Her shoes?' I looked up. The wave of nausea had passed and my breathing was normal. 'Her feet were bare when. . . ? Yes, of course. She must have kicked them off as she tried to escape. What else did you find?'

'Her bag had a purse and wallet inside, and make-up, but there were no car keys. You did say she was driving a car?' I nodded and the policewoman made a note. 'She was wearing a wedding ring and pearl earrings. Also a watch, a cream blouse, red suit and – '

'What about the brooch?' I asked. 'She was wearing a large cameo brooch I'd given her for Christmas.'

The policewoman checked her list. 'It isn't here. That could explain the jagged tear on the jacket. If it came off in the struggle it might be on the beach. Thank you, that may be very helpful. Could you give me a full description please?'

'It was fifteen-carat gold, late Victorian, and it had a grey background with a scene of the Three Graces . . . The salesman warned me that the catch wasn't secure when I bought it.' I choked on a sob. 'I was going to have a safety chain put on later . . .'

'You have no idea who she was going to meet?'

I shook my head, then frowned as I remembered what Anne had said about Zena's brief involvement. 'I did once overhear her husband accusing her of having met a man. And – and I've seen someone lurking in the shadows at Hazeling on three separate occasions. I thought it was a prowler, and when we had a break-in just before Christmas I was sure that he had been watching for his chance.'

'You might be correct in thinking that, Mrs Drayton. On the other hand, Mrs Courteney could have been meeting someone she didn't want her husband to know about.'

'Her friend might know more about that. I could give you her number . . . and perhaps you could let her know what happened?' The policewoman nodded. I pressed a trembling hand to my lips, feeling the tears start to fall. 'I'm sorry,' I choked. 'Sorry to be so stupid.'

'Quite understandable.' The officer looked at me in concern. 'Is there someone at home to be with you?'

'My husband is driving down from London this morning. He's going to take me back with him.'

'Your husband,' she said, making a note. 'Was he not with you at Hazeling over Christmas?'

'He went back to London on Boxing Day afternoon,' I said. 'He – he had something he wanted to do, and I stayed on at the house. I was asleep when he left, but it must have been around three.'

She nodded, and wrote it all down. 'So he would have been in London at the time Mrs Courteney died. Don't look so upset, Mrs Drayton. We have to check these things. Sometimes wives are the last to find out about their husbands' affairs.'

'Piers didn't even like Zena very much,' I said. 'My husband is devoted to me. I'm quite positive there are no other women in his life – and certainly not Zena.'

'You are probably right,' she said. 'The attack on Mrs Courteney has all the signs of being a frenzied assault by someone not in their right mind. In many cases of murder we find that it was done by a member of the family, but in this instance I doubt it. I would say from a personal point of view that whoever killed her was insane at the time.'

'At the time?' I stared at her, struck by her phrasing. 'Surely someone who could do that would have to be permanently insane?'

249

'Or a split personality,' she suggested. 'Some form of schizophrenia.'

'Even so, it would be bound to surface every now and then. People would realize something was wrong, surely?'

The policewoman frowned and looked thoughtful. 'Most of the murderers I've seen have seemed normal. Some of them were so calm afterwards that it was hard to believe that they actually did it, and some of them were so clever at hiding their emotions – ' She broke off as a male colleague came into the room. A few whispered words took place between them and then she turned to me with a smile. 'Your husband is here, Mrs Drayton.'

'Piers?' I jumped up, feeling nervous as I remembered his telephone call the previous evening. 'I drove over in my stepfather's car. Do you think. . . ?'

'Don't worry about it,' the policewoman said. 'One of our officers will take it back for you. He can put the keys through the front door if no one is there.'

'Thank you. Is there anything else, or can I go now?'

'You've been very helpful, Mrs Drayton. If we need to contact you again, we have your London address, don't we?'

'Yes.' I looked directly at her. 'I hope you catch whoever did it. Zena didn't deserve to die like that.'

'No one does. It's something you never get used to, however long you're on the force.'

'I suppose not,' I said. 'Well, goodbye then.'

I walked out of the waiting room and into the main station. Piers was standing by the desk, a look of impatience on his face. As soon as he saw me, he came to greet me, taking me in his arms to hold me close to his chest.

'I'm sorry, darling,' he whispered. 'If I'd been here you wouldn't have had to go through all this.' He looked down at me, his expression contrite. 'Forgive me. Please. I shouldn't have left you like that – and I shouldn't have said those stupid things last night. I'm so damned jealous.'

'I know.' I drew a sobbing breath of relief. His black mood was over. 'Let's go home, Piers.'

'I've got your things in the car,' he said, smiling now. 'You don't want to go back to Hazeling for anything, do you?'

'I don't care if I never go there again,' I said.

'Now don't forget, you're taking my black suit to the cleaners,' Piers said as he picked up his briefcase and headed for the door. 'And you have to confirm that booking for your birthday party.'

'I'm not likely to forget,' I replied, a little irritated by his manner. Since our return from Hazeling ten days earlier, Piers had been as tender and attentive as when we were first married, but now for some reason I found his excessive care of me suffocating. He was forever reminding me to do things, as if he thought I was incapable of the simplest task.

'But you do forget, darling,' he said, with a smile that carried a hint of reproach. 'You left the taps running in the bath yesterday, and the day before you forgot to switch off the electric fire when you went out.'

'But I'm sure I turned it off before I left. And I remembered the bath in time.'

'The fire was on when I came in,' Piers reminded me. 'I wasn't criticizing you, Aline. Anyone can forget things. You mustn't worry about it.'

'I'm not,' I said, but I lied. It was worrying, and I knew it was true. My memory was sometimes haphazard these days, but it was because I was always tired.

Piers kissed my cheek and left. Determined not to do anything stupid, I went to the telephone and rang the Café de Paris. They had provisionally booked a private suite for my birthday but I had to confirm the numbers. It was just a small party for a few friends, and Piers had insisted that it should go ahead despite Zena's death.

'It's a very special birthday for you,' he said when I suggested that we should just ask Tony and Julie to dinner. 'Nothing can change what happened. Besides, you didn't even like Zena very much, remember?'

'What an odd thing to say . . .' I faltered and stopped. Any mention of Zena was enough to make me feel guilty. I was possibly the last person she'd spoken to before she met her murderer. Perhaps there was something I could have done or said that would have prevented it happening. 'That last afternoon, she was just upset over the pictures.'

Piers had a speculative expression in his eyes. 'I've always suspected Zena of having pushed you down the stairs. She was a jealous little cat, Aline. Don't break your heart over her.'

I nodded, pretending to go along with him, but his careless attitude towards Zena's murder disturbed me. Surely he could see that it didn't matter whether or not I'd liked Zena. She had been Michael's wife and she was dead, the victim of a brutal murder. The sight of her bruised and battered face lived in my mind, and I saw it every time I closed my eyes. When Piers said things that sounded callous, he wasn't the man with whom I'd fallen in love. At least, it revealed another side to him, a side I didn't much like.

With a struggle, I brought my wandering thoughts back into line. Piers had asked me to do something else. What was it. . . ? For a moment I couldn't think. My mind seemed to have blanked out. It had happened once or twice since our return from Hazeling. I thought the sleeping pills might be to blame, but without them I lay awake all night, haunted by the memory of Zena's face. I went over and over the whole thing in my head. Who could have done such a thing? The police were no nearer to finding out, though they had discovered Zena's car. It had been abandoned in an old sandpit miles away, but the police thought some youths had been joy-riding in it, and any evidence it might have contained had been destroyed.

My thoughts had wandered again, but now I remembered. Piers had asked me to take his black suit to the cleaners . . . Or was it the grey? I tried to recall his exact words: he'd said black just before he left, but earlier I was sure he'd said the pale grey one. That was his favourite and could do with a clean. I decided to take both to be sure of getting it right.

I went through to the bedroom and looked in the wardrobe. Piers' grey suit was hanging right at the front. I took it down. He had a habit of leaving things in pockets, so I went through them. This time there were a couple of letters, both in white envelopes with a curious blue print on them. I'd noticed them a few times before. I laid them on the table at Piers' side of the bed and looked for his black suit.

It wasn't in the wardrobe, but both Piers and I had overflowed into the spare room and I went to search there. Half an hour later, I was on the verge of tears. Piers' suit wasn't anywhere in the flat. It had to be somewhere! But where? I couldn't have taken it to the cleaners already, could I?

Telling myself I really was beginning to forget things, I went through my wallet. No cleaning tickets – so where was that suit?

I picked up the grey suit and left the flat, checking to make sure I'd turned off the kettle, the oven and the electric fire. Piers would be so annoyed with me if his suit had gone missing.

I deposited the grey suit safely at the cleaners and asked them if there were any items registered to Mr or Mrs Drayton. The assistant laughed when I told her I'd mislaid a suit, but although she searched thoroughly it couldn't be found.

'Perhaps you took it somewhere else?' she suggested.

'No, I always come here. My husband likes your gold service.'

Leaving the shop, I shivered in the bitter wind. I felt as if I might have a cold or flu coming on. My shoulders and back ached, and my head was muzzy as if from a fever.

I wished Julie were in town, but she was taking a couple of weeks' holiday to visit her mother and wouldn't be back until tomorrow.

'We had Christmas with Tony's family, so I thought it was only fair to spend the New Year with Mum,' Julie had said last time I rang her. 'But I'll be back for your birthday – that's definite.'

I went back to the flat, made myself a hot drink and curled up in front of the fire, feeling restless. There just wasn't enough to occupy me these days. If I didn't keep active, I started to brood over things, and then my imagination began to play tricks on me. Pictures flashed into my mind, just as they had after I'd left the hospital. I saw strange, distorted images of people I knew, but they were all jumbled up together so that nothing made sense any more.

What was happening to me? I'd always had the dreams, of course, but I'd been able to cope with them, to put them out of my mind once I was awake. Now I seemed unable to get a grip on things. It was frightening because I didn't understand it, but I had to fight it. I had to hang on to reality.

When I married Piers, I'd envisaged a large family which would keep me busy, but now I sometimes thought that he would be happier if we never had children. I'd already thought that I might like to set up some sort of a trust for a children's charity when I came into my inheritance, but also I needed to work. I decided to give Mr Silcott another ring about that job.

I was lucky and found him in the office.

'I was just thinking about you,' he said.

'Oh – something nice, I hope?'

'Well . . .' He hesitated. 'I'm going to clear Mrs Pearson's house next week. It's a big job, there's so much stuff to be catalogued . . .'

'Could I help? I was ringing to ask if you'd found anything for me.'

'Were you?' He sounded pleased. 'It wouldn't upset you to go to Mrs Pearson's?'

'It might a little,' I admitted, 'but I think it would be good for me in other ways.'

'I shall be with you, of course,' he said. 'I should be so grateful for your help, Aline. We can discuss your fee then, and I think I can find you enough work to give you an interest without taking over your life.'

'That's exactly what I want,' I said. 'Bless you, Mr Silcott. You'll let me know when you want me?'

'I'll ring you soon.'

I was feeling better when I put down the phone. At last I'd done something positive.

I thought I would clean the flat, but as I got out the vacuum I suddenly felt dizzy and had to sit down. My head was swimming and I was nauseated. I must be coming down with a bug of some kind. Perhaps it would be better if I put my feet up for a while. After all, Piers wasn't coming home for lunch.

I was day-dreaming when Piers came in. I started, feeling guilty, though I wasn't sure why.

'Lunch not ready, darling?' he asked.

'I didn't think you were coming home for it.'

'I said I would.' A flash of annoyance passed across his face. 'Never mind. I'll make a salad for us both.'

As he walked towards the kitchen, I remembered the cause of my guilt. I followed him, aware of a distinct reluctance to tell him the black suit was missing.

'Piers . . .' I faltered as he turned. 'I couldn't find your black suit. You wanted me to take it to the cleaners for you, but I couldn't find it.'

His brows went up in surprise. 'But it's in the wardrobe, darling, behind the brown stripe.'

'No. I looked, but it wasn't anywhere.'

'It was there this morning.' He went into the bedroom. 'I'm sure . . .' He opened the wardrobe and flicked through, and then took out a hanger. 'Here it is, Aline. Just where it was when I left.'

'But it can't be!' I stared at the suit as he laid it on the bed. How could it have been there all the time? 'But I looked everywhere, Piers. Honestly, I did!'

'Why don't you just admit you forgot about it?' His expression was that of a man under extreme provocation, trying not to be angry.

'No, Piers, I didn't forget,' I said, feeling annoyed now. 'I took your grey suit and I looked for the black one.' As I saw the doubt in his face, I snatched up the letters from the side of the bed. 'These were in the grey suit!'

Something flickered in his eyes. 'Did you read those letters, Aline?'

I blinked at him, taken off guard by his expression. Why was he looking at me like that? 'No, of course I didn't. I never read your letters – and I did search for your suit, Piers. I did . . .' I began to sob. My head ached and I felt awful.

'There's no need to cry, darling.' His voice was gentle again. 'I'm not upset about the suit. I can take it myself this afternoon.'

I tried to stop crying. 'I'll take it for you. Oh!' I pressed a hand to my head as I felt the dizziness sweep over me.

'What's wrong, darling?' Piers came to put his arm around me as I swayed. 'Aren't you well?'

'I think I may be getting flu,' I said. 'I feel so ill.'

'That doesn't suprise me in the least. You've been under a terrible strain for weeks.' He bent down to sweep me up in his arms. 'It's bed for you, Aline, and if you're no better in the morning, I shall send for the doctor.'

As he laid me down on the bed, I clutched his hand. 'I did look for the suit, Piers.'

'Anyone can overlook something, Aline. You're not yourself.'

'You – you don't think I'm having a mental breakdown, do you?' I gazed up at him, feeling scared. 'Piers, I'm not losing my mind, am I?'

Something flickered in his eyes. 'What an imagination the woman has! Of course you're not mad, darling. This is just temporary. It will go away in time. Now lie there and rest, and I'll bring your lunch on a tray.'

I closed my eyes as he walked from the room. He was being so considerate and kind, but he hadn't quite been able to hide his thoughts this time. He did think there was something wrong with me.

Most of my aches and pains had disappeared the next morning, but Piers made me stay in bed. He had decided to call the doctor anyway. I heard them talking in low voices in the hall, and then the doctor came into the bedroom alone. He smiled at me in a remote, impersonal way and went through the routine of pulse, temperature and listening to my heart through his stethoscope.

'You seem to be in good health, Mrs Drayton,' he said. 'You may have had a temperature yesterday, but you certainly haven't today.'

'I felt as if I had flu coming.'

'You hadn't been to a party the previous evening?'

'No!' I was indignant as I realized what he was implying. 'I hadn't been drinking, if that's what you mean.'

'Your husband mentioned lapses of memory . . .'

'A few perhaps,' I admitted. 'But I don't drink to excess and I don't take drugs. Nothing but the sleeping pills I was prescribed.'

He glanced at the bottle beside the bed, opened them and checked the contents. 'These are quite mild. They shouldn't affect you adversely, unless you swallow too many on top of a bottle of wine, of course.'

'I never take them if I've had a drink.'

'If I were you, I should keep the bottle in the bathroom cabinet. There's less chance of an accidental overdose that way.'

'We usually do,' I said. 'I don't remember leaving them there.'

'Ask your husband to – ' The doctor broke off as Piers came in. 'I was just saying to Mrs Drayton that it would be best to keep her sleeping tablets in the bathroom cabinet.'

'But we always . . .' Piers looked at the bottle and frowned. 'Did you get them out to show the doctor, Aline?'

'I – I don't think so.' A significant look passed between the two men. 'I may have done. I think I need a new prescription, don't I?'

'You have enough for a few days, Mrs Drayton. I'll send you a prescription at the end of the week, but please promise to keep them in the cabinet.' The doctor checked his watch. 'And now I must get on.'

I had the impression that he thought he was dealing with a neurotic woman who enjoyed imagining she was ill. As Piers went to show him out, I heard them talking about the various symptoms of acute depression.

'I don't think she is a serious case, but keep her busy. Give her something to think about.'

When Piers returned, I was already under the shower. I was upset and angry – too angry for tears. How could they talk about me like that? By the time I'd dressed, I was in control. Piers looked at me as I came out of the bedroom.

'Should you be going out, darling? It's very cold, and if you're getting flu . . .'

'The doctor said I was perfectly well,' I told him, a note of bitterness in my voice. 'Julie will be back at the clinic today. I have to talk to someone – or I really will go mad!'

Without waiting for his reply, I went out of the flat and slammed the door.

Julie's smile of welcome faded as she saw my expression. She was in her office, writing up a report, when I was shown in, but she closed the folder and came to me in concern as the tears flowed.

'What's wrong, Aline?'

'Damn!' I muttered, hunting in my bag for a tissue. 'I didn't intend to cry all over you. I just wanted to talk.'

'Friends are for crying all over,' Julie said, handing me one of her own tissues. 'Tell Momma all about it.'

256

'Oh, Julie.' I laughed, the sudden storm of emotion over. 'I'm glad you're here. You make me feel so much better.'

Julie's eyes narrowed as she realized it was serious. 'So this isn't just another lover's tiff. Is it to do with Zena's murder?'

'Indirectly, perhaps.' I drew a deep breath. 'I've been having the dreams again, and sometimes I think what I've imagined is real – and I forget to do things.'

'So do I,' she said. 'Constantly.'

'Piers and Doctor Robinson seem to think I'm suffering from acute depression. The doctor gave me a stern warning about keeping my sleeping tablets in the bathroom.'

'A sensible precaution. I hate those damned things!' Julie looked at me. 'Do you think there's something wrong with you?'

'I – I don't know. I was supposed to take Piers' suit to the cleaners yesterday. I looked everywhere and it wasn't there, but when Piers opened the wardrobe it was just where he'd said. I don't know how I could have missed it.'

'No,' Julie muttered. 'Nor do I.'

'So you think they're right then, the doctor and Piers?'

'I didn't say that, Aline.' Julie frowned again. 'Could that suit have been put back in the wardrobe?'

'How?' I stared at her. 'Even if Piers wanted to, he had no opportunity. I was with him all the time. He wasn't carrying anything when he went out or when he came in. Besides why should he hide his own suit?'

'I can't imagine,' Julie said with a shrug. 'It wasn't the end of the world, Aline. I've often searched the house for something I wanted, and then Tony comes in and puts his hands straight on it. You're probably just feeling tired and overwrought, and that's when everything gets on top of you.'

'So you think I'm making too much of it all?'

Julie's eyes slid away from mine. She busied herself with the coffee machine. When she looked at me again, she was smiling.

'Well, I'm damned sure you're not going mad, Aline. And that's my professional opinion, so you can stop worrying.'

'Oh, Julie!' Her matter-of-fact manner was reassuring. 'Thank you! Thank you for that.'

'No extra charge,' she said, and laughed. 'Anyone who has been through what you've been through recently has the right to throw a few wobblies. But you're as sane as I am, my friend. And I'll testify to that, if need be.'

'It won't come to that. I feel better just for having talked to you.'

'Good.' Her eyes had a militant glitter. 'So you're going to be twenty-five and rich next month. I hope I'm invited to the party?'

'Of course you are. Haven't you had your invitation?'

'Not yet. Perhaps it got stuck in the post.'

'But Piers posted all the invitations days ago.'

Julie pulled a wry face. 'God bless the Post Office! You had better give me the details in case it turns out to be one of those "lost in post" mysteries. Who else have you invited?'

'Oh, just a few friends, Piers' colleagues from work, Mr Silcott, Rita and Tim, Keith and Joan – that's about all. I asked Zena's friend Anne, but she couldn't manage to get up to town.'

'What about Nick?' Julie asked. 'He flew to the States over Christmas but he's back now.'

'I doubt if he would come. But you can bring him if you want. One more won't make any difference.' Before the words were out of my mouth, I was wondering what had possessed me to say them. And yet in my heart I knew.

'I'll ask him then.' Julie looked pleased.

'I'm sure he won't come.'

'It won't hurt to ask.'

'No, I don't suppose so.' I couldn't very well take back the invitation now it had been given . . . even if I'd wanted to. Piers would find it provocative, but it was time Piers discovered he couldn't have it all his own way.

Julie poured the coffee. She gave me a shy, half-anxious smile as she handed me a mug. 'Now I've got some news for you . . .'

I sensed the excitement she was trying to control. 'Julie, you're not. . . ?'

'Yes.' She nodded, looking happy. 'I'm pregnant, Aline. I went to see the doctor while I was at my mother's and it was confirmed.'

'That's wonderful! I'm so pleased for you.' I flew to hug her. 'What does Tony say?'

'He's mildly pleased.' Julie cocked an eyebrow. 'The bank has agreed to a loan on the strength of all the new orders he's getting, and of course I shall go on working for as long as I can.'

'Not too long,' I said, hugging her again. 'I know you'll refuse, Julie, but if Tony ever needs . . .'

She shook her head and smiled. 'He won't, but I've always known you would help us if we were desperate.'

'I was going to lend Zena the money for her partnership.

Maybe you're right, Julie. Maybe I bring bad luck to people I try to help.'

'Nonsense!'

'Is it? I tried to help Phyllis Pearson – and look what happened to her.'

Julie's eyes narrowed. 'I haven't forgotten.'

'What do you mean?'

'Nothing in particular.' Julie refilled her coffee mug. 'So what did Piers give you for Christmas, then?'

Her change of subject was transparently obvious.

'Too much,' I said. 'What can I buy you for the baby, Julie?'

'Anything you like,' she said, smiling. 'As far as the baby is concerned, I'm placing no restrictions on you. Not that you would take much notice if I did . . .' She shook her head in mock reproof. 'That Renzo suit is fantastic, Aline. I dread to think what you paid for it!'

'What's an arm and a leg between friends?'

We laughed together.

Piers was reading the *Financial Times* when I let myself in, loaded down with parcels. He glanced up, studying my face for a moment, and then he smiled.

'You look better, darling. Did you enjoy yourself?'

'Julie's having a baby. I've been buying her a few presents and some clothes for myself.' I met his look a touch defiantly. 'Yes, I did enjoy myself. And no, it hasn't upset me. I'm over the miscarriage now, Piers. When my body is ready, I'll get pregnant again. I'm not going to brood just because Julie has at last managed something she's wanted for ages.'

'Of course not,' he said, his eyes wary. 'I'm glad you're taking it so well. Shall we go out for a meal this evening?'

'Yes, I'd like to. I think I'll have a bath and wash my hair.' I started towards the bedroom, then stopped and looked back at him. 'Julie hasn't had her invitation to my party. You did send them, Piers?'

'Send. . . ?' He frowned and got to his feet. 'You were going to post them yourself. I offered, but you insisted.' He opened the drawer in the hall table. 'Aline, you forgot again!'

I stared at the pile of neat white envelopes and then at him. 'Piers,' I whispered. 'You said – I thought you said . . .'

Choking back a sob, I ran into the bedroom and locked the door. I hid my burning cheeks in my hands, feeling afraid. I couldn't have made a mistake like that! I just couldn't . . . Unless I really was losing my memory – and my mind.

Chapter Nineteen

The child was terrified. She ran across the saltmarshes, screaming for help, stumbling in the muddy pools as she tried to escape. He could run so much faster than she, and he was gaining on her. Her chest hurt and she found it difficult to breathe. Oh, why didn't Michael come? Why hadn't she listened to him when he told her not to stray?

Her pursuer was catching her up. She gave one last despairing cry, and then, as if the effort had been too much for her, she fell face down in the muddy sand. And then he was on her. She fought desperately, finding new strength in her terror, kicking and biting as his hands went round her throat. She looked up into his face, her eyes pleading with him. He seemed to check himself, his hold slackened as though he was suddenly unsure.

'You shouldn't have laughed,' he said. 'You saw me crying and you laughed. She laughed at me too. She laughed when I told her I was going to kill her for lying to me all that time, but she won't laugh any more . . .'

The child's lips moved. 'Please,' she whispered. 'Don't hurt me. I didn't mean to laugh at you . . .'

And then the blackness came down.

I woke in fear, and sat up in bed with an anguished cry. The room was dark and cold; very little light was showing through the heavy curtains. I shivered as I realized what had upset me. It wasn't just a dream this time; I had remembered. I could remember exactly what had happened on the marshes all those years ago. I could remember everything until just before I passed out!

Beside me in the bed, Piers stirred. He groaned and then switched on the light, blinking as he looked at me.

'Not another dream?'

'This time it was real. I saw it all just as it happened.'

'It's always seems real,' he pointed out, watching me with an intentness that betrayed his concern. 'That's what makes a nightmare so frightening.'

'You don't understand. This time I know how it happened. I remember everything.'

'Are you sure?' His eyes narrowed. 'You're certain it isn't another dream?'

'Quite certain. It was a nightmare when I thought Michael was strangling me. Everything was distorted in the dreams, Piers – like a hall of mirrors at a fairground. This was different.'

'You *were* dreaming, Aline.'

'Yes, but dreams usually fade. I can remember everything about this one.'

He threw back the bedcovers. 'I think I'll make us some tea. Switch the fire on if you're cold, darling. We could be talking all night.'

As Piers went into the kitchen, I reviewed my dream. I remembered Michael telling me not to stray. I'd been so determined to find his palette knife for him that I hadn't listened. It was just as he'd said, I'd wandered off and then . . .

Piers came in with a tray. 'So,' he said. 'Now you know who attacked you. What did he look like?'

'What?' I stared at him and blinked. 'I'm not sure . . . He was quite young, I think. Yes, only a youth really, perhaps eighteen or nineteen. He had dark hair and . . .' I sighed and shook my head.

Piers handed me a cup. 'It was just another dream, Aline. Next time it will be Michael again – or maybe even me.'

I sat in silence for a moment, thinking. Piers was convinced it was just another dream, but I wasn't so sure. I believed that for the first time I'd remembered everything just as it had happened.

'Did you hear what I said? Next time, you'll be imagining it was me chasing you.'

I blinked as I realized what Piers had said.

'You? Why should it be you?'

'Because nightmares are like that, darling. You reconstruct things that worry you in your everyday life, and play them out as if you were awake. That's the purpose of dreams, to help you sort out your problems. Except that in dreams everything can become distorted, just like your hall of mirrors. If we have a quarrel before you go to sleep one night, you could dream that I was the one trying to strangle you.'

'Oh, Piers! He – He did look a bit like you . . .' I laughed as it occurred to me for the first time.

'Only a bit?' Piers joked. 'If you keep on waking me up in the middle of the night, he might get to look a lot more like me.'

'Piers!' I giggled as I saw his teasing expression. I loved him so much when he was like this. 'I'm sorry. I hate waking you.'

'Just trying to make you laugh, darling.' He reached out to touch my cheek. 'I would never hurt you, Aline. Never cause you physical pain. I love you. You do know that?'

'Yes,' I whispered. 'Yes, of course I know, Piers.'

'We have a lot more in common than you imagine, you know.'

'What do you mean?' I was curious.

'You had a lonely, unhappy childhood, and so did I. My grandparents were very strict. My grandfather didn't drink or smoke and he believed that children should be seen and not heard. He was very mean and he used to hoard his money. I think he hated me from the day I was born . . .'

'He sounds like a throwback to the Victorian era,' I said, taking his hand. 'You haven't talked about it much.'

'It was a long time ago,' he said. 'Looking back, I see I never knew what it was like to be loved, Aline. I was never given a toy for my birthday or Christmas. It was always clothes, and usually those I needed for school . . .' He smiled ironically. 'That's probably why I always buy the best now. So you see, I do understand these moods of yours. I understand far more than you think.'

'Piers, darling,' I whispered, reaching up to kiss him. 'Thank you for telling me.'

'I left school when I was fifteen,' he went on, as if I hadn't spoken. 'My grandmother said I had to earn my living. For a while I worked in a garage. Then, after my grandparents died, I came to London. I was on my own and broke, until I met Bill. He was a strange chap, a bit of a loner, but a natural at picking out the genuine article. He took a fancy to me and I stayed with him in the rooms over his shop. It wasn't much of a place really, but better than sleeping on the streets. Bill took a fancy to me, for some reason, and he taught me a lot. I educated myself by reading everything I could . . .'

'You must have been devastated when he died.'

'I blamed myself. If I'd been there a few minutes earlier . . . I damn near killed the young thug who'd mugged him. Bill tried to pull me off and then he had another heart attack. There was nothing I could do. I watched him die in the street and I was helpless. I felt it was my fault. It haunted me for months afterwards. Sometimes it does now . . . So you see, we both have our nightmares, darling.'

'Oh, Piers.' I said. 'I've always sensed something.'

'Yes,' he said, touching the tip of my nose with one finger. 'I thought you had. So now you know my terrible secret.'

'I love you so very much.'

His eyes were sad and reflective as he gazed down at me. 'If I ever thought you didn't . . .' He laughed, his mood vanishing as suddenly as it had come. 'I'll be giving you more nightmares, darling. Forget what I said. Come here and I'll hold you until you go to sleep. Nothing bad will happen to you while I'm with you.'

As Piers took me in his arms, I felt closer to him than I had for a long time. I was so pleased that he had at last confided in me, and I believed I had inched closer to understanding that bleak look in his eyes. There were two tragedies in his life: he had lost a woman he loved in a car accident, and his friend had died in front of him on the street. Piers blamed himself because Bill had tried to stop him attacking the young thug. I knew how guilt could build up in the mind, and I understood. If Piers needed to be alone sometimes, I would know that it was because his memories had proved too painful. It was a bond between us. We had both been touched by tragedy.

I heard the telephone ringing when I emerged from the shower. I went into the hall as Piers was replacing the receiver and I looked at him inquiringly.

'No one important,' he said, frowning. 'Were you expecting a call?'

'Well, yes, I thought it might be Mr Silcott. I've been expecting him to ring for a couple of weeks now.'

'No, it was for me.' Piers smiled. 'We're not busy at the gallery at the moment. I thought I might take a few days off. We could have a day out, if you like.'

'That would be nice,' I said. 'Where shall we go?'

'We'll take a drive into the country. It will do us both good to relax.'

'Hang on then, I'll dress.'

As I was dressing, the phone rang again. Piers didn't call me so it must have been for him. I was surprised that Mr Silcott hadn't rung before this. I'd been looking forward to helping him with the cataloguing, but perhaps he'd decided he didn't need help after all.

The phone rang again just as we were leaving the flat. I went to answer it, but Piers laid a restraining hand on my arm.

'Leave it,' he said. 'It will be the gallery, and it can wait.'

'It might be important.'

There was a momentary hint of annoyance in his eyes.

'If it's important, whoever it is will ring again.' Piers argued, then smiled. 'Come on, I'm looking forward to our day out, aren't you?'

'Of course.'

I smiled back, but I was aware of a nagging voice at the back of my mind that kept asking why Piers didn't want me to answer the phone.

*

263

'Happy birthday, darling.' Piers greeted me with a kiss. 'Wake up, sleepyhead. You've got a pile of cards – and these are from me.' He laid a huge bouquet of red roses across the bed. 'And this, and this . . . and this.' He piled the prettily wrapped gifts all around me on the bed.

'You always spoil me,' I said, relieved that I'd woken without one of the headaches that seemed to plague me these days. 'Oh, Piers, this is beautiful!'

I lifted the two rows of smooth, creamy pearls from their bed of black satin. The clasp was the kind worn at the front; set with large diamonds, it was made of white gold and shaped in the form of a heart.

'I love it, darling. I think pearls are my favourite jewel of all.'

'I must remember that in future,' he said with a smile. 'Now open the others. The cards can wait.'

Recognizing the handwriting, I'd been about to open Julie's card, but I laid it aside and opened the rest of Piers' presents. As usual, there was a varied assortment: expensive silk undies, designer bags and shoes, and a very sexy black evening dress.

'I thought it would look fantastic with the pearls,' Piers said. 'You could wear it this evening, darling.'

'Yes, I shall,' I replied and leaned forward to kiss him. 'It's lovely, Piers.'

'So are you,' he said, his hand stroking my bare arm. 'I do love you. Never forget that, Aline.'

'Piers,' I whispered. 'Piers darling . . .'

And then I was in his arms. I shivered with pleasure as he began to make love to me. Piers knew just how to bring my body tinglingly, gloriously alive, and I surrendered my lips to his. We had made love too little of late, and I knew it was my fault. Too often these days I took a pill to help me sleep, and it was ruining our sex life. I had begun taking them again when I was alone at Hazeling, and after Zena's murder I had become dependent on them, and I was finding it harder and harder to do without them . . .

Piers' hand rested on my throat, his fingers tightening for a moment. I felt constricted and unable to breathe, and I looked up at him with frightened eyes. The pressure eased and he kissed me.

'My sweet Aline,' he murmured. 'Never forget that you belong to me, will you?'

Nick's card arrived by second post. I collected it on my way back from having my hair done. Opening it, I laughed at the picture of a puppy sitting in a basket of flowers. It was typical of Nick; he almost always chose humorous cards.

Nick's message was brief, 'To Aline,' he had written, 'with all my love.'

He'd signed it with a flourish and covered all the available space with a couple of huge kisses. I hesitated for a moment, wondering what to do, then put it on the shelf with the others. It was better that Piers should see it when he came home than find it hidden away somewhere.

It was really quite innocent.

'You look wonderful,' Piers said as I came out of the bedroom that evening. 'I'm proud of you, darling.'

'Thank you,' I murmured, lifting my face for his kiss. 'I feel fantastic in this dress.'

'You wore black the first night we went out together.' Piers touched my cheek with his fingertips. 'I thought you were the most beautiful woman I'd ever seen.'

'And now?'

'Now I know I was right.' He laughed as I pouted. 'You've had enough compliments for one night. Do you want a drink before we go?'

'No, I don't think so. I'd rather keep my head clear, for the moment. This is the first time for ages that I haven't had a headache.'

'That would have been too bad on your birthday. We want you looking your best tonight, darling,' Piers said, and glanced at his watch. 'I've bought a rather special vintage champagne, but we can drink that when we come back.'

He looked disappointed so I said, 'Perhaps just one then, before we go.'

'Why waste it? It will keep.' Piers picked up my cashmere wrap and put it round my shoulders. 'Let's go, darling. Everyone will be waiting . . .'

I was feeling excited as we walked into the hotel lobby with its thick carpets and mellow furnishings. Then, as I saw everyone standing in little groups, talking in hushed voices and glancing awkwardly towards us, I knew that something was wrong. I clutched at Piers' arm.

'Why isn't everyone upstairs having a drink?'

'I've no idea.' Piers looked at me hard. 'You did phone and confirm the booking?'

'Yes, of course I did.'

'Then I'd better see what's wrong. Go and talk to Julie, darling. I'll sort this out.'

265

Julie walked towards me, looking uncertain and awkward. 'They don't know anything about the party,' she said in a low voice. 'What's gone wrong, Aline?'

'I don't know,' I said, my insides churning. I felt so foolish that I could hardly look at her. 'This is awful. But I did confirm the booking, Julie. I remember distinctly.'

'Well, keep your chin up,' Julie said, kissing my cheek and then laughing as she rubbed off a smear of lipstick. 'Don't get upset, whatever happens. Just laugh at it. Everyone else is.'

'I feel so embarrassed.'

'It isn't the end of the world, love.' Julie squeezed my arm. 'If the worst comes to the worst we can all go on to a nightclub or something.'

'But I invited everyone to a party.' I was close to tears.

Piers came back to us, his face concerned and doubtful. 'You confirmed, Aline,' he said in a hushed tone. 'But apparently you rang the next day to cancel.'

'I did no such thing!' My voice rose shrilly, but a warning squeeze of my arm from Julie calmed me down. 'Honestly, Piers, I didn't.'

'Well, there was a mix-up anyway. The management are most upset. They can provide a meal for everyone, but the suite is in use and there'll be no birthday cake or the little gifts you wanted on the tables for your guests.'

'As long as we can eat,' Julie said. 'Who cares about a cake?' She raised her voice so that everyone could hear. 'It's just a little mix-up, folks.'

There was a ripple of laughter. Waiters suddenly appeared carrying trays with glasses of champagne. The awkwardness had passed, and everyone gathered round me with congratulations and gifts. They all seemed determined to make me feel that it wasn't such a tragedy. I smiled gratefully as Julie put her arm around my waist and squeezed, and my chin went up.

'I'm sorry it isn't going to be quite as we'd planned,' I said. 'But after we've eaten, I would like you all to be my guests at a nightclub.' I turned to Piers. 'Perhaps someone could phone and warn the management we're coming so they don't refuse us entry.'

'I'll do that.' Nick's voice startled me. I hadn't noticed him standing right at the back of the little crowd. 'You won't be disappointed this time, Aline.'

For a moment I looked straight into his eyes. His face was rather grim and unsmiling, but I felt somehow strengthened by an unspoken understanding. Nick was still my friend.

I was aware of Piers beside me. He was angry and his fingers gripped my arm, hurting me. 'They have the tables ready for us, Aline,' he said, his manner cold and tightly controlled. 'We shouldn't keep them waiting – they've been put to enough trouble as it is.'

I felt as if he had slapped me in front of all our guests. He believed the mix-up was my fault, and so now would everyone else. I flushed, feeling humiliated, and wanted to run away and hide. Then something made me glance at Nick again. Very deliberately, he winked at me and lifted his glass in a salute.

I had an overwhelming desire to giggle. I felt so much better knowing that he at least didn't think I was going crazy. I smiled at Nick. This was my birthday party, and I intended to enjoy it, no matter what!

Perhaps I drank too much champagne at dinner. Afterwards, it all seemed hazy in my mind. Anyway, I was in a dangerous mood by the time we moved on to the nightclub. Piers' manner had become more and more reserved as the evening wore on, and I knew he was furious, even though he appeared outwardly smiling and pleasant. Knowing how jealous he was, I ought to have refused Nick when he asked me to dance, but I was angry, too. Piers had humiliated me in front of my friends and I didn't much like it. I was tired of being treated as though I were stupid, and my mood was reckless. I loved Piers and we had – could have – a good marriage, but not if he continued to behave in this way.

'I'd love to dance with you, Nick,' I said, smiling up at him.

The music happened to be soft and dreamy as we took the floor, and relaxed by the wine, I moved naturally into my partner's arms. It felt good. Very good. Almost as if I'd never been away.

'I have to see you alone,' he said. 'I have something to show you.'

I glanced up at him again, fluttering my lashes as I flirted with him. 'What do you want to show me, Nick – your etchings?' I giggled, feeling light-headed.

'This is serious,' Nick said, then grinned as he looked down at me. 'But I guess this is neither the time nor the place. You're enjoying yourself, aren't you? Despite it all, you're having a great time. I just hope you don't pay too high a price. You weren't meant to react like this.'

I didn't know what he was talking about, so I laid my head on his shoulder, snuggling up to him. I felt sleepy and all my worries seemed far away.

'What are you mumbling about?' I asked dreamily. 'You're a good dancer, Nick. Have I ever told you what a great mover you are?'

'Oh boy!' He chuckled, amused. 'You certainly are having a good time. Someone isn't going to be too pleased, but we'll deal with that when we have to . . .'

It was true, I was enjoying myself. I liked being in Nick's arms. A part of me realized that I wasn't just paying Piers back for what he'd said earlier. I felt happier with Nick than I had with anyone for a long time. The thought jolted my euphoria. Glancing over Nick's shoulder, I caught sight of Piers. He was dancing with Julie but he looked detached, cold and uninterested, and I knew he was angry. Serves him right, I thought. Piers might be my husband, but he didn't own me. And the sooner he realized that, the better . . .

When the music stopped, I refused to let go of Nick. I stood with my arms about his waist, laughing up at him. Piers was talking to someone, but he made an excuse and came towards me. Just as he reached me, the music started again. I turned my back on him deliberately, moving into Nick's arms once more. When I looked for Piers again, he had disappeared.

I put him out of my mind. If he was sulking, let him get on with it. Abandoning my cares, I danced with Nick again and again, laughing and drinking glass after glass of champagne. I felt as if I'd been let out of prison. It was almost two hours later when everyone had begun to think about leaving that Piers reappeared. He was smiling, appparently calm and unruffled when he came and took hold of my arm, but as I felt his fingers bite into my flesh, my mood sobered.

'Say goodnight, darling,' Piers prompted. 'I think it's time we went home, don't you?'

'Where did you go?' I asked. 'Why did you disappear like that?'

'I went for a walk,' Piers replied in a controlled tone. 'I'm sure you didn't miss me. I was only gone a few minutes.'

Glancing at him, I was puzzled. Something was different but I didn't know what. I got into the taxi, sitting stiff and silent as we were driven home. When we reached the flat, I went straight to bed. Piers did not join me and I was soon asleep.

'You behaved like a tramp, making eyes at that ex-lover of yours! No doubt he'll expect you to jump back into bed with him – but that's probably what you want, if you haven't already.'

'Shut up, Piers!' I cried, surprising us both. 'Maybe I did have a little too much to drink last night, and maybe I did flirt with Nick.' I raised my eyes to his over the breakfast table, wanting there to be no possibility of a mistake. 'I did it to punish you. To pay you back for humiliating me in front of our guests. You made me look a fool and – '

'You did that without any help from me.' He glared at me. 'You were almost out on your feet when I brought you home last night.'

'At least I didn't need a damned sleeping pill!' I allowed myself the luxury of yelling. 'I confirmed that booking at the hotel, Piers. I know I did, and I didn't cancel. I may forget to turn off the fire now and then, but I'm not losing my mind. If someone cancelled it wasn't me.'

'Who else would do it?'

'I've not the remotest idea,' I said. 'Obviously, whoever it was intended to ruin my birthday, but thanks to Julie and Nick I had a good time anyway.'

'And I played no part in all this, I suppose?' His eyes were as hard and as treacherous as black ice. 'Do you imagine it was easy arranging dinner for ten people at short notice?'

'I'm sure you used your charm – and money, Piers,' I said, wanting to punish him. 'That particular combination usually gets you what you want, doesn't it?'

Piers looked at me in silence, the little pulse beating at his temple. He moved towards me and caught my wrist. His grip was painful, but I refused to let him see that he was hurting me.

'You're just like all the others,' he said, and I noticed that he was breathing heavily and his skin was beaded with sweat. 'I thought you were different but now I know you for the little slut you are.'

'If I did leave you for Nick, which I won't, it would be your own fault,' I said. 'You're impossible to live with, Piers. You and your insane jealousy . . .'

I regretted the words as soon as they were uttered but my pride wouldn't let me retract them. He must see that we couldn't go on this way.

'If that's your attitude, we have nothing to say to each other.' He picked up his briefcase and walked to the door, then turned to look at me. 'I expect to be late this evening. Don't bother waiting up for me.'

'Don't worry, I won't!'

Piers stared at me, a strange almost resigned expression in his eyes, then he inclined his head. 'It was your choice, Aline. Don't forget that.'

Then, leaving me staring after him in dismay, he went out, closing the door with a little snap.

I drew a deep, sobbing breath. What had I done? I hadn't meant the quarrel to go this far. I loved Piers. Despite everything, I loved him. I

269

didn't want to lose him and I knew I mustn't let Piers go without making up our quarrel. I was about to run out and catch him at the lift when I saw something lying on the carpet. Bending down, I saw it was the card Nick had given me. It had been ripped to shreds. The discovery made me angry again and I no longer wanted to follow Piers.

I gathered up the pieces and stared at them for several minutes as I tried to sort out the confusion of my thoughts. My love for the man I'd married hadn't changed, but the man I was living with was a different person. Why? Could it be that I was imagining things, that I *was* ill? My hands trembled as I tried to reassemble the pieces of the card. What had happened to me? I gave up on the card and buried my face in my hands, feeling confused and miserable. Behind me, the telephone rang.

'Aline.' Nick's voice made my spine tingle. 'How are you this morning?'

'I'm fine,' I replied. 'A slight headache, but that's my fault.'

'If you can't celebrate on your birthday . . .' Nick hesitated. 'What did your husband have to say about it?'

'He wasn't very pleased.' My voice was tight and controlled. 'He'll get over it.'

'Perhaps.' Nick was again hesitant. 'Could you meet me for lunch today, Aline? I think we should talk.'

'Why?' I remembered Piers' jibes and blushed. 'Last night – '

'It has nothing to do with last night. Don't worry, I haven't got the wrong idea. I knew why you were flirting with me.'

'I'm sorry, Nick,' I said, hearing a wistful note in his voice. 'I didn't mean to use you. I was just angry with Piers.'

'I was delighted to be used,' he replied dryly. 'But I do have to talk to you. It's important, Aline.'

'I don't understand, Nick.'

'And I'm not about to explain on the phone.'

I took a deep breath. 'All right. I'll meet you at twelve-thirty at L'Escargot.'

'I think somewhere less public would be advisable. Why don't you come out to Richmond?' He was silent for a moment. 'I'll book a table at a discreet Italian restaurant I know. What I have to say is going to upset you, Aline, but you have to know. Come to the shop at twelve.'

His tone was commanding, and that worried me. For Nick to talk like that something must be seriously wrong.

'Nick! Tell me now,' I cried, my stomach churning.

'Later – and don't let me down this time. If you don't turn up, I'll come looking for you.'

Nick hung up and I stared at the phone in frustration. What was that supposed to mean? For a moment I wished I hadn't agreed to meet him, but I knew his threat hadn't been an idle one. If I didn't keep my appointment, he was certain to turn up at the flat.

Chapter Twenty

I arrived at Nick's shop at five to twelve. He was serving a rather smart woman customer who seemed as if she would talk for ever, but he smiled at me as I moved away to browse through his display of china. He had managed to collect some beautiful things. There were Derby figures and a set of Chelsea flower plates, blue and white dishes with Chinese designs, delicate little coffee cups, elegant bowls with gold leaf edging and some magnificent vases that were over four feet high. The bronze horse I'd wanted to buy for Piers was still there, but it had a 'not for sale' notice propped up against it. I looked up at Nick as the customer left.

'Why isn't the horse for sale?'

'I decided to keep it,' he said, avoiding my eyes. He turned the *open-closed* notice in his glass door then smiled at me. 'Shall we go?'

'I think we should talk here, Nick. If whatever you want to tell me is so private . . .'

He hesitated and then nodded. 'Maybe it would be as well. You're not going to be pleased with me, Aline. Julie – and you – told me you didn't want me to research that old murder, but once I start something like that – '

'You finish.' He nodded, and as I saw the look in his eyes I felt a queasy sensation in my stomach. 'You had better tell me what you've discovered, then.'

Nick looked surprised, but things had changed. I'd accused Nick of being jealous and unfair, but that wasn't true. Whatever Nick had done, he had done for me. I understood that now.

Nick was silent for a moment, studying my face, then he reached inside his jacket pocket. 'These are photocopies of all the newspaper reports,' he said. 'But I managed to get an actual photograph from the paper's own files.'

'Just tell me what you've found out.' I sat down on a Victorian sofa, my knees shaking. The expression on Nick's face left me in no doubt that he thought his discoveries significant.

'The murder of Edith Dodson was similar in several ways to that of Phyllis Pearson. If there is a connection, whoever was responsible for both murders had very strong hands. Her neck was snapped . . .' I gasped and Nick's mouth tightened. He sat down opposite me, his face grim. 'In Edith Dodson's case, the police were fooled at the start into thinking it was a break-in, then they began to suspect the grandson had done it. Apparently he'd had a rotten life with his grandfather; he never let the boy have any fun or do anything other kids take for granted. Edith's neighbours said she treated her grandson worse than a dog.' Nick paused and looked at me, as if asking if I wanted him to go on. I nodded, feeling sick. 'A few weeks previously, Edith's husband fell – or was pushed – down their staircase. He died in hospital without regaining consciousness, but the wife of the farmer who owned their cottage heard a row between Edith and her grandson. It seems she blamed him for Mr Dodson's death.'

'Did – did the police arrest the Dodsons' grandson?' I asked. My mouth tasted of ashes and my hands had begun to tremble. I thrust them into my pockets so that Nick wouldn't see how upset I was.

'Supposedly he was on holiday at the time of the murder, then he disappeared. Cash went missing from the house. It seems that Mr Dodson didn't trust banks and kept several thousand pounds under the floorboards. The farmer thought he saw the grandson leaving the house late one night after the police had sealed it, and an empty biscuit tin was found abandoned when they went to investigate. Some paintings were also taken.'

'The grandson went back to the house after the murder?'

'Some weeks later, yes. To take money and various other things.'

'But surely if he murdered his grandmother, he would have taken the cash then . . .'

'The theory is that he killed her in a rage and panicked, then came back when he thought the search had died down.'

'That would take strong nerves, wouldn't it?'

'Or a compulsion to return to the scene of his crime. But you're right, only a certain type of criminal mind could cope with that. A mind that doesn't see things the way you or I would.'

I nodded, thoughtful now. 'A mind that was unbalanced?'

'Perhaps.' Nick paused, looking at me.

'Go on, there's more, isn't there?'

It all made sense to me. A horrible pattern was emerging. I felt cold and I had a sense of being in a nightmare. But this was real.

Nick was silent for a few seconds, then he held the photograph out to me. 'Does this remind you of anyone? It was taken about two years before the Dodson murder.'

273

I took it from him, my hand trembling. It was a black and white picture of a young man of about seventeen. I stared at the glaring, rebellious eyes and then I gasped. It was the face I'd seen in my dreams. The face of the man who had attacked me on the marshes!

Closing my eyes, I relived the scene on the marshes. I could smell the salty tang of the grass beneath me as I lay terrified, looking up into that face. I heard the menace in his voice as he taunted me, threatening to kill me because I'd laughed at him. I'd laughed, and for that I must die. Even though I was only eleven years old, I knew that the behaviour of my attacker was unnatural.

I believed I was about to die. Then, all at once, the madness faded from the attacker's eyes. He seemed to blink, then stared at me in surprise as he realized what he was doing . . . And then the blackness came down; I did not see him get to his feet and run away, leaving me there on the sand. But I knew that he had . . .

'Do you know who he is, Aline?' Nick's voice came to me from a distance, recalling my wandering thoughts.

I glanced up into Nick's concerned eyes. 'I – I'm not sure,' I said, amazed at how calm I sounded. 'I can see the resemblance, but that's all it is.'

'It was taken over thirteen years ago.'

'Yes, I know.' I stood up, keeping my manner light and unconcerned. 'Will you ring for a taxi for me, Nick?'

'I thought we were having lunch?' He sounded anxious, half angry. 'You aren't going to ignore this?'

'No,' I said. 'No, I'm not ignoring what you've told me – but I have to handle this in my own way.' I raised my eyes to his, hoping for understanding. 'I'm not angry and I'm not blind. I just need to be quite, quite sure.'

'Yes,' he said gently. 'I understand that, Aline. But be careful. I don't want you to have a nasty accident. You happen to be very precious to me.'

I stared up at him. 'Am I, Nick? Then why didn't you tell me that long ago?'

'I was a damned fool. I loved you, Aline. I've always loved you – perhaps too much. I was terrified that if we . . .' His voice faltered for a moment, then he looked me in the eyes. 'I was married for a couple of years but the job got in the way and I came back unexpectedly one night to find her in bed with someone else.'

'Oh, Nick!' Tears stung my eyes. 'Why didn't you tell me?'

'Pride, I suppose – and stubbornness.' He moved nearer to me, looking down into my face. I knew that he wanted to kiss me and I sensed the suppressed longing in him as his hands clenched at his sides. 'Aline, I – '

'Tell me another day,' I interrupted, knowing that if I didn't leave then I wouldn't have the strength. 'I have to go home, Nick. I have to go now.'

It wasn't until I was sitting in the taxi that I realized I was still clutching the photograph Nick had given me. I gazed down at it, a rabbit looking into the eyes of a stoat. It couldn't be . . . The whole idea was so horrible that it defied reason. I must be imagining the resemblance to my husband, but Nick had seen it first. He was convinced that the seventeen-year-old Peter Dodson and Piers Drayton were one and the same person. But Nick didn't know what I knew.

Thrusting the picture into my jacket pocket, I felt the sickness sweep over me. Peter Dodson had attacked and almost killed me that day on the saltmarshes at Blakeney. He had attacked me because I had seen him crying, and laughed. I'd laughed to see a young man in his late teens blubbering and weeping noisily like a little child. He hadn't noticed me watching him. I'd been so surprised to see anyone at all on the marshes on a cold February day, especially a stranger who screamed and shouted at the sky in an excess of emotion. My laughter had been a nervous reaction to what was a disturbing sight. The young man's grief had not seemed a normal display, but something strange and terribly private. So I'd laughed, in an awkward, uncomfortable, childish way. And then he had become aware of me.

'Why are you laughing?' he had demanded.

Something in his eyes had frightened me: a wildness, an almost insane desperation that had made me back away from him in terror. But my flight had been in vain, for Peter Dodson had pursued and caught me. In the struggle I'd been cut and bruised. He had meant to kill me, but at the last moment he had changed his mind.

My husband looked like an older Peter Dodson, calmer, more controlled. Too controlled at times – unnaturally so. I'd found that strange calm disturbing. And the way his moods could change so suddenly . . . just as Peter Dodson's had that day on the marshes.

I paid off the taxi and hurried inside the apartment building, praying that Piers hadn't returned. I needed time to think.

I made coffee, pacing the kitchen floor as I went over the events of the past few months in my mind, remembering little things Piers had told me about his childhood – things that made a horrible pattern if Piers Drayton really was Peter Dodson. He had lived with his grandparents . . . They had died within weeks of each other when he was nineteen . . . He had said his life had been made utterly miserable by his grandfather's strictness . . . He had seemed anxious when he asked if I could remember the face of the man who had attacked me on the marshes, but then he had made a joke of it all, persuading me that it was just another nightmare. It was as if he had been goading me, seeing just how far he could push me, trying to drive me into some kind of mental breakdown.

The first time we'd met, Piers had told me about the isolated cottage in Cornwall where he had been brought up. He had never been allowed to go into town and do all the things other young men did. It must have been this that caused him to grow up to hate and despise the only family he'd ever known. He'd been starved of human companionship and love, driven to the edge of despair, until eventually something inside him went haywire . . .

Shivering, I looked out of the window. It was raining hard and the sky was black. Almost as black as the despair in my heart. Was my husband the loving, generous man I'd thought, or was he a cold, calculating murderer?

'*No!*' I cried, my throat tightening with emotion. 'Not Piers. Please, don't let it be true. Please not Piers. Not Piers . . .'

The idea was so awful, I couldn't begin to accept it; but I had to know the truth. For too long, I'd blinded myself to his faults. It was time to face the facts, and there must be clues here in the flat. I'd never ever pried into Piers' personal papers, but now I was going to.

I went in to the bedroom. I knew what I was looking for – the letters in white envelopes with strange blue printing. I had a feeling that they might be the key to this mystery. Piers always made a point of collecting the post himself when they were due.

Guiltily, I began to go through Piers' pockets. There was the usual assortment of old tickets, handkerchiefs and coins, but no letters. Piers had obviously remembered the incident over the grey suit, when I'd found two of the white envelopes in his pocket and he had been so concerned that I might have read them.

I searched on through the wardrobes, flinging clothes on to the bed as I looked for some sort of evidence. But evidence of what? Was I trying to prove my husband's guilt or his innocence? At this moment I no longer knew. Terrified that Piers would return and discover me, I worked feverishly.

I pulled out drawers, tossing the contents to the floor as a growing sense of doom filled me. All the time, I was remembering . . . remembering Piers' terrible jealousy and how menacingly he had warned me never to leave him. I was remembering the nightmares and the headaches, the questioning that sometimes drove me to the edge of tears, and the coldness in his eyes when he'd discovered Michael's obsession.

After a search through every drawer and cupboard in the rest of the flat, I went back to the bedroom. There was just Piers' bedside chest to go. Breathing heavily, I wrenched out the top drawer and emptied it on to the bed. My nerves were stretched almost to the limit. I felt as if my head would burst and I wanted to scream in frustration as I scrabbled amongst his belongings. There must be something there, *something* that would tell me what I wanted to know.

There was an old wallet with a few business cards and receipts, also keys, a pocket torch, combs and cufflinks – all the usual clutter – but no white envelopes. Then I noticed the photograph. It was badly creased. I smoothed it out and turned it over. It was of me, and my blood ran cold as I saw it had been taken outside the Alhambra.

Janet Hendry had said a man was taking photographs of me that day, but I'd dismissed it as irrelevant. Yet here was the proof . . . Proof of what? That Piers had been in Granada that day . . . that he had taken a picture of a pretty girl . . . that he had followed me, perhaps?

It was odd but it proved nothing. Even so, I was feeling shaken as I went back to searching the drawers. Why had Piers never mentioned the photograph? It was another unexplained incident, another uncomfortable circumstance, but it wasn't the proof I needed. I went on with my search.

The next drawer was full of socks. The third contained underwear. The fourth was crammed with belts. I was about to close it when something caught my eye. I emptied everything on to the bed, and then my heart stood still. The brooch lay there, out of place amongst the assortment of belts, mesmerizing me, so that for several seconds I was unable to touch it or pick it up.

My mouth felt dry and I swallowed hard, trying not to panic. It was a cameo brooch with a grey stone, portraying the Three Graces; just like the one I'd given Zena for Christmas; just like the brooch she'd been wearing the night she died – the brooch that had not been on her body when it was found. *But it didn't have to be the same one.*

I paused for a moment, then, my hand shaking, I picked it up and turned it over in my palm and saw the fifteen-carat-gold mark and the young head of Victoria that the sales assistant had pointed out to me. There was the same flimsy catch . . . It *was* the same brooch.

Leaving Piers' belts on the bed, I went through to the kitchen and took the photograph Nick had given me from my jacket pocket. I laid them side by side on the table, the photo of me outside the Alhambra, the brooch and the picture of a teenage murderer, staring at the evidence in disbelief. It all fitted into the puzzle.

'But why?' I whispered. 'Why Zena?'

If Piers and Peter Dodson were one and the same person, it explained why Mrs Pearson had died. She had recognized Piers, either from the press photograph or from personal knowledge. She could even have known Edith Dodson and her grandchild; that was something I could only guess at. But she had been concerned enough to put that old newspaper cutting in an envelope with my name on it. She had been concerned for me.

But why Zena? The question kept hammering at my brain. Why did Zena have to die?

Suddenly I remembered Zena's last phonecall. *'I've got something important to tell you, Aline. I have to meet someone first and then I'll be home . . .'*

Had she wanted to tell me something about Piers? What could Zena have known that was so dangerous she had to die?

'*No!* No! No!' I covered my face with my hands. It was all a mistake. There must be a simple explanation. Piers couldn't be this evil creature I was conjuring up in my mind.

I glanced at my watch. It was gone six. Julie must have left the office by now. I had to talk to someone! Julie would understand, she would know why I couldn't go to the police. She would know why I had to be sure that this wasn't another of my nightmares, that I wasn't imagining it all. Julie was involved in psychotherapy sessions at the clinic; she would know if it was possible for someone to appear sane but do things that were so terrible they defied all reason.

Dialling her home number, I frowned as the answerphone clicked on. Damn! Well, I would simply leave a message.

'It's Aline,' I said. 'I think Nick may be right. I'm going down to Hazeling to see if I can discover any clues about Zena. I'll ring you this evening.'

I hurried through to the bedroom. Piers' belts were still on the bed. Thrusting them back into the drawer, I grabbed an overnight bag and crammed some clothes into it.

The keys to Piers' estate car were lying on the hall table. I snatched them up, slammed the flat door behind me and took the lift down to the garage. My heart was beating wildly and I was terrified Piers would return before I could escape. I couldn't face him at this moment. It might be that all my suspicions were unfounded. Perhaps I was doing him a terrible injustice, but I could no longer pretend even to myself that everything was as it should be.

I started the car and eased it out into the busy stream of rush-hour traffic. Needing to concentrate on my driving helped me to calm down. I didn't often drive these days and I had to be fully aware of what I was doing. At least I was out of the flat before Piers returned . . . but, the brooch and photographs! They were still on the kitchen table. In my hurry to leave I'd forgotten them, and I cursed myself.

I shifted the gear lever. It wasn't Zena who had pushed me down the stairs. It was Piers! I remembered the sharp tang of an unfamiliar scent just before I felt a hard push in the back. Piers had been using a new aftershave, and he'd worn it to the hospital the first time he visited me and then never again, as if he'd deliberately been testing my memory. But why had he done it?

He hadn't wanted a baby! I'd seen that look of rejection – of fear, almost – in his eyes when I'd first told him we were having a child. He had recovered himself almost immediately, and I'd been taken in by his lies.

Damn the traffic, I thought as my head throbbed. I seemed to be trapped, like a pet hamster in a cage, treading an endless wheel. The lights of the cars tailed away as far as I could see, moving slowly, oh so slowly. Yet perhaps it was better that I was behind the wheel of a car. The headache was getting worse, but I wouldn't feel safe until I was out of London, out of Piers' reach. I had to be alone to think. But my thoughts were coming thick and fast, the evidence building up to a horrible conclusion. The suit that had disappeared . . . The invitations that were never posted . . . The cancelled party . . . Were they all a part of Piers' plan to murder me? Had he been trying to drive me out of my mind? He had nearly succeeded. Perhaps I *was* mad. Perhaps this was all a delusion.

Why? Why Zena? Why had he married me? Why did he want to kill me? Why now?

The questions just went round and round in my mind and the traffic bundled closer and closer together in an endless jam.

It was dark and bitterly cold when I reached Hazeling. As I swung the car into the entrance, I caught sight of a man trapped like a startled rabbit in the car headlamps. Winding the window down, I yelled at him.

'Who are you? What are you doing here?'

For a moment he hesitated, then he turned and ran. Staring after him, I concluded that he was the prowler I'd noticed lurking in the shadows. This time, I'd been able to see his face clearly. Unshaven and dirty, he looked like a tramp. I realized that he was probably using one of the outhouses as somewhere to sleep in the cold weather, and my fear faded. He was more frightened of me than I was of him. Perhaps in the morning I might try to find him and offer him food.

I parked the estate in front of the house, and used the car lights to help me unlock the door. As it swung open, I felt the chill go through me. It was freezing! Hazeling had always been difficult to heat, but without the old coke-fired boiler to keep off the worst of the cold, it was like an iceberg. Something would have to be done about the place soon. One thing, if I left Piers I wouldn't want to live here. I switched on the hall lights and locked the car, remembering to turn off the headlamps. Then I locked and bolted the front door.

The house was cheerless, unwelcoming. The atmosphere seemed very heavy and oppressive, as if the unhappiness of Zena's last months still lingered. I thought of the dolls in the attic, waiting for her, waiting for someone who would never come. Zena was dead. Murdered. Had the dolls known that she was going to die when they called to me that night? Had they been trying to warn me?

I gave myself a mental shake. I must not let my imagination go out of control – that way lay madness. I knew the shadows were there in my mind, waiting, and if I once gave into them . . .

I switched on lights and electric fires as I hurried to the kitchen. At least I could make myself a hot drink. There wasn't any milk but I could drink my coffee black. It would keep my mind clear. Having filled the machine, I went through to the drawing room and put a match to the fire that I'd laid the day after Zena died, when I'd been waiting for news.

Feeling chilled by my thoughts as much as the cold, I watched a flame begin to lick over the damp paper and wood. It was going to be a while before the fire got going, so I returned to the kitchen. Zena had died because she had something to tell me. Was is something she had seen or overheard? Had she guessed that Piers had pushed me down the stairs? Or was it something else?

I was aware of being hungry. I'd eaten nothing since breakfast. Taking two chocolate biscuits from a new packet in the cupboard, I ate and drank, wondering where best to begin my search. I knew that the police had already been through Zena's personal belongings, but they had obviously not found anything incriminating.

What was I looking for? What kind of a clue had I hoped to find at Hazeling? Or had I merely acted on impulse, choosing it as a way of escape from Piers? *I could never go back to Piers.*

Suddenly, I knew that I did not want to. Even if most of my suspicions were proved false, I knew that Piers had attacked me on the marshes all those years ago. It was Piers who had made the strange phonecalls that started soon after my mother died, Piers who had watched me from a distance, taking an interest in my life until the day he decided to step back into it.

He must have planned everything. He must have been thinking about it for years. My flesh crawled as I realized that he had always been there, watching me, a brooding, evil shadow hanging over my life . . .

Then, I thought where I might find out about Zena's part in all this. Zena was the sort of person who would keep a diary. The chances were that the police had found it . . . on the other hand she might have hidden it very carefully.

I left my coffee unfinished on the kitchen table and ran upstairs. At the doorway to Zena's room, I hesitated, reluctant to go in. It wasn't too late to turn back. I didn't know for sure . . . Reluctantly, I acknowledged that it *was* too late. I'd refused to believe Nick when he'd suggested that Piers might have had something to do with Helena's accident. I'd ignored the warnings Julie had tried to give me time and time again. And I'd dismissed the voices in my head that had told me something wasn't quite as it should be – Piers' strange moods . . . Those abrupt changes of personality . . . But now I *had* to know.

I opened the door of Zena's room and went in. The scent of her oversweet perfume lingered in the air like an unseen presence and I felt that she was there, willing me on. She wanted me to find her diary. She wanted me to know the truth so that she could be at peace.

I tried the dressing table, chest of drawers and wardrobe shelf without result. But that was too easy; the police would have found it if it had been in an obvious place. Where would Zena hide something she didn't want anyone to find? In a coat pocket, perhaps, or. . . ?

Looking round the room, my gaze fell on Susie sitting in an old-fashioned rocking chair by the window. The doll's glass eyes seemed to fill with tears and I imagined her mouth opening and whispering my name.

'Aline, pick me up. Hold me . . .'

The room had turned suddenly colder and a shiver caught me. I stood still, unable to move. Had I heard that voice, or was it the wind? Outside the window it was still and the air was crisp with frost. Susie *had* spoken to me – or was it Zena?

The shadows were all around me, closing in on me. I fought them off. If they claimed me too soon, Piers would have won.

I walked over to the doll. Susie was dressed in a blue satin gown with lace frills and ribbon bows, her pale blonde ringlets clustered round her china face. I stretched out my hand . . . An unseen force gently propelling me, I picked her up. Tucked into her dress was something flat and hard. It was a small white leather pocket diary.

Unforgivably, I dropped Susie on to the floor, where she sprawled in a tangle of china limbs, and I left the room. My heart was jumping and fluttering as I walked slowly downstairs. Now that I'd found the diary, I was unwilling to read it. If it contained the proof I was certain it must, I would have no choice but to go to the police – and Piers would be arrested for Zena's murder.

The doubts began again. Supposing my imagination was playing tricks on me? Supposing I went to the police and Piers was innocent? My mind was suddenly flooded with pictures of Piers smiling at me, Piers reaching out for me, kissing me . . . and the pain was intolerable. I tried to make excuses for him. Zena could have given him the brooch to have a safety chain fitted. But when? She'd been wearing it when we found the paintings. Perhaps it had fallen off as Zena had rushed away that last afternoon. Piers could have picked it up. He had a habit of leaving things in his pockets. Surely he wouldn't have been foolish enough to keep it, knowing it could incriminate him?

'*Who knows what goes on in the mind of a murderer?*'

Michael's voice: the words were those he'd used just after I'd read of Phyllis Pearson's death, but I felt that he was speaking to me now from the shadows.

'Oh, Michael,' I whispered. 'Help me. Please help me.'

The fire was burning brightly in the drawing room. I poured myself a brandy and drank it to settle my nerves. Then I sat down to read Zena's diary.

Most of it referred to shopping trips, cooking or clothes, and, in-between, revealing lines that told of her deep unhappiness. Then in March I found the first relevant entry.

I met a man today. We bumped into each other and I dropped my shopping. He picked it up for me and invited me for coffee.

It was innocent enough, but a few days later she met him again – a lunch date this time. There were phonecalls and a walk on the beach at Cley . . . On the beach where she had died . . . He had given her a small present of a musical box . . . The musical box she had played over and over again in the attic . . .

So there had been someone she was interested in, at least for a while. Michael's intuition had been right.

I went on reading as the details of Zena's life were unfolded. It was all here, her unhappiness because she could not have a child, her increasing bitterness, then her anxiety over Michael's obsession and his failing health. She had been flattered by the attentions of this man, but despite it all, she had loved her husband.

I found an entry that looked as if it meant something important. Zena had underscored some of the words.

All he wanted to talk about was *her* and *her* money. I wish I'd never told him anything about the family. He's obsessed with *her*. Just like Michael!

The word *her* had been heavily underlined each time. What could it mean? I turned the pages frantically but the entries stopped after that particular day. Either the meetings had ended or Zena had no longer wished to record them.

It seemed that I was the person being discussed. Whoever Zena had been meeting had been interested in me and my inheritance – but Zena had never once named or described the man. It could have been anyone. The diary was of no value to the police or anyone else. It proved absolutely nothing.

'Oh, Zena,' I whispered. 'Why didn't you put it down? Why didn't you write his name?'

I poured myself another brandy and drank it slowly, staring into the fire. I watched the pictures in the flames as the logs blackened and fell into ashes.

Even if it had been Piers Zena was meeting, it didn't explain why he had killed her – unless she had threatened to tell me. Had she become suspicious about his reasons for marrying me? Had she threatened him with blackmail?

The brandy warmed me and eased my tensions and the ache in my heart. I'd thought Piers loved me but now it seemed that all he had wanted after all was the money.

A kind of hopelessness was creeping over me. It was all too difficult and painful and terrifying, and I wanted to slip away into the shadows . . .

★

The brandy did its work and as I curled up in front of the fire, sipping my drink, I began to feel more relaxed and even slightly hazy as I stared into the flames. One by one the pieces of the puzzle slipped into place.

Piers had planned our meeting – Tony had known him only a few weeks when he invited him to that party, and Piers must have deliberately cultivated the acquaintance. But why? Was it for the money? Tears slid down my cheeks as I realized it must have been. Piers had never loved me . . .

'Crying, Aline?'

Piers' voice startled me. I jumped and turned round, frightened. 'Piers . . .' Scrambling to my feet, I spilled some of the brandy on my skirt. 'How did you get in? I locked the door.' That wouldn't stop him. No doubt he had duplicates of all the keys. He had left our bed in the middle of that first night we were here together in order to explore. He might already have been planning my fall and perhaps my death. Seeing the look in his eyes, I gasped, 'Piers, no. Please . . .'

'You're frightened,' he said, his voice sounding calm. 'I guessed you would be here. So you've worked it all out, have you?' His glance fell on the diary. 'Zena's, I suppose. Did the stupid woman write it all down?'

'Piers . . .' The brandy made the room whirl around. 'Piers, please tell me you didn't kill Zena.'

His eyes looked into mine, sending little spiky chills through me, then he smiled. 'But you know I hate lies, Aline,' he said. 'Besides, it's too late for that, isn't it? You know too much.'

'I don't know anything, Piers.' I was trembling and my head was spinning as I put out a hand to steady myself. What was wrong with me? I tried to concentrate. 'Zena – Zena didn't name the man she was meeting. There's no proof . . .'

'But you found the brooch, and you've seen the photograph of Peter Dodson, haven't you? I suppose that was your nosey reporter friend?' Piers saw my start of fear and nodded. 'Who else would it have been? I should have killed him at the beginning. That was a mistake.' He looked at me and there was a kind of sadness in his face, as though he was reproaching me. 'Why did you betray me, Aline? I loved you. I never wanted to hurt you.'

I felt as if I were in the middle of a nightmare. He was blaming me for everything. I tried to clear my thoughts, putting a hand to my head.

'But you wanted the money. You asked Zena about the money before we married.'

'I was given nothing in this life,' Piers said. 'I was cheated of what was rightfully mine. Cheated and deceived. I was given nothing – so I've always taken what I wanted. I wanted you. The money was necessary for me to live as I was meant to live, but I didn't intend that you should die. Once you realized that you were dependent on me, I would have been good to you, Aline. You would always have been cared for, loved . . .'

He sounded so reasonable, so calm and sane – almost hurt that I had questioned his motives. I struggled to fight off the dizziness.

'You tried to make me think that I was losing my mind so that I would sign over control of the money. But Piers, it can't matter to you. Your galleries must be worth as much or more than I am.'

He laughed as I faltered, and my heart sank. There was no way of reaching him, no way of making him see reason.

'You've no idea, have you? Zena knew more about your money than you did. But then, she thought she was getting a share of it when she married Michael.' His eyes had a gloating look, as though he was enjoying this. 'You were never interested in anything as mundane as money, were you? You've never known what it's like to sleep under bridges and not know when you're going to eat again, so why should a few hundred thousand here or there mean anything? Your inheritance runs into millions, Aline. Five million plus a few hundred thousand, to be exact. The letter giving details of all the investments arrived on your birthday, but I kept it for you.'

'You what?' Anger cut through the haziness in my mind. 'How dared you? You had no right to do that.'

'But you weren't interested,' he said. There was an air of suppressed excitement about him now. 'You told me that so many times. I had to take care of the money for you. You would have given it all away. Besides, your life belonged to me, and that gave me the right.' Piers frowned as I shook my head. 'Don't you understand yet, Aline? I read about the inheritance years ago, after that day on the marshes; I wanted to know how you were. I was worried about you. You see, I cared about you even then.'

I made a smothered sound of denial and he looked hurt. 'You don't believe me, but it's true. I was sorry I'd scared you, but pleased that I'd let you live. Your life was in my hands and I let you go. When I read about the money, I knew that there was a purpose in our meeting that day. Your life belonged to me, therefore everything you owned was mine. I knew that one day I would have it all. I watched over you from a distance until I was ready. Sometimes I followed you . . . Like that day in the Alhambra. And all the time I was waiting for the right moment.'

'Don't! Please don't,' I begged. I didn't know this man saying these terrible things. It wasn't the Piers I had loved. 'I don't want to hear any more.'

'But you have to know so that you will understand.' Piers' eyes were glazed. 'It amused me when they blamed your stepfather for the attack. Oh, not in so many words, but it was hinted between the lines. No one suspected me. I didn't know that you thought it was Michael, of course; that was a bonus. It made it easier to convince you that the dreams were real. You clung to me then. You needed me.'

'And you pretended to love me!' I cried, feeling sick.

'I do love you, Aline.' Piers was smiling as he moved towards me. 'That's why your death will be gentle and painless, my darling. Not like that blackmailing little bitch Zena! She wasn't satisfied with what you were giving her; she wanted more. Much more.' His eyes moved over me caressingly and his tone was that of a lover. 'I hurt you once, my sweet little Aline, but I could never hurt you again. Even though you have betrayed me, I forgive you. Don't be frightened. I shall be gentle with you . . .'

The room was going round and round. I sat down as my legs went weak. Something was wrong with me. Three small brandies shouldn't have this effect. Piers was smiling benevolently, as if he was pleased with me. As I watched, he bent down to retrieve my brandy glass. He was wearing soft black leather gloves; he refilled my glass then took a small packet from his pocket and sprinkled some powder into the brandy, swirling it round and round until it was absorbed into the golden liquid.

'Just crushed sleeping tablets, darling,' he said. 'Nothing that will cause you pain, I promise.'

'Piers, please don't . . .'

He wasn't listening.

'I attacked you that day because you saw me crying, and no one had ever seen that before. I was angry with you for laughing. But it was more than that, of course.' Piers continued swirling the brandy, his face gentle and thoughtful as he looked at me. 'I had just discovered that my grandparents had lied to me. They had lied to me, cheated me, laughed at me . . .'

I licked my dry lips, trying to see him through the mist. 'Why did they lie to you, Piers?'

'So you didn't read the letters.' His eyelids flickered. 'I wasn't sure. I was careless. Zena read one when she stayed with us. That sealed her fate, of course. I couldn't let her live then, could I? You do understand, my darling. She would have destroyed me. I had to do it.'

Poor Zena. That's what she had wanted to tell me.

'And Phyllis Pearson – that wasn't you?'

'I recognized her. She was a friend of the old bitch and I thought she would remember and tell you everything.'

I was chilled by his manner. He seemed to have no awareness of right or wrong. It was as if he believed that whatever he chose to do was a kind of divine right that could not be questioned. He moved towards me, still smiling. 'And now it's time for your nightcap, Aline. This will make certain that your death is painless.'

'No, Piers!' I tried to rise but my legs wouldn't move. 'Please . . .'

'But you have to die, my sweet Aline,' he murmured softly. 'Don't you see that you've left me no choice? I can't let you live now that you've decided to betray me.'

'I won't tell, Piers. I'll give you the money, if that's what you want.' I was so terrified, I would have promised anything at that moment.

'But you don't keep your promises, Aline. I thought you were different, but you're like all the others. My father promised to come back for me, but he never did. He was a rich man but he left all his money to a foundation in America when he died, and gave me nothing. He abandoned me to that crazy old man and that spiteful bitch. I should have been living in a house like this. I should have been the heir to a fortune, like you, but my father hated me. He wished I'd never been born, so he left me to beatings and constant nagging . . .'

Piers' voice had begun to rise but he checked himself, advancing purposefully towards me. 'Drink this, darling. You will sleep as Hazeling burns to the ground. You said the house was a burden, and I've decided you're right. It's well insured, though. Michael saw to that before he died. It was so considerate of him to have a heart attack; it saved me the trouble of planning an accident for him.'

'Please, Piers,' I whispered. He was insane, completely insane, but I had to try to reach him. 'Please don't do this.'

He could not hear me. His mind was tuned inward, to a world of its own.

'That brandy was prepared for you when I left at Christmas,' he said. 'I thought you might get miserable and have a few drinks when you were alone here. It wasn't strong enough to kill you, just enough to make you confused. You disappointed me by coping so well. Why couldn't you have made it easy for me, Aline? Believe me, I never intended you to die.'

'Oh, Piers . . .'

I was shaking as he put his arm around me, supporting me tenderly and placing the glass to my lips. I clenched my teeth, resisting as he pressed harder. Then his hand went round my throat, his fingers exerting just sufficient pressure to hurt. As I gasped, he poured the liquid into my mouth. I choked and spat, but some of it went down.

'You shouldn't have made me do that,' Piers said, and drew me to him, his mouth whispering against my hair. 'Aline, my darling, why did you betray me? This hurts me so much.'

Gently, he lifted me in his arms, laid me on the floor and placed a cushion beneath my head. He bent over me, brushing his lips over mine. His touch made me shudder. A look of reproach came to his eyes, then he straightened up. I watched, unable to move a finger as he went over to the fireplace and dropped Zena's diary on to the fire. Piers glanced back at me and I saw that, unbelievably, he had tears in his eyes.

'The only other person I've ever cried for was my mother,' he said. Then he grasped the tongs and lifted a burning log from the grate, letting it fall on to the hearthrug. It smouldered but seemed unlikely to catch. For a moment he hesitated, then poured the contents of the brandy decanter on to the floor. There was a little *whoosh* and the rug caught. He threw a newspaper into the flames, retreating as they shot up and began to lick across the rug to the carpet. 'There, it will soon be over, Aline.'

'Piers . . .'

My lips moved but no sound came out. Piers threw some more papers on to the fire. It was burning fiercely now. My eyelids were growing heavy. I couldn't keep my eyes open any longer. I willed myself to move but I was too tired . . . too sleepy . . .

'Goodbye, my darling. Never forget that I loved you.'

Piers' voice came to me from a long, long way away. I struggled to open my eyelids. It was so difficult. The shadows were closing in on me, claiming me. Piers wasn't there any more. The flames had begun to lick up the wooden legs of a chair, and the fire was gradually spreading across the carpet towards me.

'No!' I whispered. 'I don't want to die. Help me, please. Help me . . .'

I knew I had to move. I had to crawl to the door or I would die. Already the smoke was beginning to fill my lungs. I was choking, but I couldn't move.

'Michael, help me . . . Zena . . .'

In the shadows something moved. I lifted my arm but the effort was too much. I closed my eyes once more.

Chapter Twenty-One

'Aline, I love you. Please don't die. God damn it, woman! Don't let that bastard win. You can do it.' Nick's voice broke on a sob. 'You can do it.'

My eyelids fluttered. I tried to speak but it was too much for me. There was pain but it was muted, far away, like Nick's voice. Someone grabbed my hand and held it so tightly that it hurt me.

'Bloody hell, Aline! I'm damned well not going to let you run out on me again. Wake up, damn you. Wake up!'

Since he was obviously going to give me no peace, I made a tremendous effort. 'Don't swear, Nick.' The words came out in a croaky whisper. 'My mother says it's not nice.'

It was a feeble attempt at a joke but it was the best I could do.

'Did you hear that?' There was a shout of triumphant laughter. 'Did you hear? She's going to make it. She's bloody well going to make it!' Through the mists of pain and drugs, I could hear the sound of a woman sobbing. 'Jesus, Julie! She's going to make it.'

It was a long, painful time later that I opened my eyes to see Nick sitting beside my bed. He smiled down at me.

'Feeling better, love?'

'I – I'm not sure.' I tried to sit up and failed, my head spinning. 'I feel awful. Did someone kick me in the stomach?'

'They used a stomach pump on you,' Nick said. 'Seems you took an overdose or something.'

'Like hell I did!' I glared at him. 'Piers tried to kill me.'

'I know. I wasn't sure you would remember.'

'I remember every detail,' I said bitterly. 'He drugged me and then left me to die in the fire.'

'That's about it,' Nick's eyes were serious now. 'Hazeling is in a bit of a mess, but it's repairable, I'm told. Thank God old Tom got you out before the fire reached you. You inhaled a lot of smoke but the doctors dealt with that.'

'Old Tom?' I was puzzled. 'Who is he?'

'Your resident tramp.' Nick's smile came back. 'He saw Piers leaving

289

and then he looked through the window and saw the flames, so he broke in and pulled you out. If he hadn't been there . . .' Nick's voice almost broke, then he recovered and went on, 'He'd come up to the house to tell you who he was, thinking he might have frightened you earlier. It was a miracle that he was there at exactly the right moment. In a matter of seconds you would have been engulfed by the fire.'

'Someone up there must have been looking out for me,' I said, trying to smile.

'Looks like it.' Nick's cheerful manner covered the emotion he couldn't quite suppress. 'Julie rang me when she got your message. I drove straight down, but I would have been too late. I arrived just after the fire brigade. You were being put into an ambulance.'

'So the cavalry was late, huh?'

'Oh, God, I thought you were going to die!' Nick's face suddenly contorted with grief, then he gripped my hand, making an obvious attempt at lightness. ' 'Fraid so, babe,' he said in a very bad American accent. 'Old Tom grabbed all the glory.' His smile came back and he reverted to his normal voice. 'He'll probably live on it for the rest of his life. He's a local celebrity, pictures in all the papers. Your stepfather used to give him food, but Piers told him to get lost, and threatened him with violence. He'd been on one of his periodic walkabouts, but he decided to come back that night.'

'Luckily for me.' I closed my eyes and Nick released my hand.

'Are you tired, Aline?'

'No.' I opened my eyes. 'Don't go, Nick. Don't leave me.'

'Wild horses wouldn't drag me, but Sister says not too long.' He was joking again to hide his feelings, but I wasn't fooled. 'Sorry if I look like the Cheshire Cat, but I thought you'd had it.'

'I know. I heard you swearing at me. That's why I decided to hang on.'

His hand reached for mine again. 'I'm glad you did,' he said. 'I know it's too soon, but when you're ready, I'll be around.'

'Yes,' I whispered. 'I know.' I felt the tears sting my eyes. Nick loved me, but he couldn't guess at the way I felt inside. No one could. No one could know how it felt to discover that someone you thought loved you wanted to kill you. All at once, I needed to be alone. I looked up at Nick, knowing that he would understand. He had always been my friend. 'Perhaps I am a little tired . . .'

Julie gave me flowers and grapes, then sat on my bed and ate the grapes.

'You look awful,' she informed me. 'Better than you did, but dreadful.'

'Thanks a lot!'

'No extra charge.' Julie's teasing smile faded. 'When you get out of here, you're coming home with me, Aline.'

'No, Julie.'

'Well, you can't go to Hazeling. So where are you going?'

I looked into her anxious eyes. 'Tell me about Piers. Have the police arrested him yet?'

Julie hesitated, then shook her head. 'No. He's disappeared, Aline. The police have a theory that he had another identity, another life to step into. He got away with murder once before by disappearing, and he seems to have done it again.'

'Surely he wouldn't just leave everything behind? His galleries, all his pictures, his Rolls-Royce. . . ?'

'They found the car abandoned,' Julie said with a frown. 'And the galleries were about to be taken into the hands of the receivers. He was bankrupt, Aline. He'd only managed to stave off his creditors because of his marriage to you. He'd given assurances that his debts would be met soon.'

'I see. That explains a lot, doesn't it?'

'It had to be the money, Aline.'

'I'm not sure.' I shook my head as Julie looked doubtful. 'I think there was more, much more to it, though of course he wanted control of the money. It – I was an obsession with him. He seemed to think that he was owed a fortune, and he believed that I belonged to him. Because he could have killed me that day on the marshes, he thought my life was his to do with as he pleased. It wasn't until he thought I intended to leave him for Nick that he – that he decided to kill me.'

'I suspected there was a problem after Ronnie told me that Helena had broken off her engagement before she died; Helena was Ronnie's second cousin. But I didn't want to repeat what Ronnie had said until I was sure it wasn't spite.'

'You did try to tell me, Julie. Besides, I knew there was something. I think Piers tried very hard to control it – his illness or whatever it was – until he thought I was going to leave him. That seemed to be the last straw, somehow.'

'And would you have left him for Nick?'

My gaze dropped. 'I – I don't know. Even if I hadn't discovered the truth, I doubt if I could have gone on living with him for long. He thought he could control me, Julie. Because I let him have all his own way at first, he thought I was weak and would show little resistance.'

'He didn't know you very well, did he?' Julie gave me a wry smile. 'You're not still breaking your heart over him, Aline? He is evil: a cold, ruthless killer who would have done anything to get what he wanted.'

'Is he?' I wrinkled my brow. 'I wish I was as sure as you, Julie. I can't forget the way he was at the beginning . . .' I sighed wearily. 'I expect you're right. I never really knew him. Even his name was false. He was Peter Dodson, wasn't he?'

'The police are convinced of it. Nick gave them all the evidence he'd managed to ferret out, and it seems that some fingerprints from Piers' car match those taken from the Dodson's home all those years ago.' Julie frowned. 'He's a cold-blooded murderer, Aline. He's killed at least twice, perhaps more – and the real Piers Drayton could be a victim, for all we know. You won't be safe while he's free.'

'That's why I'm not going to endanger you, Julie. He wouldn't think twice about murdering both you and Tony if he thought you were in his way.' I gripped her hand. 'Piers never liked you, Julie. I think he knew you suspected something was wrong with him. That's why he did his best to stay away from you.'

Julie's eyes darkened with worry as she looked at me. 'Then what are you going to do?'

'I'm going to disappear,' I said. 'If Piers can do it, then so can I.'

I smiled and shook my head as Julie protested, refusing to be drawn. I wasn't going to tell anyone, but I'd just realized that there was something I had to do. Something that would horrify my friend . . .

I discharged myself from hospital a few days later. As I was leaving, Nick's car drew up outside. He swore as he saw me and snatched my overnight bag.

'You're going straight back inside.'

'No.' I frowned at him. 'I've discharged myself. I'm going to take a taxi back to London, pick up some things and then buy a car. After that, I intend to find a house to rent in the county. I'm not sure where yet.'

'Julie told me you were going to disappear. That's ridiculous, Aline. You're coming to stay with me.'

'No, Nick.' I smiled at him to soften my words. 'I have to do it my way. Please, give me a little time to sort myself out.'

'But you can't bury yourself in the country, away from all your friends. It's madness, Aline – and dangerous.'

'Less dangerous than returning to London,' I said. 'Piers would know just where to look for me. It's what he would expect me to do, don't you see? He tried to kill me because he thought I was leaving him for you.'

Nick stared at me in exasperation. 'You don't know what you're doing, Aline. The man is a maniac!'

'It's what I want, Nick,' I told him firmly. 'I'm going to do it, whether you agree or not.'

'But why?' His eyes narrowed in suspicion. 'Why not let me be with you?'

'Because it's not what I want,' I said, hardening my heart as I saw the hurt in his eyes. 'I need to be alone for a while. Please understand.'

It was no use telling Nick his life would be in danger if I stayed with him; that would only make him more determined to protect me.

'I don't like it, Aline. You're hiding something . . .'

'Don't be ridiculous, Nick. The police are bound to catch Piers soon. All I have to do is keep out of the way for a while.'

'At least let me hire a bodyguard for you.'

'No!' I said harshly. He had to stay out of it for his own sake. 'Leave me alone, Nick. I know what I'm doing, believe me.'

Nick insisted on taking me to the flat to collect my things. I gave in without too much of an argument, mostly because I dreaded the thought of going back to Piers' flat, even though I knew it was the last place he would be.

It was strange and unpleasant going into the empty rooms, rather like entering the house of someone who had died. Fighting waves of panic that swept over me as I went into the bedroom that I'd so recently shared with Piers, I packed three suitcases but left the rest untouched. There would be plenty of time later to sort everything out. I wanted very little of what was there; it might be best to arrange for a firm to clear it soon. The flat belonged to the bank now, as did everything else that Piers had owned. My own possessions could be put into store or given away to a charity. I wanted nothing that Piers had given me, and I'd already instructed my lawyers to give all the expensive jewellery he'd bought me to the receivers, including my engagement ring. My wedding ring was still on my finger, a reminder of the man who had tried to kill me.

I locked the door with a crisp turn of the key. A part of my life was over, finished. I had something important to do. There would be time later to take stock of my situation and think of the future . . . if there *was* to be a future for me.

I bought a secondhand Volvo estate car that I could drive straight out of the garage. Only when I had the keys in my hand did Nick let me go.

'You'll let me know where you are?' he asked, his face strained. 'Please, Aline.'

'Of course.' I smiled at him, reaching out to touch his cheek. 'As soon as I'm settled.'

'I do love you, Aline.'

He looked so anxious and hurt that my resolve wavered. 'I know, Nick,' I said. 'And I'm sorry for doing this to you. I'm grateful for your care of me . . . and I love you. I think I always did.'

'Then why. . . ?' The pain showed in his face. I knew that he was reluctant to let me go even now. 'Just remember I'm always there if you want me.'

'Thank you, my best, my dearest friend,' I whispered, and kissed his cheek.

For a moment Nick's hands moved as though he wanted to take me in his arms, but he restrained himself. 'Take care then,' he said.

I waved, watching him in the mirror as I drove away. If he'd had any idea of where I was going or what I was planning, he would never have let me out of his sight.

It had taken three phonecalls from the hospital to discover the exact whereabouts of the Dodson's cottage, and another two to arrange for the present tenants to move out. There were sometimes advantages to having a great deal of money. Somewhere, a very surprised farm labourer was enjoying an unexpected windfall that had bought him a house of his own.

I'd lied to Nick. I knew exactly where I was going.

I drove straight to Hazeling. I was dreading seeing it for the first time since the fire and, as I drew up outside the front door, I was shaking. If there had been any other way, I would not have gone near the place; but there was something in the house I needed. I hoped it had not been destroyed by the fire.

A horrible smell of burning still hung over the place, tainting the air as I got out of the car and looked at the house. Everywhere was in a terrible mess – the walls blackened by smoke and a large gaping hole in the roof – but even though Nick had said it was repairable, I was surprised to see that so much of it was still standing. Some of the broken windows and doors had been boarded up to keep out opportunists. I had phoned from hospital to arrange for the undamaged contents to be removed and stored, but the removers had not started yet. With any luck, I would find what I wanted inside.

I broke the glass in a window at the back of the house and climbed in, then I made my way through to the hall. The stench of burning was even worse now and I had to hold a handkerchief to my nose to stop myself choking. I felt sick and shaky but I was determined to find what I'd come for.

As I reached the hall, I saw that the fire had hardly touched it, though it was smoke-blackened and running with water. The carpet squelched beneath my feet as I wrenched open the door of the cupboard beneath the stairs. For a moment I couldn't see what I wanted and I scrabbled in a pile of junk until my fingers touched the smooth wood of the box. Opening it, I saw that everything I needed was still there; it was a sign – a sign that I was meant to carry out my plans.

I closed the lid with a snap, then turned and hurried back the way I had come, climbing out of the window and almost running to the car. I was breathing hard now, and I felt a trickle of sweat run down my spine. It had taken all the nerve I possessed to come here, and now I couldn't wait to get away.

It was late in the evening when I arrived at the farmhouse. The farmer's wife was friendly and very curious about the woman who had paid a fortune to become her tenant for a few months. She gave me the key and offered to take me up to the cottage.

'That's very kind of you,' I said. 'But I think I can find it now.'

'The light switch is just inside the door to your right. I've given it a good clean right through – and the fridge is stocked just the way you asked.'

'Thank you.'

I ignored her curious gaze and went back to the car. No doubt I'd caused quite a stir in such a small community. It would probably generate a lot of gossip and might even rate a mention in the local paper.

I hoped it would. If not, I would have to find a way of creating my own publicity. It shouldn't be difficult; journalists had always seemed fascinated by my father's tragic death and my own inheritance.

The cottage was small, dismal and dark, but at least there was a fire in the kitchen and plenty of food in the larder. I switched on all the lights and the electric fires. Then I went upstairs to unpack, choosing the small bedroom at the back. Edith Dodson had been murdered in the larger one at the front.

After I'd hung my things in the wardrobe, I went into the front bedroom. No chills went down my spine, nor did I experience any sense of horror. It was just a room. I'd thought I might feel something, but no echoes of the past remained. It was a long time ago. Other people had lived here since the murder.

Going back downstairs, I made a cup of tea. Then I opened the box I'd collected from Hazeling. I picked up the gun and began to examine it.

It was growing dark as I walked through the woods behind the cottage. Around me the trees were stark and bare of their summer finery, their branches like scrawny fingers that reached out to catch at my hair and my clothes, whipping into my face as I walked. In the half-light strange shapes loomed up at me; the stump of a tree became a crouching dragon, a fallen branch a hiding place, a ring of toadstools a magic circle. I was aware of fear. Every sound was a threat, and I could hear the drumming of my own heart. I was alert, watchful, on edge, listening for every squeak, every football, every breath. Unseen life lurked in the undergrowth, rustling, terrifying and menacing because I was expecting to be followed. Wild thoughts of werewolves and demons flitted through my mind, to be replaced by a more terrifying picture still. I was being followed. Someone was behind me. I tensed, expecting to be attacked at any moment. Piers was here . . . He was going to kill me . . .

Then, somewhere out of sight, a dog whined. I whipped round as it broke free from the undergrowth, and rushed up to me, wagging its tail. I laughed at my own foolishness. Relief made me weak as I stroked its head. It was thin, smelly and obviously a stray, almost certain to be hungry. I made a big fuss of it, thankful for its company, and when I moved on it trotted at my side.

'Good boy,' I said, my fear conquered as I looked at my new friend. 'Do you want to come home with me? I've got some nice cold beef for supper. Would you like some?'

The dog barked as if it understood. I smiled, and made plans to bath and delouse it, and to include tins of dog food in my shopping. It was surprising how much better I felt now that I wasn't alone.

I'd panicked, but that was because I'd let my imagination take over. I'd thought Piers was following me, but it was far too soon. I realized that now. I'd been at the cottage only a few days. Piers was clever and ruthless, but even he could not know where I was yet. Besides, that was what I wanted; it was the reason I'd come to the cottage. I must think of a way to advertise my presence – a way to encourage my husband. Perhaps an ad in the local paper asking if anyone had lost a dog. . . ?

It was imperative that Piers should find me, because I was going to kill him.

As I let myself into the cottage, I heard the telephone. The ringing stopped as I dumped my shopping on the kitchen table and I wondered who it was. Several weeks had passed since I came to the cottage, but despite advertising in the local and district papers, no one had claimed the dog I'd named Ragamuffin. I was beginning to hope they never would.

Ragamuffin had become a friend. I cried into his shaggy coat night after night, and he licked the tears from my face, not knowing that he was helping me to heal.

When I had first arrived in Cornwall, I had felt a deadly coldness inside me, a numbness that was my only defence against the pain and bitterness that would otherwise have been unbearable. Now my feelings were beginning to change and I had at last accepted the terrible truth that Piers was a killer, and possibly devoid of normal human feelings.

Sometimes, when I remembered the touch of his lips or the sweetness of his smile, what had happened that night at Hazeling all seemed like a drug-induced fantasy; but in my heart I knew it was not. There were two separate personalities in Piers, the good and the evil, and the evil one had finally taken over.

No doubt the psychoanalysts would have a name for his condition that would make it all very sanitary and straightforward, but they had never experienced the moment of evil as I had. They had never looked into those piercing eyes as I had, and known that death was coming: known that the person they loved was going to kill them. They would never understand the agony and despair that Piers had sown in my soul. I still believed that in his own way, Piers had loved me – with a perverted love, perhaps, that sought to own rather than to protect, but the only kind of love he could give.

For myself, I'd believed in him and loved him so completely at the start, and he had turned me into a shadow player disinclined to love or trust other people. I was sickened by the memory of his touch, defiled by having known such a monster.

At times, I hated myself – and hated Piers. I knew that I had to kill him, not to save my own life, but because I had helped to turn him into the monster he had become. Perhaps if I had never come into his life, he would have managed to hold on to his sanity.

I had to kill him, because I knew that he was too clever for the police. Unless I took his life, he would kill and kill again and then disappear.

My thoughts were interrupted as the telephone rang again. I hesitated, my heart almost stopping, then I picked it up.

'Aline.' Nick's voice calmed me. 'Thank God! I've rung three times this morning already.'

'I've been shopping. Why have you been ringing?'

'Piers has been seen . . .' The words sent a little thrill of fear through me. 'He went back to the flat, but by the time the police arrived, he'd gone.'

'He must have been desperate, to try that.'

'Yes, or he doesn't know what he's doing.' Nick hesitated. 'I think you ought to know something, Aline. The police have located Peter Dodson's mother. She is in a private clinic for the mentally ill, but before that she was kept in an asylum for years. She's under sedation all the time. After her son was born, she went crazy and tried to smother him and then attacked the nurse and her own parents with a knife. When her lover discovered that there was a history of instability in the family, he disowned his son and went back to America.'

I thought for a moment. 'Piers had been paying for his mother to stay at the clinic, hadn't he?'

'Did you know all this?'

'No, but now you've told me about Piers' mother, it makes sense. He was concerned about some letters he'd left in a jacket pocket; they used to come regularly and could have been monthly statements from the clinic. He boasted that he'd killed Zena because she read one of them.'

I paused and Nick said, 'Go on, Aline. Tell me all of it now.'

'This is mostly speculation, but I think the fact that his mother was insane was what Piers meant when he said his grandparents lied to him. From little things Piers said, I think they let him believe his mother was dead – he once told me she had died of a tumour and I think that was what he wanted to believe – then one day his grandmother just threw the truth at him. Piers called her "the old bitch" and said something about her laughing at him. If it's true, she must either have been very cruel or a little unbalanced herself . . .' I drew a deep breath. 'I can't know for sure, of course, but I believe he had just learnt the truth about his mother when he attacked me on the marshes. At – at Hazeling, he told me he had only ever cried for one other person – his mother – and he was crying when I saw him on the marshes . . .'

'That makes sense,' Nick said. 'If he had just been told something like that, he must have been half out of his mind with shock and distress. He must have walked out of his grandmother's house in a daze after he killed her. Somehow he got to the marshes from Cornwall, and then he gave way to his grief.'

'I believe that's why he attacked me when I laughed. Then, when he realized what he was doing, he panicked and ran off.' I rubbed my neck to ease the tension I felt. 'Once, after we were married, when he thought I was nagging him, Piers got very upset, then he looked at me and said – '

'Yes?' Nick prompted.

'He said that the old bitch was always nagging him. He looked as if he hated me, then he seemed to come to himself and realized I wasn't her.'

'It sounds as if he really hated her. Mind you, if she threw the truth at him like that, he had cause.'

'I think it was what drove him over the edge and made him kill her.' I paused. 'It was because he believed I had betrayed him that he decided to kill me too.'

'You must come back to London,' Nick said, a note of alarm in his voice. 'Or let me come down there. It's too dangerous for you to be alone, Aline.'

'This is the last place Piers would think of looking for me.' I lied.

'Please, Aline. Go out and get in your car and drive back to London now.'

'I'm sorry, Nick,' I said. 'I came down here for a little peace. Don't worry about me, I'm fine.'

I put down the phone, then unplugged it. Piers had gone back to the flat; that was significant. If he had risked arrest to go there, it must mean that he needed the cash he kept for emergencies. He had successfully disappeared for weeks. Something must have brought him out of hiding, and I believed I knew what it must be.

Dusk was falling fast in the woods. Ragamuffin bounded far ahead of me. I'd stayed out for too long, enjoying the warm spring sunshine; now it was turning cold and the woods were lonely and frightening.

I touched the pistol in my pocket – the gun I had found in the cupboard under the stairs at Hazeling – feeling a return of confidence as my fingers curled around the metal. I was going to kill Piers. When he came – and his vanity was such that I was sure he would not be able to resist it – I was going to take his life before he took mine. Not out of vengeance, but because it had to be done.

Glancing back, I thought I saw the shadow of a man, and my heart skipped a beat. It must be Piers. But why didn't he come closer? Why did he make no attempt to catch me? Perhaps he suspected a trap. I thought about it: I was behaving too calmly. He would expect me to show fear.

I began to run. Ragamuffin barked, enjoying this new game, and jumped up at me in great excitement. Soon I was panting, my legs whipped and stung by the undergrowth as I ran through it. My fear was real now, mounting with every breath. This was what I wanted but it was terrifying.

There wasn't much further to go to the cottage. I could see the gate . . .

Inside the cottage, I left the door closed but unlocked, then turned to face what I knew was inevitable. Piers was coming for me. My heart was battering against my ribs, but my mind was clear and calm. I took the gun from my pocket and pointed it at the door. Then I heard footsteps outside. The door handle was turned. I tensed with fear, my pulse haywire. The time had come at last. He was here.

My hand trembled on the gun. I clutched my right wrist with my left hand, steadying myself. I probably had time for one shot before he attacked me, perhaps two . . . The door was opened. It swung back on its hinges, and a trickle of cold sweat ran down my spine.

Piers stood there, staring at me. Where was the monster of my imagination? Where, the devil I'd seen so often in my dreams? This was my husband, the man I loved . . .

He looked ill and his eyes pleaded with me, and I was thrown off balance by a rush of emotion.

'Aline,' Piers whispered hoarsely. 'Please don't be afraid of me. Please don't hate me. I know I deserve this. I know that I deserve to die, but please listen to me first.'

'Stay away from me, Piers,' I warned, feeling the drumming begin at my temples. My mouth was dry and I felt dizzy. 'If you take one step towards me I'll kill you. I swear it.'

'Aline, forgive me. I've been in hell ever since . . . a hell such as you could never imagine. Please let me explain.'

I felt myself being swayed by the gentle persuasiveness of his voice. The pain in my breast was crushing.

'No,' I choked, fighting my own desire to believe in his words. *My desire to believe that he had really loved me.* 'No, Piers. You tried to kill me. You left me to die in the fire at Hazeling.'

'That wasn't me,' Piers cried. 'You must know that I wasn't in control, I was insane . . .' He took a hesitant step towards me. 'I know

300

what I've done to you, Aline. Believe me, I've suffered for it. You can have no idea what it has been like.'

'Stay away, Piers.' My finger hovered over the trigger. 'How can I believe you? How do I know that this isn't a trap?'

'Aline, please,' he begged. 'I never wanted to hurt you. I love you. It was the devil in me – the devil who haunts me . . . But I can control this madness. I've done it before. I shall again. Give me a chance. Help me!'

I wavered, my hand trembling as I stared at his haggard face. 'How do I know that it isn't the devil talking now, Piers?'

'You can't know,' he said. 'I don't always know myself. But I've come to beg your pardon, Aline. To beg you to forgive me.'

'Oh, Piers!'

The tears were coursing down my cheeks. I looked at him uncertainly, my resolve weakening. Supposing he wasn't evil, but ill? Wasn't madness an illness? Didn't he deserve my understanding . . . my pity? He had tried to kill me, but perhaps the doctors were right, perhaps he couldn't help himself. He needed help.

'You need to be looked after,' I said, my arm falling to my side. 'You need help. Proper, qualified help.'

I fell silent as I saw the sudden glow in his eyes, and I knew I had said the wrong thing. Somehow I'd triggered the madness in him. In that instant his expression changed from one of wretchedness to a sinister alertness. When he came in he had been Piers, now he was someone else – someone who wanted to kill me.

'Put the gun down, Aline,' he murmured. 'Why don't you give it to me? You know you're not going to use it. You couldn't shoot me. You haven't got the strength to do it, have you?'

I faltered and was lost.

Piers sprang at me. We grappled for the weapon, and as his fingers tightened around my wrist, it fell to the floor. I screamed several times as I struggled against Piers, kicking, scratching and biting in an effort to break free, but Piers was too strong for me. His hands were around my throat, pressing hard, restricting the flow of air. I was choking, dying . . .

Then the door was flung open. Surprised, Piers let go of me and swivelled round. I slumped to the floor, gasping for breath. Then, through the blur of darkness in front of my eyes, I became aware of what was happening around me. There was a fight going on. The two men crashed into the furniture and wrestled desperately on the ground.

As the mist cleared, I saw it was Nick – and I was terrified Piers would kill him. I looked for the gun. It was still on the floor. I knew I had to get

301

it; it was important to reach the gun. Dizzily, I crawled on my hands and knees towards it. I had to kill Piers before he killed Nick.

Before I could reach the gun, Piers yelled and punched Nick in the stomach, winding him and making him stagger back. As Nick struggled to recover his breath, Piers reached for the gun. He picked it up, his eyes wild as he whirled round, looking for me. I was on my knees only a few paces away from him. Piers stared down at me, and as he saw the horror and fear in my eyes, his finger tightened on the trigger. Then he paused, his face twisting with sudden agony.

'Forgive me,' he cried. 'I loved you.'

And then as I watched, he put the gun to his temple and fired.

It was a long time afterwards, when the police – who had arrived soon after the shooting – and the ambulance had been and gone, that I stopped shaking. The police had taken the gun, and my statement. It hadn't been said, but I knew that some kind of action might be taken over my possession of the weapon.

'It was very foolish of you to come here alone, Mrs Drayton,' the police inspector had said. 'I must warn you that we may be questioning you again about your reasons for having that gun.'

'Surely that's clear enough,' Nick had explained. 'Your people had failed to find her husband and she was terrified. She needed it for protection.'

'Yes, sir.' The inspector had been impassive. 'I'll make a note of your comments in my report.'

When at last we were alone, Nick made coffee and brought it to me as I sat in front of the fire, my hand on Ragamuffin's head. The dog looked at the man suspiciously, but settled down as I reassured him. I took the mug Nick offered and frowned.

'You know why I had the gun, of course?'

'You wanted to kill him, didn't you? That's why you came here, isn't it?' Nick looked grim. 'Did you think I wouldn't guess what you were up to?'

I met his eyes, then nodded. 'I thought that I had to kill him,' I whispered. 'I – I thought he was evil.'

'Did you really think you could kill him?'

'I – I don't know.' The admission was forced out of me. 'I wanted to kill him, Nick. That's what he did to me: he's made me as evil as he was.'

'Don't ever say that again!' Nick took hold of my hands, pulling me to my feet. 'You're not like him, Aline. He was insane. You couldn't have done it.'

I went limp as he let me go. 'He's destroyed me, Nick. I feel so empty, so ugly . . .'

'Time,' he said briskly.

'At least he's dead now. I shan't need to be afraid of him any more.'

'You need not have been afraid. You've been watched over all the time.' Nick nodded as I stared in surprise. 'Did you imagine that either Julie or I would let you be here without a twenty-four-hour guard? He was outside, telephoning the police, when I arrived.'

'That's how they got here so fast.' I smiled ruefully. 'You hired a bodyguard . . . No wonder I'd thought I was being followed so often. I should have known – shouldn't I?'

'Yes.' He was unsmiling. 'You should.'

'I'm sorry,' I said. 'I haven't been thinking straight since the fire.'

'That's understandable. You've been through a terrible experience. But it's over now.'

It was over. Piers was dead. Reliving his terrible death in my mind, I gasped. In those brief seconds before he shot himself, I'd seen the horror in my husband's eyes and known he had realized that he could no longer control his madness. Rather than suffer incarceration in an asylum for the rest of his life, he had decided to end it.

'Nick.' I looked at him, a silent appeal in my eyes. 'Oh, Nick!'

He grabbed me as I started to tremble again, and held me tight as the shudders turned into sobs of grief. Nick touched his lips to my hair, soothing and comforting until I quietened.

'I don't know what to do,' I said at last. 'I feel so – so tainted.' I couldn't look at him. 'I feel as if I can't go on.'

'You have to fight it, Aline. Come back to London and make a new life for yourself. Julie misses you, and so do I. Leave this cottage and come back with me now.'

I gazed up at him, still in the grip of despair. 'But I can't give you what you want, Nick. I can't love ever again.'

'I'm not asking you to love me. Just be my friend. And you *can* love – you love that wretched dog!' Nick laughed as Ragamuffin pushed between us, bristling with jealousy.

'That's different,' I said. 'How can I ever forget . . . How can I ever live with the memory of what . . .' I couldn't finish. 'I just want to go away, Nick; to hide, and pretend that I'm someone else, that I was never married to Piers and I don't have an inheritance. The money is a curse. I've always thought so, and now . . .' I was talking wildly and I knew it.

I was close to breaking down once more. He took hold of my

shoulders and gave me a little shake. 'Stop feeling sorry for yourself, Aline. So you've had a bad time, but it isn't the end of the world.' I looked up, startled as I sensed his anger. 'You say you don't want your inheritance, but that's just negative. Think of all the good you could do with it. Think of all the sick children or starving families you could help.'

I was silent as I absorbed Nick's challenge. Then I felt something stir and glow to life inside me.

'Yes,' I said. 'I could do that, couldn't I, Nick? Before the fire, I had thought of turning Hazeling into a home for handicapped children. I could rebuild it and set up a trust fund . . .'

'Then do it, Aline.' Nick held both my hands and looked tenderly into my eyes, his anger gone now. 'Don't let that bastard win!'

'No,' I said, beginning to smile. 'I won't.'

Chapter Twenty-Two

'Tony is out for the evening,' Julie said, as she welcomed me into her flat, 'so we can relax and talk for as long as you like.'

'Thanks.' I smiled. 'That was tactful of Tony. I do need to talk, Julie.'

'I've opened a bottle of wine.' She looked doubtful. 'You're not still taking those sleeping tablets?'

'No.' I pulled a face. 'Sometimes I can't sleep, but I'd rather read than take a pill.'

'Good.' Julie nodded her approval. 'You look much better, Aline.'

'I feel fine.'

'Have you signed the partnership papers yet?'

'Yes, this morning. Gerald wanted to change the name to Silcott and Marlowe, but I asked him not to. I prefer to keep in the background.'

'But you're pleased you've done it?'

'Yes, there's no problem there. I ought to have suggested it months ago. I was afraid of offending Mr Silcott – Gerald – but he's delighted. The extra capital will help him expand and it has given me an interest. We're going to hold special jewellery sales every three months, and that will be my project.'

'It sounds exciting,' Julie said. 'And there's Hazeling, of course. How are the builders getting on with the restoration?'

'I haven't been down, but Nick seems to think I'll be pleased. He met the architect a couple of weeks ago. Because Hazeling Manor is a listed building, we've had to be so careful . . .'

'I should imagine so.' A wail from the bedroom interrupted Julie. 'It seems young madam is awake. Excuse me, Aline. I shan't be long.'

'May I come and see Sarah?'

'Of course.' Julie looked pleased. 'She's growing so fast and changing all the time.'

We went through to the bedroom. Julie lifted the crying child. The tears ceased as if by magic and she gurgled up at her mother, her wide blue eyes fringed with seductive lashes.

'She's a real charmer,' I said.

'She knows how to get her own way.' Julie laughed. 'I expect I spoil her.'

'Why not?' I said. 'She's gorgeous.'

'Yes, she is. Tony adores her.'

I waited while Julie soothed the baby, then put her back in her cot and led the way back to the sitting room. She poured wine for us both, then looked up. 'Are you going to tell me?'

I laughed and sipped my wine. 'Am I so transparent?'

'Something is bothering you.'

'Nick has asked me to marry him.'

'So.' Her brows went up. 'What's the problem?'

'I'm not sure there is one. I care very deeply for Nick, as you know . . .'

'But?'

'I want to be sure, Julie. When I married Piers I was swept off my feet. I don't want to make another mistake.'

'Nick isn't Piers.'

'Of course not! I didn't mean that. Nick has been wonderful these past months. I don't know how I would have managed without him. He's even been keeping Ragamuffin in his back garden for me, because I can't have a dog in my flat.'

'Then what are you worrying about?'

'It's me,' I said in a hesitant voice. 'I've never been able to explain why I rushed into marriage with Piers.' I twisted my wineglass with nervous fingers. 'It – it was a kind of compulsion, Julie. I think I was attracted to Piers because I sensed he represented danger.' My cheeks flushed. 'It was almost as if I recognized him . . . As if I were compelled to go back and play out that scene on the marshes over again.'

'That doesn't surprise me.' Seeing that she had startled me, Julie smiled. 'You're not the first to feel that way, Aline. At the clinic we see several cases where a child who has been abused by a drunken father will seek out the same type of man as a husband. Similarly, a woman who has been sexually abused will sometimes reject a gentle lover in favour of a man she knows will hurt her. It's a way of asking to be punished for what they see as their guilt.'

'Does that make me a case for psychiatric treatment?' I blushed as she laughed, then blurted out my fears. 'Supposing I marry Nick and make him miserable because I can't respond to him?'

'I don't think that's likely, Aline. And no, in my opinion, you don't need treatment. For years you've had a guilt complex, but you told me that you'd forgiven Michael – and your mother?' I nodded. 'I think you'll find that that was your problem. It was because you believed Michael might have abused you that you needed to play out the scene again. You had to prove to yourself that it wasn't him, and now you have. So now you can forgive yourself.'

'Yes,' I agreed, her sensible words easing my tension. 'The nightmares have gone, and I've stopped feeling guilty. Michael's obsession wasn't my fault.'

'Of course it wasn't,' Julie said. 'And what's wrong with being attracted to a man who seems slightly dangerous? A lot of women are. Piers was mentally ill, but you couldn't have known that. The strain of his financial worries, guilt and jealousy – and possibly the fear of being kept under sedation, like his mother, for the rest of his life – pushed him over the edge. It was a tragedy that he wasn't caught when he murdered Edith Dodson. If he had been given treatment then, he might have been a different man. He might even have been able to lead a normal life once his rehabilitation was completed.'

'Oh, Julie.' I leant over and kissed her cheek. 'Thank you, you've made me feel much better.'

'Respect yourself, Aline,' my friend said. 'You're a nice person. Believe it. You're the only one who's ever doubted it.'

I laughed and blushed. 'And you're great, Julie. I'll never be able to thank you enough.'

'Just invite me to the wedding.'

'Nick . . .' I held my breath as he looked up from the brass lamp he was polishing. 'I'd like to go down to Hazeling this weekend. Will you come with me?'

'Of course.' He frowned and laid down his cloth. 'Are you sure you're ready?'

'Yes, quite sure.' I smiled at him. 'Could we leave Friday lunchtime and make a weekend of it?'

'I don't see why not. I'll get someone to mind the shop for a few days, and look after that dog of yours. We could take a trip round Norfolk, visit a few antique shops, eat some good food . . .'

'That sounds great,' I said. 'I'd like to visit Blakeney again. You've never been to the Quay, have you?'

'No.' There was surprise in Nick's eyes, but he didn't voice his doubts. 'Where shall we stay?'

'Why not the Blakeney Hotel? I'll make the reservations, shall I?'

'Fine.' Nick's expression was guarded. 'You seem happy today.'

'I am,' I assured him. 'I'll pick you up tomorrow.'

'Do you fancy lunch today?'

'No time. I'm having my hair done, then I have a valuation for the saleroom and I'm collecting a new car. I've bought a Mercedes.'

'So we're travelling in style, then?'

'It's about time,' I said. 'I'll see you, Nick.'

Laughing at the slightly disbelieving expression in his eyes, I left the shop.

It was June and the sun was shining when we left London. Nick had immediately fallen in love with the sports car I'd bought in a mood of indulgence. I handed him the keys.

'You drive,' I said. 'I'll relax!'

What I wanted was to watch him as he eased the car through the busy traffic. His face was so familiar, so dear to me. I'd hurt Nick badly once, and I would do anything rather than hurt him again. He deserved to be loved, but despite my talk with Julie, I was still afraid to take that final step. I loved Nick, but was I in love with him? I hoped that this weekend would tell me.

Because Nick didn't know Norfolk well, we took the journey slowly after leaving Norwich, enjoying the feeling of freedom that comes with a stolen holiday. At Cromer we parked the car and wandered on the wide green at the clifftop, looking down at the sea. We found a restaurant offering fresh crab salad, and ate our meal with the relish of children let out of school.

Nick's eyes sparkled as he looked at my windblown hair. 'This was a good idea. I'm enjoying myself.'

'So am I,' I said. 'Let's go on to Sheringham. You've got to see everything.'

He caught my hand, understanding my mood. 'You drive. I want to absorb the scenery.'

It was pretty now, with the pink may blossom and wild roses strewn in the hedgerows. Gardens flourished behind red-brick walls, with delphiniums, aquilegia, iris and deep-scented pinks. We drove along the coast road as much as possible, calling in at Sheringham late in the afternoon. Down a little side street near the sea front, we found a small antique shop, and managed to catch the owner before he locked up for the night.

Nick bought a tea caddy; it was early Georgian, made of mahogany inlaid with satinwood. Then his eyes fell on a jewellery cabinet.

'May we see that tray of rings?' he asked, and when it was brought out, he picked an old rose-gold signet in the shape of a heart with an almandine garnet at its centre. 'Yes, I think we'll take that, too.'

Outside, Nick slipped the ring on the little finger of my left hand. 'Fits perfectly,' he said. 'I thought it would.'

'Thank you, Nick. It's lovely.'

'It's nothing,' he said. 'Where now?'

I glanced at my watch. 'It's too late to go to Hazeling this evening. I think we'll go on to the hotel.'

'You're in the driving seat.'

I smiled and took the keys. Nick was having a great time, and so was I.

We passed Cley on our way to Blakeney, but the beach where Zena had died couldn't be seen from the road – only the flat stretches of the marshes, a windmill on the horizon and a narrow road leading towards the high ridge of shingle.

Entering Blakeney a short time later, I drove down the lane leading to the Quay, past red-brick and pebble-dashed houses, shops and pubs, then turned right past the channel, which was high enough for small boats to put out, stopping at last in the hotel forecourt.

Nick had been watching me for the last few miles. I knew that he was wondering what was behind my sudden decision to come down. He was silent and thoughtful as he took our cases from the car and we went inside.

'I'd like a bath before dinner,' I said. 'Shall we meet in the bar?'

'Whatever you say.'

If Nick was disappointed that I'd booked separate rooms, he didn't show it.

We ate late in the evening, lingering over our coffee and brandy.

'We'll go to Hazeling first thing tomorrow,' Nick said. 'Then we can wander where the fancy takes us.'

'Good idea,' I said. 'Goodnight, Nick.'

I kissed his cheek and went into my room.

Hazeling no longer showed any signs of the fire. It was empty, the undamaged contents having been stored while the rebuilding was going on. I was surprised to see that – apart from necessary changes – it looked much the same, and I said so to Nick.

'You saw the plans, Aline. The architect has tried to keep to the original structure as much as possible.'

'Yes.' I smiled at him. 'I'm glad I didn't come sooner.'

'You're not upset now?' His brows went up as I shook my head.

'No, I'm not upset, Nick. I'm glad Hazeling is being restored. I can't wait to see it full of children.' I walked back to the car. 'Let's go now.'

'Where first?'

'I don't mind. I think there's an antique shop on the way to Holt, and a very good one in Burnham Market.' I laughed up at him. 'We could have lunch in Wells at a fabulous restaurant called The Moorings, if you like. They do a marvellous butterscotch pudding.'

'We'll just drive,' he said, catching my mood, 'and see where we end up.'

We drove past the wide stretches of the Moreston marshes, past beautiful stands of woodland and a little stream, the wayside bright with red poppies, purple mallow and yellow gorse. Entering Wells, we turned left on to the main quay, which was also the centre of the town.

For a while we wandered by the quayside, inhaling the salty tang of the sea breezes. Wells-next-the-Sea was a holiday resort, but also a working port – the centre of the whelk industry – and several boats were bringing in their catch of shellfish. After lunch, we drove on to Holkham and visited the Hall and the pottery.

All along this part of the coast there was a succession of small harbours, and we visited most of them, taking detours down narrow winding roads just for the fun of seeing where they came out.

'This is Admiral Nelson's country,' I told Nick. 'His father was the rector at Burnham Thorpe.'

At Burnham Deepdale, we saw a wonderful church and got out to take photographs. It was pebble-dashed and had an unusual round tower that made it stand out from the others in the area. Just down the road, we stopped and ate fresh lobster in a tiny restaurant.

'If we go on like this I'm going to get fat,' I said, but Nick laughed and shook his head.

It was very late in the evening when we returned to Blakeney.

'What time do you want to leave tomorrow?' Nick asked.

'After lunch,' I said. 'I'd like to walk on the marshes before we go.' Hesitantly, I kissed his cheek. 'Goodnight. Thank you for today.'

'It was good for me, too,' he said. 'Goodnight, Aline.'

Alone in my room, I took a bath, then pulled on a satin robe and stood by the window, looking out at the marshes. In the moonlight they were beautiful but lonely and eerie. Sighing, I turned back to the bed, then paused. This wasn't what I'd planned for the weekend, but I'd expected

Nick to make the first move. He was waiting for me, but I couldn't say, 'Nick, I want to sleep with you.' Or could I?

Well, why not? I smiled as I moved towards the door. It had been my idea to come and Nick could only throw me out.

It was a matter of seconds before he opened his door. He was wearing a short towelling robe. His legs and feet were bare, and his hair was damp. He opened the door wider for me to come in. 'Couldn't you sleep?'

'I don't feel like sleeping,' I said. 'That's why I'm here.'

'Aline . . .' I heard his indrawn breath and saw the sudden hope in his eyes. 'I wasn't sure . . . I didn't want to assume too much.'

'Darling Nick,' I murmured, reaching out to untie the belt of his robe and slide my arms around his body, which was still cool from the shower. 'What did you imagine this was all about?'

'You booked separate rooms.' He smiled as I nuzzled his neck. 'I'm not a mind-reader, Aline.'

'I couldn't book just one. I was waiting for things to happen naturally.'

'And I spoilt your plans by behaving like a perfect gentleman.' Nick was grinning now. 'I'm sorry, darling. Then again, perhaps not. I think I'm going to enjoy being seduced.'

'Damn you,' I said. 'Are you going to kiss me or not?'

'Patience, woman,' he teased. 'This has been a shock for my delicate nerves. I hope you intend to make an honest man of me.'

'Nick!'

Laughing, he pulled me to him, his lips caressing mine with infinite tenderness. I felt a swift surge of desire and my mouth opened beneath his. Nick wrenched the satin tie at my waist and pushed the robe back, kissing my neck and my breasts. I shivered, feeling ripples of sensation as he flicked at the nipples with the tip of his tongue.

'Yes, oh yes,' I whispered. 'That feels so good, Nick.'

He gathered me up in his arms and carried me to the bed, where we clung to each other, our hands stroking and exploring. Never before had it been this good between us, and I knew that it had been my fault. Nick had always been gentle and tender, but I had not known how to respond. I hadn't told him what was good for me. I hadn't helped him to please me. Now I was free of the shadows and there were no restraints.

'Nick . . . darling . . . Now . . .' I cried.

Afterwards, we lay talking, holding each other close. We talked for ages, slept, and made love again, then talked some more. There were no barriers between us, no shadows from the past. At last we fell asleep.

*

311

We had breakfast in bed, took a bath together and then went for a walk. Hand in hand, we strolled beside the channel, looking at the boats drawn up on the sandy slope. The sun was shining and it was warm. People were on the footpaths and the flood bank, enjoying a day out. The marshes no longer looked sinister to me, but wild and beautiful, a glorious place to be with the man I loved.

'That's Michael's,' I said, pointing out a crab boat with a pink hull. 'It was built here in Blakeney. See, it's called the *Siren Song*.'

'Shall we take it out at high tide?'

'I don't know if the engine is working,' I said. 'It hasn't been used for a while. I'll ask Stratton Long Marine to overhaul it. We can go out when we come down again.'

'We are coming, then?' Nick looked into my eyes. 'You're really over it, Aline? No more bad dreams?'

'I'm over it.' I smiled and held his hand to my cheek. 'I think I'll buy a little cottage somewhere in the area. Then we can come as often as we want. You do like it down here?' I was anxious.

'It's great,' he said, his eyes bright with mischief. 'Especially at night.'

'Oh, Nick,' I whispered, my throat catching. 'I can't believe I'm so lucky, after the way I treated you . . .'

'Forget it,' he said. 'It was my fault as much as yours. After that last quarrel, I realized what a fool I'd been. I was going to tell you that I'd made up my mind to give up my job and settle down. I'd discovered that you were more important to me than anything else.'

'And when you came back . . .' I choked.

'Hush,' he said, silencing me with a kiss. 'No more recriminations. And while we're on the subject, one of the reasons I wouldn't sell you that bronze horse was because I'd got carried away at the auction. I paid too much for the damned thing. I couldn't sell it to you or anyone else.'

'Nick.' I smiled at him. 'And I thought . . .'

'I'm not saying I wasn't jealous. I *was*. But I'm not the kind to carry it to extreme lengths.'

'Will you forgive me for all the things I said to you?'

'I already have.' He squeezed my hand. 'Besides, it's in the past. We have the future to look forward to. That's all that matters.'

'Yes.' The shades of duplicity, suffering and violent death that lay at the back of my mind shifted and, like the sun bleaching the midday shadow, lightened and retreated. The gulls circled overhead, their loud cries triumphant in the sunlight, and my spirit soared with them.

*

The sun was hot as I stepped forward to cut the satin ribbon and formally announce that the Michael Courteney Home for handicapped children was open. I handed the scissors back to Matron with a smile, and sat down as the older woman proposed a vote of thanks.

'I'm sure that I don't have to tell anyone here how grateful we all are to Mrs Winters for her tireless work these past months, and for the endowment of the Hazeling trust fund which will allow our work to go on here in the future.'

There was a round of clapping and then everyone went inside for tea. In the hallway was a large cabinet with the more valuable of Zena's dolls on display; all the other toys were in the children's playroom. I'd discussed it with Anne, and she had agreed that it was what Zena would have wanted.

For some time, I was kept busy talking to the press and officials invited for the opening. At last I was able to make my excuses and find Julie, who was rocking her little girl, now almost a year old.

'It all seemed to go very well,' Julie said. 'Are you pleased?'

'Yes.' I smiled. 'Yes, I am. I was a bit worried about the new hospital wing, but they've made a good job of it, don't you think?'

'Marvellous,' Julie said, looking at me thoughtfully. 'You don't regret letting it go, do you?'

'No, of course not. We would never have used it. We're quite happy spending weekends in our cottage, and Ragamuffin loves it.'

'That's good.' Julie looked at me. 'There's nothing wrong, is there?'

'No. Why?'

'You seem a little withdrawn,' Julie said. 'As though you're not really here.'

'Oh dear.' I pulled a face and laughed. 'Sorry. I was thinking about something Matron said, but I'll stop now if you'll let me hold Sarah for a moment.'

I took the baby in my arms, making a conscious effort to talk to my friend. Julie knew me too well and I wanted to keep my secret to myself for just a little longer.

Nick kicked and muttered something in his sleep. I shook him gently. 'Wake up, darling. You're having a bad dream.'

Nick opened his eyes and looked at me apologetically. 'Sorry, Aline. I was playing rugby. Good Lord, it's years since I gave it up.' He gave a rueful laugh. 'Did I wake you?'

'No, I was thinking about something.'

'Would you like a cup of tea?'

'Yes please.'

As Nick left the room, I sat up in bed, staring at my own reflection in the mirror. Nick's dream hadn't really been a nightmare, just one of those strange ones that keep you tossing all night. I smiled as he returned with two mugs of tea.

'So how did it feel handing Hazeling over, then?' he asked.

'Good,' I assured him. 'It's been a long haul but it was worth it. It was the best thing that could happen. You didn't mind that I named it after Michael?'

'Of course not.' Nick gave me a wicked look. 'It was a bit of luck finding those last two pictures tucked away in his studio. I like the one of you as Diana the huntress – very sexy!'

I laughed, blushing as I thought about the rather revealing pictures Nick had discovered. I'd wondered at the time if Nick would be angry, but he'd pounced on them triumphantly and carried them back to hang in the flat, declaring that he enjoyed looking at them.

'Nick . . .' I hesitated, still a little afraid of his reaction to my news. 'Nick, I've got something to tell you.'

'Yes.' His eyes were anxious as I looked at him. 'I knew there was something on your mind. Fire away.'

'It's just that . . .' I took a deep breath. 'I think Julie guessed. She kept hinting but I wouldn't tell her until I'd told you. I only got the confirmation this morning . . .'

The anxiety faded from his eyes, and he started to smile. 'She dropped a few hints to me,' he said. 'Is it true – are we having a baby, Aline?'

'Yes.' I held my breath. 'Do you mind?'

I needn't have asked. Nick gave a great whoop of joy and did an Indian war dance round the bedroom. By the time he came back to sweep me up in his arms, I was laughing.

'That sounds as if you're mildly pleased,' I said.

'Just a bit,' he murmured, and kissed me. 'It will do for a start, anyway. I want at least six of the little blighters.'

The last tiny doubt fled. I would fill my life with laughter and love and Nick's children. The shadows were banished forever.